Praise for Brian Lumley
and the Necroscope® saga

"Lumley uses language deftly to conjure his alien universe, and both setting and characters are vivid and engaging. Fans of the Necroscope series and this Vampire World series will undoubtedly enjoy this adventure."

—*Publishers Weekly* on *The Last Aerie*

"Lumley never oversteps the delicate line between blood-chilling horror and cold gruel. An accomplished word-smith, Lumley wields a pen with the deft skill of a surgeon, drawing just enough blood to titillate without offending his readers." —*The Phoenix Gazette*

"Since reading Lumley's Necroscope series, I know that vampires really do exist!"
 —H. R. Giger, Academy Award–winning artist for *Alien*

"A vampire adventure for the Tom Clancy set. The plot is interesting and features plenty of political and military intrigue." —*Fangoria* on *Necroscope: Avengers*

"Lumley's imagination always works overtime and new concepts are fired at the reader with amazing regularity."
 —*Ashland News* on *Necroscope: Resurgence*

TOR BOOKS BY BRIAN LUMLEY

THE NECROSCOPE® SERIES
Necroscope
Necroscope II: Vamphyri!
Necroscope III: The Source
Necroscope IV: Deadspeak
Necroscope V: Deadspawn
Blood Brothers
The Last Aerie
Bloodwars
Necroscope: The Lost Years
Necroscope: Resurgence
Necroscope: Invaders
Necroscope: Defilers
Necroscope: Avengers
Necroscope: The Touch
Necroscope: Harry and the Pirates

THE TITUS CROW SERIES
*Titus Crow Volume One: The Burrowers Beneath &
The Transition of Titus Crow*
*Titus Crow Volume Two: The Clock of Dreams &
Spawn of the Winds*
Titus Crow Volume Three: In the Moons of Borea & Elysia

THE PSYCHOMECH TRILOGY
Psychomech
Psychosphere
Psychamok

OTHER NOVELS
Demogorgon
The House of Doors
Maze of Worlds
Khai of Khem
The House of Cthulhu
Tarra Khash: Hrossak!
Sorcery in Shad

SHORT STORY COLLECTIONS
Fruiting Bodies and Other Fungi
The Whisperer and Other Voices
Beneath the Moors and Darker Places
Harry Keogh: Necroscope and Other Weird Heroes!

BRIAN LUMLEY

NECROSCOPE IV
DEADSPEAK

TOR®

A TOM DOHERTY ASSOCIATES BOOK
NEW YORK

This is a work of fiction. All the characters and events portrayed in this book are either products of the author's imagination or are used fictitiously.

NECROSCOPE® IV: DEADSPEAK

Copyright © 1990 by Brian Lumley

Necroscope® is a registered trademark of Brian Lumley.

All rights reserved.

A Tor Book
Published by Tom Doherty Associates, LLC
175 Fifth Avenue
New York, NY 10010

www.tor-forge.com

Tor® is a registered trademark of Tom Doherty Associates, LLC.

ISBN 978-0-7653-6385-5

First Edition: May 1990
Second Edition: December 2003
Third Edition: September 2009

Printed in the United States of America

10 9 8 7 6 5 4 3 2 1

For Stavros Dendrinos

Prologue
Harry Keogh:
A Résumé and Chronology

One: Necroscope

CHRISTENED HARRY "SNAITH," IN EDINBURGH, 1957, Harry is the son of a psychic-sensitive mother, Mary Keogh (who is herself the daughter of a "gifted" expatriate Russian lady), and Gerald Snaith, a banker. Harry's father dies of a stroke the following year, and in the winter of 1960 his mother marries again, this time choosing for a husband a Russian by the name of Viktor Shukshin. Like Mary's mother before him, Shukshin has fled the USSR, a supposed "dissident," which perhaps accounts for Mary's initial attraction to him in what will soon become an unmitigated mismatch.

Winter of 1963: Harry's mother is murdered by Shukshin at Bonnyrig outside Edinburgh, where he drowns her under the ice of a frozen river. He alleges that, while skating, she crashed through a thin crust and was washed away; there was nothing he could do to save her; he is "distraught, almost out of [his] mind with grief and horror." Mary Keogh's body is never found; Shukshin inherits her isolated Bonnyrig house and the not inconsiderable monies left to her by her first husband.

Within six months the infant Harry (now Harry "Keogh") has gone to live with an uncle and his wife at Harden on the northeast coast of England. The arrangement is more than satisfactory to Shukshin, who could never stand the child.

Harry commences schooling with the roughneck children of the colliery village. A dreamy, introspective sort of child, he is a loner, develops few friendships (with fellow pupils, at any rate), and thus falls easy prey to bullying and the like. And as he grows towards his teens, so his daydreaming spirit, psychic insight, and instincts lead him into further conflict with his teachers. But he is not lacking in grit—on the contrary.

Harry's problem is that he has inherited his maternal forebears' mediumistic talents, and that they are developed (and still developing) in him to an extraordinary degree. He has no requirement for "real" friends as such, because the many friends he *already has* are more than sufficient and willing to supply his needs. As to who these friends are: they are the myriad dead in their graves!

Up against the school bully, Harry defeats him with the telepathic assistance of an *ex*-ex-army physical training instructor; a man who, before the fall from sea cliffs which killed him, was expert in many areas of self-defence. Punished with mathematical homework, Harry receives help from an ex-headmaster of the school; but in this he almost gives himself away. His current maths teacher is the son of Harry's coach, where he lies "at rest" in Harden Cemetery, and as such he very nearly recognises his father's hand in Harry's work.

In 1969 Harry passes examinations to gain entry into a technical college at West Hartlepool a few miles down the coast, and in the course of the next five years until the end of his formal (and orthodox) education, does his best to tone down use of his talents and extraordinary skills in an attempt to prove himself a "normal, average student"—except in one field. Knowing that he will soon need to support himself, he has taken to writing; even by the time he finishes school he has seen several short pieces of fiction in print. His tutor is

a man once moderately famous for his vivid short stories—
who has been dead since 1947. But this is just the beginning;
under a pseudonym and before he is nineteen, Harry has
already written his first full-length novel, *Diary of a
Seventeenth-Century Rake*. While falling short of the best-
seller lists, still the book does very well. It is not so much a
sensation for its storyline as for its amazing historical au-
thenticity . . . until one considers the qualifications of Harry's
co-author and collaborator: namely, a seventeenth-century
rake, shot dead by an outraged husband in 1672!

Summer of 1976. In a few months Harry will be nineteen.
He has his own unassuming top-floor flat in an old three-
story house on the coast road out of Hartlepool towards Sun-
derland. Perhaps typically, the house stands opposite one of
the town's oldest graveyards . . . Harry is never short of
friends to talk to. What's more, and now that his talent as a
Necroscope has developed to its full, he can converse with
exanimate persons even over great distances. He needs only
to be introduced or to have spoken to one of the teeming
dead, and thereafter can always seek him out again. With
Harry, however, it's a matter of common decency that he
physically go and see them: that is, to attend them at their
grave sides. He does not believe in "shouting" at his friends.

In their turn (and in return for his friendship) Harry's dead
people love him. He is their pharos, the one shining light in
their eternal darkness. He brings hope where none has ever
before existed; he is their single window, their observatory
on a world they had thought left behind and gone forever.
For contrary to the beliefs of the living, death is not The End
but a transition to incorporeality, immobility. The flesh may
be weak and corruptible, but mind and will go on. Great
artists, when they die, continue to visualise magnificent can-
vases, pictures they can never paint; architects plan fantastic,
faultless, continent-spanning cities, which can never be built;
scientists follow through the research they commenced in life
but never had time to complete or perfect. Except that now,
through Harry Keogh, they may contact one another and
(perhaps more importantly) even obtain knowledge of the

corporeal world. And so, while they would never deliberately burden him, all the trials and tribulations of Harry's countless dead friends are his, and his troubles are theirs. And Harry does have troubles.

At his flat in Hartlepool, when he is not working, Harry entertains his childhood sweetheart, Brenda, who will shortly fall pregnant and become his wife. But as his worldly scope widens, so a shadow from the past grows into an obsession. Harry dreams and daydreams of his poor murdered mother, and time and again in his darkest nightmares revisits the frozen river where she died before her time. Finally he resolves to take revenge on Viktor Shukshin, his stepfather.

In this, as in all things, he has the blessing of the dead. Murder is a crime they cannot tolerate; knowing the darkness of death, anyone who deliberately takes life is an abhorrence to them!

Winter of 1976 and Harry goes to see Shukshin, confronting him with evidence of his guilt. His stepfather is plainly dangerous, even deranged, and Harry suspects he'll now try to kill him, too. In January of '77 he gives him the opportunity. They skate on the river together, but when Shukshin moves in for the kill, Harry is prepared. His plan goes wrong, however; they *both* fall through the ice and emerge together by the riverbank. The Russian has the strength of a madman and will surely drown his stepson . . . But no, for Harry's *mother* rises from her watery grave to drag Shukshin down!

And Harry has discovered a new talent; or rather, he now knows how far the dead will go in order to protect him— knows that in fact they will rise from their graves for him!

Harry's talent has not gone unnoticed: a top-secret British intelligence organization, E-Branch (''E'' for ESP), and its Soviet counterpart are both aware of his powers. He is no sooner approached to join the British organization than its head is killed, taken out by the Romanian spy and necromancer Boris Dragosani. A ghoul, Dragosani rips open the dead to steal their secrets right out of their blood and guts;

by butchering the top man in E-Branch, he now knows all the secrets of the British espers.

Harry vows to track him down and even the score, and the teeming dead offer their assistance. Of course they do, for even they are not safe from a man who violates corpses! What Harry and the dead don't know is that Dragosani has been infected with vampirism: he has the vampire egg of Thibor Ferenczy *inside* him, growing there, gradually changing him and taking control. More, Dragosani has murdered a colleague, Max Batu the Mongol, in order to steal the secret of his killing eye. He can now kill at a glance!

Time is short and Harry must follow Dragosani back to the USSR—to Soviet E-Branch headquarters at the Chateau Bronnitsy, where the vampire is now Supremo—and there kill him. But how? Harry is no spy.

A British precog (an agent with the ability to scan vague details of the future) has foreseen Harry's involvement not only with vampires but also in connection with the twisted figure-8 sigil of the Möbius strip. To get to Dragosani he must first understand the Möbius connection. Here at least Harry is on familiar ground; for August Ferdinand Möbius has been dead since 1868, and the dead will do anything for Harry Keogh.

In Leipzig Harry visits Möbius's grave and discovers the long-expired mathematician and astronomer at work on his space-time equations. What he did in life he continues, undisturbed, to do in death; and in the course of a century he has reduced the physical universe to a set of mathematical symbols. He knows how to bend space-time and ride his Möbius strip out to the stars! Teleportation: an easy route into the Chateau Bronnitsy—or anywhere else, for that matter. Fine, but all Harry has is an intuitive grasp of maths— and he certainly doesn't have a hundred years! Still, he has to start somewhere.

For days Möbius instructs Harry, until his pupil is sure that the answer lies right here, just an inch beyond his grasp. He only needs a spur, and . . .

The East German GREPO (Grenz Polizei) have their eye

on Harry. On the orders of Dragosani they try to arrest him in the Leipzig graveyard—and this is the spur he needs. Suddenly Möbius's equations are no longer meaningless figures and symbols: they are a doorway into the strange immaterial universe of the Möbius Continuum! Harry conjures a Möbius door and escapes from the GREPO trap; by trial and error he learns how to use this weird and until now entirely conjectural parallel universe; eventually he projects himself into the grounds of Soviet E-Branch HQ.

Against the armoured might of the Chateau Bronnitsy, Harry's task seems nigh impossible: he needs allies. And he finds them. The chateau's grounds are waterlogged, peaty, white under the crisp snow of a Russian winter—but not frozen. And down in the peat, preserved through four centuries since a time when Moscow was sacked by a band of Crimean Tartars, the *remains* of that butchered band stir and begin to rise up!

With his zombie army Harry advances into the chateau, destroys its defences, seeks out and kills Dragosani and his vampire tenant. In the fight he, too, is killed; his body dies; but in the last moment his mind, his will, transfers to the metaphysical Möbius Continuum.

And riding the Möbius strip into future time, Harry's id is absorbed into the unformed infant mentality . . . of his own son!

Two: Wamphyri!

AUGUST 1977. DRAWN TO HARRY JR.'S ALL-ABSORBING MIND like an iron filing to a magnet, like a mote in a whirlpool, the Harry Keogh identity is in danger of being entirely sub-sumed, dislocated, wiped clean. As the child's perceptions expand, how much of his father's id will be left? Will anything *at all* of Harry Sr. remain?

Harry's one avenue of freedom lies in the Möbius Contin-uum. He can still use it at will—but only when his infant son is asleep, and only as an incorporeal entity. That's Harry's big problem now: the fact that he doesn't have a body. And another is this: that while exploring the infinity of the future timestream, he has noted among the myriad blue life threads of mankind a scarlet thread—a vampire in our midst. And worse, the thread crosses young Harry's in the very close future!

Harry investigates. (He is incorporeal, but so are the dead; he can still communicate with them and they are still in his debt.) In September 1977 he speaks to the spirit of Thibor Ferenczy—no longer undead but truly extinct, a vampire no

9

more—where his tomb keeps watch on the cruciform hills under the *Carpatii Meridionali*; and to Thibor's "father," Faethor Ferenczy, where he died in a World War II bombing raid on Ploiesti towards Bucharest, where even today the ruins lie overrun with weeds and brambles.

Even dead, vampires are devious, the worst liars imaginable; even dead they tempt, taunt, terrorize if they can. But Harry has nothing to lose and Thibor has much to gain. With one exception, Harry Keogh is Thibor's last remaining contact with a world he once planned to rule. One exception, yes . . .

In 1959 the vampire had "infected" a pregnant woman. Using the arts of the Wamphyri, he had touched and tainted her foetal male child—and willed it that one day this man as yet unborn would remember him and return to the cruciform hills in search of his "true" father.

And now it is 1977 and Yulian Bodescu, not yet eighteen years old, is a strange, precocious, and . . . yes, even occasionally frightening young man. To know him too well is to know fear and revulsion. Thibor Ferenczy's taint has taken full hold on him; his blood and soul are corrupt; he is a fledgling vampire.

Yulian's mother is English; his father, a Romanian, is dead. Mother and son live alone together at Harkley House in Devon. His life is a constant tug-of-war between frustration and lust, hers is lived like a chicken penned with a fox; she knows he is evil and capable of greater evil, but fears him too greatly for public accusation. Also, having protected him since childhood, she still dares hope that he will change in the fullness of time. And indeed he is changing—rapidly—but not for the better.

Yulian half guesses, half knows what he is; he constantly dreams of stirless trees, black hills in the shape of a cross, a tomb in a silent glade on a hillside . . . and of the Old Thing in the Ground which once lay waiting there. *And* of what it left behind to wait for him! The scarlet vampire thread which was once Thibor and is now Yulian tugs at him, beckoning him to attend his "father." And this is that selfsame thread which Harry Keogh has seen crossing his own infant son's pure blue thread in the Möbius Continuum's future-time stream.

But even as Harry plays cat-and-mouse word games with the anciently wise, utterly devious, and immemorially evil Wamphyri, so the espers of British E-Branch have staked out Harkley House in Devon. Telepaths, they are only waiting for Harry to give them the word and they will move in on Harkley and try to destroy Yulian and any other infected person whom they may find there. And they will do this because they know that if any such person—or thing—breaks out . . . then vampirism could spread like a plague through the length and breadth of the land, even the world!

Also, in Romania, Alec Kyle and Felix Krakovitch, current heads of their respective ESPionage organizations, have joined forces to destroy whatever remains of Thibor Ferenczy in the black earth of the cruciform hills. They succeed in burning a monstrous *remnant*—but not before Thibor sends Yulian a dream message and warning. For Thibor had hoped to use his English "son" as a vessel, and in him rise up again to resume his vampire existence, but now that his last vestiges are destroyed . . .

. . . Instead he turns to vengeance. Thibor is gone forever, dead and gone like all the teeming dead. But just like them his mind remains. And in the dream he sends to Yulian he tells all and lays the blame on E-Branch, and especially on Harry Keogh. What E-Branch has done to Thibor, it also plans to do to Yulian Bodescu. But Keogh is the one to watch out for, the only one who poses any real threat. Only destroy him . . . and Yulian may pick off the rest of his enemies in his own good time, one by one. And he vows to do just that.

As for destroying Keogh: that should be the very simplest thing. Harry Keogh is incorporeal, a bodiless id, his own infant son's sixth sense. Only remove the child, and the father goes with him . . .

Meanwhile Harry has learned all he can of vampire history, of means to destroy them, of ancient ground which may still require cleansing of their evil. He initiates E-Branch's attack on Harkley House.

In the USSR, however, Felix Krakovitch has been killed and Alec Kyle, head of E-Branch, is falsely accused of his murder. Russian espers have taken Kyle to the Chateau Bronnitsy where they are using a combination of high technology and ESP to drain him of all knowledge. That is: *all* knowledge! The most severe form of brainwashing and intelligence gathering, the treatment will leave him literally brain dead, a husk, a body robbed of its governing mind. And when the body dies, Kyle will be dumped in West Berlin with never a mark on him. That, at least, is the plan . . .

In the interim Yulian Bodescu has not been idle. For a long time he has been breeding something in Harkley's cellars; his Alsatian dog is more than a dog; Bodescu has raped and vampirized a visiting aunt and cousin and even infected his own mother. The house, when E-Branch's men attack, is discovered to be a place of total lunacy, mayhem, and nightmare!

Bodescu escapes, the only survivor as Harkley House goes up in cleansing fire. Intent on destroying the Keogh child, he heads north for Hartlepool. His trail is bloody and littered with E-Branch agents when finally he enters the house and climbs to Brenda Keogh's top-floor flat. The mother tries to protect her child and is hurled aside. Harry Jr. is awake; his mind *contains* Harry Keogh; the monster is upon them, powerful hands reaching . . .

Harry can do nothing. Trapped in the infant's whirlpool id, he knows that they are both about to die. But then . . .

Go, little Harry tells him. *Through you I've learned what I had to learn. I don't need you that way any longer. But I do need you as a father. So go on, get out, save yourself.* The mental attraction which binds Harry to his son's mind has been relaxed; he can now flee into the Möbius Continuum; but . . . he can't!

"You're my son. How can I go, and leave you here with . . . with this?"

But Harry Jr. has no intention of being left behind. He has

12

his father's knowledge; he *is* a mature mind in the body of an infant, lacking only experience; they *both* flee to the Möbius Continuum!

The child has inherited much more than this, however. What the father could do, the infant son can do in spades. Harry Jr. is a Necroscope of enormous power. In the ancient cemetery just across the road, the dead answer his call. They come out of their graves, shuffle, flop, crawl from the graveyard and into the house, and up the stairs. Bodescu flees but they trap him and employ the old time-tested methods of eradication: the stake, decapitation, cleansing fire . . .

Harry Keogh is free, but free to do what? Incorporeal, he must eventually be absorbed by the Möbius Continuum . . . or perhaps be expelled elsewhere, elsewhen. However bodiless, he is still a "foreign body" in Möbius's enigmatic emptiness of mathematical conjecture.

Except . . . there is a force—an attraction other than Harry Jr.'s infant id—a vacuum to be filled. It is the vacuum of Alec Kyle's drained mind, and when Harry explores, he is sucked in irresistibly to reanimate the brain-dead esper.

It is late September 1977, and Harry Keogh, Necroscope and explorer of the metaphysical Möbius Continuum, has taken up permanent residence in another man's body; indeed, to all intents and purposes, and to anyone who doesn't know better, he *is* that other man. But Harry is also the natural father of a most unnatural child, a child with awesome *super*natural powers.

Harry employs ultra-high explosives to blow the Chateau Bronnitsy to hell, then rides the Möbius strip home to seek out his wife and child . . . only to discover that they have disappeared. Not alone from England but from the face of the earth.

Indeed, entirely out of this universe!

Three: The Source

IN 1983 IN THE URALS, THERE OCCURS THE PERCHORSK INcident: an "industrial accident" according to the Soviets, but an accident of some magnitude. In fact the Russians, seeking an answer to the USA's proposed Star Wars, have built and tested a laser-type weapon to create a shield against incoming missiles. The experiment is a failure; there is a blowback in the weapon; in the deeps of the Perchorsk Pass havoc is wreaked as the fabric of space-time itself receives a terrible wrenching. The world's intelligence agencies, including British E-Branch, are interested to discover what Moscow is hiding up there under the snow and ice and mountains—curious to know what, *exactly*, the Perchorsk Projekt really is or was.

A year later, and something (a UFO?) is tracked from Novaya Zemlya on a course which takes it west of Franz Josef Land and on a beeline for Ellesmere Island. Mig interceptors have been sent up from Kirovsk south of Murmansk. The "object" is two miles higher than the Migs when they catch up with it, but it sees them, descends, and destroys them.

14

Their debris is lost in snow and ice some six hundred miles from the pole and a like distance short of Ellesmere. A USAF AWACS reports the Migs lost from its screens, presumed down, but hotline Moscow is curiously cautious, even ambiguous: "What Migs? What intruder?"

The Americans, angrily: "This thing is coming out of your airspace; if it sticks to its present course, it will be intercepted, forced to land. If it fails to comply or acts hostile, it may even be shot down."

And unexpectedly: "Good!" from the Russians. "We renounce it utterly. Do with it as you see fit."

Two USAF fighters have meanwhile been scrambled up from a strip near Port Fairfield, Maine. The AWACS guides them to their target; at close to Mach II they've crossed the Hudson Bay from the Belcher Islands to a point two hundred miles north of Churchill. The AWACS is left behind a little, but their target is dead ahead at 10,000 feet. They spot it . . .

. . . And take it out—no questions asked—one *look* at it is enough reason to fire on the thing! Equipped with experimental air-to-air Firedevils, the USAF planes succeed where the Migs paid the price. The thing burns, blows apart over the Hudson Bay, crashes to earth. The AWACS has caught up, gets the whole thing on film. Eventually British E-Branch is invited (a) to a picture show, and (b) to offer an educated opinion . . . a guess . . . *anything* will be appreciated.

E-Branch keeps its expert opinion to itself—for the sanity of the world! Reason: the thing from Perchorsk was obviously similar—*very* similar—to the monstrosity that Yulian Bodescu bred in his cellars, also to the Thibor Ferenczy remnant burned on the cruciform hills of Romania. Except that by comparison they were pigmies and this one was a giant—and armoured! In a nutshell, it was a thing of vampire protoflesh, and E-Branch suspects that the Russians at Perchorsk made it: an incredible biological experiment which perhaps broke free of its controlled or test environment!

This is one theory, at least. But not the only one . . .

E-Branch contrives to put a contact inside the Perchorsk

Projekt to act as a spy and telepathic transmitter. Before he is discovered they learn enough to convince them of the world-threatening evil of the place, even enough to cause them to reestablish their old contact with Harry Keogh . . .

It is 1985. Eight years since Yulian Bodescu died and Harry wrecked the Chateau Bronnitsy, eight long years since his half-deranged wife and her necroscopic child fled, apparently right out of this world. And ever since then he's been looking for them. They are not dead, for if they were, the teeming dead would know it and likewise Harry Keogh. But if they're alive . . . then Harry no longer knows where to search. He has exhausted every bolthole, searched . . . everywhere.

Darcy Clarke, head of E-Branch, goes to see Harry at his Edinburgh home. He starts to tell him about Perchorsk but Harry isn't interested. As Clarke fills in the details, however, Harry's interest picks up. His old enemies the Soviet mindspies have established a cell at Perchorsk to block metaphysical prying. They're obviously hiding something big, something very unpleasant. They have a regiment of troops up there in the mountains, equipped with real firepower—for what? Who is likely to attack the Urals? Who do the Russians think they're keeping out? *What* are they keeping in?

"We think they're doing something with genetics," Clarke tells Harry. "We think they're breeding warrior vampires!"

Even now Harry is only half-swayed; but at last Clarke plays his trump.

The British spy in Perchorsk, Michael J. Simmons, has vanished; the very best of E-Branch's espers can't find him; they believe he's alive (he hasn't been "cancelled," or their telepaths would know) but they don't know *where* he's alive. Which precisely parallels Harry's own problem! Perhaps, by some weird freak of coincidence, Harry Jr., Brenda Keogh, and the Perchorsk spy are all in the same place. To be doubly sure that E-Branch aren't just using him to their own ends, Harry asks his myriad dead friends to look into it. Is there a recent arrival in their teeming ranks by the name of Michael J. Simmons? But . . .

There is not. Simmons isn't dead, he's simply not here . . .

Harry investigates and discovers that the accident at the Perchorsk Projekt has blown a hole in space-time, a "grey hole" leading to a world "parallel" with our own; also that the world on the other side is the spawning ground of vampires, indeed *The Source* of all vampire myth and legend.

He talks again to the long-dead August Ferdinand Möbius, to the devious mind of the extinct Faethor Ferenczy, and to more recent friends among the legions of the dead; until finally he discovers an alternate route into the vampire world. And what a monstrous world that is!

Sunside is hot, a blazing desert; Starside is the realm of the Wamphyri, where their aeries stand kilometer-high close to the mountain pinnacles which divide the planet. On Sunside the Travellers, the original Gypsies, wander in bands and tribes through the verdant foothills of the central range; active during the long days, they burrow in dark holes and caves through the shorter fear-filled nights. For when the sun sets on Sunside—that's when the Wamphyri come a-hunting.

Travellers, and Trogs (a primitive aboriginal race), are to the Wamphyri what the coconut is to Earth's tropical islanders. They form a large part of their diet, provide slaves, workers, women; even when they die or are disposed of, there is rarely any waste. Their remains go to feed Wamphyri "gas beasts," "siphoneers," and "warriors," which are themselves fashioned of transmuted Trogs and Travellers. Their grotesquely *altered,* fossilized bodies decorate the vertiginous, glooming castles of the Wamphyri, are even formed into furniture or hardened into exterior sheaths, so protecting the aerie properties of their vampire masters against the elements.

As for the Lords of these rearing keeps . . .

The Wamphyri are monstrous, warlike, jealous of their territories and possessions, forever scheming and feuding. There is nothing a vampire hates and distrusts more than another

17

vampire. And no one they *all* hate and distrust more than the Dweller in His Garden in the West.

Following a nightmare series of adventures and misadventures, a party of Travellers—including Jazz Simmons and the beautiful telepath Zek Föener—have joined forces with the Dweller. By the time Harry Keogh arrives, the Wamphyri have set aside all personal arguments and disputes to unite against their common enemy, preparatory to invading the Garden, the Dweller's territory in the hills. Of all the awesome Wamphyri Lords, only the Lady Karen, a gorgeous once-Traveller whose vampire tenant has not yet reached full maturity, reneges and flees to the Dweller, warning him of the coming war.

The battle is joined; the Lords Shaithis, Menor Maimbite, Belath, Volse Pinescu, Lesk the Glut, and many others, with all their hybrid warriors and Trog minions, against the Dweller and his small party of humans.

But Harry Keogh is with the Dweller, and the Dweller is . . . Harry Jr.! By means of a timeslip, Harry Jr. is not the mere boy his father expected but grown to a young man in a golden mask, and this is the world to which he has transported his poor demented mother—for her safety and peace of mind! Yes, and until now he has provided amply for all her needs—and his own. For individually the Wamphyri Lords were no match for him and his "science." Now that they are united, however . . . Harry Sr. has arrived just in time.

By ingenious use of the Möbius Continuum, and of the Necroscope powers of father and son, Shaithis and his vampire army are defeated, their aeries destroyed, all but the Lady Karen's. She goes back there, and Harry Keogh visits her. He seeks to free her of her vampire, not for her sake but for his son's—for the Dweller has become infected with vampirism. Harry will use Karen to test a theory, to provide, he hopes, a cure.

He drives Karen's vampire out and destroys it. Alas, he also destroys her. She had *been* Wamphyri, and now she is a shell. When one has known the magnified emotions—the freedom from guilt, timidity, and remorse—the sheer *lust* and *power* of the Wamphyri . . . what is there after that? Nothing, and she throws herself from the aerie's battlements.

But the Dweller still has a vampire in him, and back in the Garden where his band of Travellers are rebuilding their shattered lives and homes . . . Harry Jr. is ever more aware of his father's hooded eyes, watching him intently . . .

I: Castle Ferenczy

Still an hour short of midday, two peasant wives of Halmagiu village wended their way home along well-trodden forest tracks. Their baskets were full of small wild plums and the first ripe berries of the season, all with the dew still glistening on them. Some of the plums were still a little green . . . all the better for the making of sharp, tangy brandy! Dark-robed, with coarse cloth headsquares framing their narrow faces, the women cheerfully embroidered tidbits of village gossip to suit their mood, their teeth flashing ivory in weathered leather as they laughed over especially juicy morsels.

In the near distance, blue wood smoke drifted in almost perpendicular spirals from Halmagiu's chimneys; it formed a haze high over the early-autumn canopy of forest. But closer, in the trees themselves were other fires; cooking smells of spiced meats and herbal soups drifted on the still air; small silver bells jingled; a bough creaked where a wild-haired,

20

dark-eyed, silent, staring child dangled from the rope of a makeshift swing.

There were gaudy caravans gathered in a circle under the trees. Outside the circle: tethered ponies cropped the grass, and bright-coloured dresses swirled where bare-armed girls gathered firewood. Inside: black iron cooking pots suspended over licking flames issued puffs of mouth-watering steam; male Travellers tended their own duties or simply looked on, smoking their long, thin-stemmed pipes, as the encampment settled in. Travellers, yes. Wanderers: Gypsies! The *Szgany* had returned to the region of Halmagiu.

The boy on the rope in the tree had spotted the two village women and now uttered a piercing whistle. All murmur and jingle and movement in the Gypsy encampment ceased upon the instant; dark eyes turned outwards in unison, staring with curiosity at the Romanian peasant women with their baskets. The Gypsy men in their leather jackets looked very strong, somehow fierce, but there was nothing of animosity in their eyes. They had their own codes, the Szgany, and knew which side their bread was greased. For five hundred years the people of Halmagiu had dealt with them fairly, bought their trinkets and knickknacks, and left them in peace. And so in their turn the Gypsies would work no deliberate harm against Halmagiu.

"Good morning, ladies." The Gypsy king (for so the leaders of these roving bands prided themselves, as little kings) stood up on the steps of his wagon and bowed to them. "Please tell our friends in the village we'll be knocking on their doors—pots and pans of the best quality, charms to keep away the night things, cards to read, and keen eyes that know the lie of a line in your palm. Bring out your knives for sharpening and your broken ax handles. All will be put to rights. Why, this year we've even a good pony or two, to replace the nags that pull your carts! We'll not be here long, so make the best of our bargains before we move on."

"Good morning to you," the oldest of the pair at once answered, if in a breathless fashion. "And be sure I'll tell

21

them in the village." And in a hushed aside to her companion: "Stay close; move along with me; say nothing!"

As they passed by one of the wagons, so this same older woman took a small jar of hazelnuts from her basket and a double handful of plums, placing them on the steps of the wagon as a gift. If the offering was seen, no one said anything, and in any case the activity in the camp had already resumed its normal pace as the women headed once more for home.

But the younger one, who hadn't lived in Halmagiu very long, asked, "Why did you give the nuts and plums away? I've heard the Gypsies give nothing for nothing, do nothing for nothing, and far too often *take* something for nothing! Won't it encourage them, leaving gifts like that?"

"It does no harm to keep well in with the fey people," the other told her. "When you've lived here as long as I have, you'll know what I mean. And anyway, they're not here to steal or work mischief." She gave a small shudder. "Indeed, I fancy I know well enough why they're here."

"Oh?" said her friend wonderingly.

"Oh, yes. It's the phase of the moon, a calling they've heard, an offering they'll make. They propitiate the earth, replenish the rich soil, appease . . . their gods."

"Their gods? Are they heathens, then . . . ? What gods?"

"Call it Nature if you like!" the first one snapped. "But ask me no more. I'm a simple woman and don't wish to know. Nor should you wish to know. My grandmother's grandmother remembered a time when the Gypsies came. Aye, and likely her granny before her. Sometimes fifteen months will go by, or eighteen—but never more than twenty-one—before they're back again. Spring, summer, winter: only the Szgany themselves know the season, the month, the time. But when they hear the calling, when the moon is right, when a lone wolf howls high up in the mountains, then they return. Yes, and when they go, they always leave their offering . . ."

"What sort of offering?" The younger woman was more curious than ever.

"Don't ask," said the other, hurriedly shaking her head.

"Don't ask." But it was only her way; the younger woman knew she was dying to tell her; she bided her time and resolved to ask no more.

But in a little while, fancying that they'd strayed too far from the most direct route back to the village, she felt obliged to enquire, "But isn't this a long way round we're taking?"

"Be quiet now!" hushed the older woman. "Look!"

They had arrived at a clearing in the forest at the foot of a gaunt outcrop of grey volcanic rock. Bald and domed, with several humps, this irregular mound stood perhaps fifty feet high, with more forest beyond, then sheer cliffs rising to a fir-clad plateau like a first gigantic step to the misted, grimly forbidding heights of the Zarundului massif. The trees around the base of the outcrop had been felled, all shrubs and undergrowth cleared away; at its summit, a cairn of heavy stones stood like a small tower or chimney, pointing to the mountains.

And up there, seated on the bare rock at the foot of the cairn, working with a knife at a shard of stone which he held in his lap—a young man: Szgany! He was intent upon his work, seeing nothing but the stone in his hands. He gazed down across a distance of little more than one hundred feet—gazed seemingly head-on, so that the women of the village must surely be central to his periphery of vision—but if he saw them he gave no sign. And indeed it was plain that he did not see them, only the stone which he worked. And even at that distance, clearly there was something . . . not quite right with him.

"But . . . what's he doing up there?" the younger of the two enquired in a hoarse whisper. "He's very handsome, and yet . . . strange. And anyway, isn't this a forbidden place? My Hzak tells me that the great stone of the cairn is a very special stone, and that—"

"*Shhh!*" the other once again cautioned her, a finger to her lips. "Don't disturb him. They don't take kindly to being spied upon, the Szgany. Not that this one will hear us anyway. Still . . . best to be careful."

"He won't hear us, you say? Then why are we talking in

23

whispers? No, I *know* why we're whispering: because this is a private place, like a shrine. Almost holy.''

"*Un*holy!" the other corrected her. "As to why he won't notice us—why, just look at him up there! His skin's not so much dark as slate grey, sickly, dying. Eyes deep-sunken, burning. Obsessed with that stone he's carving. He's been called, can't you see? He's mazed, hypnotised—doomed!"

Even as the last word left her lips, so the man on the rock stood up, took up his stone, and ground it firmly into position on the rim of the cairn. It sat there side by side with many dozens of others, like a brick in the topmost tier of a wall, and anyone having seen the ritual of the carving would know that each single stone of that cairn was marked in some weird, meaningful way. The younger woman opened her mouth to say something, but her friend at once anticipated her question.

"His name," she said. "He carved his name and his dates, if he knows them. Like all the other names and dates carved up there. Like all the others gone before him. That rude stone is his headstone, which makes the cairn itself a graveyard!"

Now the young Gypsy was craning his neck, looking up, up at the mountains. He stood frozen in that position for long moments, as if waiting for something. And high in the grey-blue sky a small dark blot of cloud drifted across the face of the sun. At that, the elder of the two women gave a start; she herself had become almost hypnotised, stalled there and without the will to move on. But as the sun was eclipsed and shadows fell everywhere, she grabbed the other's elbow and turned her face away. "Come," she gasped, suddenly breathless, "let's be gone from here. Our men will be worried. Especially if they know there are Gypsies about."

They hurried through the shadows of the trees, found the track, soon began to see the first wooden houses on Halmagiu's outskirts, where the forest thinned down to nothing. But even as they stepped out from the trees into a dusty lane and their heartbeats slowed a little, so they heard a sound from behind and above and far, far beyond.

Not quite midday in Halmagiu, the sun coming out from

behind a small, stray cloud; the first days of true winter still some seven or eight weeks away—but every soul who heard that sound took it as a wintry omen anyway. Aye, and some took it for more than that.

It was the mournful voice of a wolf echoing down from the mountains, calling as wolves have called for a thousand, thousand years and more. The two women paused, clutched their baskets, held their breath and listened. But:

"There's no answering cry," said the younger eventually. "He's alone, that old wolf."

"For now." The other nodded. "Aye, alone—but he's been heard all right, take my word for it. And he *will* be answered, soon enough. Following which . . ." She shook her head and hurried on.

The other caught up with her. "Yes, following which?" she pressed.

The older woman peered at her, scowled a little, finally barked, "But you must learn to listen, Anna! There are some things we don't much talk about up here—so if you want to learn, then when they *are* talked about, you must listen!"

"I was listening," the other answered. "It's just that I didn't understand, that's all. You said the old wolf would be answered, soon enough. And . . . and then?"

"Aye, and then," said the older one, turning towards her doorway, where bunches of garlic dangled from the lintel, drying in the sun. And over her shoulder: "And then—the very next morning—why, the Szgany will be gone! No trace of them at all except maybe the ashes in their camp, the ruts in the tracks where their caravans have rolled, moving on. But their numbers will have been shortened by one. One who answered an ancient call and stayed behind."

The younger woman's mouth formed a silent "O."

"That's right," said the first, nodding. "You just saw him—adding his soul to those other poor souls inscribed in the cairn on the rock . . ."

That night, in the Szgany camp:

The girls danced, whirling to the skirl of frenzied violins

25

and the primal thump and jingle of tambourines. A long table stood heavy with food: joints of rabbit and whole hedgehogs, still steaming from the heat of the trenches where they'd baked; wild-boar sausages, sliced thin; cheeses purchased or bartered in Halmagiu village; fruit and nuts; onions simmering in gravy poured from the meats; Gypsy wines and sharp, throat-clutching wild-plum brandy.

There was a festival atmosphere. The flames of a central fire, inspired by the music, leaped high and the dancers were sinuous, sensuous. Alcohol was consumed in large measure; some of the younger Gypsies drank from a sense of relief, others from fear of an uncertain future. For those who had been spared this time around, there would always be other times . . .

But they were Szgany and this was the way of things; they were His to the ends of the earth, His to command, His to take. Their pact with the Old One had been signed and sealed more than four hundred years ago. Through Him they had prospered down the centuries, they prospered now, they would prosper in all the years to come. He made the hard times easier—aye, and the easy times hard—but always He achieved a balance. His blood was in them, and theirs in Him. And the blood is the life.

Only two amongst them were alone and private. Even with the girls dancing, the drinking, the feasting, still they were alone. For all of this noise and movement around them was an assumed gaiety, wherein they could scarcely participate.

One of them, the young man from the cairn, sat on the steps of an ornately carved and painted wagon, with a whetstone and his long-bladed knife, bringing the cutting edge to a scintillant shimmer of silver in the flicker of near-distant firelight. While in the yellow camplight behind him where the door stood open, his mother sat sobbing, wringing her hands, praying for all she was worth to One who was not a god—indeed, to One who was the very opposite—that He spare her son this night. But praying in vain.

And as one tune ended and bright skirts whispered to a halt, falling about gleaming brown limbs, and mustached men

quit their leaping and high-kicking—in that interval when the
fiddlers sipped their brandy before starting up again—then
the moon showed its rim above the mountains, whose misted
crags were brought to a sudden prominence. And as mouths
gaped open and all eyes turned upwards to the risen moon,
so the mournful howl of a wolf drifted down to them from
unseen aeries of rock.

For a single moment the tableau stood frozen . . . but the
next saw dark eyes turning to gaze at the young man on
the caravan steps. He stood up, looked up at the moon and
the crags, and sighed. And sheathing his knife, he stepped
down to the clearing, crossed it on wooden legs, headed for
the darkness beyond the encircling wagons.

His mother broke the silence. Her wail, rising to a shriek
of anguish, was that of a banshee as she hurled herself from
their caravan home, crashed down the wooden steps, came
reeling after her son, her arms outstretched. But she did not
go to him; instead she fell to her knees some paces away, her
arms still reaching, aching for him. For the chief of this band,
their "king," had stepped forward to embrace the young
man. He hugged him, kissed him on both cheeks, released
him. And without more ado the chosen one went out of the
firelight, between the wagons, and was swallowed by darkness.

"Dumitru!" his mother screamed. She got to her feet,
made to rush after him—and flew into the arms of her king.

"Peace, woman," he told her gruffly, his throat bobbing.
"We've seen it coming a month now, watched the change in
him. The Old One has called and Dumitru answers. We knew
what to expect. This is always the way of it."

"But he's my son, my son!" she sobbed wrackingly into
his chest.

"Aye," he said, his own voice finally breaking, sending
tears coursing down his leathery cheeks. "And mine . . .
mine too . . . aye."

He led her stumbling and sobbing back to their caravan,
and behind them the music started up again, and the dancing,
and the feasting and drinking . . .

27

* * *

Dumitru Zirra climbed the ramparts of the Zarundului like a fox born to those heights. The moon lit a path for him, but even without that silver swath he would have known the way. For there was guidance from within: a voice inside his head, which was not his voice, told him where to step, reach, grasp. There were paths up here, if you knew them, but between these hairpin tracks were vertiginous shortcuts. Dumitru chose the latter, or someone made that choice for him.

Dumiitruuu! the dark voice crooned to him, drawing out his name like a cry of torment. *Ah, my faithful, my Szgaaany, son of my sons. Step here, and there, and here, Dumiitruuu. And here, where the wolf stepped—see his mark on the rock? The father of your fathers awaits you, Dumiitruuu. The moon is risen up and the hour draws niiigh. Make haste, my son, for I'm old and dry and shrivelled close to death—the true death! But you shall succor me, Dumiitruuu. Aye, and all your youth and strength be miiine!*

Almost to the treeline the youth laboured, his breath ragged and his hands bloody from the climbing, to the blackest crags of all, where a vast ruin humped against the final cliff. On the one side a gorge so sheer and black it might descend to hell, and on the other the last of the tall firs shielding the tumbled pile of some ancient keep, set back against sheer-rising walls of rock. Dumitru saw the place and for a moment was brought up short, but then he also saw the flame-eyed wolf standing in the broken gates of the ruin and hesitated no more. He went on, and the great wolf led the way.

Welcome to my house, Dumiitruuu! that glutinous voice oozed like mud in his mind. *You are my guest, my son . . . enter of your own free will . . .*

Dumitru Zirra clambered dazedly over the first shattered stones of the place, and mazed as he was, still the queer aspect of these ruins impressed him. It had been a castle, of that he was sure. In olden times a boyar had lived here, a Ferenczy—Janos Ferenczy! No question of that, for down all the ages since the time of Grigor Zirra, the first Szgany "king," the Zirras had been sworn in allegiance to the Baron

Ferenczy and had borne his crest: a bat leaping into flight from the mouth of a black urn, with wings outspread, showing three ribs to each wing. The eyes of the bat were red, likewise the ribs of its wings, made prominent in scarlet, while the vessel from which it soared was in the shape of a burial urn.

Aye, and now the youth's deep-sunken, staring eyes picked out a like design carved on the shattered slab of a huge stone lintel where it lay half-buried in debris; and indeed he knew that he stood upon the threshold of the great and ancient *patron* of the Zirras and their followers. For it was that same sigil as described which even now was displayed on the sides of Vasile Zirra's caravan (however cleverly obscured in the generally ornate and much-convoluted lacquer and paintwork designs). Similarly old Vasile, Dumitru's father, wore a ring bearing a miniature of this crest, allegedly passed down to him from time immemorial. This would have been Dumitru's one day—had he not heard the calling . . .

Some little way ahead of Dumitru the great wolf growled low in its throat, urging him on. He paused, however, uncertain where the shadows of fallen blocks obscured his vision. The front edge of the ruin seemed to have been tossed (tossed, yes, as by some enormous explosion in the guts of the place) out to and beyond the rim of the gorge, where still a jumble of massive stones and slates were spread in dark confusion, so that Dumitru supposed a large part of the castle had gone down into the gorge.

As to what could have caused such destruction, he had no—

But you hesitate, my son, came that monstrous mental voice, oozing like a slug in his mind, overriding and obliterating all matters of question and conjecture and will. That voice which had completely overwhelmed and taken control of him during the course of the last four or five weeks, making him its zombie. *And I see that it is as I suspected, Dumiitruuu . . . you are strong-willed! Good! Very good! The strength of the will is that of the body, and the strength of*

29

the body is the blood. Your blood is strong, my son, as it is in all your race . . .

The great wolf growled again and Dumitru stumbled after. The youth knew he should flee this place, run headlong, break his bones in the dark and crawl if he must—anything but carry on. And yet he was powerless against the lure of that ancient, evil voice. It was as if he had made some promise he could not break, or as if he kept the promise of some long-dead and honoured ancestor, which was inviolable.

Now, guided by the voice in his head, he stumbled among leaning menhir blocks in search of a certain spot; now he went on all fours, clearing away fresh-fallen leaves, damp grey lichens, and shards of black rock; now he discovered (or merely uncovered, for the voice had told him it would be here) a narrow slab with an iron ring, which he lifted easily. A blast of foul air struck his face, filled his lungs, made him more dizzy yet where he crouched over the black and reeking abyss; and when at last his head cleared—of the fumes, at least—he was already descending into nightmare depths.

Now the voice told him: *Here, here my son . . . a niche in the wall . . . torches, a bundle, and matches all wrapped in a skin . . . aye, better than the flints of my youth . . . light one torch and take two more with you . . . for be sure you'll need them, Dumiitruuu . . .*

The stone stairwell spiralled; Dumitru descended nitrous steps, obliged to clamber in places where the stair had collapsed. He reached a buckled floor littered with blocks of fire-blackened masonry; another trapdoor; the descent continued through dankly echoing bowels of earth. Down, ever down, to sinister and sentient nether pits . . .

Until at last:

Well done, Dumiitruuu, the dark voice complimented him— a voice that smiled monstrously, invisibly, whose owner was well pleased with himself—his pleasure grating like a file on the nerve-endings of the young man's brain. And suddenly . . . Dumitru might have bolted. For a split second he was his own man again—he knew he stood on the very threshold of hell!

But then that alien intelligence closed like a vise on his mind; the inexorable process started five weeks ago guided him towards its logical conclusion; the strength of free will flickered like a guttering candle in him, almost extinguished. And . . .

Look about you, Dumiitruuu. Look and learn what are the works and mysteries of your master, my son . . .

Behind Dumitru on the stone staircase, the great flame-eyed wolf. And before him—

The lair of a necromancer!

Such things were legends amongst the Szgany, tales to be told about the campfires in certain seasons, but neither Dumitru nor any other who might view this scene would require any special knowledge or explanation save that of his own imagination, his own instinct. And wide-eyed and gape-mouthed, with his torch held high, the youth wandered unsteadily through the *ordered* remnants and relics of chaos and madness.

Not the chaos of the upper regions, which was purely physical, for these secret nether vaults had suffered little of the destruction of the higher levels; they were preserved, pristine under the dust and cobwebs of half a century. No, this was a *mental* chaos: the knowledge that these were the works of a man or men—or, again taking into account all manner of Szgany myth and legend, the works of things disguised as such.

Of the vaults themselves:

The stonework was ancient, indeed hoary. Nitre-streaked and yet not noticeably damp, in places the masonry even showed signs of dripstone concretion. Wispy stalactite strings depended from the high-vaulted ceilings; and around the edges of the rooms, where the floor had been not so frequently trodden, smooth-domed stalagmite deposits formed small nodes or blisters on the roughly fitted flags. Dumitru was no archaeologist, but from the primitive roughness of the dressed stone and the poor condition of the ancient mortar alone, even he would have dated the castle—or at least these secret regions of the castle—as being some eight or nine hundred years old. It would need to be at least that for the formation of these calcium deposits—or else the solutions seeping from above must be heavily laced with crystalline salts.

There were numerous archways, uniformly eight feet wide and eleven high, all wedged at their tops with massive keystones, some of which had settled a little from the unimaginable tonnage of the higher levels. The ceilings—none of them less than fourteen or fifteen feet tall at apex—were vaulted in an interlocking design similar to the archways; in several places massive blocks had fallen, doubtless shaken loose by whatever blast had doomed the place, shattering the heavy flags of the floor like schoolroom slates.

Beyond the archways were rooms all of a large size, all with archways of their own; Dumitru had descended to a maze of ancient rooms, where the tenant of this broken pile had practised his secret arts. As to the nature of those arts:

So far, with the single exception of his first terrified guess, Dumitru had avoided conjecture. But this was no longer possible. The walls were covered in frescoes which, however faded, told the entire tale; and many of the rooms contained undeniable evidence of a much more solid, much more frightening nature. Also, the voice in his head, now cruel and full of glee, would not permit of his ignorance: it *desired* that he know the way of these old matters.

Necromancy, you thought, Dumitru, when first your torch cast back the shadows down here, the voice reiterated. *The resurrection of defunct salts and ashes back into life for the purpose of interrogation. The history of the world, as it were, from the horse's mouth, from the reanimated, imperfect wraiths of them that lived it. The unravelling of ancient secrets, and perhaps even the foretelling of the dimly distant future. Aye, divination by use of the dead . . . ! That is what you thought.*

Well, (and after a small pause the voice gave a mental shrug) *and you were right—as far as you went. But you did not go far enough. You have avoided looking . . . you avoid it even now! What, and are you my son, Dumitru, or some puling babe in arms? I thought I had called strong wine in unto myself, only to discover that the Szgaaany have been brewing water all these years! Ha-haa-haaa! But no . . . I make jokes . . . don't be so angry, my son . . .*

. . . It is anger, is it not, Dumiitruuu? No? Fear, perhaps?

You fear for your life, Dumiitruuu? The voice had sunk to a whisper now, but insidious as the drip of a slow acid. *But you shall have your life, my son—in me! The blood is the life, Dumiitruuu—and that shall go on and on . . . aaand . . .*

But there! Now the voice sprang alive, became merry. *Why, we were grown morose, and that must never be! What? But we shall be as one, and live out all our life together. Do you hear me, Dumiitruuu . . . ? Well?*

"I . . . I hear you," the youth answered, speaking to no one.

And do you believe me? Say it—say that you believe in me, as your father's fathers believed in me.

Dumitru was not sure he did believe, but the owner of the voice squeezed inside his head until he cried out, "Yes . . . ! Yes, I believe, just as my fathers believed."

Very well, said the voice, apparently placated. *Then don't be so shy, Dumiitruuu: look upon my works without averting your eyes, without shrinking back. The pictures painted and graven in the walls—the many amphorae in their racks—the salts and powders contained in these ancient vessels . . .*

In the flaring torchlight Dumitru looked. Racks of black oak standing everywhere, and on their shelves numberless jars, urns: amphorae, as the voice had termed them. Throughout these rooms in this subterranean hideaway, there must be several thousands of them, all tight-stoppered with plugs of oak in leaden sheaths, all with faded, centuries-stained labels pasted to them where handles joined necks. One rack had been shattered, thrown aside by a falling ceiling stone; its jars had been spilled, some of them breaking open. Powders had trickled out, forming small cones which themselves had taken on the dust of decades, and when Dumitru looked at these spilled . . . remains . . . ?

See how fine they are, these essential salts, whispered the voice in his head, which now contained a curiosity of its own, as if even the owner of that voice were awed by this ghoulish hoard. *Stoop down, feel them in your hands, Dumiitruuu.*

The youth could not disobey; he sifted the powders, which were soft as talc and yet free as mercury; they ran through his fingers and left his hands clean, without residue. And while he handled the salts in this fashion, so the Thing in his mind gave a mental sniff: it seemed to *taste* of the essence of what it had bade Dumitru examine. And:

Ah . . . he was a Greek, this one! the voice informed. *I recognise him—we conversed on several occasions. A priest from Greek land, aye, who knew the legends of the Vrykoulakas. He'd crusaded against them, he said, and carried his crusade across the sea to Moldavia, Wallachia, even to these very mountains. He built a grand church in Alba Iulia, which possibly stands there even to this day, and from it would go out among the towns and villages to seek out the monstrous Vrykoulakas.*

Individuals of the townspeople would name their enemies, often knowing them for innocents; and depending on the power or stature of the accuser, the "Venerable" Arakli Aenos—as this one was called—would "prove" or "disprove" the accusation. For example: if a famous boyar gave evidence that such and such persons were bloodsucking demons, be sure that the Greek would discover them as such. But only let a poor man bring such a charge, however faithfully, and he might well be ignored or even punished for a liar! A witchfinder and a fake, old Aenos, who upon a time accused even myself! Aye, and I must needs flee to escape them from Visegrad, who came to put me down! Oh, I tell you, it was a very troublesome business, that time.

But . . . time settles many a score. Ashes to ashes, dust to dust. When he died, they buried the old fraud in a lead-lined box in Alba Iulia, beside the church he'd built there. What a boon! For just exactly as had been intended, so the imperish-

able lead of his coffin sufficed to keep out the seepage and worms and all manner of rodent malefactor—until a time one hundred years later when I dug him up! Oh, yes—we conversed on several occasions. But in the end, what did he know? Nothing! A fraud, a faker!

Still, I evened the score. That pile of dust you sifted there: Arakli Aenos himself—and ah, how he screeaaamed *when I gave him back his form and flesh, and burned the dog with hot ironsss! Ha-haa-haaa!*

Dumitru hissed his horror and snatched back his fingers from the strewn "salts." He slapped his hands as if they, too, were burned with hot irons, blew on them, wiped them trembling down his coarsely woven trousers. He lurched upright and backed away from the broken urns, only to crash into another rack which stood behind him. He fell sprawling in dust and powder and salts; but his confusion had served to clear his mazed mind a little—which the owner of the voice at once recognised, so that now he tightened his grip.

Steady now, steady, my son! Ah, I see: you think I torment you to no purpose—you believe I derive pleasure from such instruction. But no, no—I deem it only fair that you should know the gravity of the service you perform. You make unto me a considerable offering: of succor, sustenance, replenishment. Wherefore I grant you knowledge . . . for however short a time. Now stand up, stand tall, hear well my words, and follow their directions.

The walls, go to the walls, Dumiitruuu. Good! Now trace the frescoes—with your eyes, my son, and with your hands. Now look and learn:

Here is a man. He is born, lives his life, dies. Prince or peasant, sinner or saint, all go the same way. You see them there in the pictures: holy men and blackguards alike, moving swiftly from cradle to grave, rushing headlong from the sweet, warm moment of conception to the cold, empty abyss of dissolution. It is the lot of all men, it would seem: to become one with the earth, and all the lessons learned in their lives wasted, and their secrets remaining secret unto them alone forever . . .

35

On?

But some there are whose remains, by circumstance of their interment—like the Greek priest, perhaps—remain intact; and others, perhaps cremated and buried in jugs, whose powdered ashes are kept apart from the earth and pure. There they lie, a crumbled bone or two, a handful of dust, and in them all the knowledge of their waking seasons, all the secrets of life and sometimes of death—and maybe even conditions between the two—which they took with them to the grave. All lost.

And again I say . . . oh?

And you will say: but what of knowledge in books, or knowledge passed down by word of mouth, or carved in stone? Surely a learned man, if he so desire, may leave his knowledge behind him for the benefit of others to come after?

What? Stone tablets? Bah! Even the mountains are worn down and the epochs they have known blown away as dust. Word of mouth? Tell a man a story and by the time he retells it the theme is altered. After twenty tellings it may not even be recognised! Books? Given a century and they wither, two and they become so brittle as to snap, three—they crumble into nothing! No, don't speak of books. They are the most fragile of things. Why, there was once in Alexandria the world's most wondrous library . . . and where, pray, are all of those books now? Gone, Dumiitruuu. Gone like all the men of yesteryear. But unlike the books, the men are not forgotten. Not necessarily . . .

And again, what if a man does not desire to leave his secrets behind him?

But enough of that for now; for see, the frescoes are changed. And here is another man . . . well, at least we shall call him a man. But strange, for he is not alone conceived of man and woman. See for yourself: for parent he has . . . but what is this? A snake? A slug? And the creature issues an egg, which the man takes in unto him. And now this most fortunate person is no longer merely human but . . . something else. Ah! And see—this one does not die but goes on and on! Always! Perhaps forever.

36

Do you follow me, Dumiitruuu? Do you follow the pictures on the wall? Aye, and unless this very special One is slain by some brutal man who has the knowledge—or dies accidentally, which may occur upon a time—why, then he will go on forever! Except . . . he has needs, this one. He may not sustain himself like ordinary men. Rather, he knows better sources of sustenance! The blood is the life . . .

Do you know the name of such a one, my son?

"I . . . I know what such men are called," Dumitru answered, for all the world speaking to a vault empty of life other than his own. "The Greeks call them 'Vrykoulakas,' as you have made mention; the Russians 'Viesczy'; and we Travellers, the Szgany, we call them 'Moroi'—vampires!"

There is another name, said the voice, *from a land far, far away in space and time. The name by which they know themselves: Wamphyri!* And for a moment, perhaps in a certain reverence, the voice paused. Then:

Now tell me, Dumiitruuu: do you know who I am? Oh, I know, I'm a voice in your head, but unless you're a madman, the voice must have a source. Have you guessed my identity, Dumiitruuu? Perhaps you've even known it all along, eh?

"You are the Old One." Dumitru gulped, his Adam's apple bobbing, throat dry as a stick. "The undead, undying patron of the Szgany Zirra. You are Janos, the Baron Ferenczy!"

Aye, and you may be a peasant but you're in no wise ignorant, answered the voice. *Indeed I am that one! And you are mine to command as I will. But first a question: is there one among your father Vasile Zirra's band whose hands are three-fingered? A child, perhaps, male, born recently, since last you Szgany were here? Or perhaps a stranger you've seen on your travels, who desired to join your company?*

A strange question, some would think, but not Dumitru. It was part of the legend: that one day a man would come with three fingers on his hands instead of the usual four. Three broad, strong fingers and a thumb to each hand; born that way and natural enough; neither surgically contrived nor even grotesque to look upon. "No," he answered at once. "He has not come."

37

The voice gave a mental grunt; Dumitru could almost see the impatient shrug of broad, powerful shoulders. And: *Not come*, the voice of Janos Ferenczy repeated him. *Not yet come . . .*

But . . . the attitude of the unseen presence was mercurial; it changed in a moment; disappointment was put aside and resignation took its place. *Ah, well, and so I wait out the years. What is time to the Wamphyri anyway, eh?*

Dumitru made no answer. In examining the faded frescoes, he had reached a part of the wall which showed several very gruesome scenes. The frescoes were like a tapestry, telling a story in pictures, but these pictures were straight out of nightmare. In the first, a man was held down by four others, one to each limb. A fifth tormentor in Turkish breeches stood over him with a curved sword raised high, while a sixth knelt close by with a mallet and sharp stake of wood. In the next picture the victim had been beheaded and the stake driven through him, pinning him down—but a huge, fat, sluglike worm or snake was emerging from his severed neck, so that the men about him reared back in horror! In a third picture the men had encircled the Thing with a ring of torches and were burning it; likewise the head and body of its once-host, upon a pile of faggots. The fourth and penultimate scene of the set was of a priest, swinging his censer in one hand, while with the other he poured the vampire's ashes into an urn. Presumably it was a rite of exorcism, of purification. But if so, then it was mistaken, wasted.

For the final scene was of the same urn, and above it a black bat in flight, rising like a phoenix from the ashes. Indeed, the very sigil of the Ferenczy! And:

Aye, said Janos darkly, in Dumitru's head, *but not until the advent of the three-fingered man. Not until he comes, the true son of my sons. For only then may I escape from one vessel into the next. Ah, for there are vessels and there are vessels, Dumiitruuu, and some of them are of stone . . .*

Again the youth's mind had started to unmaze itself. Of his own will, suddenly he saw how low his torch had burned where he'd placed it in a stone bracket on the wall. He took it down and tremblingly lit another from it, waving it a little to get the flame going. And licking his dry lips, he looked at the myriad urns and wondered which one held his tormentor. How easy it would be to shatter the thing, scatter its dust, thrust his torch amongst those sentient remains and see if they'd burn a second time.

Janos was not slow to note the resurgence of Szgany will, or to read the threat in the mind he'd mastered. He chuckled voicelessly and said, *Ah, not here, not here, Dumiitruuu! What? You'd have me lie among scum? And could it be I heard you thinking treacherous thoughts just then? Still, you'd not be of the blood if you didn't, eh?* And again his evil chuckle, following which: *But you were right to rekindle your torch: best not let the flame die, Dumiitruuu, for it's an exceeding dark place you've come to. Also, there's yet a thing or two I want to show you, for which we'll need the light. Now see, there's a room to your right, my son. Go in through the archway, if you will, and there discover my true lair.*

Dumitru might have struggled with himself . . . but useless; the vampire's grip on his mind had returned more solid than ever. He did as instructed, passing under the arch and into a room much like the others except for its appointments. No racks of amphorae or frescoed walls here; the place was more habitation than warehouse; woven tapestries were on the walls, and the floor was of green-glazed tiles set in mortar. Centrally, a mosaic of smaller tiles described the prophetic crest of the Ferenczy, while to one side and close to a massive fireplace stood an ancient table of dense, black oak.

The wall hangings were falling into moldering tatters and the dust lay as thick here as anywhere, but yet there was a seeming anomaly. Upon the desk were papers, books, envelopes, various seals and waxes, pens and inks: *modern* things by comparison with anything else Dumitru had seen. The Ferenczy's things? He had assumed the Old One to be dead—or undead—but all of this seemed to suggest otherwise.

No, the baron's viscous mental voice contradicted him, *not mine but the property of . . . shall we say, a student of mine? He studied my works, and might even have dared to study*

39

*me! Oh, he knew well enow the words to call me up, but he
did not know where to find me, nor even that I was here at
all! But alas, I fancy he's no more. Most likely his bones
adorn the upper ruins somewhere. It shall delight me to discover them there one day, and do for him what he might so
easily have done for me!*

While the voice of Janos Ferenczy so darkly and yet ob-
scurely reminisced, so Dumitru Zirra had crossed to the table. There were copies of letters there, but not in any
language he could read. He could make out the dates, though,
from fifty years earlier, and something of the far-flung postal
addresses and addressees. There had been a M. Raynaud in
Paris, a Josef Nadek in Prague, one Colin Grieve in Edinburgh, and a Joseph Curwen in Providence; oh, and a host
of others in the towns and cities of as many different lands
again. The writer to all of these names and addresses, as
witness his handwriting on the browned paper, was one and
the same person: a certain Mr. Hutchinson, or "Edw. H."
as he more frequently signed himself.

As for the books: they meant nothing to Dumitru. A peasant, however much travelled and practised in certain tongues
and dialects, such titles as the *Turba Philosophorum,* Bacon's
Thesaurus Chemicus, and Trithemius's *De Lapide Philosoph-
ico* meant nothing to him. Or if they did, he made no real
connection.

But in one book which still lay open, and despite the dust
lying thick on its pages, Dumitru saw pictures which did
mean something, and something quite horrific. For there, in
painstaking and pain-giving detail, were shown a series of
the most hideous and brutal tortures, the like of which caused
him—even half-hypnotised as he was—to flinch and draw
back a little, distancing himself from the page. But in the
next moment, his eyes were drawn to the rest of that room's
appurtenances, which until now had not impressed themselves upon his mind; that is, to the great manacles fastened
to the walls by heavy chains, to certain badly corroded implements idly tossed to the floor in one corner, and to the

several iron braziers which still contained the ashes of olden fires!

Before he could give these items any further attention, however, if he had wanted to:

Dumiitruuu, crooned that gurgling voice in his head, *now tell me: have you ever thirsted? Have you ever wandered in a dry desert, with never sight or sign of water, and felt your throat contract to a throbbing ulcer through which you can scarce draw breath? Well, possibly you may have known a time when you* felt *dry as salt, which might help you understand something of the way I feel now. But only something of it. Certainly you have never been* as *salt. Ah, if only I could describe* my *thirst, my son!*

But enough; I'm sure now that you perceive something of my arts, my meaning, my power and destiny, and that the requirements of One such as I have importance far above any question of common life and lives. And the time has come to introduce you to the final mystery, wherein we both shall know the most exquisite ecstasies. The great chimney, Dumiitruuu—go in.

Go into a chimney, a fireplace? Dumitru looked at it, felt the urge to draw back from it, and could not. Massively built, the fire-scarred hole was all of four feet wide and five high, arched over and set with a central keystone at its top; he need stoop only a little to pass inside. Before doing so, he lit another torch—a pause which Janos Ferenczy saw as a sign of hesitancy. *Quickly now, Dumiitruuu,* the awful voice urged, *for even in dissolution—no, especially in dissolution—my need is not to be kept waiting. It is such that I cannot endure it.*

Dumitru passed into the fireplace, held up his torch to light the place. Above him soared a wide, scorched flu, which angled back gradually into the wall. Holding his torch away, the youth looked for light from above and saw only darkness. That was not strange: the chimney must pass through several angles in its climb to the surface, and of course it would be blocked where the upper regions lay in ruins.

Bringing the torch close again, Dumitru saw iron rungs set in the sloping back wall of the flue. In its heyday, the castle's

41

chimneys would need sweeping from time to time. And yet . . . there was no accumulation of soot such as might be expected; apart from a superficial scorching, the chimney seemed hardly used at all.

Oh, it has been used, my son. Janos Ferenczy's mental voice chuckled obscenely. *You shall see, you shall see. But first, step aside a little. Before you ascend there are those who must descend! Small minions of mine, small friends . . .*

Dumitru crushed back against a side wall; there came a fluttering, rapidly amplified by the chimney into a roar, and a colony of small bats whose hurtling bodies formed an almost solid shaft rushed down and out from the flue, dispersing into the subterranean vaults. For long moments they issued from the flue, until Dumitru began to think they must be without number. But then the roaring in the chimney diminished, a few latecomers shot by him, and all was silence once more.

Now climb, said the Ferenczy, again closing his grip on the mind of his mental slave.

The rungs were wide and shallow, twelve inches apart, and set very firmly into the mortar between stones. Dumitru found that he could carry his torch and, using only his feet and one hand, still climb easily enough. After only nine or ten rungs the chimney narrowed considerably, and after as many again flattened through about forty-five degrees to become little more than an upward sloping shaft. Within the space of a further twenty feet the rungs petered out and were replaced by shallow slablike steps; the "floor" then levelled out entirely and the "ceiling" gradually receded to a height of some nine or ten feet.

Now Dumitru found himself in a narrow, featureless stone passageway no more than three feet wide and of indeterminate length, where a feeling of utmost dread quickly enveloped him, bringing him to a crouching halt. Trembling and oozing cold sweat—with his heart fluttering in his chest like a trapped bird, and clammy perspiration sticking his clothes to his back and thighs—the youth thrust out his torch before him. Up ahead in the shadows where they flickered beyond the full range of illumination, a pair of yellow triangular eyes—wolf eyes and feral—floated low to the floor and reflected the torch's fitful light. They were fixed upon Dumitru.

An old friend of mine, Dumiitruuu. Janos Ferenczy's voice crawled in his mind like mental slime. *Just like the Szgany, he and his kith and kin have watched over me many a year. Why, all manner of curious folk might come wandering up here but for these wolves of mine! Did he perhaps frighten you? You thought him below and behind you, and here he is ahead? But can't you see that this is my bolt hole? And what sort of a bolt hole, pray, with only one way in and out? No, only follow this passage far enough, and it emerges in a hole in the face of the sheer cliff. Except . . . you shall not be required to go so far . . .*

The voice scarcely bothered to disguise its threat; the Ferenczy would not be denied his due now; his grip on Dumitru's mind and will tightened like a vise of ice. And: *Proceed,* he coldly commanded.

Ahead of the youth the great wolf turned and loped on, a grey shadow that merged with the greater darkness. Dumitru followed, his step uncertain, his heart pounding until he thought he could actually hear the blood singing in his ears, like the ocean in the whorl of a conch. And he wasn't the only one who could hear it.

Ah, my son, my son! The voice was a gurgle of monstrous anticipation, of unbridled lust. *Your heart leaps in you like a stag fixed with a bolt! Such strength, such youth! I feel it all! But whatever it is that causes such panic in you, be sure it is almost at an end, Dumiitruuu . . .*

The passage widened; on Dumitru's left the wall as before, but on his right a depression, a trench running parallel, cut in the solid rock—indeed in bedrock—that deepened with each pace he took. He extended his torch out over the rim and looked down, and in the deepest section of the trench saw . . . the rim and narrow neck of . . . of a black urn, half-buried in dark soil!

The rim of the urn—like a dark pouting mouth, with lips that seemed to expand and contract loathsomely in the flick-

43

ering light—stood some five feet below the level of Dumitru's path. Beyond the urn, the bed of the trench had been raised up. Cut in a "V," like a sluice, it sloped gently downwards to a raised rim channelled into a narrow spout which projected directly over the mouth of the urn; in the other direction, the V-shaped bed sloped upwards and out of sight into shadows. The raised rim of rock and carved spout above the urn looked for all the world like guttering over a rain barrel, and like guttering they were stained black from the flow of some nameless liquid . . .

For several long moments Dumitru stood trembling there, gasping, not fully understanding what he saw but knowing with every instinct of his being that whatever it was, this contrivance was the very embodiment of evil. And as he oozed cold, slimy sweat and felt his entire body wracked with shudders, so the voice of his tormentor came again in his staggering mind:

Go on, my son, that terrible voice urged. *A pace or two more, Dumiitruuu, and all will become apparent. But carefully, very carefully—don't faint or fall from the path, whatever you do!*

Two more paces, and the youth's bulging eyes never leaving that terrible urn, nor even blinking—until he saw the place where the trench came to an end: a black oblong like an open grave. And as the light of his torch fell within—what that terrible space contained!

Spikes! Needle-sharp fangs of rusted iron, filling that final gap side to side and end to end. Three dozen of them at least—and Dumitru knew their meaning, and the Ferenczy's terrible purpose in an instant!

Oh? Ha-haa-haaa! Ha-haaa! Terrible laughter filled Dumitru's mind, if not his ears. *And so finally it's a battle of wills, eh, my son?*

A battle of wills? Dumitru's will hardened; he fought for control of his mind, his young, powerful muscles. And: "I . . . won't . . . kill myself for you . . . old devil!" he gasped.

Of course you won't, Dumiitruuu. Not even I can make you do that, not against your will. Beguilement has its limits, you see. No, you won't kill yourself, my son. I shall do that. Indeed—I already have!

Dumitru found his limbs full of a sudden strength, his mind free at last of the Ferenczy's shackles. Licking his lips, eyes starting out, he looked this way and that. Which way to run? Somewhere up ahead a great wolf waited; but he still had his torch; the wolf would back off before its flaring. And behind him . . .

From behind him, in this previously still place, suddenly the air came rushing like a wind—fanned by a myriad of wings! The bats!

In another moment the crushing claustrophobia of the place crashed down on Dumitru. Even without the bats, whose return seemed imminent, he knew he could never find courage to retrace his steps down the false flue, and then through the castle's vaults with their graveyard loot, and on up that echoing stone stairwell to the outside world. No, there was only one way: forward to whatever awaited him. And as the first bats came in a rush, so he hurled himself along the stone ledge—

Which at once tilted under his weight!

And:

Ahaaa! said the awful voice in his head, full of triumph now. *But even a big wolf weighs much less than a man full-grown, Dumiitruuu!*

Opposite the spiked pit, the ledge and entire section of wall that backed it—an "L" of hewn stone—tilted through ninety degrees and tossed Dumitru onto the spikes. His single shriek, of realisation and the horror it brought combined, was cut off short as he was pierced through skull and spine and most of his vital organs—but not his heart. Still beating, his heart continued to pump his blood—to pump it out through the many lacerations of his impaled, writhing body.

And did I not say it would be an ecstasy, Dumiitruuu? And did I not say I'd kill you? The monster's gloating words came floating through all the youth's agonies, but dimly and fading, as was the agony itself. And that was the last of Janos Fer-

45

enczy's torments, his final taunt; for now Dumitru could no longer hear him.

But Janos was not disappointed. No, for now there was that which was far more important—an ancient thirst to quench. At least until the next time.

Blood coursed down the V-shaped channel, spurted from the spout, splashed down into the mouth of the urn to wet whatever was inside. Ancient ashes, salts—the chemicals of a man, of a monster—soaked it up, bubbled and bulked out, smoked and smouldered. Such was the chemical reaction that the obscene lips of the urn seemed almost to belch . . .

In a little while the great wolf came back. He passed scornfully under the bats where they chittered and formed a ceiling of living fur, stepped timidly where the pivoting floor and wall of the passage had rocked smoothly back into place, and paused to gaze down at the now silent urn.

Then . . . he whined deep in the back of his throat, jumped down into the pit and up onto the runnelled slab above the urn, and crept timidly between the spikes to a clear area at the head of the trench. There he turned about and began to free Dumitru's drained body from the spikes, lifting the corpse from them one at a time.

When this was done, he'd jump up out of the pit, which wasn't deep here, reach down and worry the body out, and drag it to the Place of Many Bones, where he could feed at will. It was a routine with which the old wolf was quite familiar. He'd performed this task on several previous occasions.

So had his father before him. And his. And his . . .

II: Seekers

SAVIRSIN, ROMANIA; EVENING OF THE FIRST FRIDAY IN August 1983; the *Gaststube* of an inn perched on the steep
mountainside at the eastern extreme of the town, where the
road climbs up through many hairpin bends and out of sight
into the pines.

Three young Americans, tourists by their looks and rig,
sat together at a chipped, ages-blackened, heavily grained
circular wooden table in one corner of the barroom. Their
clothes were casual; one of them smoked a cigarette; their
drinks were local beers, not especially strong but stinging to
the palate and very refreshing.

At the bar itself a pair of gnarled mountain men, hunters
complete with rifles so ancient they must surely qualify as
antiques, had guffawed and slapped backs and bragged of
their prowess—and not only as hunters of beasts—for over an
hour before one of them suddenly took on a surprised look,
staggered back from the bar, and with a slurred oath aimed
himself reeling through the door out into the smoky blue-
grey twilight. His rifle lay on the bar where he'd left it; the

47

bartender, not a little gingerly, took it up and put it carefully away out of sight, then continued to wash and dry the day's used glasses.

The departed hunter's drinking companion—and partner in crime or whatever—roared with renewed laughter; he slapped the bar explosively, finished off the other's plum brandy and threw back his own, then looked around for more sport. And of course he spied the Americans where they sat at their ease, making casual conversation. In fact, and until now, their conversation had centered on him, but he didn't know that.

He ordered another drink—and whatever they were drinking for them at the table; one for the barman, too—and swayed his way over to them. Before filling the order, the barman took his rifle, too, and placed it safely with the other.

"Gogosu," the old hunter growled, thumbing himself in his leather-clad chest. "Emil Gogosu. And you? *Touristi*, are you?" He spoke Romanian, the dialect of the area, which leaned a little towards Hungarian. All three, they smiled back at him, two of them somewhat warily.

But the third translated, and quickly answered, "Tourists, yes. From America, the USA. Sit down, Emil Gogosu, and talk to us."

Taken by surprise, the hunter said, "Eh? Eh? You have the tongue? You're a guide for these two, eh? Profitable, is it?"

The younger man laughed. "God, no! I'm with them—I'm one of them—an American!"

"Impossible!" Gogosu declared, taking a seat. "What? Why, I never before heard such a thing! Foreigners speaking the tongue? You're pulling my leg, right?"

Gogosu was peasant Romanian through and through. He had a brown, weather-beaten face, grey bullhorn mustaches stained yellow in the middle from pipe-smoking, long sideburns curling in towards his upper lip, and penetrating grey eyes under bristling, even greyer brows. He wore a patched leather jacket with a high collar that buttoned up to the neck, over a white shirt whose sleeves fitted snug at the wrist. His fur *caciula* cap was held fast under the right epaulet of his jacket; a half-filled bandolier passed under the left epaulet, crossed his chest diagonally, fed itself up under his right arm and across his back. A wide leather belt supported a sheath and hunter's knife, several pouches, and his coarsely woven trousers which he wore tucked into his climber's pigskin-calf boots. A small man, still he looked strong and wiry. And all in all, he was a picturesque specimen.

"We were talking about you," their interpreter told him.

"Eh? Oh?" Gogosu looked from one face to the next all the way round. "About me? So I'm a figure of curiosity, am I?"

"Of admiration," the wily American answered. "A hunter, by your looks, and good at it—or so we'd guess. You'd know this country, these mountains, well?"

"There isn't a man knows 'em better!" Gogosu declared. But he was wily, too, and now his eyes narrowed a little. "You're looking for a guide, eh?"

"We could be, we could be." The other slowly nodded. "But there are guides and there are guides. You ask *some* guides to show you a ruined castle on a mountain and they promise you the earth! The very castle of Dracula, they say! And then they take you to a pile of rocks like someone's pigsty collapsed! Aye, ruins, Emil Gogosu, that's what we're interested in. For photographs, for pictures . . . for mood and atmosphere!"

The barman delivered their drinks and Gogosu tossed his straight back. "Eh? Eh? You're going to make one of those picture things, right? Moving pictures? The old vampire in his castle, chasing the girls with the wobbling breasts! God, yes, I've seen 'em! The pictures, I mean, down in old Lugoj, where there's a picture house. Not the girls, no . . . sod all wobbly tits round here, I can tell you! Withered paps at best in this neck of the woods, my lads! But I've seen the pictures. And that's what you're looking for, eh? Ruins . . ."

Oddly, and despite the brandy he's consumed, the old boy seemed to have sobered a little. His eyes focused more readily, became more fixed in their orbits as he studied the Americans each in his turn. First there was their interpreter. He was a queer one for sure, with his knowledge of the tongue and what all. He was tall, this one, a six-footer with inches to spare, long in the leg, lean in the hip, and broad at the shoulders. And now that Gogosu looked closer, he could see that he wasn't just American. Not all American, anyway.

"What's your name, eh? What's your name?" The hunter took the young man's hand and made to tighten his grip on it . . . but it was snatched back at once and down out of sight under the table.

"George," the owner of the refused hand quickly replied, reclaiming Gogosu's startled-to-flight attention. "George Vulpe."

"Vulpe?" The hunter laughed out loud and slapped the table, making their drinks dance. "Oh, I've known a few Vulpes in my time. But George? What kind of a name is George to go with a name like Vulpe, eh? Now come on, let's be straight, you and I . . . you mean *Gheorghe*, don't you?"

The other's dark eyes darkened more yet and seemed to brood a very little, but then they relaxed and exchanged grin for grin with the grey eyes of their inquisitor. "Well, you're a sharp one, Emil," their owner finally said. "Sharp-eyed too! Yes, I was Romanian once. There's a story to it, but it's not much . . ."

The gnarled old hunter returned to studying him. "Tell it anyway," he said, giving Vulpe a slow once-over. And the young man shrugged and sat back in his chair.

"Well, I was born here, under the mountains," he said, his voice as soft as his deceptively soft mouth. He smiled and flashed perfect teeth. *So they should be,* Gogosu thought, *in a man only twenty-six or -seven years old.* "Born here," Vulpe repeated, "yes . . . but it's only a dim and distant memory now. My folks were Travellers, which accounts for my looks. You recognised me from my tanned skin, right? And my dark eyes?"

"Aye." Gogosu nodded. "And from the thin lobes of your ears, which would take a nice gold ring. And from your high forehead and wolfish jaw, which aren't uncommon in the

Szgany. Oh, your origins are obvious enough, to a man who can see. So what happened?''

"Happened?'' Again Vulpe's shrug. "My parents moved to the cities, settled down, became 'workers' instead of the drones they'd always been.''

"Drones? You believe that?''

"No, but the authorities did. They gave them a flat in Craiova, right next to the new railway. The mortar was rotten and shaky from the trains; the plaster was coming off the walls; someone's toilet in the flat above leaked on us . . . but it was good enough for work-shy drones, they said. And until I was eleven that's where I'd play, next to the tracks. Then . . . one night a train was derailed. It ploughed right into our block, took away a wall, brought the whole place crashing down. I was lucky enough to live through it, but my people died. And for a while I thought I'd be better off dead, too, because my spine had been crushed and I was a cripple. But someone heard about me, and there was a scheme on at the time—an exchange of doctors and patients, between American and Romanian rehabilitation clinics—and because I was an orphan I was given priority. Not bad for a drone, eh? So . . . I went to the USA. And they fixed me up. What's more, they adopted me, too! Two of them did, anyway. And because I was only a boy and there was no one left back here''— yet again, his shrug—"why, I was allowed to stay!''

"Ah!'' said Gogosu. "And so now you're an American. Well, I'll believe you . . . but it's strange for Gypsies to leave the open road. Sometimes they get thrown out and go their own ways—disputes and what have you in the camps, usually over a woman or a horse—but rarely to settle in towns. What was it with your folks? Did they cross the Gypsy king or something?''

"I don't know. I was only a boy,'' Vulpe answered. "I think perhaps they feared for me: I was a weak little thing, apparently, a runt. At any rate, they left the night I was born, and covered their tracks, and never went back.''

"A runt?'' Gogosu raised an eyebrow, looked Vulpe up and down yet again. "Well, you'd not know it now! But they

51

covered their tracks, you say? That's it, then. Say no more. There'd been trouble in the camp, for sure. I'll give you odds your father and mother were secret lovers, and she was promised to another. Then you came along, so he stole her away. Oh, it happens."

"That's a very romantic notion," Vulpe said. "And who knows? You could be right . . ."

"My God, we're ignorant!" Gogosu suddenly exploded, beckoning to the barman. "Here's you and me chatting in this old tongue of ours, and your two friends bewildered and left out entirely. Now let me get you all another drink and then we'll have some introductions. I want to know why you're here, and what I can do to help, and how much you'll pay me to take you to some *real* ruins!"

"The drinks are on us," said Vulpe. "And no arguments. God, do you expect us to keep up with you, Emil Gogosu? Now slow down or you'll have us all under the table before we've even got things sorted out! As for introductions, that's easy."

He clasped the shoulder of the American closest to him. "This great gangly one is Seth Armstrong, from Texas. They build them tall there, Emil, as you can see. But then it's a big state. Why, your entire Romania would fit into Texas alone three times over!"

Gogosu was suitably impressed. He shook hands with Armstrong and looked him over. The Texan was big and raw-boned, with honest blue eyes in an open face, sparse straw-coloured hair, arms and legs as long and thin as poles. His nose was long over a wide, expressive mouth and a heavy, bristly chin. Just a little short of seventy-eight inches, Armstrong, even seated, came up head and shoulders above the others.

"Hah!" said the hunter. "This Texas would *have* to be big to accommodate such as him!"

Vulpe translated, then nodded in the direction of the third member of his group. "And this one," he said, "is Randy Laverne from Madison, Wisconsin. It mightn't be so mountainous up there, but believe me, it can get just as cold!"

"Cold?" said Gogosu. "Well, that shouldn't bother this one! I envy him all that good meat on his bones—and all the good meals it took to put it there—but it's not much use in climbing. Me, I'm able to cling to the rocks snug as a lichen, in places where gravity would get him for sure!"

Vulpe translated and Laverne laughed good-naturedly. He was the youngest and smallest (or at least the shortest) of the three Americans: twenty-five, freckle-faced, way overweight, and constantly hungry. His face was round and topped with wavy red hair; his green eyes friendly and full of fun; the corners of his eyes and mouth running into mazes of laugh lines. But there was nothing soft about him: his huge hands were incredibly strong, a legacy of his blacksmith father.

"Very well," said George Vulpe, "so now we know each other. Or rather, you know us! But what about you, Emil? You're a hunter, yes, but what else?"

"Nothing else!" said Gogosu. "I don't need to be anything else. I've a small house and a smaller woman in Ilia; in the summer I hunt wild pig and sell meat to the butchers and skins to the tailors and boot makers; in the winter I take furs and kill a few foxes, and they hire me to shoot the occasional wolf. And so I make a living—barely! And now maybe I'll be a guide, too. Why not? For I know the heights as well as the eagles who nest in 'em!"

"And the odd ruined castle? You can show us one of those, too?"

"Castles abound," said Gogosu. "But you told me there are guides and guides. Well, so are there castles and castles. And you're right: anyone can show you a tumble of old boulders and call it a castle. But I, Emil Gogosu, can show you a *castle*!"

The Americans Armstrong and Laverne got the gist of this and became excited. Armstrong, in his Texas drawl, said, "Hey, George, tell him what we're really doing here. Explain to him how close he was when he talked about Dracula and vampires and all."

"In America," Vulpe told the hunter, "all over the world, in fact, Transylvania and the *Carpatti Meridionali* are fa-

53

mous! Not so much for their dramatic beauty or gaunt isolation as for their myths and legends. You talked of Dracula,
who had his origins in a cruel Vlad of olden times . . . but
don't you know that every year the tourists flock in their
droves to visit the great Drakul's homeland and the castles
where he's said to have dwelled? Indeed it's big business.
And we believe it could be even bigger.''

"Pah!" said Gogosu. "Why, this whole country is steeped
in olden lore and superstitious myths. This impaler Vlad's
just a one of them.'' He leaned closer, lowered his voice,
and his eyes went big and round. "I could take you to a castle
old as the mountains themselves, a shattered keep so feared
that even today it's left entirely alone in a trackless place,
like naked bones under the moon, kept secret in the lee of
haunted crags!" He sat back and nodded his satisfaction with
their expressions. "There!"

After Vulpe had translated, Randy Laverne said, "Wow!"
And more soberly: "But . . . do you think he's for real?"

And the hunter knew what he'd said. He stared straight and
frowning into Laverne's wide eyes and instructed Vulpe,
"You tell him that I shot the last man who called me a liar
right in his backside! And you can also tell him this: that in
these ruins I know, there's a great grey wolf keeps watch even
today. And that's a fact, for I've tried to shoot him, too!"

Vulpe began to translate, but in the middle of it the hunter
started to laugh. "Hey! Hey!" he said. "Not so serious! And
don't take my threats too much to heart. Oh, I know my
story's a wild-sounding thing, but it's true all the same. Pay
me for my time and trouble and come see for yourselves.
Well, what do you say?"

Vulpe held up a cautionary hand and Gogosu looked at it
curiously in the moment before it was withdrawn. It had felt
strange, that hand, when he'd grasped it. And there'd been
something not quite right about it when Vulpe had clasped
the gangling Armstrong's shoulder. Also, Vulpe seemed shy
about his hands and kept them out of sight most of the time.
"Now wait," said the young expatriate Romanian, reclaim-

ing the hunter's attention. "Let's first see if we're talking about the right place."

"The *right* place?" said Gogosu, puzzled. "And just how many such places do you think there are?"

"I meant," Vulpe explained, "let's see if maybe we've heard of this castle of yours."

"I doubt it. You'll not find it on any modern maps, and that's for sure. I reckon the authorities think that if they leave it alone—if they just ignore it for long enough—then maybe it'll finally crumble away! No, no, you've not heard of this place, I'm sure."

"Well, let's check it out anyway," said Vulpe. "You see, the deeds, territories, and history of the original Dracula—I mean of the Wallachian prince from whom Dracula took his name—are well chronicled and absolutely authentic. An Englishman turned the fact into fiction, that's all, and in so doing started a legend. Then there was a famous Frenchman who also wrote about a castle in the Carpathians and possibly started a legend or two of his own. And finally an American did the same thing.

"Now the thing is, this American—his name would mean nothing to you—has since become very famous. If we could find *his* castle . . . it could be the Dracula story all over again! Tourists? Ah, but you'd see some *touristi* then, Emil Gogosu! And who knows but that you'd be chief guide, eh?"

Gogosu chewed the centre of his mustache. "Huh!" he finally snorted; but his eyes had grown very bright and not a little greedy. He rubbed his nose, finally said, "Very well, so what do you want to know? How can we decide if the castle I know and the one you're looking for is one and the same, eh?"

"It might be simpler than you think," said Vulpe. "For example, how long has this place of yours been a ruin?"

"Oh, it blew up before my time," Gogosu answered with a shrug—and was at once astonished to see Vulpe give a great start. "Eh?"

But already the American was translating to his friends, and astonishment and wonder were mirrored in their faces, too. Finally Vulpe turned again to the hunter. "Blew up, you say? You mean . . . exploded?"

"Or bombed, yes," said Gogosu, frowning. "When a wall falls, it falls, but some of these walls have been blasted outwards, hurled afar."

Vulpe was very excited now, but he tried not to show it. "And did it have a name, this castle? What of its owner before it fell? That could be very important."

"Its name?" Gogosu screwed up his face in concentration. He tapped his forehead, leaned back in his chair, finally shook his head. "My father's father had old maps," he said. "The name of the place was on them. That's where I first saw it, and when I first decided to go and see it. But its name . . . it's gone now."

Vulpe translated.

"Maps like this one?" said Armstrong. He produced a copy of an old Romanian map and spread it on the table. It soaked up a little beer but otherwise was fine.

"Like this one, aye." Gogosu nodded. "But older, far older. This is just a copy. Here, let me see." He smoothed the map out, stared at it in several places. "Not shown," he said. "My castle is not shown. Just a blank space. Well, that's understandable enough. Gloomy old place. It's like I said: they'd like to forget it. Legends? You don't know the half of it!" And a moment later: *"Ahhh!"* He jerked back in his seat and clutched at his forehead with both hands.

"Jesus!" cried Laverne. "Is he okay?"

"Okay, yes . . . Okay!" said Emil Gogosu. And to Vulpe: "Now I remember, Gheorghe. It was . . . Ferenczy!"

Vulpe's bottom jaw, and those of his friends, fell open. "Jesus!" said Laverne again, this time in a whisper.

"The Castle Ferenczy?" Armstrong reached over and grabbed the hunter's forearm.

Gogosu nodded. "That's it. And that's the one, eh?"

Vulpe and the others fell back in their seats, gaped at each other; they acted bewildered, confused, or simply astonished. But at last Vulpe said, "Yes, that's the one. And you'll take us to it? Tomorrow?"

"Oh, be sure I will," said Gogosu. "For a price!" And he looked at Vulpe's hands, where he'd spread them on the table, holding down the map. Vulpe saw where the hunter was looking, but this time made no attempt to hide his hands away. Instead he merely raised an eyebrow.

"An accident?" the old Romanian asked him. "If so, they patched you up rather cleverly."

"No," Vulpe answered, "no accident. I was born like this. It's just that my parents always taught me to hide them away, that's all. And so I do, except from my friends . . ."

Because of the mountains, the sun seemed a little late in rising. When it did, it came up hot and smoky. At 8:30 the three Americans were waiting for Gogosu on the dusty road outside the inn, their packs at their feet, peaked caps on their heads with tinted visors to keep out the worst of the sun. The old hunter had told them he'd "collect" them here, at this hour, though they hadn't been sure exactly what he'd meant.

Randy Laverne had just drained a small bottle of beer and put it down to one side of the inn's doorstep when they heard the rattle and clatter of a local bus. These were so rare as to be near fabulous; certainly the arrival of one such demanded a photograph or two; Seth Armstrong got out his camera and started snapping as the beaten-up bus came lurching out of the pines and down the serpentine road towards the inn.

The thing was a wonderful contraption: bald tyres, bonnet vibrating to a blur over the backfiring engine, windows bleary and fly-specked. The driver's window was especially bloody, from the eviscerations of a thousand suicided insects; and Emil Gogosu was leaning out of the folding doors at the front with a huge grin stamped on his leathery face, waving at them, indicating they should get aboard.

The bus shuddered to a halt; the driver grinned, nodded, and held up a roll of brown tickets; Gogosu stepped down and helped the three strap their packs to running boards which went the full length of this ancient vehicle. Then they were aboard, paid their fare, collapsed or were shaken into bone-jarring seats as the driver engaged a low gear and let the one-in-five decline do the work of his engine.

George Vulpe was seated beside Gogosu. ''Okay,'' he said when he'd recovered his breath, ''so where are we going?''

''First the payment,'' said the hunter.

''Old man,'' Vulpe returned, ''I've this feeling you don't much trust us!''

''Not so much of the 'old'—I'm only fifty-four,'' said Gogosu. ''I weather easy. But even so, I didn't get this old without learning that it's sometimes best to collect your pay *before* the fact! Trust has nothing to do with it. I don't want you falling off a mountain with my wages in your pocket, that's all!'' And he burst into laughter at Vulpe's expression.

But in another moment: ''We're going down to Lipova where we'll pick up a train to Sebis. Then we'll try to hitch a ride on a cart to Halmagiu village. And *then* we start climbing! Actually it's a`long cut. You know what that is? The opposite to a shortcut. You see, the castle is only, oh, maybe fifty kilometers from here as the crow flies—but we're not crows. So instead of crossing the Zarundului we're going round 'em. Can't cross 'em anyway; no roads. And Halmagiu is a good base camp for the climb. Now don't go getting all worried: it's not *that* much of a climb, not in daylight. If an 'old man' like me can do it, you young 'uns should shoot up there like goats!''

''Couldn't we have taken the train from Savirsin all the way?'' Vulpe wanted to know.

''If there was one scheduled. But there isn't. Don't be so eager. We'll get there. You did say you had six days left before you have to be in Bucuresti to catch your plane? So what's the hurry? The way I reckon it we should be in Sebis before noon—if we make the connection in Lipova. There *may* be a bus from Sebis to Halmagiu, which would get us there by, oh, two-thirty at the latest. Or we hitch rides . . . on trucks, carts, what have you. So we could get in late, and have to put up there for the night. Anytime after four is too late—unless you maybe fancy sleeping on the mountain?''

''We wouldn't fancy that, no.''

"Hah!" Gogosu snorted. "Fair-weather climbers! But in fact the weather *is* fair. Too damned warm for me! There'd be no problems. A big tin of Hungarian sausages in brine— they come in cheap from across the border—a loaf of black bread, a cheap bottle of plum brandy, and a few beers. What . . . ? A night under the stars in the lee of the crags, with a campfire burning red and the smell of resin coming up off the pines, would do you three the world of good. Your lungs would think they'd died and gone to lung heaven!" He made it sound good.

"We'll see," said Vulpe. "Meanwhile, we'll pay you half now and the rest when we see these ruins you've promised us." He took out a bundle of *leu* and counted off the notes— probably more money than Gogosu would normally see in a month, but very little to him and his companions—then topped up the hunter's cupped palms with a pile of copper *banis*, "shrapnel" or "scrap metal" to the three Americans. Gogosu counted it all very carefully and finally tucked it away, tried to keep a straight face, but couldn't hold it. In the end he grinned broadly and smacked his lips.

"That'll keep me in brandy for a while," he said. And more hurriedly: "A *short* while, you understand."

Vulpe nodded knowingly. "Oh, yes, I understand," and smiled as he settled back in his half of the seat.

From behind, the strident, excited voices of Armstrong and Laverne grew loud to compensate for the rumble and clatter of the bus; in front an old woman sat with a huge wire cage of squabbling chicks in her lap; a pair of hulking young farmers were hunched on the other side of the central aisle, discussing fowl pest or some such and arguing over a decades-browned copy of *Rumanian Farming Life*. There was a family group in the rear of the bus—all very smart, incongruous, uncomfortable, and odd looking in almost-modern suits and dresses—possibly on their way to a wedding or reunion or some such.

To Vulpe's American companions it must all have seemed very weird and wonderful, but to Gheorghe—to *George*—

himself it was . . . like home. Like coming home, yes. And yet as well as poignant it was also . . . puzzling.

He'd felt it ever since they got off the plane a fortnight ago, something he'd thought burned out of him in the fifteen long years since his doctor had taken him to America and come back without him. He'd wanted it to be burned out, too, that bitterness which had come with being orphaned. For in those first years in America he had *hated* Romania and couldn't even be reminded of his origins without retreating into black depression. It was one of the reasons he'd come back now, he supposed: to be able to shrug off the shroud of the place and finally say, "There was nothing here for them . . . nothing here for me . . . I escaped!"

In short he had expected the place, the entire country, to depress him and make him bitter all over again—but for the last time—and that afterwards he really would be free of it, glad that it was gone and finally forgotten. He had felt that he'd be able to get down out of that plane, look around, and shrug and say to himself, "Who needs it?"

But he'd been wrong.

What pain there'd been had quickly drained away; instead of feeling alienated, it was as if Romania had at once taken hold of him and told him, "You were a part of this. You were part of the blood of this ancient land. Your roots are here. You *know* this place, and it knows you!"

Especially here on these dusty roads and tracks under the mountains, these lanes and forest ways and high passes, these valleys and crags and forbidding desolations of sky-piercing rock. These dark woods and rearing aeries. Such places were in his blood, yes. If he listened hard enough, he could hear them surging there like a tide on a distant shore, calling to him. Something was calling to him, certainly . . .

"Tell me again," said Gogosu, digging him in the ribs.

Vulpe started and was back in the bus, drawn down from his flight of fancy. If that's what it had been. "What? Tell you what?"

"Why you're here. What it's all about. I mean, I'm damned if I can understand you vampire fanciers!"

"No," said Vulpe, shaking his head, "that's why *they* are here." He tilted his head back, indicating the two in the seats behind. "But it's only one of my reasons. Actually . . . well, I suppose I really wanted to know where I was born. I mean, I lived in Craiova as a boy, but that's not the same as being under the mountains. But up here . . . I guess this is it. And now I've seen it and I'm satisfied. I know what it's about and what I'm about. I can go away now and not worry about it anymore."

"The other reason you're here, then," the hunter insisted. "This thing about ruined castles and what all."

Vulpe shrugged, sighed, then gave it his best shot: "It has to do with romance. Now that's something *you* should understand easily enough, Emil Gogosu. What, you? A Romanian? Speaking a romance language, in a land as full of romance as this one? Oh, I don't mean the romance of a boy and girl—I mean more the romance of mystery, of history, of myths and legends. The shiver in our spines when we consider our past, when we wonder who we were and where we came from. The mystery of the stars, worlds beyond our ken, places the imagination knows but can't name or conjure except from old books or scraps of moldering maps. Like when you suddenly remembered the name of your castle.

"It's the romance of tracking down legends, and it infects people like a fever. Scientists go to the Himalayas to seek the Yeti, or hunt for Bigfoot in the North American woods. There's a lake in Scotland—do you know where I mean?—where every year they sweep the deep water with echo sounders as they seek evidence of a survivor out of time.

"It's the fascination in a fossil, the proof that the world was here and that creatures lived in it before we did. It's this love man has for tracking things down, for leaving no stone unturned, for chipping away at coincidence until it's seen that nothing is accidental and everything has not only a cause but a result. It's . . . a synchronicity of soul. It's the mystique of stumbling across the unknown and making it known, of being the first to make a connection.

"Scientists study the fossil remains of a fish believed to be extinct for sixty million years, and pretty soon discover that the same species is still being fished today in the deep waters off Madagascar! When people got interested in the fictional Dracula, they were astonished to discover there'd been a real-life Vlad the Impaler . . . and they wanted to know more about him. Why, he might well have been forgotten, except an author—whether intentional or otherwise—gave him life. And now we know more about him than ever.

"In England in the sixth century there *might* have been a King Arthur—and people are still looking for him today! Searching harder than ever for him. And it's possible he was just a legend . . .

"Right now in America—right across the world, in fact—there are societies dedicated to researching just such mysteries. Me, Armstrong, and Laverne, we're members of one of these groups. Our heroes are the old-time writers of books of horror whose like you don't much find these days, people who felt a sense of wonder and tried to transfer it to others through their writing.

"Well, fifty years ago there was an American author who wrote a novel of dark mystery. In it he mentioned a Transylvanian castle, which he called the Castle Ferenczy. According to the story the castle was destroyed by unnatural forces in the late 1920's. My friends and I came out here to see if we could find just such a pile. And now you tell us it's real and you can actually show us the tumbled boulders. It's . . . a perfect example of the kind of synchronicity I've been talking about.

"But if you've romance in your soul . . . well, perhaps it's more than just that. Oh, we know that the name Ferenczy isn't uncommon in these parts. There are echoes from the past; we know there were boyars in Hungary, Wallachia, and Moldavia with the name of Ferenczy. We've done a little research, you see? But to have found you was . . . it was marvellous! And even if your castle isn't really what we expect, still it will have been marvellous. And what a story we'll have to tell our society when we all meet up again back home, eh?"

Gogosu scratched his head, offered a blank stare.

"You understand?"

"Not a word," said the old hunter.

Vulpe sighed deeply, leaned back, and closed his eyes. It was obvious he'd been wasting his time. Also, he hadn't slept too well last night and believed he might try snatching forty winks on the bus. "Well, don't worry about it," he mumbled.

"Oh, I won't!" Gogosu was emphatic. "Romance? I'm done with all that. I've had my share and finished with it. What? Long-legged girls with their wobbly breasts? *Hah!* The evil old bloodsucking *moroi* in their gloomy castles can take the lot of 'em for all I care!"

Vulpe began to breathe deeply and said, "Umm . . ."

"Eh?" Gogosu looked at him. But already the young American was asleep. Or appeared to be. Gogosu snorted and looked away.

Vulpe opened one eye a crack and saw the old hunter settle down, then closed it again, relaxed, let his mind wander. And in a little while he really was asleep . . .

The journey passed quickly for George Vulpe. He spent most of it oblivious to the outside world, locked in the land of his dreams . . . strange dreams, in the main, which were forgotten on the instant he opened his eyes in those several places where the journey was broken. And the closer he drew to his destination, the stranger his dreams became; surreal, as dreams usually are, still they seemed paradoxically "real." Which was even more odd, for they were not visual but entirely aural.

It had been Vulpe's thought that the land itself called to him, and in the back of his sleeping mind that idea remained uppermost; except that now it was not so much Romania as a whole (or Transylvania in its own right) which was doing the calling but a definite location, a specific genius loci. The source of that mental attraction was Gogosu's promised castle, of course, which now seemed provisioned with a dark and guttural (and eager?) voice of its own:

63

I know you are near, blood of my blood, flesh of my flesh, child of my children. I wait as I have waited out the centuries, feeling the brooding mountains closing me in. But . . . there is now a light in my darkness. A quarter century and more gone by since first that candle flickered into being; it came when you were born, and it strengthened as you grew. But then . . . I knew despair. The candle was withdrawn afar; its light diminished; it dwindled to a distant sputtering speck and was extinguished. I thought your flame dead! Or perhaps . . . not put out but merely placed beyond my reach? And so I put myself to the effort, reached out in search of you, and found you faintly gleaming in a distant land—or so it was my fond preference to believe. But I could not be sure, and so I waited again.

Ah! It's easy to wait when you're dead, my son, and all hope flown. Why, there's precious little else to do! But harder when you're undead and trapped between the pulsing tumult of the living and the vacuous silence of a shunned and dishonoured grave, tenant neither of one nor the other, denied the glory of your own legend; aye, even denied your rightful place in the nightmares of men . . . For then the mind becomes a clock which ticks away all the lonely hours, and one must learn to modulate the pendulum lest it go out of kilter! Oh, indeed, for the mind is finely balanced. Only let it race and it will soon shake itself to shards, and in the end wind down to madness.

And yes, I have known that terror: that I should go mad in my loneliness, and in so doing forsake forever all dreams of resurrection, all hope of . . . of being, as once I was!

Ah! Have I frightened you? I sense a shrinking? But no, this must not be! An ancestor, a grandfather . . . nay, your very father is what I am! That selfsame blood which runs in your veins once ran in mine. It is the river of life's continuity. There can be no gulf—except perhaps the gulf of ages flown— between such as you and I. Why, we might even be as one! Oh, yes! And indeed—we—shall—be . . . friends, you'll see.

"Friends . . . with a place?" Vulpe mumbled in his sleep. "Friends with . . . the spirit of . . . a place."

*The spirit of . . . ? Ah! I see! You think that I'm an echo
from the past! A page of history torn forever from the books
by timorous men. A dark rune scored through, defaced from
the marble menhir of legends and scattered as dust—because
it wasn't pretty. The Ferenczy is gone and his bones are crumbled away; his ghost walks impotent amid the scattered ruins,
the vastly tumbled masonry of his castle. The king is dead—
long live the king!* Hah! *You cannot conceive that I am, that
I . . . remain! That I sleep like you and only require . . .
awakening.*

"You're a dream," said Vulpe. "I'm the one who needs
waking up!"

*A dream? Oh, yes! Oh, hahaa! A dream which reached
out across the world to draw you home at last. A* powerful
*dream, that, my son—which may soon become reality,
Gheorrrghe . . .*

"Gheorghe!" Emil Gogosu elbowed him roughly. "God,
what a man for sleeping!"

"George!" Seth Armstrong and Randy Laverne finally
shook him awake. "Jesus, you've slept most of the day!"

"What? Eh?" Vulpe's dream receded like a wave, leaving
him stranded in the waking world. Just as well, for he'd feared
it was beginning to suck him under. He'd been talking to
someone, he remembered that much, and it had all seemed
very real. And yet now . . . he couldn't even be sure what it
had been about.

He shook his head and licked his lips, which were very
dry. "Where are we?"

"Almost there, pal," said Armstrong. "Which is why we
woke you up. You sure you're okay? You haven't got a fever
or something? Some local bug?"

Vulpe shook his head again, this time in denial. "No, I'm
okay. Just catching up on a load of missed sleep, I suppose.
And a bit disoriented as a result." Memories came flooding
in: of catching a train in Lipova, hitching a ride on the back
of a broken-down truck to Sebis, paying a few extra *bani* to
loll on a pile of hay in a wooden-wheeled, donkey-hauled

65

cart straight out of the Dark Ages, en route for Halmagiu. And now:

"Our driver's going thataway," said Laverne, pointing along a track through the trees. "To Virfurileo, home and the end of the line for him. And Halmagiu's thataway." He pointed along a second track.

"Seven or eight kilometers, that's all," said Gogosu. "Depending on how fast you're all willing to crack along, we could be there in an hour. And plenty of time left over to shake off the dust, eat a meal, moisten our throats a bit, *and* climb a mountain before nightfall—if you're up to it. Or we could take our food with us, make camp, eat and sleep in the ruins. And how would that be for a story to take back home to America, eh? Anyway, it's up to you."

They brushed straw from their clothes, climbed into their packs, and waved the driver of the cart farewell as he creaked from sight around a bend in the forest track. And then they, too, got under way. Randy Laverne uncapped a bottle of beer, took a swig, and passed it to Vulpe, who used it to wash his mouth out.

"Almost there." Armstrong sighed, gangling along pace for pace with the sprightly Gogosu. "And if this place is half of what it's cracked up to be . . ."

"I'm sure it will be," said Vulpe quietly. And he frowned, for in fact he really was sure it would be.

"Well, we'll know soon enough, George," said Laverne, his short legs hurrying to keep up.

And from some secret cave in the back of Vulpe's mind: *Oh, yes. Soon now, my son. Soon now, Gheorrrghe . . .*

At something less than five miles, the last leg of their journey wasn't much at all; in the previous week the Americans had trekked close to twenty times that distance. They got into Halmagiu in the middle of the afternoon, found lodgings for the following night (not for tonight because Gogosu had already talked them into spending it on the mountain), washed up, changed their footwear, and had a snack al fresco on the

open wooden balcony of their guest house where it overlooked the village's main street.

"What you have to remember," their guide had told them
in an aside as they negotiated the price of their rooms, "is
that these people are peasants. They're not sophisticated like
me and used to the ways of foreigners, city dwellers, and
other weird types. They're more primitive, suspicious, superstitious! So let me do the talking. You're climbers, that's
all. No, not even that, you're . . . ramblers! And we're not
going walking up the Zarundului but the Metalici."

"What's the difference?" Vulpe asked him later when they
were eating. "Between the Zarundului and the Metalici, I
mean?"

The old hunter pointed northwest over the rooftops, to a
serrated jaw of smoky peaks, gold-rimmed with sunlight.
"Them's the Metalici," he said. "The Zarundului are behind
us. They're grey . . . always. Grey green in the spring, grey
brown in the autumn, grey in the winter. And white, of
course. The castle is right up on the tree line, backed up to
a cliff. Aye, a cliff at its back and a gorge at its front. A
keep, a stronghold. In the old days, one hell of a place to
crack!"

"I meant"—Vulpe was patient—"why shouldn't the locals
know we're going there?"

Gogosu wriggled uncomfortably. "Superstitious, like I
said. They call those heights the 'Szgany Mountains,' because the travelling folk are so respectful of them. The locals
don't go climbing up there themselves, and they probably
wouldn't like us doing it, neither."

"Because of the ruins?"

Again Gogosu wriggled. "Can't say, don't know, don't
much care. But a couple of winters ago when I tried to shoot
an old wolf up there . . . why, these people treated me like
a leper! There are foxes in the foothills that raid the farms,
but they won't hunt or trap 'em. They're funny that way,
that's all. The grandfathers tell ghost stories to keep the young
'uns away, you know? The old wampir in his castle?"

"But they'll see us headed that way, surely?"

"No, for we'll skirt round."

Vulpe was wary. "I mean, we're not moving onto government property or something, are we? There isn't a military training area or anything of that nature up there, is there?"

"Lord, *no!*" Gogosu was getting annoyed now. "It's like I said: stupid superstition, that's all. You have to remember: if a young 'un dies up here, and no simple explanation for it, they still put a clove of garlic in his mouth before they nail the lid down on him! Aye, and sometimes they do a lot more than that, too! So leave it be before you get me frightening myself, right?"

Seth Armstrong spoke up. "I keep hearing this word 'Szgany.' What's it mean?"

Gogosu didn't need an interpreter for that one. He turned to Armstrong and in broken English said, "In the Germany is *Zigeuner, da?* Here is Szgany. The road peoples."

"Gypsies," said Vulpe, nodding. "My kind of people." He turned and looked back into the dusty yellow interior of the inn's upper levels, looked into the rooms, across the stairwell and out *through* the rear wall. It was as if his gaze was unrestricted by the matter of the inn. Tilting his head back, he "looked" at the grey, unseen mountains of the Zarundului where they reared just a few miles away, and pictured them frowning back at him.

And thought to himself, *Maybe the locals are right and there are places men shouldn't go.*

And unheard (except perhaps as an expression of his own will, his own intent, which it was not) a chuckling, secretive, dark, and sinister voice answered him: *Oh, there are, my son. But you will, Gheorrrghe, you will . . .*

The climb was easy at first. Almost 5:00 P.M. and the sun descending steadily towards the misted valley floor between Mount Codrului and the western extremity of the Zarandului range; but Gogosu confident that they'd reach the ruins before twilight, find a place to camp inside a broken wall, get a fire going, eat, and eventually sleep there in the lee of legends.

"I wouldn't do it on my own," he admitted, picking his

way up a stepped ridge towards a chimney in a crumbling buttress of cliff. "Lord, no! But four of us, hale and hearty? What's to fear?"

Vulpe, the last in line, paused to translate and look around. The others couldn't see it, but his expression was puzzled. He seemed to recognize this place. Déjà vu? He let his companions draw away from him.

Armstrong, directly behind their guide, asked, "Well, and what is there to fear?" He reached back to give Laverne a hand where he puffed and panted.

"Only one's own imagination," said Gogosu, understanding the question from its modulation. "For it's all too ready to conjure not only warrior ghosts out of the past but a whole heap of mundane menaces from the present, too! Aye, the mind of man's a powerful force when he's on his own; there's plenty of scope up ahead for wild imaginings, I can tell you. But apart from that . . . in the winter you might observe the occasional wolf, wandering down here from the northern Carpatii." His tone of voice contained a careless shrug. "They're safe enough, the Grey Ones, except in packs . . ."

The old hunter paused at the base of the chimney, turned to see how the others were progressing where they laboured in his tracks.

But Vulpe had skirted the ridge and was moving along the base of the cliffs to a point where they cut back out of sight around a corner. "Oh?" the old hunter hailed him. "And where are you off, then, Gheorghe?"

The young American looked up and back. His face was pale in the shadow of the cliff and his forehead furrowed in a frown of concentration. "You're making hard work of it, my friend," he called out, his voice echoing from crag to crag. "Why climb when you can walk, eh? There's an old track here that's simplicity itself to follow. The way may be longer but it's faster, too—and a sight kinder to your hands and knees! I'll meet you where your route and mine come together again halfway up."

"Where our routes . . . ?" Gogosu was baffled at first,

then annoyed and not a little sarcastic. "Oh, I see!" he yelled. "And you've been this way before, eh?"

But Vulpe had already turned into the reentry and out of sight. "No," his voice came echoing. "It's just instinct, I suppose."

"Huh!" Gogosu snorted. "Instinct!" But then, as he started in to tackle the chimney, he gave a chuckle. "Oh, let him go," he said. "He'll double back soon enough when the track runs out and the shadows start to creep. Mark my words, it won't be long before he's seeing wolves in every shrub—and by God, how he'll hurry to catch up then!"

But he was wrong. An hour later when the way was steeper and the light beginning to fail, they reached the broad ledge of a false plateau and found Vulpe stretched out, chewing on a twig, waiting for them. He'd been there some time, it seemed. He nodded when he saw them, said, "The rest of the way's easy."

Gogosu scowled and Armstrong merely returned Vulpe's nod, but Laverne was hot and angry. "Taking a bit of a chance there, weren't you, George?" he growled. "What if you'd got lost?"

Vulpe seemed surprised by the testiness in his friend's voice. "Lost? I . . . I didn't even consider it! Fact is, I seem to be something of a natural at this sort of thing."

Nothing more was said and they all rested for a few minutes. Then Gogosu stood up. "Well," he said, "half an hour more and we're there." He bowed stiffly to Vulpe from the waist and added, "If you'd care to lead the way . . . ?"

His sarcasm was wasted; Vulpe took the lead and made easy going of the final climb; they reached the penultimate crest just as the sun sank down behind the western range.

The view was wonderful: blue-grey valleys brimming with mist, and the mountains rising out of it, and smoke from the villages smudging the sky where the distant peaks faded from gold to grey. The four men stood on the rim of a pine-clad saddle or shallow fold between marching rows of peaks. Gogosu pointed. "Along there," he said. "We follow the rising ground through the trees until we hit the gorge. There, where the mountain is split, set back against the cliff—''

"The ruins of the Ferenczy's castle," Vulpe anticipated him.

The hunter nodded. "And just enough light to settle in and get a fire going against the fall of night. Are we all ready, then?"

But George Vulpe was already leading the way.

As they went, the eerie cry of a wolf came drifting on the resin-laden air, gradually fading into mournful ululations.

"Damn *me*!" Gogosu cursed as he stumbled to a halt. He cocked his head on one side, sniffed at the air, listened intently. But there was no repeat performance. Unslinging his rifle from behind his back, he said, "Did you hear that? And can you credit it? It's a sure sign of a hard winter to come, they say, when the wolves are as early as this."

And turning aside a little from the others, he made sure his weapon was loaded . . .

III: Finders

In the hour before midnight a mist came up that lapped at the castle's stones and filled in the gaps between so that the ancient riven walls seemed afloat on a gently undulating sea of milk. Under a shining blue-grey moon whose features were perfectly distinct, George Vulpe sat beside the fire and fed it with branches gathered in the twilight, watched the occasional spark jump skyward to join the stars, and blink out before ever they were reached.

He had volunteered for first watch. Having slept through most of the day, he would in any case be the obvious choice. Emil Gogosu had insisted there was no real need for anyone to remain awake, but at the same time he had not objected when the Americans worked out a roster. Vulpe would be first and take the real weight of it, Seth Armstrong would go from 2:00 A.M. till 4:30, and Randy Laverne would be on till sevenish, when he'd wake Gogosu. That suited the old hunter fine; it would be dawn then anyway and he didn't believe in lying abed once the sun was up.

Both Gogosu and Armstrong were now fast asleep: the first

72

wrapped in a blanket and wedged in a groove of half-buried stones with his feet pointing at the fire, and the last in his sleeping bag, using his jacket wadded over a rounded stone as a pillow. Laverne was awake, barely; he had eaten too many of the boiled Hungarian sausages and too much of the local black bread; his indigestion kept burping him awake just as he thought he was going under. He lay farthest from the fire in the shadows of the castle's wall, his sleeping bag tossed down on a bed of living pine twigs stripped from the branches of trees where they encroached on the ruins. Facing the fire, he was drowsily aware of Vulpe sitting there, his occasional motion as he shoved the end of this or that branch a little deeper into the red and yellow heart of incandescence.

What he was not aware of was the insidious change coming over his friend, the gradual submersion of Vulpe's mind in a strange reverie, the pseudo-memories which passed before his eyes, or limned themselves in the eye of his mind, like ghostly pictures superimposed on the flickering flames. Nor could he know of the hypnotic vampiric influence which even now wheedled and insinuated itself into Vulpe's conscious and subconscious being.

But when a branch burned through and fell sputtering into the heart of the fire, Laverne knew it and started more fully awake. He sat up . . . in time to see a dark shadow pass into even greater darkness through a gap in the old wall. A shadow that moved with an inexorable, zombielike rigidity, like a sleepwalker, its feet causing eddies in the lap and swirl of creeping mist. And he knew that the shadow could only have been George Vulpe, for his sleeping bag was empty where it lay crumpled against a leaning boulder in the glow of the fire.

Laverne's mind cleared. He unzipped himself from his bed, sought his climbing shoes, and pulled them on. With fingers which were still leaden from sleep, he drew laces tight and tied fumbling knots. Still rising up from his half sleep, he nevertheless hurried. There had been something in the way George moved: not furtive but at the same time silently . . . yes, like a sleepwalker. He'd been that way, sort of, all day:

sleeping through the journey, not entirely with it even when he was fully awake. And the way he'd climbed up here, like it was something he did every Friday morning before breakfast!

Passing close to Gogosu and Armstrong where they lay, Laverne thought to wake them . . . then thought again. That would all take time, and meanwhile George might easily have toppled headfirst into the gorge, or brained himself on one of the many low archways in the ranks of tottering walls. Laverne knew his own strength; he'd be able to handle George on his own if it came to it; he didn't need the others and it would be a shame to rouse them for nothing. So he'd take care of this himself. The only thing he mustn't do, if in fact George was sleepwalking, was shock him awake.

Careful where he stepped through the inches-deep ground mist, Laverne followed Vulpe's exact route, passed through the same gap in the wall, and moved deeper into the ruins. They were extensive, covering almost an acre if one took into account those walls which had fallen or been blasted outwards. Away from the sleepers and the firelight, he switched on a pocket torch and aimed its beam ahead. The ground rose up a little here, where heaps of tumbled stones stood higher than the lapping mist, like islands in some strange white sea.

In the torch beam, caught in the moment before he passed behind a shattered wall, George Vulpe paused briefly and looked back. His eyes seemed huge as lanterns, reflecting the electric light. George's eyes . . . and the eyes of something else!

They were there only for a single moment, then gone, blinking out like lights switched off. A pair of eyes, low to the ground, triangular, feral . . . A wolf?

Laverne swung his beam wildly, aimed it this way and that, crouched down a little, and turned in a complete circle. He saw nothing, just ragged walls, mounds of stones, empty archways, and inky darkness beyond. And a little way to the rear, the friendly glow of the campfire like a pharos in the night.

They'd made a wise choice not to start exploring this place in the twilight; it was just too big, its condition too dangerous; and maybe Laverne had been mistaken to leave the others sleeping.

But . . . a wolf? Or just his imagination? A fox, more likely. This would be the ideal spot for foxes. There'd be room for dens galore in the caves of these ruins. And hadn't Gogosu mentioned how the locals wouldn't shoot or hunt the foxes who raided from up here? Yes he had. So that's what it had been, then, a fox . . .

. . . Or a wolf.

Laverne had a pocketknife with a three-inch blade; he took it out, opened it up, and weighed it in his hand. Great for opening letters, peeling apples, or whittling wood! But in any case better than nothing. Christ! *Why* hadn't he shaken the others awake? But too late for that now, and meanwhile George was getting away from him.

"George!" he whispered, following on. "George, for Chrissakes! Where the hell are you?"

Laverne reached the corner of crumbling wall where Vulpe had disappeared. Beyond it lay a large area silvered by moonlight, which might once have been a great hall. On the far side, behind a jumble of broken masonry and shattered roof slates, the silhouette of a man stood outlined from the waist up. Laverne recognised the figure as George Vulpe. Even as he watched, it took a step forward and down in that stiff, robotic way, until only the head and shoulders were showing. Then another step, and the head might be a round boulder atop the pile; another and Vulpe had vanished from sight.

Into what? A hole or half-choked stairwell? Where did the idiot think he was going? How did he *know* where he was going? "George!" Laverne called again, a little louder this time; and again he went in pursuit.

Beyond the pile of rubble, there where a small area of debris had been cleared away down to the original stone flags of the floor, a hole gaped blackly, descending into the bowels of the place. At one end of the hole or stairwell a long, narrow, pivoting slab had been raised by means of an iron ring and now leaned slightly out of the perpendicular away from the space it had covered. Laverne flashed his torch into the gap, saw stone steps descending. Carried on a stale-tasting updraft came a whiff of something burning, mingled with musk and less easily identified odours; glimpsed in the darkness down below, the merest flicker of yellow light, immediately disappearing into the unknown depths.

The paunchy young American paused for a brief moment, but the mystery was such that he had to follow it up. "George?" he said again, his whisper a croak as he squeezed down into the hole.

After that . . . it was easy to lose track of time, direction, one's entire orientation. Moreover, the pressure spring in Laverne's torch had lost some of its tension; battery contact was weak, which resulted in a poor beam of light that came and went; so that every so often he had to give the torch a nervous shake to restore its power.

The stone steps were narrow and descended spirally, winding round a central core which was solid enough in itself. But outwards from the spiral all was darkness and echoing space, and Laverne hated to think how far he might fall if he slipped or stumbled. He made sure he did neither. But how would George Vulpe be faring, sleepwalking in a place like this? *If* he was sleepwalking . . .

Finally a floor was reached, with evidence of a fire or explosion on every hand in the shape of scorched and blackened walls and fallen blocks of carved masonry; and here a second trapdoor slab; then more steps leading down, ever down . . .

Occasionally Laverne would see the flaring of a torch—a real torch—down below at some undetermined depth, or smell its smoke drifting up to him. But never a sound from Vulpe, who must have known this place extremely well to negotiate its hazards so cleanly and silently. How he could *possibly* have known it so well was a different matter. But Laverne felt his anger rising commensurate to the depths in which he descended. Surely he and Seth Armstrong were the victims of a huge joke, in which Gogosu was possibly a participant no less than Vulpe? Ever since last night when they'd met the old hunter, it had been as if this entire venture were preordained, worked out in advance. By whom? And hadn't George been born here? Hadn't he lived here—or if not here exactly, in Romania?

And finally Vulpe's descent into the black guts of this place, when he thought the others were asleep . . . what little "surprise" was he planning now? And why go to such elaborate lengths anyway? If he'd known of this place and been here before—as a boy, perhaps—couldn't he have let them in on it? It wouldn't have been any the less fascinating for that.

"The Castle Ferenczy!" Laverne snorted now to himself. "Shit!" And how many *leu* had Vulpe coughed up, he wondered, to get old Gogosu to play his part in this farce?

Very angry now, he stepped down onto a second floor, where he paused to call out more loudly yet, "George! What the *fuck* are you up to, eh?"

His cry disturbed the air, brought down rills of dust from unseen heights and ceilings. As its echoes boomed out and came back distorted and discordant, Laverne nervously explored the place with the smoky, jittery beam of his torch.

He was in the vaults, the place of frescoed walls, many archways, centuries-blackened oaken racks, urns, and amphorae, festoons of cobwebs, and layers of drifted dust. And there were footprints in the dust, quite a few of them. The most recent of these could only be Vulpe's. Laverne followed the direction they took—and ahead caught a glimpse of flaring torchlight where it lit the curve of an archway before disappearing.

You bastard! Laverne thought. *You'd have to be deaf not to know I'm back here! You've got a hell of a lot of explaining to do, good buddy! And if I don't like what you have to—*

From above and behind, on the stone stairs where they wound up into darkness, there came the soft pad of feet and a softer whining. A pebble, disturbed, came clattering down the steps. Then all was silence again.

Shaking like a leaf, suddenly cold and clammy, Laverne aimed his torch up the stairwell. *"Jesus!"* he gasped. *"Je-*

sus!'' But there was nothing and no one there. Or perhaps a shadow, drawing back out of sight?

Laverne stumbled across the stone-flagged floor of the great room, through an archway, and into other rooms beyond it. His ragged breathing and muffled footfalls seemed to echo thunderously, but he made no effort to be silent. He must shorten the distance between Vulpe and himself right now and find out exactly what the bastard was doing down here! The glow of Vulpe's torch came again, and the resinous stench of its burning; Laverne plunged in that direction, through drifts of dust, salts, and chemicals where they lay spilled on the floor, until . . .

. . . This room was different from the others. He paused under the archway prior to entering, cast about with his weakening beam.

Mouldy tapestries on the walls; a tiled floor inlaid with a pictorial mosaic which illustrated some strange, ancient motif; a desk thick with dust, laid out with books, papers, and other writing implements. A massive fireplace and chimney breast—and the flickering glow of a naked flame coming down *out* of that fireplace! George Vulpe had stepped . . . inside there?

Finding not a little difficulty in breathing, Laverne gasped: ''George?'' He quickly crossed the room and stooped a little to aim his feeble beam of light up under the low arch of the fireplace. In there, fixed in a bracket in the rear wall, he saw Vulpe's smoky, flaring torch . . . but no Vulpe.

A hand fell on Laverne's shoulder!

''Jesus God!'' he cried out as adrenaline pumped and he snapped erect. The back of his head crunched into collision with the keystone of the arch over the fireplace; he reeled away across the room, and for a moment Vulpe was trapped in his torch's beam; the other stood there silent as a ghost, his hand still reaching out towards him.

Laverne went to his knees on the floor, clutched at the back of his head. His hand came away wet with blood. Sick and dizzy, he kneeled there. He was lucky he hadn't brained himself! But anger quickly replaced his pain. He found his orientation, again aimed his torch where last he'd seen Vulpe. But Vulpe—sleepwalker, clown, asshole, or whatever he was—wasn't there. Only a fading flicker of yellow fire from within the chimney breast.

Laverne staggered to his feet. He found his knife lying where he'd dropped it close to the chimney. He closed it and put it away. He wouldn't need a knife for the beating he was going to give "Gheorghe" Vulpe. And when he was done with him, the bastard could find his own way back out of here—if he had the strength for it!

Steadier now, gritting his teeth, Laverne went again to the fireplace. He ducked inside and at once saw the rungs in the back wall of the flue. From up above he heard sounds: the echoing scrape of shoes, a low cough. And: *What goes up,* he thought, *must come down!* Maybe he should wait right here for the idiot. Except that was when Vulpe screamed!

Laverne had never heard a scream like it. It followed close on a nerve-rending grating sound—like massive surfaces of rock sliding together—and rose to a vibrating falsetto crescendo before shutting off at highest pitch. And as its echoes died away, they were followed by a glottal gurgling and gasping. Vulpe was going, "Ak . . . ak . . . ak . . . ak," as if choking: a sort of slow death rattle. Laverne, his hair standing on end, didn't actually know what a death rattle sounded like, but he felt that if the sound were suddenly to speed up to *ak-ak-ak-ak,* then that would be his friend's last gasp!

"Oh, Jeeesus!" he whined, and drove himself clattering up the rungs and through the flue to the place where it curved through ninety degrees to become a passage. Twenty or twenty-five paces ahead, there lay Vulpe's torch still flickering fitfully and giving off black smoke where it teetered on the rim of a trench cut in the stone floor to the right of the passageway.

But of Vulpe himself . . . no sign. Only the choking, agonised "Ak . . . ak . . . ak" sounds, which seemed to be coming from the trench.

"George?" Laverne hurried forward—and came to an abrupt halt. Beyond the guttering brand, where neither its light nor his own torch beam could reach, triangular eyes floated in the darkness, unblinking, unyielding, unnerving.

Laverne wasn't an especially brave man, but he wasn't a coward either. Whatever the creature was up ahead—fox, wolf, or feral dog—it wouldn't much care for fire. He lumbered forward, snatched up the smouldering torch, and waved it overhead to get it going again. A *whoosh* of flame at once rewarded his efforts and the gathering shadows were driven back. Likewise the creature along the passageway; Laverne caught a glimpse of something grey, slinking, canine, before it was swallowed up in gloom. He also caught a glimpse of something in the trench—

—Which drove him back against the wall like a blow from some huge fist!

Gasping his shock, his horror—feeling his blood running cold in his veins—Laverne tremblingly held out the torch over the trench. His disbelieving eyes took in the bed of spikes and the figure of his friend, crucified and worse, upon them. George Vulpe squirmed there, impaled through his cheek, neck, shoulders, and arms; nailed through his back, buttocks, and thighs; issuing blood from each dark gash and puncture, which coloured the rusty spikes and flowed in thickly converging streams around and between his twitching feet, into the channel and down towards the stone spout.

"Mother of God!" Laverne croaked.

"*Ak! . . . ak! . . . ak!*" said Vulpe, the words bursting in bloody bubbles from his pallid lips.

And along the passageway the great old Grey One growled low in his throat and paced slowly, stiff-legged, into full view.

Vulpe was finished, that much was plain. An army of nurses with a ton of bandages between them couldn't have stopped him bleeding his last, not now. Laverne couldn't save him, neither from the bed of spikes nor from the wolf. On nerveless legs he backed off, shuffling crablike, sideways back along the passage, back towards the shallow steps leading to the false flue. It was all over for George—everything was over for him—and now Laverne must think only of himself. And as Vulpe's blood commenced to gurgle from the carved stone spout into the mouth of the urn, so the overweight American backed away faster yet . . .

. . . And paused abruptly, wobbling like a jelly there in the narrow mould of the passageway.

In front, the wolf, its face a snarling mask in the torchlight; between, the dying man on his torture bed of spikes; and now . . . now there was something else. Behind!

No longer breathing, Laverne cranked his head round like a nut on a rusty bolt. At first he made little of what he was seeing. All the edges were indistinct, weirdly mobile. The ceiling seemed to have lowered itself, the passage to have narrowed, the floor to have become heaped with . . . something. Something furry. Something that rustled and flopped!

Laverne's eyes bugged as he thrust out his torch in that direction, bugged more yet as several small parts of that anomalous furriness detached themselves from the moving walls and darted by him in fluttering swoops and dives. Bats! A colony of bats! And more of them clustering to the walls, floor, and ceiling even as he grimaced his disgust.

He looked back the other way. The wolf had come to a standstill; its ears were pointed into the trench, its attention centered on the urn. Cold as death, reeling and panting for air, Laverne looked where it looked. He looked, saw, and knew that he was on the verge of fainting. His blood was pooling, his senses whirling—but he also knew that he *dared not* faint! Not in this nightmare place, and certainly not now.

The urn was belching! Puffs of vapour, like small smoke rings, were issuing from its obscene mouth. Black slime, bubbling up from within, was blistering on the cold rim like congealing tar. As Vulpe's blood was consumed, so something was forming and expanding within the urn. A catalyst, his blood *transformed* what was within!

Hypnotised by horror, Laverne could only watch. A mottled blue-grey tentacle of slime, crimson-veined, slopped upwards out of the mouth of the urn and into the stone spout. Elongating, it slid like a snake along the trail of blood to where Vulpe lay transfixed. Sentient, it curled round his right leg where it was bent at the knee, surged along the impaled thigh and across his belly, crept over his palpitating chest. He continued to gasp, "Ak! . . . ak! . . . argh!"—but agony had very nearly inured him, numbed him into a mental limbo, and loss of his life's blood was quickly finishing the job.

Somehow, summoning up his last ounce of strength from the very roots of his will, Vulpe managed to lift his face up off the spike which pierced his right cheek and lower jaw; and conscious to the last, he saw what reared on his chest and even now formed a flat, swaying, blind cobra head!

His bloody jaws flew open—perhaps in a scream, though none came—and the leech thing at once drove itself into his yawning mouth and down his straining gullet! He convulsed on the spikes; his lips split at their corners as his jaws were forced apart and the now corrugated, pulsating bulk of the thing thrust into him.

The urn was empty now, steaming and slimed where the "tail" of the leech had snaked free. But still Vulpe gagged and frothed and bled from his nostrils as the horror filled him. His neck was fat from its passage into him; his eyes stood out as if to burst from their sockets; his three-fingered hands tore free of the spikes and grasped at the monster raping his throat, trying to tear it out of him. To no avail.

In another moment the entire creature had entered him— and still he tossed on the spikes, flopped his head this way and that, slopped blood and mucus all around.

"Oh, Jesus! Oh, great God in heaven!" Laverne wailed. "Die, for Christ's sake!" he instructed Vulpe. "Let it go! Be still!" And it was as if George Vulpe heard him. He *did* let it go, he *was* . . . suddenly . . . still.

The entire scene stood frozen, timeless. The great wolf, a statue blocking the way forward; the bats, almost completely choking Laverne's single route of exit; the drained and hideously refilled body of his friend, motionless on its bed of spikes. Only the flickering torch in Laverne's hand had any life of its own, and that, too, was dying.

In one badly shaking hand the firebrand, and in the other his pocket torch; Randy Laverne could never have said how he'd hung on to either one of them. But now, snarling his outrage and terror, he turned to the wall of bats and thrust at it with his smoking, guttering torch. They didn't retreat but clustered to the firebrand, smothered it with their scorching, crackling bodies, put it out! A dozen dead or dying bats fell to the floor of the passage, were ploughed under by the creeping furry tide of their cousins where they wriggled and flopped forward.

Laverne went a little mad then. He screamed hoarsely, brokenly; he panted, gasped, and screamed again; he lashed out with his arms in the near darkness and aimed the failing beam of his electric torch this way and that all around, never giving himself a moment's time to see anything.

He did *not* see George Vulpe wrench himself upright, free of the spikes in the trench, or the way his gashes had stopped bleeding and were mending themselves even now. Nor did he see him climb up from the trench, fondling the old wolf's ears and smiling. Especially, he did not see that smile. No, his act of dropping the electric torch and sliding semiconscious down the wall to crumple on the floor of the passage was occasioned by none of these things but by Vulpe's sudden appearance, his rising up there, directly before him.

By that and by his redly glaring eyes, and his entirely *alien*, phlegm-clotted voice, saying, "My friend, you came to this place of your own free will. And I believe you are . . . bleeding?" Vulpe's nostrils opened wide, sniffed, and his eyes became fiery slits in that preternaturally pale face. "Indeed, I'm sure you are. Now really, someone should see to that wound—before something gets into it . . ."

Emil Gogosu woke up to find someone kneeling close by. It was young Gheorghe, one hand shaking the hunter awake, the other holding a warning finger to his lips. *"Shhh!"* he hushed.

"Eh? What is it?" Gogosu whispered, at once wide-awake and peering about in the night. The fire was burning low, its heart redly reflecting from Vulpe's eyes. "Dawn already? I don't believe it!"

"Not dawn," the other replied, also in a whisper, however

hoarse and urgent. "Something else." He stood up. "Come, bring your gun."

Gogosu unrolled himself from his blanket, reached for his rifle, and came lithely to his feet. He prided himself that his bones didn't ache.

"Come," Vulpe said again, stepping carefully so as not to wake Armstrong.

As they left the campfire and the ruins behind and the darkness began to close in, the hunter caught at Vulpe's arm. "Your face," he said. "Is that . . . blood? What's been going on, Gheorghe? I didn't hear anything."

"Blood, yes," the other answered. "I was keeping watch. I heard something out here, in the trees there, and went to see. It might have been a dog or fox—even a wolf—but it attacked me. I fought it off. I think it may have bitten my face. And it's still out here. It was following me as I came back for you."

"Still out here?" Gogosu turned his head this way and that. The moon was down a little, its grey light coming through hazy clouds. The hunter saw nothing, but still the young American led the way.

"I thought maybe you could shoot it," said Vulpe. "You said you'd tried to shoot a wolf up here before."

"I have, that's right," Gogosu answered, hurrying to keep up. "I hit him, too, for I heard him yelp and saw the trail of blood!"

"Well," said the other, "and now another chance."

"Eh?" The hunter was puzzled. Something wasn't quite right here. He tried to get a good look at his companion in the pale moonlight. "What's wrong with your voice, Gheorghe? Frog in your throat? Still shaken up, are you?"

"That's right," said Vulpe, his voice deeper yet. "It was something of a shock . . ."

Gogosu came to a halt. Something was definitely wrong. "I see no wolf!" he said, the tone of his voice an accusation in itself. "Neither wolf nor fox nor . . . anything!"

"Oh?" said the other, also pausing. "Then what's that?" He pointed and something moved silently, low to the ground, grey-dappled where moonlight formed pools under the trees. It was there, then gone. But the hunter had seen it. As if in confirmation, a low growl came back to them out of the night.

"Damn me!" Gogosu breathed. "A Grey One!" He brushed past Vulpe, crouched low, ran forward under the trees.

Vulpe came after, caught up with him, pointed off at a tangent. "There he goes!" he rasped.

"Where? Where? God, you've the eyes of a wolf yourself!"

"This way," said Vulpe. "Come on!"

They came out of the trees, reached the piled scree at the foot of rearing crags. The younger figure breathed easy, but Gogosu was already panting for air. "Lord," he gulped, and finally admitted it: "But my legs aren't as young as yours."

"What?" said Vulpe, half turning towards him. "Oh, but I assure you they are, Emil Gogosu. Centuries younger, in fact!"

"Eh? What?"

"There!" said the other, pointing yet again. "Under that tree there!"

The hunter looked—brought his rifle up to his shoulder— saw nothing. "Under the tree?" he said. "But there's nothing there. I—"

"Give me that," said Vulpe. And before the other could argue, he'd taken the gun. Aiming at nothing in particular, he said, "Emil, are you *sure* you shot a wolf up here that time?"

"What?" The old hunter was outraged. "How many times do you need telling? Aye, and I damn near got him, too! You can wager he bears the scar to prove it!"

"Calm down, calm down!" said the other, his voice dark as the night now. "No need for wagering, Emil, for I've *seen* that gouge in his flank where your bullet burned his hide! Oh, yes, and just as you remember him, so he remembers you!"

And as suddenly as that the hunter knew that this wasn't Gheorghe Vulpe. He looked deep into his shadowed face, hissed his terror and shrank down—and saw the Grey One crouched to spring, silhouetted on top of a mound of sliding scree. It snarled, sprang . . . Gogosu snatched at his rifle where the other seemed to hold it oh so lightly . . . try snatching an iron bar from the window of a cell.

The wolf struck and knocked him down, away from this awful stranger he'd thought a friend. Its fangs were at his throat, slavering there. He went to cry out, but already those terrible teeth had met through his windpipe, turning his scream to a scarlet froth that flew like a brand across a wrinkled grey brow over vengeful yellow eyes . . .

"You let me sleep late!" was Seth Armstrong's first reaction when he found himself prodded awake. The moon was down, the ground mist gone, the fire almost dead.

"Are you complaining?" said the man seated close by, who at first glance was George Vulpe.

"No." Armstrong shook his head, as much to free it from sleep as in answer. "I guess I was exhausted. Must be the altitude."

"Good," said the other. "I'm glad you enjoyed your sleep. Sleep is a necessity, however wasteful. Why should we sleep when there's a life to be lived, eh? I shall not sleep again in . . . oh, a long time."

Armstrong was almost awake now. "What?" he said, and sat up. He might have jumped up, but the barrel of Gogosu's rifle was prodding him in the chest. And a lean grey wolf, lying prone on its belly like a dog, with paws stretched forward towards him, was gazing directly into his eyes! One of its ears stood stiffly erect; the other, twitching, lay close to its elongated skull. The wolf might be half-grinning, or half-snarling; whichever, its quivering muzzle was splashed with scarlet.

"Jesus H. Christ!" Armstrong snatched back his feet, which got tangled in the lower half of his sleeping bag.

"Be still," commanded the one who he still believed was Vulpe. "Do as you're told and he won't attack you, and I won't squeeze this trigger."

"Geor—Geor—George!" Armstrong finally found his voice. "That's a bloody wolf there!"

"Bloody, yes," said the other.

"So sh-sh-*shoot* the bastard!" Armstrong's face was deathly white in pale blue starshine.

"Eh?" said the seated man, cocking his head curiously on one side, for all the world as if he hadn't heard right. "I should shoot him? I should reward an old and trusted friend by shooting him? No, I think not." He picked up a dry branch and tossed it onto the bed of hot ashes, where small flames lingered still. Sparks showered up and the flames leaped higher, and Armstrong saw the bloodied holes in the other's clothing, his torn, rapidly mending face, the pits of hell which were his eyes.

"Christ—Christ—*Christ*!" the big, gangling man gasped. "George, what the hell's happening here?"

"Be still," the other said again, his head still tilted at an angle. For long moments he stared into Armstrong's terrified face, studying it, perhaps thinking something over. And eventually: "You're a big man and strong, and I cannot be alone in the world. Not now, and not for some time. I have things to learn, places to go, things to do. I will need instruction. I must be taught before I may . . . teach? I got something from Gheorghe's mind, you see, before he honoured the covenant. But not enough. Perhaps I was too eager. It is understandable."

"George." Armstrong licked his lips, which were parched. "George, listen." He reached out a trembling hand to the other—but the old wolf's muzzle at once cracked open to display jaws like a bone vise. He lifted his belly off the earth, crept closer.

"I *said* be still!" said the one with the rifle, lifting it until its foresight pressed against Armstrong's bobbing Adam's apple. "If the Grey One understands my wishes, why can't you? Or perhaps you're a fool, in which case I'm wasting my time. Is that it? Am I wasting my time? Should I be done with it, simply squeeze this trigger and make a fresh start?"

"I'll . . . I'll be still!" Armstrong gasped, his voice a

hoarse whisper, cold sweat starting out on his brow. "I'll be still! And . . . and don't worry, George. I'll help you. God, yes, whatever bug you've picked up, I'll help you!"

"Oh, I know you will," said this—this stranger?—still staring from his crimson eyes.

"I'll do . . . anything you say," said Armstrong. "Anything at all."

"Yes, that too," said the other, nodding. And having made up his mind: "Very well, and shall we start with something simple? Look into my eyes, Seth Armstrong." He moved the barrel of the rifle aside to lean closer, until his terrible mesmeric face was only a foot away. "Look deep, Seth. Look under the skin of my eyes, into the blood and the brains and the very landscape of my mind. The eyes are the windows of the soul, my friend, did you know that? Portals on one's dreams and passions and aspirations. Which is why *my* eyes are red. Aye, for the soul behind them has been torn asunder and eaten by a scarlet leech!"

His words conjured seething horror, but more than that they inspired awe, a creeping paralysis, a lassitude of terror. Armstrong knew what it was: hypnotism! He could feel his mind going under. But Vulpe—or whoever this was in Vulpe's body—had been right: Seth Armstrong was strong. And before his will could be subverted utterly—

—He batted the rifle aside, so that it was directed at the wolf, and reached for the throat of his tormentor. "I'm going to have me . . . a piece of . . . you, George!" he panted.

As the Texan's fingers closed on Vulpe's windpipe, so that *facsimile* gave a grunting cry and clawed at his face. The three fingers of his left hand hooked in the corner of Armstrong's lower lip, tearing it. Armstrong howled his pain, bit down hard on the smallest of Vulpe's fingers, severed it at the central knuckle in the moment before the other dragged his hand free.

The rifle went off, its flash startling and the *crack* of its discharge reverberating from the peaks. The great wolf knew something about guns; unharmed, fur bristling, still he whined and backed away.

Gurgling and clutching at his damaged hand, Vulpe had reared to his feet. Armstrong spat out Vulpe's little finger, which hung from his mouth on a thread of blood and gristle. The Texan now had possession of the rifle and knew how to use it. But even as he tried to turn the weapon on the madman, so Vulpe recovered and kicked it from his hands.

Somehow Armstrong burst free of his sleeping bag, but as he lurched to his feet he felt something clinging to his face and moving there. And shaking with laughter, the mad thing which had been George Vulpe pointed at Armstrong—at his face. He pointed with his freakish left hand, where all that remained of the third finger was now a bloody stump.

The Texan put up a hand and slapped at the finger on his cheek, clawed at it. It climbed higher, with a life of its own, and gouged at the corner of his right eye. Armstrong howled as it dug in, dislodged the eyeball, and entered the socket. With his eye hanging on his cheek, he danced and screamed and clutched at his face; but he couldn't dislodge the thing, which burrowed like an alien worm into his head.

"Jesus God!" he screamed, falling to his knees and tearing at the rim of the empty orbit. And: "J-J-Jesus G-G-God!" he gurgled again as he ripped the flopping eye loose and vampire flesh put out exploratory tendrils into his brain.

On his knees, he shuffled spastically, blindly towards the fire, and shuddered to a halt. He coughed and shuddered again, and toppled forward like a felled tree.

But the Vulpe anomaly stepped forward, caught his collar with its good hand, and swung him to one side, turning him onto his back. "Ah, no, Seth!" the thing said, standing over him. "Enough is enough. For if you burn, it will take time in the healing, and I would be up and gone from here."

"Ge-o-o-orge!" the other coughed and gagged.

"No, no, my friend, no more of that," said the monster, smiling hideously. "From now on you must call me Janos!"

More than five and a half years later . . . the balcony of a hotel room in Rhodes, overlooking a noisy, jostling, early-morning street only a stone's throw from the harbour . . .

89

salty-sweet air breezing in across the sea from Turkey, thinning out the clouds of blue exhaust smoke, the pungent miasma of the bakeries, the many odours of the breakfast bars, refuse collectors, and humanity in general in this, the nerve centre of the ancient Greek port.

It was the middle of May 1989, the tourist season only just beginning and already threatening to be a blockbuster, and the sun was a ball of fire one third of the way up the incredibly blue dome of the sky. A "dome" because you couldn't take it in in its entirety but must close your eyes to a squint, thus rounding off the corners and turning your periphery of vision to a shadowy curve. That was how Trevor Jordan felt about it, anyway, who had thrown back maybe one or two Metaxas too many the night before. But it was early yet, just after 8:00 A.M., and he guessed he'd recover in a little while; though by the same token he knew the town would get a lot noisier, too.

Jordan had breakfasted on a boiled egg and single piece of toast and was now into his third cup of coffee—the British "instant" variety, not the dark brown sludge which the Greeks drank from thimble-sized cups—which he calculated was gradually diluting whatever brandy remained in his system. The trouble with Metaxa, as he'd discovered, was that it was extremely cheap and very, *very* drinkable. Especially while watching the nonstop belly-dancing floor show in a place called the Blue Lagoon on Trianta Bay.

He groaned and gently fingeréd his forehead for the fifth or sixth time in a half hour. "Sunglasses," he said to the man who sat with him, similarly attired in dressing gown and flip-flops. "I have to buy a pair. Christ, this glare could take your eyes out!"

"Have mine," Ken Layard told him, grinning as he passed a pair of cheap, plastic-framed shades across their tiny breakfast table. "And later you can buy me new ones."

"Will you order more coffee?" Jordan groaned. "Say, a bucketful?"

"I thought you were knocking it back a bit last night," the other answered. "Why didn't you tell me you'd never been to the Greek islands before?'' He leaned over the balcony rail, called down and attracted the attention of a waiter serving breakfast to other early risers on a terraced lower level, then lifted the empty coffeepot and jiggled it suggestively.

"How do you know that?" said Jordan.

"What, that this is new to you? No one who's been here before drinks Metaxa like that—or ouzo for that matter!"

"Ah!" Jordan remembered. "We started off on ouzo!"

"*You* started off on ouzo," Layard reminded him. "I was getting atmosphere, local colour. You were getting drunk."

"Yes, but did I enjoy myself?"

Layard grinned again, shrugged, and said, "Well . . . you didn't get us thrown out of anywhere." He studied the other in his self-inflicted discomfort.

An experienced but variable telepath, Jordan could be forceful when he needed to be; usually, though, he was easygoing, transparent, an open book. It was as if he personally would like to be as readable as other people's minds were to him, as if he were trying to make some sort of physical compensation for his metaphysical talent. His face reflected this attitude: it was fresh, oval, open, almost boyish. With thinning fair hair falling forward above grey eyes and a crooked mouth which straightened out and tightened whenever he was worried or annoyed, everyone who knew Trevor Jordan liked him. Having the advantage of knowing about it when people *didn't* like him, he simply avoided them. But Jordan was rangy-limbed and athletic despite his forty-four years, and his sensitivity should not be misread; there was plenty of determination in him, too.

They were old friends, these two, who went back a long way. They could clown with each other now because of their past, in which there'd been times when there was little or no room for clowning; times and events, in fact, so outré even in their weird world that they'd receded now to mere phantoms of mind and memory. Like bad dreams or tragedies (or even drunken nights), best forgotten.

There was nothing so deadly strange in their current mission—though certainly it was serious enough—but still Jordan realised he'd been in error the previous night. He put on the sunglasses, frowned, and sat up straighter in his cane chair. "I didn't draw attention to us or anything stupid like that?"

"Lord, no," said the other. "And anyway I wouldn't have let you. You were just a tourist having himself a good time, that's all. Too much sun during the day, and too much booze through the night. And what the hell, there were plenty of other Brits around who made you look positively sober!"

"And Manolis Papastamos?" Jordan was rueful now. "He must have thought me an idiot!"

Papastamos was their local liaison man, second-in-command of the Athens narcotics squad, who had come across to Rhodes by hydrofoil to get to know the pair personally and see if there was anything he could do to simplify their task. But he'd also proved to be something of a hell-raiser, even a liability.

"No." Layard shook his head. "In fact he was more under the influence than you were! He *said* he'd join us on the harbour wall at ten-thirty to see the *Samothraki* dock—but I doubt it. When we dropped him off at his hotel, he looked like hell. On the other hand . . . they do have remarkable constitutions, these Greeks. But in any case we'll be better off without him. He knows who we are but not what we are. As far as he's concerned we're part of customs and excise, or maybe New Scotland Yard. It would be hard to concentrate with Manolis around making conversation and creating a mental racket. I hope to God he stays in bed!"

Jordan was looking and feeling a little healthier; the sunglasses had helped somewhat; fresh coffee arrived and Layard poured. Jordan watched his easy movements and thought, *Just like a big brother. He looks after me like I was a snot-nosed kid. He always has, thank God!*

Layard was a locator, a scryer without a crystal ball. He didn't need one; a map would do just as well, or an inkling of his quarry's location. A year older than Jordan, he stood a blocky seventy inches tall, with a square face, dark hair and complexion, expressive, active eyebrows and mouth. Under a forehead lined from accumulated years of concentration, his eyes were very keen and (of course) far-seeing, and so darkly brown as to border on black.

As he looked at Layard through and in the privacy of dark lenses, Jordan's thoughts went back twelve years to Harkley House in Devon, England, where he and the locator had formed their first real partnership and worked as a team for the very first time. Then as now they'd been members of E-Branch, that most secret of all the Secret Services, whose work was known only to a handful of "top people." Unlike now, however, their work on that occasion had been far less mundane. Indeed, there had been nothing at all mundane about the Yulian Bodescu affair.

Memories, deliberately suppressed for more than a decade, sprang once more into being, full-fleshed and fantastic in Jordan's ESP-endowed mind. Once more he held the crossbow in his hand, chest-high and aimed dead ahead, as he listened to the *hiss* of jetting water and the girl's voice humming that tuneless melody from beyond the closed door, and wondered if this were a trap. Then—

He kicked open the door to the shower cubicle—and stood riveted to the spot! Helen Lake, Yulian Bodescu's cousin, was utterly beautiful and quite naked. Standing sideways on, her body gleamed in the streaming water. She jerked her head round to stare at Jordan, her eyes wide in terror where she fell back against the shower's wall. Her knees began to buckle and her eyelids fluttered.

But this is just a frightened girl! he told himself—in the moment before her thoughts branded themselves on his telepathic mind.

Come on, my sweet! *she thought.* Ah, just touch me, hold me! Just a little closer, my sweet . . .

Then, jerking back away from her, he saw the carving knife in her hand and the insane glare in her demonic eyes! As she drew him effortlessly towards her and lifted her knife in a gleaming arc, so he pulled the crossbow's trigger. It was an automatic thing, his life or hers.

God! The bolt nailed her to the tiled wall; she screamed like the damned soul she was and jerked herself free of splin-

tering tiles and plaster, staggering to and fro in the shower's shallow well. But she still had the knife, and Jordan could do nothing but stand there with his eyes bulging, mouthing meaningless prayers, as she advanced on him yet again . . . !

. . . Until Ken Layard shouldered him aside—Layard with his flamethrower—whose nozzle he directed into the shower to turn it into a blistering, steaming pressure cooker!

"God help us!" Jordan gasped now, as he'd gasped it then. He blotted the unbearable memories out, came reeling back to the present. In the wake of mental conflict, crisis, his hangover seemed twice as bad. He breathed deeply, used the tips of his fingers to massage the top of his head where it felt split, and wondered out loud, "Christ, what brought that on?"

Layard's eyes were wide; he bent forward across the table and grasped Jordan's forearm. "You too?" he said.

Jordan broke an unspoken rule among E-Branch espers: he glanced into Layard's mind. Receding, he felt the echoes of similar memories and at once broke the contact. "Yes, me too," he said.

"I could tell by your face," Layard told him. "I've never seen you look like that since . . . that time. Maybe it's because we're working together again?"

"We've worked together plenty." Jordan flopped back in his chair, suddenly felt exhausted. "No, I think it's just something that was squeezed up in there and had to be out. Well, it took its time—but it's out now and gone forever, I hope!"

"Me too," Layard agreed. "But both of us at the same time? And why now? We couldn't be farther away in time and space than we are right now from Harkley House."

Jordan sighed and reached for his coffee. His hand trembled a little. "Maybe we picked it up from each other and amplified it. You know what they say about great minds thinking alike?"

Layard relaxed and nodded. "Especially minds like ours, eh?" He nodded again, if a little uncertainly. "Well, maybe you're right . . ."

* * *

By 9:45 the two were down on the northern harbour wall, seated on a wooden bench which gave them a splendid view right across the Mandraki shallows and harbour to the Fort of St. Nikolas. To their left the Bank of Greece stood on its raised promontory, its white-banded walls and blue windows reflected in the still water, while on their right and to the rear of the promenade sprawled Rhodes New Town. Mandraki, being mainly a shallow-water mooring, was not the commercial harbour; that lay a quarter mile south in the bay of the historic, picturesque and Crusader-fortified Old Town, beyond the great mole with the fort at its tip. But their information was that the drug runners moored up in Mandraki, taking on water and some small provisions there, before proceeding to Crete, Italy, Sardinia, and Spain.

A little cannabis resin would be dropped off here, by night (probably swum ashore by a crewman in swim trunks and fins), and likewise in various ports of call along the way. But the great mass of the stuff—*and* the main cargo, which was cocaine—was destined for Valencia, Spain. From where, eventually, a lot of it would find its way to England. Such had been its route and destination in the past. Meanwhile the E-Branch agents had the task of determining (a) how much of the white powder was aboard; and (b) if the amount was small, would a preemptive bust simply serve to tip their hands to the drug barons; and (c) where was the stuff kept if it was aboard.

Only a few months ago a boat had been stripped to the bones in Larnaca, Cyprus, and nothing had been found. But of course, that one had been handled by the Greek Cypriot police, whose "expertise" perhaps lacked that little something extra—like coordination or even intelligence! This time it would be a combined effort, terminating in Valencia before the bulk of the stuff could be off-loaded. And this time, too, the boat—a wallowing, wooden, round-bottomed barrel of an old Greek thing called the *Samothraki*—would be stripped not just to her bones but to the very marrow. And in the interim Jordan and Layard would shadow her along her route.

Dressed in tourist-trade "American" caps with hugely projecting peaks, bright, open-necked, short-sleeved shirts, cool slacks, and leather sandals, and equipped with binoculars, they now awaited the arrival of their quarry. Since they went allegedly incognito, their mode of dress might seem almost outlandish, but by comparison with the more lurid tourist groups they could easily be too conservative. And that was to be avoided.

They had been silent for some time; there was something of a mood on both of them; Jordan blamed the Metaxa and Layard said it was "bad gut" brought on by greasy food. Whichever, it interfered a little with their ESP.

"It's . . . cloudy," Jordan complained, frowning. Then he shrugged. "But you don't know what I mean, do you?"

"Sure I do," Layard answered. "We called it mindsmog in the old days, remember? A kind of dull mental static, distorting or blocking the pictures? Or obscuring them in a sort of . . . well, almost in a damp, reeking fog! When I reach out and search for the *Samothraki*, I can feel it there like a welling mist in my mind. A dampness, a darkness, a smog. But how to explain it in a place like this? It's weird. And it doesn't come from the boat especially but—I don't know—from everywhere!"

Jordan looked at him. "How long since we came up against other espers?"

"In our work, you mean? Just about every time we do an embassy job, I suppose. What are you getting at?"

"You don't think it's likely there are other agents on the same job? Russians, maybe, or the French?"

"It's possible." It was Layard's turn to frown. "The USSR's narcotics problem is growing every day, and France has been in the shit for years! But I was thinking: what if they're on the other side? I mean, what if the runners themselves are using espers? They could well afford to, and that's a fact!"

Jordan put his binoculars to his eyes, turned his head, and scanned the coastline from the fort on the mole all the way to the heart of the Old Town where it rose behind massive walls. "Have you tried tracking it?" he said. "I mean, after all's said and done, you're the locator. But me, I've a feeling the source is somewhere in there."

Layard's keen eyes followed the aim of Jordan's binoculars. A big, white, expensive-looking motor cruiser lolled at anchor in Mandraki's narrow, deep-water channel; beyond that a handful of caiques were moored inshore, or came and went, most of them full to the gunnels with tourists; a farther quarter mile and the Old Town's markets and streets were a hive, literally buzzing where the hill rose in a mass of churches and white and yellow houses, burning in the morning sunlight. Except that all was in motion, he might well have been looking at a picture postcard. The scene was *that* perfect.

Layard stared for long moments, then snapped his fingers, sat back, and grinned. "That's it!" he finally said. "You got it first time."

"Eh?" Jordan looked at him.

"And of course it would have to be worse for you than for me. For I only find things. I don't read minds."

"Do you want to explain?"

"What's to explain?" Layard looked smug. "Your tourist's map of the Old Town is the same as mine. Except you probably haven't read it. Okay, I'll put you out of your misery. There's an insane asylum on the hill."

"Wha-?" Jordan started, then put down his binoculars and slapped his knee. "That has to be it!" he said. "We're getting the echoes of all of those poor sick bastards locked up in that place!"

"It looks like it." Layard nodded. "So now that we know what it is, we should try to screen it out, concentrate on the job in hand." He looked out to sea through the mouth of the harbour and became serious in a moment. "Especially since it appears the *Samothraki*'s just a wee bit on the early side!"

"She's out there?" Jordan was immediately attentive.

"Five or ten minutes at the most." Layard nodded. "I just picked her up. And I'll give you odds she's in and dropping anchor by quarter past the hour."

Both men now took to watching the entrance to the harbour, so missing a sudden burst of activity aboard the big, privately owned motor cruiser. A canopied caique ferried out a small party from steps in the harbour wall; two men went aboard the sleek white ship, which soon weighed anchor; powerful engines throbbed as she turned almost on her own axis and nosed idly back along the deep-water channel. Black awnings with fancy scalloped trims gave her foredeck shade, where a black-clad figure now lounged in one of several reclining deck chairs. A tall man in white stood at the rail, looking towards the harbour mouth. He wore a black eyepatch over his right eye.

The white leisure craft was very noticeable now, but still it hovered on the periphery of the espers' vision, its screw idling where it waited in the deep-water channel. Both of them now held binoculars to their eyes, and Jordan had stood up, was leaning forward against the harbour wall as the *Samothraki* came chugging into view around the mole.

"Here she comes," he breathed. "Right between the old boy's legs!" He sent his telepathic mind reaching across the water, seeking out the minds of the captain and crew. He wanted to know the location of the cocaine . . . if one of them should be thinking about it right now . . . or about its ultimate destination . . .

"What old boy's legs?" Layard's voice came to him distantly, even though he was right here beside him. Such was Jordan's concentration that he'd almost entirely shut out the conscious world.

"The Colossus," Jordan husked. "Helios. One of the Seven Wonders of the ancient world. That's where he stood—right there, straddling that harbour mouth—until 224 B.C."

"So you did read your map after all!" breathed Layard.

The old *Samothraki* was coming in; the sleek white modern vessel was going out; the former was obscured by the latter as they came up alongside each other—and dropped their anchors.

"Shit!" said Jordan. "Mindsmog again! I can't see a damn thing through it!"

"I can feel it," Layard answered.

Jordan swept his glasses along the sleek outline of the white vessel and read off its name from the hull: the *Lazarus*. "She's a beauty," he started to say, and froze right there. Centred in his field of view, the man in black on the foredeck was seated upright in his chair; the back of his head was visible; he was looking at the old *Samothraki*. But as Jordan fixed him in his binoculars, so that oddly proportioned head turned until its unknown owner was staring straight at the esper across one hundred and twenty yards of blue water. And even though they were both wearing dark glasses, and despite the distance, it was as if they stood face-to-face!

WHAT? a powerful mental voice grunted its astonishment full in Jordan's mind. A THOUGHT THIEF? A MENTALIST?

Jordan gasped. What the hell did he have here? Whatever it was, it wasn't what he'd been looking for. He tried to withdraw but the other's mind closed on his like a great vise . . . and squeezed! He couldn't pull out! He flopped there loosely against the harbour wall and looked at the other where he now stood tall—enormous to Jordan—in the shade of the black canopy.

Their eyes were locked on each other, and Jordan straining so hard to look away, redirect his thoughts, that he was beginning to vibrate. It was as if solid bars of steel were shooting out from the other's hidden eyes, across the water and down the barrel's of Jordan's binoculars into his brain; where even now they were hammering at his mind as they drove home their message.

WHOEVER YOU ARE, YOU HAVE ENTERED MY MIND OF YOUR OWN FREE WILL. SO . . . BE . . . IT!

Layard was on his feet now, anxious and astonished. For all that he'd experienced little or nothing of the telepath's shock and, indeed, terror, still he could tell by just looking at him that something was terribly wrong. With his own mind full of mental smog and crackling, buzzing static, he reached to take Jordan's sagging weight—in time to guide and lower the telepath to the bench as he collapsed like a jelly, unconscious in his arms . . .

IV: Lazarides

THAT SAME NIGHT:

The *Lazarus* lay moored to a wharf in the main harbour, entirely still and darkly mirrored in water smooth as glass; three of the four crewmen had gone ashore, leaving only a watchkeeper; the boat's owner sat at a window seat upstairs in the most disreputable taverna of the Old Town, looking out and down across the waterfront. Downstairs a handful of tourists drank cheap brandy or ouzo and ate the execrable food, while the local layabouts, bums, and rejects in general laughed and joked with them in English and German, made coarse jokes *about* them in Greek, and scrounged drinks.

There were three or four blowsy-looking English girls down there, some with Greek boyfriends, all the worse for wear and all looking for the main chance. They danced or staggered to sporadic bursts of recorded bouzouki music, and later would dance more frantically, gaspingly, horizontally, to the accompaniment of slapping, sweating, ouzo-smelling flesh.

Upstairs was out of bounds to such as these, where the

owner of the taverna carried out the occasional shady deal, or perhaps drank, talked, or played cards with some of his many shady friends. None of these were around tonight, however, just the landlord himself, and a young Greek whore sitting alone in the alcove leading to her business premises— a small room with a bed and washbasin—and the man who now called himself Jianni Lazarides, occupying his window seat.

The fat, stubble-chinned proprietor, called Nichos Dakaris, was here to serve a bottle of good red wine to Lazarides, and the girl was here because she had a black eye and couldn't ply her trade along the waterfront. Or rather, she wouldn't. It was her way of paying Dakaris back for the beatings he gave her whenever he was obliged to cough up hush money to the local constabulary for the privilege of letting a prostitute use his place. If not for the fact that he felt the urge himself now and then, he probably wouldn't let her stay here at all; but she paid for her room "in kind" once or twice a week as the mood took Dakaris, on top of which he got forty percent of her take. Or would get it if she only used her room and wouldn't insist on free-lancing in Rhodian back alleys! Which was his other reason for beating her.

As for Jianni Lazarides: he also had his reasons for being here. This was the venue for his meeting with the Greek "captain" of the *Samothraki* and a couple of his cohorts, when he would look for an explanation as to how and why someone had been selling tickets for their assumed "covert" drug-running operation. Actually he already knew why, for he'd had it from the mind of Trevor Jordan; but now he wanted to hear it from Pavlos Themelis himself, the *Samothraki*'s master, before deciding how best to detach himself from the affair.

For Lazarides had put good money into this allegedly safe business (which now appeared to be anything but safe), and he wanted his money back or . . . payment in kind? For money and power were gods here in this era no less than in all the foregone centuries of human avarice, of which Lazarides had more than an obscure knowledge. And indeed there

101

were easier, safer, more guaranteed ways to make and use money in this vastly complex world; ways which would not attract the attention of its lawkeepers, or at any rate not too much of it.

Money was very important to Lazarides, and not just because he was greedy. This world he'd emerged into was overcrowded and threatening to become even more so, and a vampire has his needs. In the old times a boyar would be given lands by some puppet prince or other, to build a castle there and live in seclusion and, preferably and eventually, something of anonymity. Anonymity and longevity had walked hand in hand in the old days; you could not have one without the other; a famous man must not be seen to live beyond his or any other ordinary creature's span of years. But in those days news travelled slowly; a man could have sons; when he "died," there would always be one of those ready and waiting to step into his shoes.

Likewise in the here and now, except that news and indeed men no longer travelled slowly, because of which the world was that much smaller. So . . . how then to build an aerie, and all unnoticed, in these last dozen years of this twentieth century? Impossible! But still a very rich man could purchase obscurity, and with it anonymity, and so go about his business as of old. Which begged a second question: how to become very rich?

Well, Janos Ferenczy thought he had answered that one more than four hundred years ago, but now in the guise of Lazarides he wasn't so sure. In those days a gem-encrusted weapon or large nugget of gold had been instant wealth. Now too, except that now men would want to know the source of such an item. In those days a boyar's lands and possessions— or loot—had been his own, no questions asked. And only let him who dared try to take them away! But today such baubles as a jewelled hilt or a solid gold Scythian crown were "historic treasures," and a man may not trade with them without first satisfying a good many—far *too* many—queries as to their origin.

Oh, Janos knew the source of his wealth well enow; indeed, here it sat in this window seat, overlooking a harbour in the once powerful land of Rhodos! For the very man who "discovered" and unearthed these treasures in the here and now was the selfsame one who buried them deep in the earth more than four hundred years ago! How better to prepare for a second coming into the world, when one has foreseen a long, long period of uttermost dark?

And having retrieved these several caches, these items of provenance put down so long ago, surely it would be the very simplest thing to transfer them into land, properties of his own, the territories and possessions of a Wamphyri Lord? Oh, true, an aerie was out of the question, even a castle . . . but an island? An island, say, in the Greek sea, which had so many?

Ah, if only it could have been that easy!

But places change, nature takes her toll, earthquakes rumble and the land is split asunder, and treasures are buried deeper still where old markers fall or are simply torn down. The mapmakers then were not nearly so accurate, and even a keen memory—the very keenest vampire memory—will fade a little in the face of centuries . . .

Janos sighed and glanced out of the window at the harbour lights, and at those measuring the leagues of ocean, lighting their ships like luminous inchworms far out on the sea. The odious proprietor had gone now, back downstairs to serve ouzo and watered-down brandy and count his takings. But the bouzouki music still played amidst bursts of coarse laughter, the would-be lovers still danced and groped, and the young whore remained seated in her alcove as before.

The hour must be ten, and Janos had said he would contact his American thrall about then. Well, and he would . . . in a while, in a while.

He poured a little wine for himself, good and deep and red, and watched the way his glass turned to blood. Aye, the blood was the life—but not in a place like this! He would sup when he would sup, and meanwhile the wine could ease his parch. What was it after all but the plaguey unending thirst of the vampire, which one must either tame or die for? Or at least, tame within certain limits . . . And Janos wasn't shrivelled yet.

The whore had heard the chink of his glass against the bottle. Now she looked across, her surly mouth pouting; she, too, had a glass, which was empty.

Janos felt her eyes on him and turned his head. Across the room she took note of his straight-backed height, dark good looks, and expensive clothing, and wondered at the dark-tinted spectacles which shielded his eyes. But at the distance she could not see how coarse and large-pored was his skin, how wide and fleshy his mouth, or the disproportionate length of his skull, ears, and three-fingered hands. She only knew that he looked powerful, detached, deep. And certainly he was not a poor man.

She smiled, however unprettily, stood up, and stretched—which had the desired effect of lifting her pointed breasts—and crossed to Janos's window seat. He watched her swaying towards him and thought, *Of your own free will!*

"Will you drink it all?" she asked him, cocking a knowing eyebrow. "All to yourself . . . all *by* yourself?"

"No," he said at once, his expression remaining entirely ambivalent, "I require very little . . . of this."

Perhaps his voice surprised her: it was a growl, a rumble, so deep it made her bones shiver. And yet she didn't find it displeasing. Still, its force was sufficient that she took a pace to the rear. But as she drew back, so he smiled, however coldly, and indicated the bottle. "Are you thirsty, then?"

Was he a Greek, this man? He knew the tongue, but spoke it like they did in some of the old mountain villages, which modern times and ways would never reach. Or perhaps he wasn't Greek after all; or maybe he was, but many times removed, by travel and learning and the exotic dilution of far, foreign parts.

The girl didn't normally ask, but now she said, "May I?"

"By all means! As I have said, my real requirements lie in another direction."

Was that a hint? He must know what she was, surely? Should she invite him through the alcove and into her curtained room? Then, as she filled her glass . . . it was as if he had read her mind!—though of course that wouldn't be too difficult. "No," he said, with a slight but definite shake of his great head. "Now you must leave me alone. There are matters to occupy my mind, and friends will soon be joining me here."

She threw back her wine, and smiling, he refilled her glass before repeating, "Now go."

And that was that; the command was irresistible; she returned to her bench under the alcove. But now she couldn't keep her eyes off him. He was aware of it but it didn't seem to bother him. If he had *not* commanded her attention, then he might feel concerned.

Anyway, it was now time for Janos to discover what Armstrong was doing. He put the girl out of his mind, reached out with his vampire senses along the waterfront to the mole, and into the shadows there where massive walls reached up out of the still waters. No bright lights there, just heaps of mended nets, lobster pots, and the floats and amphoraelike vases with which the fishermen caught the octopus. And the ever-faithful Armstrong, of course, waiting for his master's commands.

Do you hear me, Seth?

"I'm here, where I should be," Armstrong whispered into the shadows of the mole, as if he talked to himself. He made no mention of the hunger, which Janos could feel in his mind like an ache. That was good, for a master's needs must always come first; but at the same time a man should not forget to reward a faithful dog. Armstrong would receive his reward later.

I now seek out the mentalist, the Englishman, Janos briefly explained, *and him I shall send to you. The other English will doubtless accompany him. That one is not required, for he can only hinder my works. One of them can tell us as much as two. Do you understand?*

Armstrong understood well enough—and again Janos felt the hunger in him. So much hunger that this time he commanded, *You will neither mark him nor take anything from him—nor yet give him anything of yourself! Do you hear me, Seth?*

"I understand."

Good! I suggest that he receive a stunning blow—say, to the back of the neck?—and that he then fall in the water where it is deep. Look to it, then, for if all is well, I shall send them to you soon.

Without more ado he then sent his vampire senses creeping amidst the bright lights of the New Town, searching among the hotels and tavernas, in and around the bars, fast-food stalls, and nightclubs. It was not difficult; the minds he sought were different, possessed some small powers of their own. And one of them at least had already been penetrated, damaged, almost destroyed. Indeed it was going to be destroyed, but not just yet. Time enough for that when Janos knew all that it knew. And from the single glimpse he had stolen before crushing down on that mind and driving it to seek sanctuary in oblivion, he was certain that it knew a great deal.

The mind of a mentalist, aye . . . a "telepath," as they called them now. But if Janos had caught the thought-thief spying on him (or if not on him directly, at least spying on the drug-running operation of which he was a part), how much then had he discovered *before* he was caught? Enough to make him dangerous, be sure! For in the moment of shutting him down Janos had sensed that the mindspy knew what he was! And that must never be. What? To be discovered as a vampire here in this modern world? Oh, some might scoff at such a suggestion—but others would not. This mentalist was just such a one, and there'd been echoes in his mind which hinted he knew of others. An entire nest of them!

Janos detected and seized upon a wave of frightened thoughts. He knew the scent of them. It was a mind he had encountered before, recently, which like a familiar face he now recognised. Terrified, cringing thoughts they were, bruised and battered to mental submission—but rising now once more to consciousness. He tracked them like a bloodhound, and entering that shuddering mind knew at once that this was the one and he'd made no mistake . . .

* * *

Ken Layard attended Trevor Jordon in the latter's hotel room. Their single rooms were side by side, with access from a corridor. For twelve hours solid the telepath had lain here now: six of them as still as a corpse, under the influence of a powerful sedative administered by a Greek doctor, four more in what had seemed a fairly normal sleeping mode, and the rest tossing and turning, sweating and moaning in the grip of whatever dream it was that bothered him. Layard had tried to wake him once or twice, but his friend hadn't been ready for it. The doctor had said he'd come out of it in his own good time.

As for what the trouble was: it could have been anything, according to the doctor. Too much sun, excitement, drink—a bug which had got into his system, perhaps? Or a bad migraine—but nothing to worry about just yet. The tourists were always going down with something or other.

Layard turned away from Jordan's bed, and in the next moment heard his friend say, "What? Yes—yes—I will." He spun on his heel, saw Jordan's eyes spring open, watched him push himself upright into a seated position.

There was a jar of water on Jordan's bedside table; Layard poured him a glass and offered it to him. Jordan seemed not to see it. His eyes were almost glazed. He swung his legs out of the bed, reached for his clothes where they were draped over a chair. The locator wondered: Is he sleepwalking?

"Trevor," he quietly said, taking his arm, "are you . . . ?"

"What?" Jordan faced him, blinked rapidly, suddenly looked him full in the face. His eyes focused and Layard guessed that he was now fully conscious, and apparently capable. "Yes, I'm okay. But . . ."

"But?" Layard prompted him, while Jordan continued to dress himself. There was something almost robotic about him.

The telephone rang. As Jordan went on dressing, Layard answered it. It was Manolis Papastamos, wanting to know how Jordan was doing. The Greek lawman had come on the

107

scene only seconds after Jordan's collapse; he'd helped Layard get him back here and called in the doctor.

"Trevor's fine," Layard answered his anxious query. "I think. He's getting dressed, anyway. What's happening your end?"

Papastamos spoke English the same way he spoke Greek: rapid-fire. "We're watching the boats—both of them—but nothing," he said. "If anything has come ashore from the *Samothraki*, it couldn't have been very much, and certainly not the hard stuff, which is about what we expected. I've checked out the *Lazarus*, too; unlikely that there's any connection; its owner is one Jianni Lazarides, archaeologist and treasure seeker, with good credentials. Or . . . let's just say he has no record, anyway. As for the crew of the *Samothraki*: the captain and his first mate are ashore; they may have brought a very little of the soft stuff with them; they're watching a cabaret at the moment, and drinking coffee and brandy. But more coffee than brandy. Obviously they plan on staying sober."

Jordan had meanwhile finished with dressing and was heading for the door. He moved like a zombie, and his clothes were the same ones he had worn this morning. But the nights were still chilly; plainly he hadn't so much chosen these light, casual clothes as taken them because they'd been handy. Layard called after him, "Trevor? Where do you think you're going?"

Jordan looked back. "The harbour," he answered automatically. "St. Paul's Gate, then along the mole to the windmills."

"Hello? Hello?" Papastamos was still on the phone. "What now?"

"He says he's going to the windmills on the mole," Layard told him. "And I'm going with him. There's something not right here. I've known it all day. Sorry, Manolis, but I have to hang up on you."

"I'll see you down there!" Papastamos quickly answered, but Layard only caught half of it as he was putting the phone down. And then he was struggling into his jacket and following Jordan where he made his way doggedly downstairs into the lobby, then out of the door and into the Mediterranean night.

"Aren't you going to wait for me?" he called out after him, but Jordan made no answer. He did glance back, once, and Layard saw his eyes staring out of his sick-looking face like holes punched in pasteboard. Plainly he wasn't going to wait for him, or for anyone else for that matter.

Layard almost caught up with his robotic partner as Jordan crossed a road heading for the waterfront, but then the lights changed, engines revved, and mopeds and cars started rolling in the scrambling, death-wish, devil-take-the-hindmost fashion of Greek traffic. In that same moment he found himself separated from Jordan by bumper-to-bumper metal; and by the time the exhaust fumes had cleared and the lights changed again, the telepath had disappeared into milling groups of people where they thronged the streets. Hurrying after him, Layard knew he'd lost him.

But at least he knew where he was going . . .

Jordan felt that he was fighting it for all he was worth, every step of the way, even knowing it was useless. It was like being drunk in a strange place and among strangers, when you lie on your back and the room spins. It actually seems to spin, the corners of the ceiling chasing each other like the spokes of a wheel. And there's nothing you can do to stop it because you know it isn't really spinning—it's your mind that's spinning, inside the head on top of your body. *Your* bloody head and body, but they won't obey you . . . you can't make them do what you want no matter how hard you try!

And all the time you can hear yourself trapped in your own skull like a fly in a bottle, buzzing furiously and banging repeatedly against the glass, and saying over and over again, "Oh, God, let it stop! Oh, God, let it stop! Oh, God . . . let . . . it . . . *stop*!"

It's the alcohol—the alien in your system, which has taken control—and fighting it only makes you feel that much worse. Try lifting your head and shoulders up off the bed and everything spins even faster, so fast you can feel the centrifugal force dragging you down again. Force yourself to your feet and you stagger, you turn, begin to spin with the room, with the entire bloody universe!

But only lie still, stop fighting it, close your eyes tight, and cling to yourself . . . eventually it will go away. The spinning will go away. The sickness. The buzzing of the fly in the bottle—which is your own battered, astonished, gibbering psyche—will go away. And you'll sleep. And it's possible the strangers will roll you and rob you blind.

Roll you? They could steal your underpants—even rape you, if they felt inclined—and you couldn't stop them, wouldn't feel it, wouldn't even suspect.

It was a replay of Jordan's first violent experience with alcohol. That had been when he'd started university and got homesick—of all bloody things! A couple of fellow students, college comedians thinking to have a little fun at his expense, had spiked his drinks. Then they'd played a few tricks on him in his room. Nothing vicious: they'd rouged his cheeks, given him a Cupid's-bow mouth, fitted him up with a garter belt and stockings, and stuck a Mickey Mouse johnnie on his dick.

He woke up cold, naked, ill, not knowing what had happened, wanting to die. But a day or two later when he was sober, he'd tracked them down one at a time and beaten the living shit out of them! Since when he'd only ever got physical when there was no other way around it.

But by God, he wished he could get physical now! With himself, with this mind and body which wouldn't obey him, with whoever it was that was doing this to him. For that was the terrible thing: he knew it was someone else doing it to him, jerking him about like a puppet on a set of strings, and there was *still* nothing he could do about it!

Stop! he kept telling himself. *Get a grip of yourself. Sit down . . . throw up . . . hold your head in your hands . . . wait for Ken. Do anything—but of your own free will!* But before his runaway body could even begin to obey such instructions:

AH . . . BUT IT IS *NOT* FREE! YOU CAME SPYING,
INVADED MY MIND—AN ANT IN A WASP'S NEST! SO
NOW PAY THE PRICE. GO ON: PROCEED JUST AS YOU
ARE. GO TO THE WINDMILLS.

That terrible, gonging, magnetic voice in his head—that
will which superimposed itself over his will—that telepathic,
hypnotic command of some one or thing as powerful, more
powerful, than anything he'd ever imagined before, which
made a mockery of resistance more surely than any Mickey
Finn.

Jordan's legs felt like rubber—almost vibrating, twanging
at the knees—as he strained to hold them back. As well hold
back opposite magnetic poles, or a moth from a candle. And
still he followed the waterfront to the mole, and along its
rocky neck, until the ancient windmills stood visible there
against a horizon of dark ocean.

Dressed all in black, Seth Armstrong was waiting, crouching in the shadows where the seawall was shaped like a castle's battlements, after the style of the old Crusaders whose
works were still visible all around. He let Jordan go stumbling by, looked back into the darkness of the mole, under
the winking lights of Rhodes Old Town where it sprawled on
the hill.

He heard footsteps, running, and a voice, panting:

"Trevor? For Christ's sake, slow down, will you? Where
the hell do you th—" And Armstrong struck.

Layard saw something big, black, gangling, step out of the
shadows. One eye glared at him from a slit in a black bala-
clava. Gasping, he skidded to a halt, spun on his heel to
flee—and Armstrong rabbit-punched him down to the night-
shining cobbles of the path. Out like a light, Layard lay
crumpled at the foot of the seawall. And Jordan, feeling the
strictures on his will slacken a little, turned back.

He saw the large, dark, mantislike figure of Armstrong
bent over Layard's unconscious form, saw his friend hoisted
aloft on powerful shoulders—and ejected through one of the
wall's embrasures, out into thin air! A moment more and
there came a splash—then the *chop . . . chop . . . chop* of

111

Brian Lumley

disturbed water gradually settling—and finally, as the figure in black now turned towards him—

—More running footsteps!

The beam of a torch cut the night, slashing it to left and right like a white knife through a black card.

And Manolis Papastamos' voice, just as sharp, slicing the silence: "Trevor, Ken, where are you?"

Be careful! the alien voice in Jordan's mind commanded, but the order was the merest whisper and no longer directed at him. It no longer dominated but merely advised. And he knew that his telepathic mind had simply "overheard" instructions meant for some other, meant in fact for the man in black. *Do not allow yourself to be caught or recognised!*

Splashing sounds from below the wall, and a gurgling cry! Ken Layard was alive! But Jordan knew for a fact that the locator couldn't swim! He forced his legs to carry him to the wall, where he could look out through an embrasure. And all the while he was aware of his controlling alien, confused and furious, mewling like a scalded cat in the back of his mind. But no longer fully in control.

Papastamos came running, a small, slim, streamlined shape in the night, and Jordan saw the long-limbed, gangling figure in black back off into the shadows. "Man-Manolis!" he forced his parched throat to croak. "Look out!"

The Greek lawman came to a halt, breathlessly called out, "Trevor?" and flashed his torch beam full in Jordan's face.

The shadows erupted and Armstrong smashed a blow to Papastamos' face. The Greek rode with it, went sprawling. His torch fell with him, clattering, its beam slithering everywhere. The man in black was running back along the mole towards the town. Papastamos cursed in Greek, snatched at the torch where it rolled past him, aimed it after the fleeing figure. Its beam trapped an elongated human shadow, jerking on the seawall like a giant crab escaping to the sea. But Papastamos was armed with more than just a torch.

His Beretta Model 92S barked five times in rapid succession, slinging a five-spoked fan of lead after the scuttling

112

shadow. A wailing cry of pain and a gasped, *"Uh—uh—uh!"* came back, but the footsteps didn't stop running.

"M-M-Manolis!" Jordan hadn't let up on his battle with the clamp on his will. "K-K-Ken . . . is . . . in . . . the . . . sea!"

The Greek got up, ran to the seawall. From below came a gurgling and gasping, the slosh of water windmilled by flailing arms. And without a thought for his own safety, Papastamos climbed up into the embrasure and launched himself feetfirst into the harbour . . .

In his window seat upstairs in the Taverna Dakaris, Janos Ferenczy's three-fingered right hand closed on his wineglass and applied pressure until the glass shattered. Wine and fragments of glass, and a little blood, too, were squeezed out from between his tightly clenched fingers. If he felt any pain, it didn't show in his gaunt-grey face, except perhaps in the tic jerking the flesh at one corner of his mouth.

"Janos . . . master!" Armstrong spoke to him from a little over three hundred yards away. "I'm shot!"

How badly?

"In the shoulder. I'll be useless to you until I heal. A day or two."

Sometimes I think you have always been useless to me! Go back to the boat. Try not to be seen.

"I . . . I haven't got the telepath."

I know, fool! I shall see to it myself.

"Then be careful. The man who shot me was a policeman!"

Oh? And how do you know that?

"Because he shot me! His gun. Ordinary people don't carry them. But even without it, I guessed what he was as soon as I saw him. He was expecting trouble. Policemen look the same in whatever country."

You are a veritable mine of information, Seth! The vampire's thoughts were scathingly sarcastic. *But I take your point. And since it now seems I may not take this thought-thief for my own, I shall find some other way to . . . examine*

113

him. His own telepathy shall be his undoing. His mind is receptive to the thoughts of others, which until now has made him a big fish in a little pond. Ah, but now he has a shark to contend with! For I was a mindspy five centuries before he was born!

"I'm going back to the boat," Armstrong confirmed.

Good! And if any of my crew are ashore, be sure to call them back. And Janos thrust the other out of his mind.

He returned to Jordan, where he had staggered to a seat underneath one of the antique windmills and sat there in moon-and starlight. Jordan was exhausted, totally drained by the mental battle he'd fought with his unknown adversary, but not so far gone that he couldn't appreciate what he'd come up against.

The last time Jordan had experienced anything like this had been the autumn of '77, at Harkley House in Devon. Yulian Bodescu. And it had taken Harry Keogh to clear up that mess! And was this like that? he wondered. Had he and Ken Layard sensed the presence of . . . of this Thing, even before it had become entirely apparent to them? Or apparent to him, anyway? All the pieces were starting to fit together now, and the picture they were forming was—terrible! Cannabis resin, cocaine? They were commonplace, even harmless, compared to this.

E-Branch must be put in the picture at once! The thought was like an invocation:

E-BRANCH? That deep, seething voice was there inside Jordan's head again, and mental jaws were tightening on his mind. WHAT IS THIS E-BRANCH? And pinned there by the sheer *weight* of the vampire's telepathic power, Jordan could only squirm as the monster commenced a minute, painful examination of all his most private thoughts . . .

Janos might have examined Jordan all night, except he was interrupted. Looking down out of his window, he saw the bearded, big-bellied Pavlos Themelis, master of the *Samothraki*, making his way across the street towards the Taverna Dakaris. He was a little late, coming to meet with the man he called Jianni Lazarides; but coming anyway, and Janos couldn't continue to dig away at Jordan's mind and hold a conversation with Themelis at the same time.

This morning he had found himself under the scrutiny of a thought thief, reached out, and delivered a blow to the other's mind. It had been an instinctive reaction which nevertheless served to give the vampire time to think. Jordan was strong, however, and had recovered. Well, and now Janos must strike again at that mind—a different sort of blow—and one from which the English mindspy would *not* recover. Not without a deal of help, anyway.

Driving his vampire senses deep into Jordan's psyche, Janos found the door of sanity locked, bolted, and barred against all mankind's worst fears. And chuckling, he turned the key, took down the bars, threw back the bolts—and opened the door!

That was enough . . . and now he would know just exactly where to find Jordan whenever he desired to continue his examination. It was done with only moments to spare, for already the *Samothraki*'s master was coming up the stairs.

As Pavlos Themelis and his first mate entered the room, they saw the Greek prostitute cleaning away Janos's broken glass and offering him her own. Unmoved, he accepted it, said, "Go now."

As she made to get by the huge drug runner, Themelis grabbed her arm in a fist like a ham, caught her round the waist, and swung her off her feet. He turned her over and her skirts fell down over her furious face. Themelis sniffed between her legs and roared, "Clean drawers! Open crotch, too! Good! I may see you later, Ellie!"

"Not if I see you first!" she spat at him as he set her on her feet. Then she was down the stairs, through the taverna, and out onto the street.

From down below Nichos Dakaris' hoarse voice bellowing after her as she went into the night: "Bring 'em back alive, my girl! Bring 'em right back here where I can see the colour of their money!" This was followed by gales of coarse laughter, then more bouzouki music as before.

115

Pavlos Themelis took a seat across the table from the man he knew as Jianni Lazarides. The chair groaned as he sat down on it and parked his elbows on the table. He wore his peaked captain's hat tilted on one side, which he supposed gave him an irresistible piratical look. It wasn't a bad ploy: no one would normally suspect anyone who looked so roguish of being a rogue! "Only one glass, Jianni?" he growled. "Prefer to drink alone, do you?"

"You are late!" Janos had no time for banter.

Themelis' first mate, a short, squat, torpedo of a man, had remained at the head of the stairs, from where he carefully scanned the room. Now he called down to Dakaris, "Glasses, Nichos, and a bottle of brandy. Good stuff, too, *parakalo*!" And finally he picked up a chair and carried it to the table by the window seat. Seating himself, he asked Themelis, "Well, and has he explained himself?"

Behind his dark glasses, Janos narrowed his eyes. "Oh? And is there something I should explain?"

"Come, come, Jianni!" Themelis chided. "You were supposed to come aboard us this morning in the harbour, not go sliding off in your pretty white ship as if you'd been stung in the arse or something! We'd pull alongside, you'd come over and see the stuff—of which there's a kilo for you, if you've the use for it—and then we'd collect your valuable contribution on behalf of our mutual sponsor! A show of good faith on both sides, as it were. That was the plan, to which you were party. Except . . . it didn't happen!" His easygoing look suddenly turned sour and his tone hardened. "And later, when I've parked up the old *Samothraki* and I'm wondering what the bloody fuck, I get this message saying we'll meet here instead, tonight! So now tell me, are you *sure* there's nothing you'd like to explain?"

"The explanation is simple!" Janos barked. "It could not happen the way it was planned because we were being watched! By men on the harbour wall, with binoculars. By policemen!"

Themelis and his second-in-command glanced at each other a moment, then turned again to Janos. "Policemen, Jianni?"

Themelis raised a bushy eyebrow. "You know this for a fact?"

"Yes," said Janos, for in truth he did now know it for a fact; he'd had it direct from the English thought thief. "Yes, I am certain. I cannot be mistaken. And I would remind you that right from the start of this venture I have insisted upon complete anonymity and total isolation from its mechanics. I must *not* be left vulnerable to any sort of investigation or prosecution! I thought that was understood."

Themelis narrowed his eyes, slanted his mouth in a sneer . . . then turned his bearded face away as Nichos Dakaris came labouring up the stairs. "Huh!" Themelis' torpedolike second-in-command grunted as Dakaris slammed down glasses and a bottle of brandy on the table. "What happened, Nick? Did you have to send out for it?"

"Very funny!" said Dakaris over his shoulder as he left. "But not nearly so amusing when you consider that *some* of my customers actually pay me! Friends I can always use, but nonpaying customers who also insult me . . . ?" Then he'd gone back downstairs.

Themelis had taken the opportunity to compose himself. Now he said, "It's nothing new to be watched by the police. Everyone is watched by the police! You have to keep your nerve, that's all, and not panic."

"I know how to keep my nerve well enough," said Janos. "But unless I'm mistaken, there is aboard the *Samothraki* an amount of cocaine worth ten million British pounds or two billion drachmae. Which is to say two *hundred* billions of leptae! I had no idea such monies existed. Why, five hundred years ago a man could buy an entire kingdom with such a sum and still have enough left over to hire an army to guard it! And you tell me to keep my nerve and not panic? Now let me tell you something, my fat friend: the difference between bravery and cowardice is discretion, between a rich man and a cutpurse it's not being caught, and between freedom and the dungeon it's the ability to walk away from ill-laid plans!"

As he spoke the frowns on the faces of the others grew

deeper, confused, and far more concerned. To be frank, the master of the *Samothraki* (whose criminal nature had ever held sway over caution, resulting in a string of convictions) wondered what on earth he was prattling on about! In his younger days Themelis had collected coins. But the lepta? To his knowledge the last of those had been minted in 1976—in twenties and fifties denominations only, because of their minuscule value! To calculate modern sums of money in leptae had to be a sure sign of madness! Why, it would take five hundred to buy one cigarette! And as for Lazarides' use of the term "dungeon" in place of "jail" . . . what was one supposed to make of the man? How could anyone look so young and think so archaic?

Themelis' second-in-command was thinking much the same things; but over and above everything else Lazarides had said, his final statement—of intention?—stood out in starkest definition. Something about walking away? Was he looking for an out?

"No threats, Jianni, or whatever your name is," this one now growled. "We're not the type to threaten easily, Pavlos and me. We don't want to hear any more talk about anyone walking away from anything. No one walks away from us. It's hard to walk with broken legs, and even harder if it's your spine!"

Janos had been stroking his glass with the long fingers of his left hand, watching Themelis' face rather than that of his loudmouth companion. But now his three-fingered hand stopped its stroking and his head slowly turned until he gazed directly into that one's eyes. Janos seemed to crouch down a little into himself on the low window seat—from fear, or was it something else?—and his left hand slid snakelike from the long, narrow table to hang by his side. The thug could almost feel the intensity of Janos's gaze coming right through those enigmatic dark lenses at him. And:

"You accuse me of making threats?" Janos finally answered, his voice so quiet and deep that it might simply be a series of bass grunts rather than speech proper. "You have the audacity to believe that I might find it necessary to threaten such as you? And then—as if that weren't more than enough—you in your turn threaten me? You *dare* to threaten . . . me?''

"Have a care for your bones!'' the other hissed, his lips drawing back from yellow teeth as he perched himself on the very rim of his chair, tilting it forward to shove his bullet head a little closer. "You smart-talking, oh-so-clean, high-and-mighty bastard!''

Janos's left arm and hand hung out of sight below the rim of the table. But instead of drawing back more yet, he, too, had leaned his face forward. And now—

—In a movement so swift and flowing it was quicksilver, the vampire shot out his large, long-fingered hand a distance of fifteen inches under the table and bunched up the other's scrotum so deep in his groin that his testicles flopped into his palm. Twisting and squeezing at the same time, Janos needed only to nip with his chisel-tipped nails and tear with his great strength to castrate the other right through his threadbare lightweight trousers! Yes, and the fool knew it.

His bottom jaw fell open and he snapped upright in his chair, crowding the table. He squirmed, gagging as his eyes flew wide open in his face. He was the merest moment away from becoming a eunuch, and he could do . . . nothing! Only let him begin to react violently and Janos could finish the job in a split second.

The vampire increased the pressure, drew his arm in under the table—and his victim inched himself forward and off his chair, reached across the bolted-down table, and grasped its rim in both hands to maintain his balance and take the strain off his balls. And still Janos held him there; and still he fixed him with his eyes, which were only inches away now. But where a moment ago the vampire's face had been slate grey with rage, now he merely smiled, however sardonically.

Gurgling, with tears streaming from eyes which were standing out like marbles in his purpling face, the agonised thug knew how utterly helpless he was. And suddenly it dawned on him that not only was it possible for Janos to do the unthinkable, but it was also probable!

"N-no—*no*!" he managed to gasp.

That was what Janos had been waiting for; he read it in the other's mind as well as in his wet, rubbery face; he recognised and accepted his submission. And in one viciously coordinated movement he gave a final twist and a squeeze, then released and thrust the man away.

Sending his chair flying, the thug crashed over on his back. Gasping and sobbing, he rolled himself into an almost foetal position, with his hands down between his thighs. And there he remained, rocking and moaning in his agony.

All of which had gone unheard by the people in the taverna down below, where "Zorba's Dance" and its attendant clapping and stamping had drowned everything out. But in any case, there hadn't been a lot to hear.

Pavlos Themelis was pale now, his face twitching behind his great beard. At first he hadn't known what was going on, and by the time he had known, it was over. And meanwhile Lazarides had scarcely turned a hair. But now, seeming to flow to his feet as sinuous as a snake, he stood up and towered over the table.

"You are a fool, Themelis," he grunted, "and that one is a bigger fool. But . . . a deal is a deal, and I have already invested too much in this business to abandon it now. And so it seems I must see it through. Very well, but at least let me give you some good advice: in future, be more careful."

He made as if to leave, and Themelis got quickly out of his way, gasping, "But we still need your money, or some gold at least, to see the job done!"

Crossing the floor, Janos paused. He appeared to give it a moment's thought, then said, "At three in the morning, when all the coast guards and petty law officers are asleep in their beds, weigh anchor and meet me three sea miles due east of Mandraki. We will conclude our business there, far out of sight and sound of land. Is it agreed?"

Themelis nodded, his Adam's apple bobbing. "Count on it," he said. "The old *Samothraki* will be there."

And on the floor his partner continued to writhe and groan

and sweat out his gradually easing pain; and Janos, going downstairs, didn't even look at him . . .

It was after eleven and the streets of the Old Town near the waterfront were much quieter. Janos walked in the shadows wherever possible, his long stride more a lope as he quickly put distance between himself and the Taverna Dakaris. But he was not unobserved. Greek policemen in civilian clothes, hiding in even deeper shadows, saw him go and ignored him. They didn't know him; he wasn't the reason they were here; why would they be interested in him? No, their quarry was one Pavlos Themelis, who was still inside the taverna.

Their brief had been to follow him, check out his contacts, see if he was passing any stuff around—but *not* to pull him in or hinder him in any way. There was bigger stuff going down, and when the ax fell, someone up top wanted to make sure it came down not only on the master and crew of the *Samothraki* but on the entire organisation, and came down hard. It was perfectly obvious that Nichos Dakaris was part of it, too, and his rancid taverna a likely distribution point.

In short, Janos Ferenczy's luck was holding.

But the lackadaisical Greek policemen were not the only ones to see him leave the Dakaris; Ellie Touloupa was watching, too, looking down from a vantage point one level up and a block away, where an old stone arch supported a narrow, walled alley. She saw him take his departure and noted his route: towards a small jetty in the main harbour, where people came ashore in their tenders from the yachts and pleasure craft. Ellie wasn't stupid: she had done a little quiet checking up on this Lazarides and knew that the sleek white *Lazarus* was his. So where else would he be going?

Perhaps he had a woman aboard—but if so, what was keeping him ashore, drinking on his own in a flea pit like Nichos Dakaris' place? Maybe he had problems. Well, and Ellie had a way with problems. Anyway, she found him exciting, and who could say but that there might be some money in it, too? Why, she might even end up aboard his boat for the night!

So her thoughts ran as she put out her cigarette, descended

121

to the lower level, and hurried through a maze of cobbled alleys to a spot where she might intercept him. And intercept him she did, at a junction of dark, high-walled streets not fifty feet from the jetty.

Janos, arriving at the junction, was aware of her at once. Her breathing was still laboured, from hurrying, and her high heels skittered a little on the cobbles as she came to a halt in the shadows. She felt that he could even see her (though how he saw at all in those dark glasses she couldn't say) as he slowed his pace and turned his head to look straight in her direction.

Then . . . it was a strange feeling: to want him to know that she was there, but at the same time almost fearing his knowing it. Should she stand still, hold her breath, hope that he would carry on by? Or—

But too late.

"You," he said, taking a step towards the shadows where she stood. "But this is a lonely place, Ellie, and by now there should be customers for you, back at Nick's."

As he stepped in, so she stepped a little out of the shadows. They stood close, half silhouettes in the darkness of old stone walls. And there and then she knew she would have him, the way she always knew it. "I thought I might come aboard your boat," she said breathlessly.

Another pace and he drove her back into the darkness, until she leaned against the wall. "But you may not," he answered, with a slow shake of his head.

"Then—*ah*!" she drew breath sharply as his hand grasped her narrow waist just above the hip. "Then . . . I think perhaps I would like you to fuck me here—right now—against this wall!"

He chuckled, but without humour. "And should I pay for something you so obviously desire?"

"You've already paid," she answered, beginning to pant as his free hand opened her blouse. "Your wine . . ."

"You sell yourself cheaply, Ellie." He lifted her skirts, moved even closer.

"Cheaply?" she breathed against his neck. "For you it's free!"

Again his chuckle. "Free? You give yourself freely? Ah, but this world is filled with surprises! A whore, and yet so innocent."

She parted her legs and sucked at him, and expanded as he slid into her. He was massive! He surged within her, filling her and yet still surging! The sensation was one such as she'd never known or even imagined before. Was he some sort of god, some fantastic Priapus? "Who . . . are . . . you?" She gasped the words out, knowing full well who he was. And before he could answer: "What . . . are . . . you?"

Janos was aroused now—his hunger, if nothing else. One hand tugged at her breasts while the other reached behind and under her. He continued to surge; not thrusting but simply elongating into her. And now his fingers had found her anus, and they too seemed to be surging.

"Ah! Ah! Ah!" she gasped, her eyes wide and shining in the darkness and her mouth lolling open.

And finally, grunting, he answered her question with one of his own. "Do you know the legend of the Vrykoulakas?" His hand left her breasts and took away the dark glasses from his eyes—which burned crimson as coals in his face!

She inhaled air massively, but before she could scream, his chasm of a mouth had clamped itself over the entire lower half of her face. And his tongue also surged, into and down her convulsing throat. While in her mind:

Ah, I see you do *know the legend! Well, and now you know the reality. So be it!* Inside her body his vampire proto-flesh spread into every cavity, putting out filament rootlets which burrowed in her veins and arteries like worms in soil, without damaging the structure. And even before she had lost full consciousness, Janos was feeding.

Tomorrow they would find her here and say she had died of anaemia, and not even the most minute autopsy would discover anything to the contrary. Nor would there be any— *progeny*—of this most delicious fusion. No, for Janos would see to it that nothing of him remained in her to surface later and cause him . . . problems.

As for the life he was taking: what of it? It was only one of many hundreds. And anyway, what had she been but a whore? The answer was simple: she had been nothing . . .

Three and a half hours later and three miles due east of Rhodes Town, the *Samothraki* lay as if becalmed on a sea like a millpond. Quite extraordinarily, in the last ten or fifteen minutes a writhing fret had developed, quickly thickening to a mist and then to a fog. Now damp white billows were drifting across the old ship's decks, and visibility was down to zero.

The first mate, still tender from his brush with Janos Ferenczy, had just brought Pavlos Themelis up onto the deck to see for himself. And Themelis was rightly astonished. "What?" he said. "But this is crazy! What do you make of it?"

The other shook his head. "I don't know," he answered. "Crazy, like you said. You might expect it in October, but that's six months away." They moved to the wheelhouse, where a crewman was trying to get the foghorn working.

"Forget it," Themelis told him. "It doesn't work. God, this is the Aegean! Foghorn? I never once used it! The pipes will be full of rust! Anyway, she works off steam and we've precious little up. So make yourself useful, go take a turn stoking. We have to move out of this."

"Move?" said the first mate. "Where to?"

"The hell out of this!" Themelis barked. "Where do you think? Into clear water, somewhere where the *Lazarus* isn't likely to come barging up out of nowhere and cut us in half!"

"Speak of the devil!" the other growled low in his throat, his little pig eyes full of hate where they stared through the condensation on the cabin window at the sleek white shape which even now came ghosting alongside, her reversed screws bringing her to a dead halt in the gently lapping water.

The grey, mist-wreathed crew of the *Lazarus* tossed hawsers; the ships were hauled together, port to portside; ancient tyres festooning the *Samothraki*'s strakes acted as buffers, keeping the hulls apart. All was achieved by the light of the deck lamps, in an eerie silence where even the squealing of the tyres as they were compressed and rubbed between the hulls seemed muted by the fog.

For all that the *Lazarus* was a modern steel hull, as broad as the *Samothraki* but three metres longer, still she sat low in the water when her screws were dead or idling. The decks of the two ships were more or less level, and with little or no swell to mention, transfer would be as simple as stepping from one ship to the next. And yet the crew of the white ship, all eight of them, simply lined the rail; while her master and his American companion stayed back a little, gaunt scarecrow figures under the awnings of the foredeck. The cabin lights, blazing white through the fog, gave their obscure shapes silvery silhouettes.

At the port rail of the *Samothraki*, Themelis and his men grew uneasy. There was something very odd here, something other than this weird, unnatural fog. "This Lazarides bastard," Themelis' sidekick grunted under his breath, "bothers me . . ."

Themelis offered a low snort of derision. "Something of an understatement, that, Christos," he said. "But keep your balls out of his way and you should be okay!"

The other ignored the gibe. "The mist clings to him," he continued, shivering. "It almost seems to issue *from* him!"

Lazarides and Armstrong had moved to the gate in the rail. They stood there, leaning forward, seeming to examine the *Samothraki* minutely. There was nothing to choose between them in height, Themelis thought, but plenty in bearing and style. The American shambled a little, like an ape, and wore a black eye patch over his right eye; in his right hand he carried a smart black briefcase, full of money, one hoped. And Lazarides beside him, straight as a ramrod in the night and the fog, affecting those dark glasses of his even now.

But silent? Why were they *so* silent? And what were they waiting for? "So here we are then, Jianni!" Themelis shook off the black mood of depression which had so suddenly threatened to envelop him, opened his arms expansively, glanced around, and nodded his satisfaction. "Privacy at last, eh? In the heart of a bank of fog, of all bloody things! So . . . welcome aboard the old *Samothraki*."

And at last Lazarides smiled. "You are inviting me aboard?"

"Eh?" said Themelis, taken aback. "But certainly! How else may we get our business done?"

"How indeed," said the other, with a grim nod. And as he crossed between ships, so he took off his dark glasses. Armstrong came with him, and the rest of his men, too, clambering over the rails. And the crew of the *Samothraki* backed stumblingly away from them, knowing now for a fact that something—almost everything—was most definitely wrong here. For the crew of the *Lazarus* were like flame-eyed zombies to a man, and their master . . . he was like no man they'd ever seen before.

Pavlos Themelis, seeing the transformation in the face of the man called Lazarides as he stepped aboard the *Samothraki*, thought his eyes must be playing him tricks. His first mate saw it, too, and frantically yanked his gun from its underarm holster.

Too late, for Armstrong towered over him. The American used his briefcase to bat the gun aside even as it was brought into view, then grabbed the man's gun hand and wrestled the weapon round to point at its owner's head. Bullet Head didn't stand a chance. Armstrong pointed the gun into his ear and said, *"Hah!"* And his victim, seeing the American's one eye burning like sulphur—and his forked, crimson tongue, flickering in the gape of his mouth—simply gave up the ghost.

"That one," said Janos to Themelis, almost casually, *"was* a fool!" Which was Armstrong's signal to pull the trigger.

As his head flew apart in crimson ruin, Christos was tossed like a rag doll over the rail. Sliding down between the hulls, his body was crushed and ground a little before being dumped into the mist lying soft on the sea. The hole he made in it quickly sealed itself; the echo of the shot which had killed him, caught by the fog and tossed back, was still ringing . . .

126

"Holy Mother of . . . !" Themelis breathed, helpless as his men were rounded up. But as Janos advanced on him he backed away and again, disbelievingly, observed the length of his head and jaws, the *teeth* in his monstrous mouth, the weird scarlet blaze of his terrible eyes. "J-J-Jianni?" the Greek finally got his brain working. "Jianni, I—"

"Show me this cocaine." Janos took hold of his shoulder with a steel hand, his fingers biting deep. "This oh so valuable white powder."

"It—it's below . . ." Themelis' answer was a mere breath; he could not, dare not, take his eyes from the other's face.

"Then take me below," said Janos. But first, to his men: "You did well. Now do as you will. I know how hungry you are."

Even below decks Themelis could hear the screams of his crew; and he thought, *What, Christos Nixos a fool? Maybe, but at least he didn't know what hit him!* And he wondered how long before his screams would be joining the rest . . .

Forty minutes later the *Lazarus'* diesels coughed into life and she drew slowly away from the now silent, wallowing *Samothraki*. The fog was lifting, stars beginning to show through, and soon the horizon would light with the first crack of a new day.

When the *Lazarus* was a quarter mile away, the doomed ship blew apart in a massive explosion and gouting fire. Bits of her spiralled or fluttered back to the foaming sea and were put out, leaving only their drifting smoke. She was no more. In a few days pieces of her planking might wash ashore, maybe a body or two, possibly even the bloated, fish-eaten corpse of Pavlos Themelis himself . . .

V: Harry Keogh Now: Ex-Necroscope

HARRY WOKE UP KNOWING THAT SOMETHING WAS HAPPEN-
ing or about to happen. He was propped up in the huge old
bed where he'd nodded off, his head against the headboard,
a fat, black-bound book open in his slack hands. *The Book
of the Vampire*: a so-called factual treatise which examined
the elemental evil of the vampire down through all the ages
to modern times. It was light reading for the Necroscope,
and many of its "well-authenticated cases" little more than
grotesque jokes; for no one in the world—with one possible
exception—knew more about the legend, the source, the truth
of vampirism than Harry Keogh. That one exception was his
son, also called Harry, except that Harry Jr. didn't count
because in fact he wasn't "in" this world at all but . . .
somewhere else.

Harry had been dreaming an old, troubled dream: one
which mingled his life and loves of fifteen years gone by with
those of the here and now, turning them into a surreal kalei-
doscope of eroticism. He had dreamed of loving Helen, his
first groping (mental as well as physical) sexual experience;

and of Brenda, his first true love and the wife of his youth; so that however strange and overlapping, these had been sweet and familiar dreams, and tender. But he had also dreamed of the Lady Karen and her monstrous aerie in the world of the Wamphyri, and it seemed likely that this was the dreadful dream which had started him awake.

But somewhere in there had been dreams of Sandra, too, his new and—he hoped—lasting love affair, which because of its freshness was more vivid, real, and immediate than the others. It had taken the sting of poignancy from some of the dream, and the cold clutch of horror from the rest of it.

That was what he had been dreaming about: making love to the women he had known, and to one he knew now. And also of making love to the Lady Karen, whom mercifully he had never known—not in that way.

But Sandra . . . they'd made love before on several occasions—no, on many occasions, though rarely satisfactorily—always at her place in Edinburgh, in the turned-down green glow of her bedside lamp. Not satisfactory for Harry, anyway; of course he couldn't speak for Sandra. He suspected, though, that she loved him dearly.

He had never let her know about his—dissatisfaction? Not merely because he didn't want to hurt her, more especially because it would only serve to highlight his own deficiency. A deficiency, yes, and yet at the same time something of a paradox. Because by comparison with other men (Harry was not so naive as to believe there had been no others) he supposed that to Sandra he must seem almost superhuman.

He could make love to her for an hour, sometimes longer, before bringing himself to climax. But he was not superhuman, at least not in that sense. It was simply that in bed he couldn't seem to get switched on to her. When he came, always it was with some other woman in his mind's eye. Any other woman: the friend of a friend or some brief, chance encounter; some cover girl or other; even the small girl Helen from his childhood, or the wife Brenda from his early manhood. A hell of a thing to admit about the woman you think you love, and who you're fairly sure loves you!

His deficiency, obviously, for Sandra was very beautiful. Indeed, Harry should consider himself a lucky man—everybody said so. Maybe it was the cool, green, subdued lighting of her bedroom that turned him off: he didn't really care for green. And her eyes were greenish, too. Or a greeny blue, anyway.

That's why her part of this dream had been so different: in it they had made love and it had been good. He had been close to climax when he woke up . . . when he'd come awake knowing that something was about to happen.

He woke up in his own bed, in his own country house near Bonnyrig, not far out of Edinburgh, with the book still in his hands. And feeling its weight there . . . so maybe that's what had coloured his dreams. Vampires. The *Wamphyri*. Not surprising, really: they'd coloured most of his dreams for several years now.

Outside, dawn was on the brink; faint streamers of light, grey green, filtered through the narrow slits of his blinds; they tinted the atmosphere of his bedroom with a faint watercolour haze, a wash of subdued submarine tints.

Half-reclining there, becoming aware, coming back to life, he felt a tingle start up in his scalp. His hair was standing up on end. So was his penis, still throbbing from the dream. He was naked, electrically erect—and now aware and intent.

He *listened* intently: to murmuring plumbing sounds as the central heating responded to its timer, to the first idiot twitterings of sleepy birds in the garden, to a world stretching itself in the strengthening dawn outside.

Harry rarely slept more than an hour or two at a stretch, and dawn was his favourite time—normally. It was always good to know that the night was safely past, a new day under way. But this time he felt that something was happening, and he *gazed* intently through the faint green haze, turning his eyes to stare at the open bedroom door. Drugged by sleep, he saw everything with soft edges, fuzzy and indistinct. There was nothing sharp in the entire room. Except his inexplicable intentness, which seemed odd when matched against his blurred vision.

130

Anyone who ever started awake after a good drunk would know how he felt. You half know where you are, you half want to be somewhere special, you are half-afraid of not being where you should be; and even when you know where you are, you're still not quite *sure* you're there, or even that you are you. Part of the "never again" syndrome.

Except that Harry had not been drinking—not that he could remember, anyway.

The other thing that invariably affected him on those occasions when he woke up like this—the thing which had used to frighten him a great deal, but which he'd thought he was used to—was his paralysis. The fact that he could not move. It was only the transition from sleep to waking, he knew that, but still it was horrible. He had to force gradual movement into his limbs, usually starting with a hand or a foot. He was paralysed now, with only his eyes to command of all his various parts. He made them stare through the open bedroom door into the shadows beyond.

Something was happening. Something had awakened him. Something had robbed him of the satisfaction of spilling himself into Sandra and enjoying it for once. Something was in the house . . .

That would account for his tingling scalp, his hair standing erect at the back of his neck, his wilting hard. A perfume was in the air. Something moved in the shadows beyond the bedroom door: a movement sensed, not heard. Something came closer to the door, paused just out of sight in darkness.

Harry wanted to call out, "Who's there?" but his paralysis wouldn't let him. Perhaps he gurgled a little. A shape emerged partly from the shadows. Through the submarine haze he saw a navel, the lower part of a belly with its dark bush of pubic hair, the curve of soft feminine hips and the tops of thighs where they might show above dark stockings. She stood (whoever she was) just beyond the door, her flesh soft in the filtered light. As he watched she transferred her weight from one unseen foot to the other, her thighs moving, her hip jutting. Above the belly, soft in the shadows, there would be breasts large and ripe. Sandra had large breasts.

131

It was Sandra, of course.

Harry's voice still refused to work, but he could now move the fingers of his left hand. Sandra must be able to see him, see how she was affecting him. His dream was about to become reality. The blood coursed in his veins and began to pound once more. In the back of his mind, faintly, he asked himself questions. And answered them.

Why had she come?

Obviously for sex.

How had she got in?

He must have given her a key. He didn't remember doing so.

Why didn't she come forward more clearly into view?

Because she wanted to see him fully aroused first. Perhaps she had not wished to wake him until she was in bed with him.

Why had she waited so long to show him that she could be sexually aggressive? She'd taken the initiative before, certainly, but never to this extent.

Maybe because she sensed his uncertainty—feared that he might be having second thoughts—or perhaps because she suspected he had never fully enjoyed her.

Well, and maybe she was right.

Staring was causing his right eye to jump, both eyes to water. It was the poor light. Harry willed his left hand to move, stretched it out, pulled the cord that closed the window shutters—to shut out a little more of the faint, greeny-grey light. That left the room in near darkness—thin dim green stripes on a black velvet background. And that was what she'd been waiting for.

Now she moved forward, olive-fleshed. She must be wearing stockings; a T-shirt, too, rolled up to show her navel. Sexy, dismembered by darkness, her thighs, belly, and navel floated towards him, hips moving languidly, green-striped. She got onto the bed, kneeling, her thighs opening, and inched forward. The dark cleft was visible in her bush of pubic hair. She was so silent. And so light. The bed did not sink in where she crept towards him. Harry wondered, *How does she do that?*

She began to lower herself onto him—slowly, so slowly—the dark cleft widening as her body settled to its target. He arched his back, straining up towards her . . . but why couldn't he feel her knees gripping his hips? Why was she so weightless?

Then, suddenly and without warning, his flesh was crawling. Lust fled him in a moment. For somehow—instinctively, intuitively—he knew that this was not Sandra. And worse, he knew that he couldn't rightly say *what* it was!

His left hand fumblingly found the light cord, pulled it.

Light flooded the room blindingly.

At the same time the cleft in her bush of pubic hair sprang open like a mechanical thing! White-gleaming, yawning jaws of salivating needle teeth set in bulging, obscenely glistening pink gums shot down from the gaping lips to snap shut on him in a vise of shearing agony!

Harry screamed, rammed himself backwards in his bed, banged his head savagely on the headboard. Galvanised, his hands stabbed out, striking murderously for a face, a throat—striking instinctively at features . . . which weren't there!

Above the navel—nothing! And below the upper thighs—nothing!

She—it—was a lower abdomen, a disembodied vagina with cannibal teeth which were chomping on him! And his blood hot and red and spurting as the thing feasted on his genitals and munched them up like so much slop. *And a crimson eye that snapped suddenly open, glaring at Harry from the orbit which he had mistaken for a navel!*

"And that's it, Harry?" Dr. David Bettley, an E-Branch empath retired early for the sake of his shaky heart, gazed at his visitor from beneath half-lowered, bushy eyebrows.

"Isn't it enough?" the other answered, with some animation. "Christ, it was enough for me! It scared the living daylights out of me. Yes, even out of *me*! I mean, don't think I'm bragging but that's no easy thing to do. It's just that this damn dream was so . . . so real! We all have nightmares, but this one . . .'' He shook his head, gave an involuntary shudder.

''Yes, I can see how badly it affected you,'' said Bettley concernedly. ''But when I say 'that's it,' it isn't to make light of your experience. I'm simply asking, was there any more?''

''No.'' Harry shook his head. ''For that's when I *actually* came awake. But if you mean more reaction to it? You'd better believe there was! Look, I was weak as a kitten. I'm sure I was in shock. I felt physically sick, almost threw up. Also, I emptied my bowels—and I'm not ashamed to admit that I only just made it to the toilet! I don't mean to be crude, but that dream literally scared the shit out of me!'' He paused, slumped back in his chair, and lost a little of his animation. He looked tired, Bettley thought.

But eventually he struggled upright again and continued. ''Afterwards . . . I prowled the house with all the lights blazing, with a meat cleaver in my hand. I searched for the thing everywhere. For an hour, two, until full daylight. And most of that time I was shaking like a leaf. It was only when I'd stopped shaking that I finally convinced myself it was a dream.'' He suddenly laughed, but his laughter was shaky even now. ''Hey! I nearly called the police. Can you picture that? I mean, you're a psychiatrist, but how do you think they'd have taken my story, eh? Maybe I'd have been in to see you a day or two earlier!''

Dr. Bettley steepled his fingers and stared deep into the other's eyes. Harry Keogh was maybe forty-three or -four (his body, anyway) but looked five years younger. Except Bettley knew that his mind was in fact five years younger again! It was a weird business dealing with—even looking at—a man like Harry Keogh. For Bettley had known this face and body before, when it belonged to Alec Kyle.

The doctor shook his head and blinked, then deliberately avoided Harry's eyes. It was just that sometimes they could be so very soulful, those eyes of his . . .

As for the rest of him:

Harry's body had been well fleshed, maybe even a little

overweight, once. With its height, however, that hadn't mattered a great deal. Not to Alec Kyle, whose job with E-Branch had been in large part sedentary. But it had mattered to Harry. After that business at the Chateau Bronnitsy—his metempsychosis—he'd trained his new body down, got it to a peak of perfection. Or at least done as best he could with it, considering its age. That's why it looked only thirty-seven or -eight years old. But better still if it was only thirty-two, like the mind inside it. A very confusing business . . . and the doctor shook his head and blinked again.

"So what do you make of it?" Keogh asked. "Could it be part of my problem?"

"Your problem?" Bettley repeated him. "Oh, I'm sure it is. I'm sure it could only be part of your problem—unless of course you haven't put me fully in the picture."

Harry raised an eyebrow.

"About your feelings towards Sandra. You've mentioned a certain ambivalence, a lack of desire, even a slackening of potency. It could be that you're taking your loss out on her—mentally, inside your head—blaming her for the fact that you're no longer . . ." He paused.

"A Necroscope?" Harry prompted.

"Possibly." Bettley shrugged. "But . . . on the other hand you also seem ambivalent towards your loss. I have to tell you that sometimes I get the feeling you're glad it's gone, glad you can no longer talk to . . . to . . ."

"To the dead," said Harry sourly. And: "Well, you're half-right. Sometimes it's good to be just normal, ordinary. Let's face it, most people would consider me a freak, even a monster. So you're half-right. But you're also half-wrong." He lay back in the chair again, closed his eyes and stroked his brow.

Bettley went back to studying him.

Grey streaks, so evenly spaced as to seem deliberately designed or effected, were plentiful in Harry's russet-brown, naturally wavy hair. It wouldn't be too many years before the grey overtook the brown; even now it loaned him a certain erudition, gave him the look of a scholar. Ah, but in what strange and esoteric subjects? And yet Harry wasn't like that at all. What, a black magician? A twentieth-century wizard? A necromancer? No, just a Necroscope, a man who talked to the dead—or used to.

Of course, he had other talents, too. Bettley looked at him sitting there, so tired looking, his hand to his brow. The *places* this man had been! The *means* he'd used to go there, and to return. What other man had ever used an obscure mathematical concept as a . . . a spaceship, or a time machine?

Harry opened his eyes and caught Bettley staring at him. He said nothing, merely stared back. That's what he was here for: to be stared at, to be examined. And Bettley was good at his job, and discreet. Everybody said so. He had many admirable qualities. Must have, else E-Branch would never have taken him on. And again Harry wondered, *Is he still working for them?* Not that it would matter a great deal, for Bettley was easy to talk to. It was just that Harry so hated subterfuge.

The doctor continued to stare into Harry's eyes. They were soulful as ever, and somehow defensive; but at the same time it seemed that Harry needed this close contact. Honey brown, those eyes; very wide, very intelligent, and (strange beyond words) very innocent! Genuinely innocent, Bettley knew. Harry Keogh had not asked to be what he was, or to be called upon to do the things he'd done.

Bettley forced himself back to the job in hand. "So I'm half-wrong," he said. "You would like your talents back, to be a 'freak' again—your words, Harry. But what will you do with those talents if they do return to you? How will you use them?"

Harry gave a wry smile. His teeth were good and strong, not quite white, a little uneven; they were set in a mouth which was usually sensitive but could tighten, becoming caustic and even cruel. Or perhaps not so much cruel as unyielding, single-minded.

"You know, I scarcely knew my mother," he dreamily answered. "I was too young, just a baby, when she died. But

I got to know her . . . later. And I miss her. A boy's best friend is his mum, you know? And . . . well, I have a lot of friends down there.''

''In the ground?''

''Yes. Hell, we had some good conversations!''

Bettley almost shuddered, fought it down. ''You miss talking to them?''

''They had their problems, wanted to air their views, wondered how things had gone in the world of the living. Some of them worried a lot, about people they'd left behind. I was able to reassure them. But most were merely lonely. Merely! But I knew what it was like for them. I could feel it. It was hell to be that lonely. They needed me; I was somebody to them; and I suppose I miss them needing me.''

''But none of this explains your dream,'' the doctor mused. ''Maybe it has no explanation—except fear. You've lost your friends, your skills, those parts of yourself that made you unique. And now you're afraid of losing your manhood.''

Harry narrowed his eyes a little and began to pay more attention; he looked at Bettley more piercingly. ''Explain.''

''But isn't it obvious? A disembodied female thing—a dead thing, a vampire thing—devours your core, the parts of you that make you a man. She was fear, *your* fear, pure but not so simple. Her vampire nature was straight out of your own past experience. You don't like being normal, and the more you have to endure it the more afraid of it you get to be. It's all tied up to your past, Harry: it's all the things you've lost until you're afraid of losing anything else. You lost your mother when you were a child, lost your own wife and child in an unreachable place, lost so many friends and even your own body! And finally you've lost your talents. No more Möbius Continuum, no more talking to the dead, no more Necroscope . . .''

Harry was frowning now. ''What you said about vampires made me remember something,'' he said. ''Several things, in fact.'' He went back to rubbing his brow.

''Go on,'' Bettley prompted him.

''I have to start some way back,'' Harry continued, ''when

137

I was a kid at Harden Modern Boys. That's a school. I was a Necroscope even then, but it wasn't something I much liked. It used to make me dizzy, sick even. I mean it came naturally to me, but I knew it wasn't. I knew it was very *un*natural. But even before that I used to . . . well, see things.''

Bettley was an empath; now he felt something of what Harry felt and the short hairs began to rise at the back of his neck. This was going to be important. He glanced down at a button on his side of the desk: it was still red, the tape was still running. "What sort of things?" he asked, hiding his eagerness.

"I was an infant when my stepfather killed my mother," the other answered. "I wasn't on the scene, and even if I had been, I wasn't old enough for it to impress me. I couldn't possibly have understood what was happening, and almost certainly I wouldn't have remembered it. And I couldn't have reconstructed it later from overheard conversations because Shukshin's account of the 'accident' had been accepted. There was no question of his having murdered her—except from me. It was a nightmare I used to have: of him holding her there under the ice, until she drifted away. And I saw the ring on his finger: a cat's-eye set in a thick gold band. It came off when he drowned her and sank to the bottom of the river, and fifteen years later I knew where to go back and dive for it.''

Bettley felt a tingling in his spine. "But you were a Necroscope—*the* Necroscope—and read it out of your dead mother's mind. Surely?''

Harry shook his head. "No, because it was a dream I had from a time long before I first consciously talked to the dead. And in it I 'remembered' something I couldn't possibly remember. It was a talent I'd had without even recognising it! You know my mother was a psychic medium, and her mother too? Maybe it was something that came down from them. But as my greater talent—as a Necroscope—developed, so this other thing was pushed into the background, got lost.''

"And you think all of this has something to do with this new dream of yours? In what way?''

Harry's shrug was lighter, no longer defeatist. "You know how when someone goes blind he seems to develop a sixth sense? And people handicapped from birth, how they seem to make up for their deficiencies in other ways?"

"Of course," the doctor answered. "Some of the greatest musicians the world's ever seen have been deaf or blind. But what . . . ?" And then he snapped his fingers. "I see! So you think that the loss of your other talents has caused this . . . this atrophied one to start growing again, is that it?"

"Maybe"—Harry nodded—"maybe. Except I'm not just seeing things from the past anymore but from the future. My future. But vaguely, unformed except as nightmares."

It was Bettley's turn to frown. "A precog, is that what you think you're becoming? But what has this to do with vampires, Harry?"

"It was my dream," the other answered. "Something I'd forgotten, or hadn't wanted to remember, until you brought it back to me. But now I remember it clearly. I can *see* it clearly."

"Go on."

"It's just a little thing." Harry shrugged again, perhaps defensively.

"But best if we have it out in the open, right?" Bettley spoke quietly, clearing the way for Harry without openly urging him on.

"Perhaps." And in a sudden rush of words: "I saw red threads! The scarlet life threads of vampires!"

"In your dream?" Bettley shivered as gooseflesh crept on his back and forearms. "Where in your dream?"

"In the green stripes where the light came through the blinds," Harry answered. "The stripes on her belly and thighs, in the moment before that hellish thing fastened on me. They were green-tinted, almost submarine, but as my blood began to spurt they turned red. Red stripes streaming off her body into the dim past, and also into the future. Writhing red threads among the blue life threads of humanity. Vampires!"

The doctor said nothing, waited, felt the other's horror—

and fascination—washing out from him, welling into the study like a sick, almost tangible flood tide. Until Harry shook his head and cut it off. Then, abruptly, he stood up and headed a little unsteadily for the door.

"Harry?" Bettley called after him.

At the door Harry turned. "I'm wasting your time," he said. "As usual. Let's face it, you could be right and I'm frightened of my own shadow. Self-pity, because I'm nothing special anymore. And maybe scared because I know what *could* be out there waiting for me, but probably isn't. But what the hell—what will be will be, we know that. And the time is long past when I could do anything about it or change any part of it."

Bettley shook his head in denial. "It wasn't a waste, Harry, not if we got something out of it. And it seems to me we got a lot out of it."

The other nodded. "Thanks anyway," he said, and closed the door behind him. The doctor got up and moved to his window. Shortly, down below, Harry left the building and stepped out into Princes Street in the heart of Edinburgh. He turned up his coat collar against the squalling rain, tucked his chin in, and angled his back to the bluster, then stepped to the kerb and hailed a taxi. A moment later and the car had whirled him away.

Bettley returned to his desk, sat down, and sighed. Now he was the one who felt weak; but Keogh's psychic essence— a near-tangible "echo" of his presence—was already fading. When it had faded into nothing, the empath rewound his interview tape and dialled a special number at E-Branch HQ in London. He waited until he got a signal, then placed the handset into a cradle on the tape machine under his desk. At the press of a button, Harry's interview began playing itself into storage at E-Branch.

Along with all of his other interviews . . .

In the back of the taxi on the way to Bonnyrig, Harry relaxed and closed his eyes, leaned his head against the seat, and tried to recall something of that other dream which had bothered him on and off for the last three or four years, the one about Harry Jr. He knew what the dream was in essence— what had been done to him, how, and why—but its fine detail eluded him. The what and how part was obvious: by use of the Wamphyri art of fascination, hypnotism, Harry Jr. had made his father an *ex*-Necroscope, at the same time removing or cancelling his ability to enter and manoeuvre in the Möbius Continuum. As to why he'd done it:

You would destroy me if you could, he heard his son's voice again, like a record played a hundred times, until he knew every word and phrase, every mood and emotion or lack of it, by heart. *Don't deny it, for I can see it in your eyes, smell it on your breath, read it in your mind. I know your mind well, Father. Almost as well as you do. I've explored every part of it, remember?*

And now, under his breath, Harry answered again as he'd answered then, "But if you know that much, then you know I'd never harm you. I don't want to destroy you, only to cure you."

As you "cured" the Lady Karen? And where is she now, Father? It hadn't been an accusation; there'd been no sarcasm in it, no sourness; it was just a statement of fact. For the Lady Karen had killed herself, which Harry Jr. knew well enough.

"The thing had taken too strong a hold on her," Harry had insisted. "Also, she'd been a peasant, a Traveller, without your understanding. She couldn't see what she'd gained, only what she thought she'd lost. She didn't have to kill herself. Maybe she was . . . unbalanced?"

You know she wasn't. She was simply Wamphyri. And you drove her vampire out and killed it. You thought it would be like killing a tapeworm, like lancing a boil or cutting out a cancer. But it wasn't. You say she couldn't see what she'd gained. Now tell me, Father, what you think the Lady Karen had gained?

"Her freedom!" Harry had cried in desperation, and in sudden horror of himself. "For God's sake, don't prove me wrong in what I did! I'm no bloody murderer!"

141

No, you're not. But you are a man with an obsession. And I'm afraid of you. Or if not afraid of you, afraid of your goals, your ambitions. You want a world—your world—free of vampirism. An entirely admirable objective. But when you've achieved that aim . . . what then? Will my world be next? An obsession, yes, which seems to be growing in you even as my vampire is growing in me. I'm Wamphyri now, Father, and there's nothing so tenacious as a vampire—unless it's Harry Keogh himself!

Can't you see how dangerous you are to me? You know many of the secret arts of the Wamphyri, and how to destroy them; you can talk to the dead, travel in the Möbius Continuum—even in time itself, however ephemerally. I ran away from you, from your world, once. But now, in this world, I've fought for my territories and earned them. They're mine now and I'll not desert them. I'll run no more. But I can't take the chance that you won't come after me, daren't accept the risk that you won't be satisfied. I'm Wamphyri! I'll not suffer your experiments. I'll not be a guinea pig for any more "cures" you might come up with.

"And what of me?" Harry had spoken up then, even as he now whispered the words to himself. "How safe will I be? I'm a threat to you, you've admitted as much. How long before your vampire is ascendant and you come looking for me?"

But that won't happen, Father. I'm not a peasant; I do have knowledge; I shall control myself as a clever addict controls his addiction.

"And if it gets *out* of control? You, too, are a Necroscope. And in the Möbius Continuum there's nothing you can't do, nowhere you can't go, and always carrying your contamination with you. What poor bastard will get *your* egg, son?"

At which Harry Jr. had sighed heavily and taken off his golden mask. His scars from the battle in the Garden had healed now; there was nothing much to be seen of them; his vampire had been busy repairing him, moulding his flesh as his father feared it would one day mould his will. *So you see*

142

we're at stalemate, he'd said. And his eyes had opened into huge crimson orbs.

"No!" Harry gasped out loud, now as he'd gasped it then. Except that then it had been the last thing he'd said for quite some time, until he'd woken up at E-Branch. Whereas now:

"Whazzat, Chief?" his dour-faced driver glanced back at him, frowning and puzzled. "But did ye no say Bonnyrig? Ah surely hope so, 'cos we're a'most there!"

The real world crashed down on Harry. He was sitting upright, stiff and pale, with his bottom jaw hanging slightly open. He licked his dry lips and looked out through the taxi's windows. Yes, they were almost there. And:

"Bonnyrig, yes, of course," he mumbled. "I was . . . I was daydreaming, that's all." And he directed the other through the village and to his house . . .

North London in late April 1989; a fairly rundown bottom-floor flat in the otherwise "upwardly mobile" district of Highgate just off Hornsey Lane; two men, apparently relaxed, talking quietly over drinks in a large sitting room lined with bookshelves full of books and many small items of foreign, mainly European bric-a-brac . . .

Very untypical of his race, Nikolai Zharov was slender as a wand, pale as milk, almost effeminate in his affectations. He used a cigarette holder to smoke Marlboros with their filters torn off, spoke excellent English albeit with a slight lisp, and had in general a rather limp-wristed air. His eyes were dark, deep set and heavy-lidded, giving him an almost-drugged appearance which belied the alert and ever-calculating nature of his brain.

His hair was thin and black, swept back, lacquered down with some antiseptic-smelling Russian preparation; under a thin, straight nose his lips were also thin in a too-wide mouth. A pointed chin completed his lean look; he appeared the sort who might easily bend but never break; "real men" may be tempted to look at him askance but they wouldn't push their luck with him. Out in the city's streets Zharov would certainly warrant a second glance, following which the observer would very likely look away. The Russian would tend to make people feel uneasy.

He made Wellesley uneasy, for a fact, though the latter tried hard to conceal it. As owner of the flat, Wellesley was worried someone might have seen his visitor coming here, or even followed him. Which would be one hell of a difficult thing to explain away. For Wellesley was a player in the intelligence game, and so was Zharov, though ostensibly they worked for different bosses.

At five feet eight inches tall Norman Harold Wellesley was some five or six inches shorter than the spindly Russian; he had more meat on him, too, and more colour in his face. Too much colour. But it wasn't his stature or mildly choleric mottling that put him at a disadvantage. His current mental agitation hailed not so much from physical or even cultural disparities of race and type as from fear pure and simple. Fear of what Zharov was asking him to do.

In answer to which he had just this moment replied, "But you must know that's plainly out of the question, not feasible, indeed little short of impossible!" Explosive-seeming words, yet uttered quietly, coldly, even with a measure of calculation. A calculated attempt to dissuade Zharov from his course, or perhaps reroute it a little, even knowing that he wasn't the author of the "request" he'd made but merely the delivery boy.

And the Russian had obviously expected as much. "Wrong," he answered, just as quietly, but with something of a cold smile to counter the other's flush. "Not only is it entirely possible but imperative. If, as you have reported, Harry Keogh is on the verge of developing new and hitherto unsuspected talents, then he *must* be stopped. It is as simple as that. He has been a veritable plague on Soviet ESPionage, Norman. A disaster, a mental hurricane . . . a psiclone? Oh, our E-Branch survives, lives on despite all his efforts, but barely." Zharov shrugged. "On the other hand, perhaps we should be grateful to him: his, er, *successes* have made us more than ever aware of the power of parapsychology—its importance—in the field of spying. The problem is that as a weapon he gives your side far too much of an edge. Which is why he has to go . . .''

If Wellesley had been paying any real attention to Zharov's argument, it hardly showed. "You will recall—" he now started to reply. "I mean, you have probably been informed—that my initial liability was a small one? Very well, I owe your masters a small favour—I'm in their debt, let's say—but not such a large debt even now. And their interest rates are way too high, my friend. Beyond my limited ability to pay. I'm afraid that's my answer, Nikolai, which you must take back with you to Moscow.''

Zharov sighed, put down his drink, and leaned back in his chair. He stretched his long legs, folded his arms across his chest, and pursed his lips; he allowed his heavy eyelids to droop more yet. The pupils of his dark eyes glinted from their cores, and for several long moments he studied Wellesley where he was seated on the opposite side of a small occasional table.

Wellesley's red hair was receding fast. At forty-five he was perhaps six or seven years the Russian's senior, and looked every day of it. A generally unattractive man, he had one redeeming feature: his mouth, which was firm, well shaped, and housed an immaculate set of teeth. Other than that, his nose was bulbous and fleshy, his watery blue eyes too round and staring, and his excess of colouring brought the large freckles of his forehead into glaring yellow prominence. Zharov concentrated on Wellesley's freckles a moment more before straightening up again.

"Ah, détente!" he tut-tutted. "Glasnost! What have they brought us to when we must bargain with debtors? Why, in the good old days we would simply send in the debt collectors! Or perhaps the bullyboys? But now . . . the gentleman's way out: bankruptcy, receivership! Norman, I'm very much afraid you're about to go bankrupt. Your cover is about to be"—he formed his mouth into a tube and puffed cigarette smoke through it in a series of perfect rings—"blown!"

"Cover?" Wellesley's eyes narrowed suspiciously and his colour deepened more yet. "I have no cover. I am what I appear to be. Look, I made a mistake and I understand I must pay for it. Fine—but I'm not about to kill for you! Oh, you'd like that, wouldn't you?—for me to turn a small debt into a massive great overdraft! But it's not on, Nikolai. So go ahead, Comrade, drop me in it. 'Bankrupt' me, if that's the threat. I'll lose my job and maybe my liberty for a while, but not forever. But if I play your game, I'm a goner! I'd be in even deeper. And what will it be next time, eh? More treachery? Another murder? What you're doing is blackmail and you know it, but I'm not having any. So do your worst and kiss any 'favours' I owe you good-bye forever!''

"Bluff." Zharov smiled. "And nicely played, too. But bluff all the same." His smile fell from his face and he stood up. "Very well, I call: you are a mole, a sleeper!"

"A sleeper?" Wellesley's fists shook where he held them clenched at his sides. "Well, and maybe I was—but never activated. I've done nothing wrong."

Zharov smiled again but it was more a grimace. He gave a small shrug of his thin shoulders and headed for the door. "That will be your side of it, of course."

Wellesley jumped to his feet and got to the door first. "And where the hell do you think you're going?" he rasped. "We've resolved nothing!"

"I have said all I had to say," said the other, coming to a halt and standing perfectly still. After a moment's pause he carefully reached out and took his overcoat from a peg. "And now"—his voice had deepened a little and his thin mouth twitched in one corner—"now I am leaving." He took thin, black leather gloves from a pocket of the overcoat and swiftly pulled them on. "And will you try to stop me, Norman? Believe me, that would be something of an error."

Wellesley had never been much for the physical side of things; he believed the other well enough. He backed off a little, said, "So what will happen now?"

"I shall report your reticence." Zharov was forthright. "I shall say you no longer consider your debt outstanding, that you wish it written off. And they shall reply: no, we wish *him* written off! Your file will be 'leaked' to someone of responsibility in one of your own intelligence branches, and—"

"My file?" Wellesley's watery eyes began a rapid, nervous blinking. "A few dirty pictures of me and a whore snapped through one-way glass in a grubby Moscow hotel all of twelve years ago? Why, in those days that sort of stuff was ten-a-penny! It was dealt with on a day-to-day basis! Tomorrow I shall go and make a clean breast of that old . . . *affair*! And what will your side do then, eh? Moreover, I'll name names— yours specifically—and there'll be no more courier jobs for you, Nikolai!"

Zharov gave a small, sad shake of his head. "Your file is somewhat thicker than that, Norman. Why, it's quite full of little tidbits of intelligence information you've passed on to us over the years. Make a clean breast of it? Oh, I should think you'll be doing that—or at least trying to—for quite a few years to come."

"Tidbits of . . . ?" Wellesley was now almost purple. "I've given you nothing—not a thing! What tidbits of . . . ?"

Zharov watched him shaking like a leaf, shaking from a combination of rage and frustration; and slowly the Russian's smile returned. "*I* know you've given us nothing," he said quietly. "Until now we haven't asked for anything. *I* also know you're innocent, more or less—but the people who count don't. And now, finally, we are asking for something. So you can either pay up, or . . ." And again his shrug. "It's your life, my friend . . ."

As Zharov reached to open the door Wellesley caught at his arm. "I need to think about it," he gasped.

"Fair enough, only don't take too long."

Wellesley nodded, gulped. "Don't go out that way. Go out the back." He led the way through the flat. "How did you come here anyway? Christ, if anyone saw you, I—"

"No one saw me, Norman. And anyway, I'm not much known over here. I was at a casino in the Cromwell Road. I came by taxi and let him drop me off a few blocks away. I walked. Now I shall walk again, and eventually get another cab."

Wellesley let him out the back door and went with him down the dark garden path to the gate. Before pulling the gate to behind him, Zharov took out a manila envelope from his overcoat pocket and handed it over. "Some photographs you haven't seen before," he said. "Just a reminder that you shouldn't take too long making up your mind, Norman. We're in a bit of a hurry, as you see. And don't try to contact me; I shall be in touch with you. Meanwhile . . . I'll have a night or two to kill. I might even find myself a nice clean whore." He chuckled dryly. "And if your lot take any pictures of me with her . . . why, I'll just keep them as souvenirs!"

When he'd gone, Wellesley went shakily back indoors. He freshened up his drink and sat down, then took out the photographs from their envelope. To anyone who didn't know better, they'd seem to be blowups of simple snapshots. But Wellesley knew better, and so would just about any agent or officer of British intelligence—or of any of the world's intelligence agencies, for that matter. The pictures were of Wellesley and a much older man. They wore overcoats and Russian fur hats, walked together, chatted in a scene where the spiral cupolas of Red Square were prominent over red-tiled rooftops, drank vodka seated on the steps of a dacha. Half a dozen shots in all, and it would seem they were bosom pals.

Wellesley's older "friend" would be in his midsixties: he was grey at the temples with a central stripe of jet black hair swept back from a high, much-wrinkled brow. He had small eyes under bushy black eyebrows, lots of laughter lines in the corners of his eyes and lips, and a hard mouth in a face which was otherwise quite jolly. Well, and he had been a jolly sort of chap in his way—and jolly murderous in other ways! Wellesley's lips silently formed his name: *Borowitz*, then spoke it out loud: "Comrade General Gregor Borowitz—you old bastard! God, what a fool I was!"

One picture was especially interesting, if only for its scenery: Wellesley and Borowitz standing in the courtyard of an old mansion or chateau, a place of debased heritage and mixed architectural antecedents. It had twin minarets jutting upwards like rotting phallus mushrooms from steeply gabled end walls; their flaking spiral decorations and sagging parapets added to a general sense of decay and dereliction. But in fact the chateau had been anything but derelict.

Wellesley had never been inside the place, hadn't even known what it housed, not then. But he knew well enough now. It was the Chateau Bronnitsy, Soviet mindspy HQ, an infamous place—until Harry Keogh had blown it to hell. It was a pity he hadn't done it just a couple of years earlier, that's all . . .

The next morning, Darcy Clarke was late for work. A bad traffic accident on the North Circular, traffic-light failure in the centre of town, and finally some dumb bastard's rust bucket parked in Darcy's space. He'd been about to let the air out of the offender's tyres when he turned up, said "Fuck you!" to Clarke's raving, and drove off!

Still fuming, Clarke used the elevator discreetly placed at the rear of an otherwise perfectly normal-looking up-market hotel to climb up to the top floor, which in its soundproof, burglar-proof, mundane-, mechanical-, and metaphysics-proofed entirety housed E-Branch, also known as INTESP. As he let himself in and shrugged out of his coat, last night's duty officer was just leaving for home.

Abel Angstrom gave Clarke the once-over and said, "Morning, Darcy. All hot and bothered, are you? You will be!"

Clarke grimaced and hung up his coat. "Nothing can go wrong that hasn't already," he grunted. "What's up?"

"The boss," Angstrom told him. "That's what's up. He's *been* up since six-thirty, locked in his office with the Keogh file. Drinking coffee by the gallon! He's watching the clock, too—been gripping each and every bloke who's come in after eight A.M. He wants you, so if I were you, I'd wear my flak jacket!"

Clarke groaned, said, "Thanks for the warning," went to the gents and tidied himself up a little.

As he was straightening his tie in a mirror, suddenly everything boiled over. To himself he rasped, "What the bloody hell? Why do I bother? Dog's-bloody-body Clarke! And Himself wants to see me, does he? Shit and damnation—it's like being in the bloody army!" He deliberately *un*straightened his tie, mussed his hair, looked at himself again.

There, that was better! And come to think of it, what did he have to fear anyway? Answer, nothing; for Clarke had a psi-talent no one had positively tagged yet; it kept him out of trouble, protecting him as a mother protects her child. He wasn't *quite* a deflector: fire a gun at him and your bullets wouldn't swerve, you'd simply miss him. Or the firing pin would come down on blanks. Or he'd somehow stumble at just the right moment. He was the opposite of accident prone. He could walk through a mine field and come out unscathed . . . and yet he still switched off the current to change a light bulb! Except this morning he wasn't in the mood for switching off anything. *Let it all hang out,* he thought, heading for the sanctum sanctorum.

When he knocked on the door, a surly voice said, "Who?"

Arrogant bastard! he thought. "Darcy Clarke."

"Come in, Clarke," and as he passed inside: "Where the hell have you been? I mean, do you work here or not?" And before he could answer: "Sit down . . ."

But Clarke remained standing. He didn't need this. He'd had it, taken all he could take of his new boss in the six months the man had been the head of E-Branch. Hell, there were other jobs; he didn't have to work for this overbearing bastard. And where was the continuity? Sir Keenan Gormley had been a gentleman; Alec Kyle a friend; under Clarke himself the branch had been efficient *and* friendly—to its friends, anyway. But this bloke was . . . hell, a boor! Gauche! A primitive! Certainly as far as internal relationships—man management—were concerned. As for talents: so what *was* the guy? A scryer, telepath, deflector, locator? No, his talent was simply that his mind was impenetrable: telepaths couldn't touch him. Some would say that made him the ideal man for the job. Maybe it did. But it would be nice if he was human, too. After serving under such men as Gormley and Kyle, working for someone like Norman Harold Wellesley was—

Wellesley was seated at his desk. Without looking up, he sighed, took a deep breath, and said, "I said—"

"That's right, I heard you," Clarke cut him short. "Good morning to you, too."

Now Wellesley looked up, and Clarke saw that he was his usual, florid self. He also saw the file on Harry Keogh spread every which way across the surface of Wellesley's desk. And for the first time he wondered what was going on.

Wellesley saw Clarke's attitude at once, knew it wouldn't be wise to try riding roughshod over him this morning. Also, he knew there was a power struggle coming up, that it had been in the wind ever since he'd taken over here. But that was something he didn't need, not right now, anyway.

"All right, Darcy," he said, tempering his tone a little, "so we've both been having a bad time. You're the second-in-command, I know that, and you believe you're due some respect. Fine, but when things go wrong—and while we're all running round being nice and respectful—I'm the one who carries the can! However you feel about it, I still have to run this place. And with this kind of job . . . who needs an excuse to be ill-mannered? That's my story. So how come *you* got out of the wrong side of bed this morning?"

Clarke thought, *What? When did he last call me Darcy? Is he actually trying to be reasonable, for Christ's sake?*

He allowed himself to be mollified, partly, and sat down. "The traffic was hell and some clown stole my parking space," he finally answered. "That's just for starters. I'm also expecting a call from Rhodes—from Trevor Jordan and Ken Layard—on that drugs job; customs and excise, and New Scotland Yard, will want to know how things are progressing. Add to that about a dozen unanswered requests from our minister responsible for esper support on unsolved major crimes, routine office admin, the Russian-embassy job I'm supposed to be supervising, and—"

"Well you can skip the embassy job for one," Wellesley was quick to break in. "It's routine, unimportant. A few extra Ivans in the country? A Russian delegation? So what? Christ, we've more on our plate than mundane snooping! But even without all that . . . yes, I can see you're up to your neck.''

"Damn right," said Clarke. "And sinking fast! So you see I wouldn't think you rude—in fact I'd probably thank you—if you simply told me to piss off and get on with my job! Except I don't suppose you'd have called me in here if there wasn't something on your mind.''

"Well, no one could ever accuse you of not getting straight to the point, could they?" said Wellesley. And for once his round eyes were unblinking and less than hostile where they searched the other out. What he saw was this:

For all his weird talent, Clarke wasn't much to look at. No one would suppose that he'd ever been the boss of anything, let alone head of the most secret branch of the British Secret Services. He was Mr. Nondescript, the world's most average man. Well, maybe not *that* indistinct, but getting on that way, certainly. Middle height, mousey-haired, with something of a slight stoop and a small paunch—and middle-aged to boot— Clarke was just about middle of the range in every way. He had hazel eyes in a face not much given to laughter, an intense mouth, and generally downcast air. And the rest of him, including his wardrobe, was . . . medium.

But he had run E-Branch; he'd been around through some pretty hairy stuff; he'd known Harry Keogh.

"Keogh," said Wellesley, the name coming off his lips like it tasted sour. "That's what's on my mind.''

"That": as if Keogh were some kind of contraption or thing and not a person at all. Clarke raised an eyebrow. "Something new on Harry?" Wellesley had been monitoring Bettley's reports himself—and keeping whatever they contained *to* himself.

"Maybe, and maybe not," Wellesley answered. And rapidly, so as not to allow Clarke time to think: "Do you know what would happen if he got his talents back?"

"Sure," and even though Clarke *did* have time to think, he said it anyway: "You'd be out of a job!"

152

Unexpectedly, Wellesley smiled. But it quickly faded from his face. "It's always good to know where one stands," he said. "So you think he'd take over E-Branch, right?"

"With his talents he could *be* E-Branch!" Clarke answered. And suddenly his face lit up. "Are you saying he's got it back?"

For a moment Wellesley didn't answer. Then: "You were his friend, weren't you?"

"His friend?" Clarke frowned, chewed his bottom lip, began to look a little worried. No, he couldn't honestly say he'd ever been a friend of Harry's, or even that he'd wanted to be. There'd been a time, though, when he'd seen some of Harry's friends in action—and he still had nightmares about it! But at last he answered, "We were . . . acquainted, that's all. See, most of Harry's real friends were sort of, well, dead." He gave a shrug. "That's what qualified them, sort of."

Wellesley stared harder at him. "And he actually did what these documents credit him with doing? Talked to the dead? Called corpses out of their graves? I mean, I'll grant you telepathy: I've seen it working in our test cubicles, and in all the criminal cases the branch has dealt with in the last six months. Even your own peculiar talent, Darcy, which is well documented even if I haven't yet seen it in action. But this?" He wrinkled his bulbous nose. "A damned . . . necromancer?"

Clarke shook his head. "A Necroscope. Harry wouldn't like you to call him a necromancer. If you've been through his file, you'll know about Dragosani. *He* was a necromancer. The dead were frightened of him; they loathed him. But they loved Harry. Yes, he talked to them, and called them up out of their graves when that was the only way to do what he had to do. But there was no pressure involved; just for them to know he was in dire straits was often sufficient."

Wellesley was aware that Clarke's voice had gone very quiet, and that the man himself was now quite pale. But still he pressed on. "You were there in Hartlepool at the end of the Bodescu affair. You actually *saw* this thing?"

153

Clarke shuddered. "I saw many . . . things. I smelled them, too . . ." He shook his head, as if to clear it of unbearable memories, and pulled himself together. "So what's your problem, Norman? Okay, so during your time here we've mainly been dealing with mundane stuff. Well, that's what we deal with, mainly. As for what Harry Keogh, Gormley, Kyle, and all the others came up against that time . . . just hope and pray it's all done with, that's all."

Still Wellesley seemed unconvinced. "It couldn't have been mass hypnotism, mass illusion, some kind of trick or fraud?"

Again Clarke shook his head. "I have this defence-mechanism thing, remember? You might be able to fool me but you can't fool it. It only gets scared when there's something there to be scared of. It doesn't run away from harmless illusions, only from real dangers. But it sure as hell propels me away from dead people and *un*dead people and things that would chew my fucking head off!"

For a moment Wellesley seemed lost for an answer to that. Eventually he said, "Would it surprise you to know that I was totally unaware of my own talent? All my life, I mean, until I applied for a job here?" (This was a lie, but Clarke couldn't know it.) "I mean, how does one know when one has a *negative* talent? If it was common everyday practice for people to read other people's minds, then I'd be a freak, the odd man out who couldn't do it and couldn't have it done to him. But it isn't common practice and so I had no measure for it. I only knew—or thought—that I had an interest in parapsychology, the metaphysical. Which is why I mistakenly put in for a transfer here. And then you people checked me out for suitability and discovered I kept my mind in a safe."

Clarke looked puzzled. "What are you trying to say?"

"I'm not sure myself. I suppose I'm trying to explain why, as the head of E-Branch, I have so much difficulty believing in what we're doing! And when you confront me with the reality of someone like Harry Keogh . . . Well, I mean, parapsychology is one thing, but this is supernatural!"

Clarke grinned one of his rare grins. "So you're human after all," he said. "Did you think you were alone in your confusion? Why, there's not a man or woman ever worked here who hasn't known the same doubts! If I had a pound for every time I've thought about it—its ambiguities, inconsistencies, and head-on contradictions—hell, I'd be rich! What, an outfit as weird as this is? Robots and romantics? Superscience and the supernatural? Telemetry and telepathy? Computerized probability patterns and precognition? Spy satellites and scryers? Of course you're confused! Who isn't? But that's what it's all about: gadgets and ghosts!''

Wellesley was a little happier. He'd managed to get Clarke on his side for once. And with what he had in mind, that's where he had to have him. "And teleportation?" he said. "Was that one of Keogh's talents, too?"

Clarke nodded. "That's what we'd call it," he said, "but it wasn't like that to Harry. He simply used doors no one else knew were there. He'd step in a door here and . . . come out somewhere else. Just about anywhere else. When I wanted to recruit him in on the Perchorsk business, I went up to Edinburgh to see him. He said okay, he'd take a chance if I would. That is, if he was going up against the unknown, he wanted me to taste a little of it, too. And he brought me back here through a thing he calls the Möbius Continuum. It was quite something, but nothing I'd ever want to do again . . .''

Wellesley sighed again and said, "I think you're right. If he got his talents back, we'd have to offer him my job. You'd like that, right?"

Clarke shrugged.

"Don't be coy, Darcy." Wellesley nodded knowingly. "It's plain as day. You'd rather have him—or anyone—as your boss than me. But what you don't seem to realise is that I'm all for it! I don't understand you or the people who work here and I don't suppose I ever will. I want out, but I know our minister responsible won't let me go until there's someone to replace me. You? No, because that would make it look like they made a mistake replacing you in the first place. But Harry Keogh . . .''

"Harry's had the best help we can give him," Clarke said.

"We've hypnotised him, psychoanalysed him, damn near brainwashed him. But it's gone. So what can you do for him?"

"It's more what *we* can do for him, Darcy."

"Go on."

"Last night I had a long talk with the Markham girl up in Edinburgh, and—"

"If there's one part of this that I really hate," Clarke heatedly cut in, "it's that we've done this to him!"

"—and she advised me to speak to David Bettley," Wellesley continued, unperturbed, "because she's worried about Keogh. Can you understand that? She does have genuine feelings for him. It may be just a job but she *is* worried about him. Or maybe you think he'd be better off on his own? Well, whichever, she satisfies two needs: one in Keogh, and one in us. The need to know what's on his mind."

"The tender art of the mindspy!" Clarke snorted.

"So I took her advice and spoke to Bettley. I got him out of bed to answer his telephone. I would have contacted him anyway, about some of his most recent reports and recordings; because in them he's given me cause to believe that Keogh is (a) about to develop some strange new talent, or (b) he's on the point of cracking up. Anyway, in the course of our conversation Bettley mentioned how Keogh first discovered this, er, Möbius thing."

"The Möbius Continuum."

"Correct. He'd apparently been on the verge of it but needed a spur. Which came when the East German GREPO found him talking to Möbius in a Leipzig graveyard. That did it, triggered his mathematical genius. He teleported—or used the Continuum—to escape from them. That's why I have his file here: I wanted to check that I had it right. And it's also why I'm double-checking with you."

"So?"

"The way I see it," Wellesley continued, "Keogh's like a computer that's suffered a power failure: the information he requires—and which E-Branch wants to use—is no longer accessible to him. Oh, it's probably still in there, but it's jammed in limbo. And so far we haven't been able to shake it loose."

"What do you propose?"

"Well, I'm still working on it. But the way I see it, if we apply just the right spur . . . with a bit of luck it could be Leipzig all over again. You see, Keogh has been having some bad dreams lately; and if what you say of him is true—oh, I don't doubt it, but nevertheless *if*—then any dream awful enough to frighten him must be really bad. But perhaps not quite bad enough, eh?"

"You want to scare him silly?"

"I want to scare him almost to death! So close to death that he escapes into the Möbius Continuum!"

Clarke sat still and silent for long moments, until eventually Wellesley leaned forward and quietly said, "Well, what do you think?"

"My honest opinion?"

"Of course."

"I think it stinks. Also, I think that if you plan to fool with Keogh you'd better take out extra insurance. And finally I think that it had better work, because if it doesn't, I'm up and gone. When this is finished, no matter how it works out, I won't be able to work with you any longer."

Wellesley smiled thinly. "But you do want me out of here, right? And so you won't . . . hinder me?"

"No, in fact I insist on being part of it. That way I can be sure that if Harry has any breaks coming, he'll get them."

Wellesley continued to smile. *Oh, he'll get his breaks, all right,* he thought. *Broken all the way through, in fact!*

And he was one of only a handful of men in the entire world who could think such things—especially here in E-Branch HQ—and be certain that no one could hear him doing it . . .

VI: Sandra

SANDRA MARKHAM WAS TWENTY-SEVEN, POSSESSED A BEAU-
tiful face and figure, and was a neophyte telepath. As yet her
talent was a fifty-fifty thing; she had very little control over
it; it came and went. But where Harry Keogh was concerned,
that might be just as well. Sometimes, in Harry's mind, she'd
read things she was sure had no right to be there—or in any
sane mind, for that matter!

She and Harry had made love only an hour ago, and afterwards he had at once fallen asleep. Sandra had come to know
Harry's habits well enough: he'd stay asleep for three or four
hours, which for him would serve as a full night's rest. As
for Sandra: she would have to sleep tomorrow, at her own
place in Edinburgh, making up the night's deficiency.

Staring right into Harry's pale, relaxed, almost little-boyish
face, she saw no sign as yet of the rapid eye movements
which would tell her that he was dreaming. So for now she,
too, could relax. It was Harry's dreams which most interested
her. That was what she tried to keep telling herself, anyway.

She worked for E-Branch. Sometimes she wished she

didn't, but she did. That was how she earned her daily bread (the meat and gravy, too), so she really shouldn't complain. And in fact there hadn't been too much to complain about, until Harry came along. At first he'd been just another job— a new friend to get close to, learn about, and try to understand—but then she'd got in deeper. It had "just happened," and afterwards she'd wanted it to happen again, and again. Until in a little while he wasn't just a job but more a way of life, not only "on her mind," as it were, but under her skin as well. And finally she'd started to suppose, and still did, that she was in love with him.

Certainly working on Harry's case (she hated thinking of it like that, but it was the truth, however she dressed it up) had been more interesting than being a human divining rod on cases the police couldn't solve. That was how E-Branch used her, usually: to eavesdrop on criminal minds—the minds of prisoners in their cells, too tough for the law to crack— looking for those damning clues which more orthodox methods couldn't turn up. Which would be satisfying enough work in itself, if only she didn't actually have to go *in* there. Because minds like those were often cesspools, which frequently left her knowing how sewers smell. And sometimes, especially if it was a brutal murder or rape, the smell could linger for a long, long time.

Which was probably the reason she'd fallen in love with Harry Keogh. Because *his* mind was a field of daisies . . . most of the time. In fact he had the gentlest mind she'd ever come across: not soft, no way! Not even naive, though there was something of that in him, too, but just . . . just gentle. Harry wouldn't much like hurting anything, or anybody . . .

With Sandra's looks it would be strange if there had been no men. There had been men, a few. But her talent wasn't something she could just switch on and off. Indeed that was its one big drawback: without so much as a by your leave, it came and went. Tonight a man would wine and dine you, take you home and kiss your hand on your doorstep, and ask to see you again. And as you were about to say yes his mind would open like a book and you would see him in there like some great rutting satyr—and you'd be in there with him. Not all men, no, but enough.

But that wasn't all; there was also the deceit; the fact that people lie. Like the neighbour in the flat next door who smiles and says, "Good morning," to you on the stairs, when she's actually thinking, *Piss off and die, you ugly bitch!* Or the hairdresser who makes small talk while he does your hair, and you suddenly hear him thinking, *God, they pay me five pounds an hour for this! She must have more money than sense, the stupid cow!*

Oh, there had been men, all right. The good-looking ones who only worried how *they* looked. And the not-so-good-lookers whose minds seethed with jealousy if anyone else even smiled at you. And then, having got safely through an entire week of evenings with a "perfect" companion, to have him make love to you and lie there beside you in your bed, wondering if he'll have time for another and still catch the last bus home.

It was life and Sandra knew it, and she'd learned to live with it ever since her middle teens when the thing had first started to develop in her. But it hadn't left much room for "love." Not until Harry, anyway.

He was such . . . an anomaly.

She'd read his file, as well as his mind. He had killed men, a great many. That's what it said in his file. But it didn't say he remembered and regretted almost every one of them, or how every now and then he'd get the urge to go back and tell them he was sorry, but really he'd had no choice. It didn't say he still had nightmares about some of the things he'd seen and done. And anyway, Sandra really couldn't believe half of the things credited (credited? Or better perhaps, ascribed?) to him. Her own talent was paranormal, yes, but what Harry could do—what he'd used to do—was supernatural. And he'd used his powers the best way he knew how. He had killed many men with them, but he'd never murdered a one.

Sandra *knew* how murderers thought, and they didn't think like Harry Keogh. Their thoughts were deep and dark as red wine, but tumbled as a rough sea, and full of shoals and eddies; while his were clear spring water over rounded pebbles. Oh, his mind could be sharp, too; there were plenty of daggers in there, if you gave him cause to whet them; but they were clearly visible at all times, not hidden away, neither afraid of themselves nor of detection. No, there were no dark corners or mean streets in Harry's mind. Or if there were, he wasn't the one to dwell on or in them.

And in that same moment, lying there beside him, Sandra knew how she'd defined him. He was, could only be, one of two things: either completely amoral, or naturally innocent! And since she knew there was no lack of morality, that made him an innocent. A bloody innocent, but nevertheless blameless. A child with blood on his hands and on his conscience and in his nightmares, which he had chosen to keep to himself except when they were unbearable, when he went to Bettley. Well, she wasn't sure what that made Bettley—a Judas priest? A father confessor who told?—but she couldn't be happy with what it made her. And the most terrible thing of all, she believed he half suspected. Which would explain why he was never completely at his ease with her, and why he couldn't seem to enjoy her the way she wanted him to, the way she enjoyed him. Christ, to have found a man like Harry, only to discover that of all men he was the one she probably couldn't have! Not the way she wanted him, anyway.

Suddenly angry with herself—wanting to throw off all the covers and leap out of bed, but caring enough that she wouldn't disturb him—she carefully removed his hand from where it lay draped diagonally across her and slid sideways out from between the sheets. And naked, she went to the bathroom.

She was neither warm nor cold nor thirsty, but she felt she had to do something. Something ordinary, to herself, to change herself physically. And that way perhaps to change her mood, too. In the daytime it would be the simplest thing: she would walk to the park and watch the smallest children at play, and know that something of their worlds of faerie would soon find their way into her own far less Elysian existence. And when that thought came, she knew for certain

161

that for someone who was usually so positive, she must now be feeling pretty damned negative. That she should need someone else's innocence to balance the weight of her own guilt!

She drank a glass of water, splashed cold water up under her arms and breasts where their lovemaking had made her perspire, towelled her flesh dry, and examined herself critically in the long bathroom mirror.

Unlike Harry, there was little or no naiveté in Sandra. There might be, except for her telepathy. But it's hard to be naive or innocent in a world where people's minds are wont to flutter open like pages in a book, and not have the power to look away but must read what's written there. The other E-Branch telepaths—people like Trevor Jordan—were luckier in this respect; they were obliged to apply, channel their talent; it didn't just come and go for them, like a badly tuned radio station.

Angry again, Sandra shook her head. There she went again: great waves of self-pity! What? Pity for herself? For this beautiful creature in the mirror? And how often had she heard it broadcast, from so many of those stations out there: *God, but what I'd give to be like her!*

Ah, if only they knew!

But how much worse if she'd been ugly . . . ?

She had large, greeny-blue, penetrating eyes over a small, tilted nose; a mouth she'd trained to be soft and uncynical; small ears almost lost in the burnish of copper hair, and high cheekbones curving down delicately to a rounded, rather self-conscious chin. Of course she was conscious of herself. Other people were, and so she had to be.

Her right eyebrow, a slightly upward-tilted line of bronze, was questioning, almost challenging. As if she were saying, "Go on—think it!" And sometimes she was.

Her smile was bright, rewarding, involuntary on those occasions when she detected complimentary thoughts. Or she might darken her high brow and narrow her eyes to knife point at some of the other things she "heard." At a glance, then, Sandra's face might well be mistaken for the face on the cover of any number of glossy, popular ladies' magazines. But on closer inspection it would be seen that there were boundless tracts of character there, too. Her twenty-seven years had not left her unblemished; there were laughter lines in the corners of her eyes, yes, but other faint lines lay parallel and horizontal on her brow, speaking volumes for the number of times she'd frowned. She was grateful that the latter didn't detract from her looks overall.

As for the rest of her:

But for two personal criticisms, Sandra's body would be near perfect, or as close as she would wish it to be. She was too large "up top," which gave her a bouncing elasticity she was afraid might typecast her, and her legs were far too long.

"Well, you might find those things a disadvantage," Harry's voice came back to her from a previous time, "but I'm all for it!" He liked it when, in their lovemaking, she'd wrap her legs right round him; or when she let her breasts dangle in his face, inviting his attentions. Her large nipples, imperfect as most nipples are, seemed a constant fascination to him, at least on those occasions when he was all there. But far too often he'd be somewhere else entirely. And now another truth dawned on her: too often she'd used her sex to trap him in the here and now, as if she were afraid that if she released him, he'd fly . . . somewhere else.

Suddenly cold, she put out the bathroom light and went back to the bedroom.

Harry lay just as she'd left him, on his side, facing left, his right arm draped in the hollow she'd occupied. And still his breathing was deep and steady, his eyelids unmoving. A brief telepathic glimpse, unbidden, defined endless, empty vaults of dream, through which he drifted looking for a door. It came and went, and Sandra sighed. There were always doors in Harry's dreams, revenant perhaps of the Möbius doors he'd once called up mathematically out of thin air.

He'd once told her, "Now that it's over I sometimes get this feeling it was all a dream, or a story read in a book of fantasy. Unreal, something I made up, or maybe an out-of-body experience. But that brings back all too clearly what it was really *like* to be incorporeal, and I know that it happened for a fact. How can I explain it? Have you ever dreamed you could fly? That you actually knew how to fly?''

''Yes,'' she'd answered, in her mildly Edinburghian Scottish accent. ''Often, and very vividly. I used to run down a steeply sloping field to take off, and soar up over the Pentland hills, over the village where I was born. It was sometimes frightening, but I remember knowing *exactly* how it was done!''

Harry had been excited. ''That's right! And waking up you tried to hang on to it, you were reluctant to let the secret vanish with the dream. And it vexed you when you were completely awake to learn that you were earthbound again. Well''—and he'd sighed as his excitement ebbed—''that's pretty much how it sometimes is for me. Like something I had in a long series of childhood dreams, but burned out of me now and gone forever . . .''

Better for you, Harry, she'd thought. *That world was a dangerous place. You're safe now.*

But not much good for E-Branch, and definitely not why she was here. On the contrary, they wanted his powers restored and didn't much care how. And she was supposed to be part of the restoration team.

She slipped into bed with him, as much for his warmth as for anything, and his free hand automatically cupped her breast. His body was lean and hard, well trained. He insisted on keeping it that way. ''It's years older than me,'' he'd once told her, without an ounce of humour, ''and so I have to look after it.'' As if it wasn't his but something he was caretaking. Hard to believe there'd been a time when it really wasn't his. But she hadn't known him—or it—then, and was glad for that.

''Umm?'' he murmured now as she moulded herself to him.

''Nothing,'' she whispered in the darkness of the room. ''Shh!''

''Umm . . .'' he said again, and instinctively drew her closer.

He was warm and he was Harry. She'd never felt so safe

with anyone before. Him with all his hang-ups, and yet when she was with him like this it was like clinging to a rock. She stroked his chest, but gently so as not to awaken or arouse him, and tried to will him into deeper sleep—

—And like a fool willed herself there instead . . .

Haaarry . . . ! Harry's ma, Mary Keogh, called to him from her watery grave, and couldn't get through to him. She never could these days, and knew why, but it didn't stop her from trying. *Harry, there's someone who's trying very hard to talk to you. He says you were friends, and that what he has to say is very important.*

Harry could hear her, but he couldn't answer. He knew that he must *not* answer, for talking to the dead had been forbidden to him. If he should try it, or even consider trying it, then once more he'd hear that irresistible voice in his mind, reinforcing those commands by means of which his Necroscope powers had been made worthless.

Under penalty of pain, you may not, Harry! Aye, great pain. Such torture that the voices of the teeming dead would be distorted beyond recognition. Such mental agony that you would never dare try again. I've no desire to be cruel, Father, but it's for your own protection—as well as mine. Faethor Ferenczy, Thibor, and Yulian Bodescu, they might well have been the last—or they might not. The Wamphyri have powers, Father! And if there are more of them hidden in your world, how long before they seek you out and find you . . . before you can find them? But they will only seek you out if they have reason to fear you. Which is why I now remove such reason utterly! Do you understand?

To which Harry had answered, "You do it for yourself. Not because you fear for me, but for you. You fear that I'll come back one day, discover you in your aerie, and destroy you! I've told you I could never do that. Obviously my word isn't good enough."

People change, Harry. You could change, too. I'm your son, but I'm also a vampire. I can't chance it that you'll not come looking for me one day with sword and stake and fire.

165

I've said it before: as a Necroscope you're dangerous, but without the dead you're impotent. Without them, no more Möbius Continuum. You can't come back here, nor seek me in the other places. And yes, this is another reason why I place these strictures upon you.

"Then you doom me to torture. It's inescapable. The dead love me. They *will* talk to me!"

They may try, but you will neither hear nor answer them! Not consciously. I hereby deny you that talent.

"But I'm a Necroscope! I talk to the dead out of habit! And what about when I grow old? If I ramble to the dead when I'm an old man, what then? Am I still bound to suffer? All my days?"

Habits are for breaking, Harry. I say it one last time, and then if you doubt me, you may try it for yourself: you may not consciously speak to the dead, and if they speak to you, you must strike their words immediately from memory or— suffer the consequences. So be it.

"And all the math Möbius taught me, am I to forget that, too?"

You have already forgotten it! That is my most immediate stricture, for I won't be invaded in my own territory! Now be done with arguing, for it's over. It . . . is . . . done!

At which Harry had felt a terrible wrenching in his mind, which made him cry out; followed by darkness; followed by . . .

. . . His return to consciousness in London, at E-Branch HQ.

That had been four years ago. He had told E-Branch all he could, helped them complete and close their files on him and all his works. He was no longer a Necroscope; he could no longer impose his metaphysical will on the physical universe; the branch should have no further use for him now. But even after they'd tried and discarded every means at their disposal to return his paranormal powers to him, still he'd been certain they wouldn't let it rest there. As a Necroscope he'd been too great an asset. They'd never forget him, and if they could get him back, they would. And so would his millions of friends, the teeming dead. Oh, Harry's actual friends—his real acquaintances among the Great Majority—numbered around one hundred only. But the rest knew *of* him. To them he would always be the one light in their eternal darkness.

And now one of them, by far the most important one to Harry, was trying to speak to him again.

Harry, oh my poor little Harry! Why won't you answer me, son? He had always been her little Harry.

"Because I can't!" he wanted to tell her—but dare not, not even asleep and dreaming. For he'd tried once before, down at the riverbank, and now remembered it only too well.

He'd gone there within the hour of his return to his home near Bonnyrig, the house which she had owned before him, and Viktor Shukshin in between. Shukshin had drowned her under the ice and left her body to float to this bight in the frozen river. There she'd settled to the bottom, to become one with the mud, the weeds, and the silt. And there she'd stayed—until the night Harry called her up again to take her revenge! Since when she'd lain here in peace, or been gradually washed away in pieces. But her spirit was here still.

And it had been there when, like so many times before, he'd gone to sit on the riverbank and look down at the water where it was untroubled and deep and dark in that slowly swirling backwater of reeds and crumbling clay bank. It had been daylight; brambles and weeds growing across the old, disused paths by the river; bird song in the shady willows and spiky blackthorns.

There were three other houses there beside his own; two of them were detached and stood in high-walled gardens extending almost to the river. They were empty and rapidly falling into disrepair, and had been up for sale for several years now. Every so often people would come to look . . . and go away shaking their heads. These were not "desirable" residences. No, it was a lonely place, which was why Harry liked it. He and his ma had used to talk in private here, and he'd never had to fear that someone might see him sitting here on his own, apparently mouthing nonsense to himself.

He hadn't known what to expect that time; he only knew that conversation was forbidden, and that there'd be a penalty to pay if he tried to break the strictures placed on his esper's mind. The acid test was the one thing E-Branch hadn't attempted, mainly because he'd refused to go so far. Darcy Clarke had been in charge then, and Darcy's talent had warned him away from pushing Harry, and Harry's friends, too far.

But there on the river Harry's mother—the spirit of the innocent girl she had been—had not been able to resist talking to her son again.

At first there had been only the solitude, the slow gurgle of the river, the bird song. But in a little while Harry's singular presence had been noted. And: *Harry?* She had come breathlessly awake in his mind. *Harry, is that you, son? Oh, I know it is! You've come home again, Harry!*

That was all she'd said to him—but it had been enough!

"Ma—don't!" he'd cried out, staggering to his feet and running, as someone ignited a Roman candle in his skull to shoot off its fireballs into the soft tissues of his brain! And only then had he known what The Dweller, Harry Jr., had really done to him.

Such mental agony that you will never dare try again! That was what his vampire son had promised, and it was what he'd delivered. Not The Dweller himself, but the post-hypnotic commands he'd left behind, sealed in Harry's mind.

And nightfall had found Harry in the long grasses by the river's edge, painfully regaining consciousness in a world where he now knew beyond any doubt that he was a Necroscope no more. He could no longer communicate with the dead. Or at least, not consciously.

But asleep and dreaming . . . ?

Haaarry . . . ! His mother's voice called to him again, echoing through the endlessly labyrinthine vaults of his otherwise empty dream. *I'm here, Harry, here.* And before he knew it, he'd turned off and passed through a door, and stood once again on the riverbank, this time in streaming moonlight. And: *Is that you, Harry?* Her hushed mental voice told him that she scarcely dared to believe it. *Have you really come to me?*

"I can't answer you, Ma!" he wanted to say, but could only remain silent.

But you have answered me, Harry! was her reply. And he knew it was so. For the dead don't require the spoken word; sufficient to think at them, if you have the talent.

Harry crumpled to the riverbank, adopted a foetal position, hugged his head with his arms and hands, and waited for the pain—which didn't come!

Oh, Harry, Harry! she said at once. *Did you think that after that first time I'd deliberately hurt you or cause you to hurt yourself?*

"Ma, I"—he tried it again, wincing expectantly as he got to his feet—"I don't understand!"

Yes you do, son, she tut-tutted. *Of course you do! It's just that you've forgotten. You forget every time, Harry.*

"Forgotten? Forgotten what, Ma? What do I forget every time?"

You forget that you've been here before, in dreams, and that what my grandson did to you doesn't count here. That's what you've forgotten, and you do it every time! Now call me up, Harry, so that I can talk to you properly and walk with you a little way.

Was that right, that he could talk to her in dreams? He had used to in the old days—waking and dreaming alike—but it wasn't like that now.

But it is *like it now, son. It's just that you need reminding each time!*

And then another voice, not his mother's, echoing more in the caverns of his memory than his sleeping mind proper.

. . . You may not consciously speak to the dead. And if they speak to you, then you must strike their words immediately from memory or—suffer the consequences . . .

"My son's voice." He sighed as understanding came at last. "So . . . how many times have we talked, Ma? I mean, since it started to hurt me . . . in the last four years, say?" And even as she began to answer him he called her up, so that she rose from the water, reached out and took his hand, and was drawn up onto the bank—a young woman again, as she'd been on the day she died.

A dozen, twenty, fifty times (a mental shrug). *It's hard to say, Harry. For always it's more difficult to get through to you. And oh, how we've missed you, Harry.*

"We?" He took her hand and they walked along the dark river path together, under a full moon riding high through a cloud-wispy sky.

Me . . . and all your friends, the teeming dead. A hundred there are all eager to hear your gentle voice again, son; a million more who would ask what you said; and all the rest to enquire how you're doing and what's become of you. And as for me: why, I'm like an oracle! For they know that I'm the one you speak to most of all. Or used to . . .

"You make me feel like I've forsaken some olden trust," he told her. "But there never was one. And anyway, it isn't so! I can't help it that I can no longer talk to you. Or that I can't remember the times when I do. And how has it become difficult to get through to me? You called me and I came. Was that so difficult?"

But you don't always come, Harry. Sometimes I can feel you there, and I call out to you, and you shy away. And each time the waiting grows longer between visits, as if you no longer cared, or had forgotten us. Or as if, perhaps, we'd become a habit? Which you now desire . . . to break?

"None of that is true!" Harry burst out. But he knew that it was. Not a habit which *he* would break, no, but one which was being broken for him—by his fear. By his terror of the mental torture which talking to the dead would bring down on him. "Or if it is true," he said, more quietly now, "then it's not my fault. My mind would be no good to you burned out, Ma. And that's what will happen if I push my luck."

Well, (and suddenly he was aware of a new resolve in her voice, and of the strengthening of her cold fingers where they gripped his hand) *then something must be done about it! About your situation, I mean—for there's trouble brewing, son, and the dead lie uneasy in their graves! Do you remember I told you, Harry, there was someone who wanted to talk to you? And how what he had to say was important?*

"Yes, I remember. Who is he, Ma, and what is it that's so important?"

He wouldn't say, and his voice came from far, far away. But it's strange when the dead feel pain, Harry, for death usually puts them beyond it!

Harry felt his blood run cold. He remembered only too well how the dead, in certain circumstances, felt pain. Sir Keenan Gormley, murdered by Soviet mindspies, had been "examined" by Boris Dragosani, a necromancer. And dead as he had been, he had felt the pain. "Is it . . . like that?" he asked his mother now, holding his breath until she answered.

I don't know how it is—she turned to him and looked him straight in the eye—*for this is something I've never known before. But, Harry, I fear for you!* And before he could even attempt to reassure her: *Oh, son, son, my poor little Harry— I fear so very, very much for you! Is it like that, you ask? And I say: will it be—can it ever be—like that again? And how, if you're no longer a Necroscope? And then I pray that it can't be. So you see, son, how I'm torn two ways. I miss you, and all the dead miss you, but if it puts you in danger, then we can do without it.*

He sensed that she was avoiding something. "Ma, are you sure you don't know who he is, this one who tried to contact me? Are you sure you don't know *where* he is, right now?"

She let go his hand, turned away, avoided his eyes. *Who he is, no,* she said. *But his voice, his mental voice, Harry, crying out like that. Oh, yes, I know where he is. And all the dead know it, too. He's in hell!*

Frowning, he took her shoulders, gently turned her until she faced him again, and said, "In hell?"

She looked at him, opened her mouth—and nothing but a gurgle came out! She coughed chokingly, spat blood . . . then straightened up, swelled out, wrenched herself free of his suddenly feeble grasp. He saw something in her mouth, forked and flickering, which wasn't a human tongue! Her

171

skin sagged and grew old, becoming wormy as centuried parchment in a moment! Flesh sloughed from her bones, revealed her skull, smoked into dust as it fell from her like a rotting shroud! She cried out her horror, turned and fled away from him along the riverbank, paused a moment over the bight, and looked back. A rancid, disintegrating skeleton, she *laughed* at him even as she toppled into the water—and he saw that her eyes glowed crimson in the moonlight, and that the teeth in her skull were sharp, curving fangs!

Nailed to the spot—fear-frozen there—Harry could only cry out after her, "Ma-aaa!" But it wasn't his mother who heard and answered him.

Haaarry! The voice came from a long way away, but still Harry whirled on the riverbank, staring this way and that in the moon-silvered night. There was no one there. *Haaarry!* It came again, but clearer in his mind. *Haaarry Keeeooogh!* And it was just as his mother had described it: a voice full of hell's own torment.

Still stunned by his mother's metamorphosis—which he knew could only be some sort of dire warning, for it was nothing she would ever deliberately engineer—Harry was at first unable to answer. But he recognised the voice's despair, its anguish, its hopelessness, as it continued to call to him.

Harry, for God's sake! If you're out there, please answer me. I know you shouldn't, I know you daren't—but you must! *It's happening again, Harry, it's happening again!*

The voice was fading, its signal weakening, its telepathic potency waning. If Harry was ever to get to the bottom of this, he must do so now. "Who are you?" he said. "What do you want of me?"

Haaarry! Harry Keogh! Help us! Its owner hadn't heard him; the voice was trailing away, beginning to merge with a wind sprung up along the riverbank.

"How?" he shouted back. "How can I help you? I don't even know who you are!" But he suspected that he did. It was a rare thing for the dead to speak to him without rapport first being established by some form of introduction. Usually he had sought them out, following which they would normally be able to find him again. Which made him suspect that he'd known this one (or these ones?) before, probably in life.

Haaarry—for God's sake find us and make an end of it!

"How can I find you?" Harry shouted into the night, wanting to cry from the sheer frustration of it. "And what's the point of it? I won't even remember, not when I'm awake."

And then—the merest whisper fading into nothing, and yet powerful enough to call up a wind that howled along the riverbank and snatched at Harry, causing him to lean into it—there came that final exhortation which chilled the ex-Necroscope's blood to ice water, sent gooseflesh creeping on his spine, and wrenched him back into the waking world.

Find us and put us down! the unknown voice implored. *Put an end to these scarlet threads right now, before they can grow. You know the way. Harry: sharp steel, the wooden stake, the cleansing fire. Do it, Harry. Please . . . do . . . it!*

Harry sprang awake. Sandra was clinging to him, trying to hold him down. He was drenched in cold sweat, shaking like a leaf; and she was frightened, too, her eyes wide from it, her mouth forming a frozen "O."

"Harry, Harry!" She lay sprawled half across him. She let go his shoulders, hugged his neck, felt his heart pounding against her breast. "It's all right, it's all right. It was a bad dream, a nightmare, that's all."

Eyes wide and darting, shivering and panting for breath, he stared all around the room and let its familiarity wash over him. Sandra had put on the light the moment his shouting had brought her awake. "What?" he said, his hands trembling where they clutched her. "What?"

"It's all right," she insisted. "A dream, that's all."

"A dream?" Her words sank in and something of the gaunt vacancy went out of his eyes. He gently pushed her away, began to sit up—then drew air in a gasp and started bolt upright! "No," he blurted, "it was more than just a dream—much more. And Christ, I have to *remember*!"

But too late; already it was receding, draining back to the

roots of his subconsciousness. "It was about . . . about"— he desperately shook his head and sent a spray of sweat flying—"my mother! No, not about her but . . . she was in it! It was . . . a warning? Yes, a warning, and . . . something else."

But that was all. It was gone, driven out against his will by the will of some other—the will, or legacy, of his son— by the post-hypnotic commands he'd planted there in Harry's mind.

"Shit!" Harry whispered, damp and shivering where he sat on the edge of the bed . . .

That had been at 4:05 A.M. Harry had had maybe three and a half hours' sleep, Sandra an hour less. When he'd finally calmed down and put on his dressing gown, then she had made a pot of coffee. And as he sat there shivering and sipping at his drink, so she had tried to bring his dream back to mind, had urged him to remember it . . . all the while cursing herself inside that she'd slept right through it! For if she had stayed awake, she might just have caught a glimpse of the terrible thing he'd experienced, whatever it had been. That was her job: help him sort out his mind and get back what he'd lost. Whether he wanted it or not, and whether or not it was good for him.

But: "No use"—he shook his head after long minutes of patient questioning—"it's gone. And probably best that it's gone. I have to be . . . careful."

Sandra had been tired. She hadn't asked why he must be careful because she knew. But she should have asked because she wasn't supposed to know. And when she'd looked at him again, his soulful eyes had been steady on her, his tousled head tilted a little on one side, perhaps questioningly. "What's your interest, anyway?" he'd wanted to know.

"Only that if you get it off your chest, you'll feel better about it." At least her lie had the ring of logic to it. "Once a nightmare is told, it's not so frightening."

"Oh? And that's your understanding of nightmares, is it?"

"I was trying to be helpful."

"But I keep telling you I can't remember, and you keep prodding away at me. It was just a dream, and no one tries *that* hard to winkle someone else's dreams out of them! Not without a damn good reason, anyway. There's something not right here, Sandra, and I think I've known it for some time. Old Bettley says it's my fault that what we have isn't exactly right for me, but now I'm not so sure . . ."

There was no answer to that and so she'd kept quiet, acted hurt, drawn apart from him. But in fact she'd known that he was the one who was hurt, and that was the last thing she wanted. And when he finally got back into bed and she joined him there, then it had become obvious how cold he was, how stiff and silent and thoughtful where he lay with his back to her . . .

A little over an hour later she was awake again, a call of nature. Harry slept on, heavy in the bed, dead to the world. That thought made her shiver a little as she rejoined him; but of course he wasn't dead, just exhausted, mentally if not physically. His limbs were leaden, his eyes still, his breathing deep, slow, and regular. No more dreams. Dawn was maybe three-quarters of an hour away.

Lying beside him, still Sandra felt distanced from him. Their relationship, she felt, was like fancy knitting, which was something she'd never been any good at. One slip of the needle and the whole thing comes undone. And that was a shame. Their lovemaking last night had been very, very good. For both of them, she knew.

To reinforce delicious, liquid memories of him inside her, she reached across him and down, taking him in her hand. And a moment later she was rewarded when he stiffened and pulsed in the tube of her fingers. An animal reaction, she knew, but she was grateful for it anyway.

Her loyalties were rapidly breaking down, splitting apart, and she knew that, too. E-Branch paid the bills, but there had to be more to life than fat pay cheques. Harry was what she wanted. He wasn't just a job anymore, hadn't been for a long time. And the time was ever drawing closer when she

175

must make the break, say to hell with the branch and tell him the whole thing; damn it, he'd probably guessed it by now anyway . . .

Drifting, her thoughts began to run in pointless circles.

Before falling asleep again, she was aware of noises in the garden where the property fronted on the river. Slow noises, shuffling, sluggish. A badger? She wasn't sure if there were any badgers up here. Hedgehogs, then . . . Not burglars, anyway . . . Not in a district as rundown as this . . . No money here . . . Badgers . . . Hedgehogs . . . A grating of stones on the gravel of the garden paths . . . Something dog-gedly busy in the garden . . .

Sandra slept in a fashion, but the noises were still on her mind. Conscious of them, she hovered on the verge of true sleep and wouldn't let herself be drawn down. But as dawn began to filter its first feeble rays of pale light through the blinds of Harry's room, the garden sounds gradually faded away. She heard the familiar creak of the old arched-over gate at the bottom of the garden, and what might have been a slow series of shuffling footsteps, and then no more.

Shortly after that the birds were singing, and Harry came up the stairs in his dressing gown with a steaming pot of coffee and biscuits on a tray. "Breakfast," he said simply. And: "We had a rough night."

"Did we?" She sat up.

"Up and down a bit." He shrugged. He was still pale but less weary looking now. And she thought she detected a new look in his eyes. Wariness? Reluctant realisation? Resolution? Hard to tell with Harry. But resolution? What had he resolved to do, to say? She must get to him before he got to her.

"I love you," she said, putting down her cup on a small bedside table. "Forget anything else and just remember that. I can't help it and don't want to, but I just love you."

"I . . . I don't know," he said. But looking at her—sitting up in his bed like that, still pink from sleep and with her nipples achingly stiff—it was hard not to want her. She knew the look in his eyes, reached out, and tugged at the cord of his dressing gown; and he was hard under there and moving with a life of his own.

Then they were clinging and she curled herself onto him; and her breasts were warm, soft, and pliant against him; and he touched her in those places where he knew she liked him to, and stroked her at the wet, mobile junction of their flesh. It was the best it had ever been, and their coffee went cold . . .

Later, downstairs, with a fresh pot beginning to bubble, he said, ''And now I could face a decent breakfast!''

''Eggs and bacon? Out on the patio?'' She thought that maybe the worst was over. She'd be able to break it to him now without fearing it would destroy everything. ''Will it be warm enough out there?''

''Middle of May?'' Harry shrugged. ''Maybe it's not so hot at that. But the sun's up and the sky is clear, so . . . let's call it invigorating rather than chilly.''

''All right.'' She turned towards the fridge but he caught her arm.

''I'll do it, if you like,'' he said. ''I think I'd enjoy making breakfast for you.''

''Fine.'' She smiled and went through the old house to the front. It was the back, really, but facing the river like that, it always seemed to her to be ''the front.''

As she opened large patio windows where they overlooked the high-walled garden, the first thing she noticed was the gate under its stone archway, hanging ajar on rusting scroll hinges. And she rembered hearing it creaking just as dawn was breaking. A puff of wind, maybe, though she couldn't remember the night as being especially breezy.

She walked down across the crazy-paving patio with its weathered garden furniture. The garden was a sun trap, seeming to gather all of the early-morning May sunlight right into itself. Already the wall of the house was warm, basking in the glow. It wouldn't at all be a bad place to live, she thought, if Harry would only get it fixed up.

He had, in fact, done a little work on the house and grounds in the last four or five years. He'd had the central heating put in, for one thing, and had at least made an effort to sort out the garden. She crossed the patio to the lawn and made her way down the gravel path which divided it centrally. The grass was longer than it should be but still manageable, barely. At the bottom of the lawned area the garden had been terraced on one side, with a shallow dry-stone wall holding back the soil. This was the alleged "vegetable garden," though the only vegetation here now consisted of large areas of stinging nettles, brambles run wild, and a huge patch of rhubarb!

She saw that several of the stones were missing from the top tier of the wall, and at once remembered the grating sounds she'd heard when she lay half-asleep. If a section of the wall had simply fallen, perhaps pushed over by an expansion of dew- or rain-sodden soil, then its debris would be lying here at the foot of the wall. But there was nothing, just a missing top tier; and for her life she couldn't see someone sneaking in here just to steal stones! Perhaps Harry would know something about it.

She carried on down to the gate and looked out across the reedy bank to the river, whose surface was inches deep in undulating mist. It was a calm scene but very eerie: the mist lying there like cream on milk, turning the river to a twining white ribbon for as far as the eye could see. She'd never seen anything quite like it before. But maybe it augured well for a warm day.

Then, closing the gate and wedging it with a half brick, she paused and sniffed at the morning air. Just for a moment then she had thought to smell something . . . gone off? Yes, gone *entirely* off, in fact. But just as quickly the smell had disappeared. So maybe that was what last night's snuffling and shuffling had been about: local nocturnal creatures sniffing at the body of some poor dead thing or other where it lay in the reeds there at the river's rim. Which might also explain the maggots squirming in a tangle on the overgrown path just outside the gate!

Maggots! *Ugh!* Loathsome things!

And there were robins on the high garden wall, too, watching her and the maggots both—speculatively, she thought. If she went away, the redbreasts would likely make short work of the horrid things. *Bon appétit!* She wasn't a bit envious.

And then, frowning, turning back from the gate and looking up the path towards the house, at last she saw where the stones from the wall had gone. Obviously it had been Harry's doing after all. He'd been laying them out as stepping-stones on the gentle slope of the lawned area. And on some whim or other, he'd caused them to form letters.

Before she could connect the letters up to see if they had any meaning, Harry appeared at the patio windows with a steaming jug of coffee, cups, milk, and sugar on a tray. "Breakfast in five minutes," he called down to her. "By the time you've poured I'll be back with the eats." And so she forgot the business with the stones and went back up the path to where he'd left the coffee on the garden table.

But halfway through breakfast she remembered and asked, "What's this thing with the stones?"

"Hmm?" Harry raised an eyebrow. "Stones?"

"In the garden, on the lawn."

"Yes," he agreed, nodding, "there are stones surrounding the lawn. What about it?"

"No," she insisted, "*on* the lawn! Stones forming letters." She smiled and teased, "What is this, Harry? Are you sending secret messages to the jumbo pilots flying into Edinburgh airport or something?"

"On the lawn?" He paused with a forkful of food halfway to his mouth. "Messages to the . . . ?" He put his fork down and, frowning now, asked, "Where on the lawn?"

"Why, just there!" She pointed. "Go and see for yourself."

He did, and she could see from the expression on his face that he knew nothing about it. She got up and joined him there, and together they stared at the peculiar stony legend. It was simple enough, looked unfinished, made no sense whatsoever:

179

K E N L
T J O R
R H

And: "Messages?" Harry said again, thoughtfully, almost to himself. For a moment longer he stared, then nervously licked his lips and glanced quickly all around the garden, peering intently here and there. Sandra wondered what he was looking for. He was suddenly quiet, very pale again, obviously seriously concerned about something.

"Harry?" she said. "Is there something . . . ?"

He sensed more than heard her worried tone of voice. "Eh?" He looked at her. "No, nothing. Some kids must have been in. So they moved a few stones around—so what?" He laughed, but there was no life in it.

"Harry," she began again, "I—"

"Anyway, you were right." He abruptly cut her short. "It's too damned cold out here! Let's get inside."

But as they gathered up the breakfast things she saw him sniff at the air, saw fresh lines of concern, of realisation— even of understanding?—gather on his brow.

"Something dead," she said, and he actually started.

"What?"

"In the reeds, down by the river. Some dead thing. There are maggots on the path. The birds are eating them." Her words were innocent enough in themselves, but now Harry looked positively haggard.

"Eating them . . ." he repeated her. And now he couldn't wait to be out of the garden and into the house.

She took the breakfast things from him and carried them through to the kitchen, then returned to his study. He was pacing the floor, pausing every now and then to look out of the patio windows and into the garden. But as she entered he came to some decision or other and tried to adopt a less hagridden look. "So what's your schedule for today?" he enquired. "Will you be drawing? What have you got on the board right now, eh?"

Just a few words but they told her a lot.

Sandra was a fashion designer—ostensibly. In fact she *did* design fashionable women's clothes and had enjoyed several small successes, but mainly it was a front for her work within E-Branch. Last night she had told Harry that she wasn't doing anything today. She had thought they might spend it together. But now, for reasons of his own, he obviously wanted her out of here. "You want me to go?" She couldn't keep the disappointment out of her voice.

"Sandra." He gave up his weak attempt at subterfuge, sighed, and looked away. "I need to be alone to do some thinking. Can you understand that?"

"And I'll be in the way? Yes, I can understand that." But her tone said she couldn't. And before he could answer: "Harry, this thing about the stones in the garden. I—"

"Look," he grated, "I don't *know* about the stones! For all I know they're only a small part . . . of . . . of . . . oh, whatever!"

"Part of what, Harry?" Surely he must hear how concerned she was?

But it seemed he didn't. "I don't know." His voice was still harsh. He shook his head, then shot her an enquiring, almost vindictive glance. "Maybe I should ask you, eh? I mean, maybe it's possible you know more about what's going on here than I do, right?"

She made no answer but began to collect up her things. When this—whatever it was—had blown over, then there'd be time enough to try to explain about her connections with E-Branch. And it would be a good time, too, to quit the branch entirely and make a clean start. With Harry, if he'd have her.

He threw some clothes on and was waiting for her in the car when she was ready. They drove along the service road from the old houses, crossed the stone bridge, and joined the major road into Bonnyrig. From the village she could get a bus into Edinburgh. She'd done it before and it was no great chore.

She hadn't meant to speak to him again right now, but getting out of the car she found herself saying, "Will I see you tonight? Should I come up here?"

"No." He shook his head. And as she turned away: "Sandra!" She looked back into his pale, troubled face. But he could only shrug helplessly and say, "I don't know. I mean I really don't."

"Will you call me?"

"Yes." He nodded, and even managed a smile. "And Sandra . . . it's okay. I mean, I know you're okay."

That took a big lead weight off her heart. Something only Harry Keogh could do as easily as that. "Yes." She leaned down and kissed him through the open car window. "We're okay, Harry. I know we're okay."

In Edinburgh, Darcy Clarke and Norman Wellesley were waiting in the road outside the sweeping terraced facade of Georgian houses where Sandra had her flat. They were in the back of Wellesley's car, parked up, with two other branch men; but as she came into view round a corner they got out of the car and met her at the door of the house. She had the ground-floor flat; without speaking, she ushered them inside.

"Nice to see you again, Miss Markham." Wellesley nodded, taking a seat.

Clarke was less formal. "How are things, Sandra?" He forced a smile.

She caught a brief glimpse of his mind and it was all worry and uncertainty. But nothing specific. Harry was in it somewhere, though, be sure. Of course he was; why else would these two be here? She said, "Coffee?" and without waiting for their answer went into her kitchen alcove. Let them do the talking.

"We have time for a coffee, yes," said Wellesley, in that oh-very-well, I-suppose-I-shall-have-to-accept way of his, as if it were his damned right! "But actually we're pretty busy and won't prolong our visit too much. So if we can get right to it: did you have plans to see Keogh tonight?"

Just like that . . . and "Keogh," not Harry. Will you be in his bed, or he in yours? Wellesley was asking. Humping again tonight, are you?

There was something about this man that got Sandra's back

up. And the fact that his mind was a complete blank—not even radiating the faintest glow—was only a small part of it. She glanced back at him from the alcove with eyes that were cold where they met his. "He said he might call me," she answered unemotionally.

"It's just that we'd prefer it if you don't see him tonight, Sandra," Clarke hurriedly put in before Wellesley could use that blunt instrument he called a tongue again. "I mean, we plan on seeing him ourselves. And we'd like to avoid, you know, any embarrassing confrontations?"

She didn't know, really. But she brought them their coffee anyway and gave Darcy a smile. She'd always liked him. She didn't like to see him uncomfortable in the presence of his boss. *Their* boss, though not for much longer. Not if things worked out as she hoped they would. "I see," she said. "So what's happening?"

"No need for you to concern yourself." Wellesley was quick off the mark. "Just routine stuff. And, I'm afraid, confidential."

And suddenly she was afraid, too . . . for Harry. More complications? Something to interfere with her own plans, which she hoped would be the best for him? It was on the tip of her tongue to tell them about the new developments, what she knew of them, but she held it back. There was that in their attitude—Wellesley's, anyway—which warned that now wasn't a good time. And anyway, it would all go in her end-of-month report, along with her resignation.

They all three finished their coffees in silence. And finally: "That's it, then," said Wellesley, standing up. "We *won't* be seeing you!"—his idea of a smart remark! He nodded, offered her a twitchy half smile, and headed for the door. She saw them out, and Wellesley's parting shot was, "So if he does, er, call you, do put him off, won't you?"

She might have answered him in kind right there and then, but Clarke gave her arm a reassuring squeeze just above the elbow, as if saying: "It's okay, I'll be there."

But why should Darcy be acting so concerned? She'd rarely seen him looking so on edge . . .

VII: Deadspeak

AFTER DROPPING SANDRA OFF IN BONNYRIG AND DURING
the short drive home, Harry stopped at a newsagent's and
bought himself a pack of twenty cigarettes. He looked at his
change but didn't try to check it. It wouldn't make any sense
to him anyway. They could rip him off every time and he just
wouldn't know it.

That was the other thing Harry Jr. had done to him: he
was now innumerate. No way he could use the Möbius Continuum if he couldn't even calculate the change from a pack
of cigarettes! Sandra saw to it that his bills were paid, or he'd
probably get that wrong, too. What price his ''instinctive
mathematics'' now, eh? The Möbius equations? What the
hell were they? What had they looked like?

And again Harry wondered, *Was it a dream?* Was that all
it had been? A fantasy? A figment of his own imagination?
Oh, he remembered how it had been, all right; but as he'd
tried to explain to Sandra, it was the way you remember a
dream, or a book you read in childhood, fast fading now.
Had he really, *really*, done all of those things? And if he had,

did he really, *really*, want to be able to do them again? To talk to the teeming dead, and step through doors no one else guessed existed to travel swift as thought in the metaphysical Möbius Continuum?

Want it? Perhaps not, but what was there without it? What was he without it? Answer: Harry Keogh, nowhere man.

Back home he went into the garden and looked at the stones again:

KENL
TJOR
RH

They meant nothing to him. But still he fixed their meaningless legend in his mind. Then he brought the wheelbarrow, loaded it up, and wheeled the stones back to the wall where . . . he paused a moment and stood frowning, before wheeling them back up to the lawn again. And there he left them, in the wheelbarrow.

For if—just *if*—someone was trying to tell him something, well, why make things harder for them?

Indoors again, Harry climbed stairs and then ladders to the attic room which no one else suspected was there—that large, dusty room with its sloping rear window, naked light bulb hanging from a roof timber, and its rows and rows of bookshelves—which was now a shrine to his obsession, if the word "shrine" were at all applicable. And of course the books themselves. All the facts and the fictions were here, all the myths and legends, all the "conclusive condemnations" and "indisputable evidences" for or against, proving, disproving, or standing in the middle ground of Harry's studies. The history, the lore, the very nature . . . of the vampire.

Which was in itself a grim joke, for how could anyone ever fully understand the nature of the vampire? And yet if any man could, then it was Harry Keogh.

But he hadn't come here today to look again at his books or delve a little deeper into the miasma of times, lands, and legends long past. No, for he believed that time itself was

185

well past for those things, for study and vain attempts at understanding. His dreams of red threads among the blue were immediate things, "now" things, and if he'd learned nothing else in his weird life, it was to trust in his dreams.

The Wamphyri have powers, Father!

An echo? A whisper? The scurry of mice? Or . . . a memory?

How long before they seek you out and find you?

No, he wasn't here to look at his books this time. The time to study an enemy's tactics is before the onslaught. Too late if he's already come a-knocking at your door. Well, he hadn't, not yet. But Harry had dreamed things, and he trusted his dreams.

He took down a piece of modern weaponry (yes, modern, though its design hadn't changed much through sixteen centuries) from the wall and carried it to a table where he laid it down on newspapers preparatory to cleaning, oiling, and generally servicing the thing. There was this, and in the corner there a sickle whose semicircular blade gleamed like a razor, and that was all.

Strange weapons, these, against a force for blight and plague and devastation potentially greater than any of man's thermonuclear toys. But right now they were the only weapons Harry had.

Better tend to them . . .

The afternoon passed without incident; why shouldn't it? Years had passed without incident, within the parameters of the Harry Keogh mentality and identity. He spent most of the time considering his position (which was this: that he was no longer a Necroscope, that he no longer had access to the Möbius Continuum), and ways in which he might improve that position and recover his talents before they atrophied utterly.

It was possible—barely, Harry supposed, considering his innumeracy—that if he could speak to Möbius, then Möbius might be able to stabilize whatever mathematical gyro was now out of kilter in his head. Except first he must be *able* to speak to him, which was likewise out of the question. For of course Möbius had been dead for well over a hundred years, and Harry was forbidden to speak to the dead on penalty of mental agony.

He could not speak to the dead, but the dead might even now be looking at ways in which they could communicate with him. He suspected—no, he more than suspected, was sure—that he spoke to them in his dreams, even though he was forbidden to remember or act upon what they had told him. But still he was aware that warnings had been passed, even if he didn't know what those warning were about.

One thing was certain, however: he knew that within himself and within every man, woman, and child on the surface of the globe, a blue thread unwound from the past and was even now spinning into the future of humanity, and that he had dreamed—or been warned—of red threads amidst the blue.

And apart from that—this inescapable mood or sensation of something impending, and something terrible—the rest of it was a Chinese puzzle with no solution, a maze with no exit, the square root of minus one, whose value may only be expressed in the abstract. Harry knew the latter for a fact, even if he no longer knew what it meant. And it was a puzzle he'd examined almost to distraction, a maze he'd explored to exhaustion, and an equation he hadn't even attempted because like all mathematical concepts it simply wouldn't read . . .

In the evening he sat and watched television, mainly for relaxation. He'd considered calling Sandra, and then hadn't. There was something on her mind, too, he knew; and anyway, what right had he to draw her into . . . whatever this was, or whatever it might turn out to be? None.

So it went; evening drew towards night; Harry prepared for bed, only to sit dozing in his chair. The dish in his garden collected signals and unscrambled their pictures onto his screen. He started awake at the sound of applause and discovered an American chat-show host talking to a fat lady who had the most human, appealing eyes Harry could imagine.

187

The show was called "Interesting People" or some such and Harry had watched it before. Usually it was anything but interesting; but now he caught the word "extrasensory" and sat up a little straighter. Naturally enough, he found ESP in all its forms entirely fascinating.

"So . . . let's get this right," the skeletally thin host said to the fat lady. "You went deaf when you were eighteen months old, and so never learned how to speak, right?"

"That's right," the fat lady answered, "but I do have this incredible memory, and obviously I'd heard a great many human conversations before I went deaf. Anyway, speech never developed in me, so I wasn't only deaf but dumb, too. Then, three years ago, I got married. My husband is a technician in a recording studio. He took me in one day and I watched him working, and I suddenly made the connection between the oscillating sensors on his machinery and the voices and instrument sounds of the group he was recording."

"Suddenly you got the idea of sound, right?"

"That's correct." The fat lady smiled, and continued, "Now, I had of course learned sign language or dactylology—which in my mind I'd called dumbspeak—and I also knew that some deaf people could carry on perfectly normal conversations, which I termed deafspeak. But I hadn't tried it myself simply because I hadn't *understood* sound! You see, my deafness was total, absolute. Sound didn't exist—except in my memory!"

"And so you saw this hypnotist?"

"Indeed I did! It was hard but he was patient—and of course it mightn't have been possible at all except he was able to use dumbspeak. So he hypnotised me and brought back all the conversations I'd heard as a baby. And when I woke up—"

"You could speak?"

"Exactly as you hear me now, yes!"

"The hell you say! Not only fully articulate but almost entirely without accent! Mrs. Zdzienicki, that's a most fascinating story and you really are one of *the* most interrrresting people we've ever had on this show!''

The camera stayed on his thin, smiling face and he nodded his head in frenetic affirmation. "Yessiree! And now, let's move on to—"

But Harry had already moved to switch off the set; and as the screen blinked out he saw how dark it had grown. Almost midnight, and the house temperature already falling as the timer cut power to the central heating system. It was time he was in bed . . .

. . . Or, maybe he'd watch just one more interview with one of these interrrresting people! He didn't remember switching the set on again, but as its picture formed he was drawn in through the screen where he found Jack Garrulous or whatever his name was adrift in the Möbius Continuum.

"Welcome to the show, Harry!" said Jack. "And we just know we're going to find you verrry interesting! Now, I've been sort of admiring this, er, place you've got here? What did you say it was called?" He held out his microphone for Harry to speak into.

"This is the Möbius Continuum, Jack," said Harry, a little nervously, "and I'm not really supposed to be here."

"The hell you say! But on this show anything goes, Harry. You're on prime time, son, so don't be shy!"

"Time?" Harry said. "But all time is prime, Jack. Is time what you're interested in? Well, in that case, take a look in here." And grabbing Garrulous by the elbow, he guided him through a future-time door.

"Interrrresting!" the other approved, as side by side they shot into the future, towards that far faint haze of blue which was the expansion of humanity through the three mundane dimensions of the space-time universe. "And what are these myriad blue threads, Harry?"

"The life threads of the human race," Harry explained. "See over there? That one just this moment bursting into being, such a pure, shining blue that it's almost blinding? That's a newborn baby with a long, long way to go. And this one here, gradually fading and getting ready to blink out?"

189

He lowered his voice in respect. "Well, that's an old man about to die."

"The hell—you—say!" said Jack Garrulous, awed. "But of course, you'd know all about that, now wouldn't you, Harry? I mean, about death and such? For after all, aren't you the one they call a necrowhatsit?"

"A Necroscope, yes." Harry nodded. "Or at least I was."

"And how's that for a talent, folks?" Garrulous beamed with teeth like piano keys. "For Harry Keogh's the man who talks to the dead! And he's the *only* one they'll talk back to— but in the nicest possible way! See, they kind of love him. So"—he turned back to Harry—"what do you call that sort of conversation, Harry? I mean, when you're talking to dead folks? See, a little while ago we were speaking to this Mrs. Zdzienicki who told us all about dumbspeak and deafspeak and—"

"Deadspeak," Harry cut him short.

"Deadspeak? Really? The hell . . . you . . . *say*! Well, if you haven't been one of the most interrrr . . ." And he paused, squinting over Harry's shoulder.

"Um?" said Harry.

"One last question, son," said Garrulous urgently, his narrowing eyes fixed on something just outside Harry's sphere of vision. "I mean, you told us about the blue life-threads sure enough, but what in all get out's the meaning of a red one, eh?"

Harry's head snapped round; wide-eyed, he stared; and saw a scarlet thread, even now angling in towards him! And:

"Vampire!" he yelled, rolling out of his armchair into the darkness of the room. And framed in the doorway leading back into the rest of the house, he saw the silhouette of what could only be one thing: that which he'd known was coming for him!

There was a small table beside his chair, which Harry had knocked flying. Groping in the darkness, his fingers found two things: a table lamp thrown to the floor and the weapon he'd worked on earlier in the day. The latter was loaded. Switching on the lamp, Harry went into a crouch behind his

chair and brought up his gleaming metal crossbow into view—
and saw that his worst nightmare had advanced into the room!

There was no denying the thing: the slate grey colour of
its flesh, its gaping jaws and what they contained, its pointed
ears and the high-collared cape which gave its skull and men-
acing features definition. It was a vampire—of the comic-
book variety! But even realising that this wasn't the real thing
(and he of all people should know), still Harry's finger had
tightened on the trigger.

It was all reaction. This body he'd trained to a peak of
perfection was working just as he'd programmed it to work
in a hundred simulations of this very situation. And despite
the fact that he'd come immediately awake—and that he knew
this thing in his room with him was a fraud—still his adrenaline was flowing and his heart pounding, and his weapon's
fifteen-inch hardwood bolt already in flight. It was only in
the last split second that he'd tried to avert disaster by ele-
vating the crossbow's tiller up towards the ceiling. But that
had been enough, barely.

Wellesley, seeing the crossbow in Harry's hand, had blown
froth through his plastic teeth in a gasp of terror and tried to
back off. The bolt missed his right ear by a hair breadth,
struck through the collar of his costume cape, and snatched
him back against the wall. It buried itself deep in plaster and
old brick and pinned him there.

He spat out his teeth and yelled, ''Jesus Christ, you idiot,
it's me!'' But this was as much for the benefit of Darcy
Clarke, back there somewhere in the dark house, as for Harry
Keogh. For even as he was shouting, Wellesley's right hand
reached inside the coat under his cape and grasped the grip
of his issue 9-mm Browning. This was his main chance.
Keogh had attacked him, just as he'd hoped he would. It was
self-defence, that's all.

Harry, taking no chances, had nocked his bow, snatched
the auxiliary bolt from its clips under the tiller of his weapon,
and placed it in the breech. In a sort of slow motion born of
the speed of his own actions, he saw Wellesley's arm straightening and coming up into the firing position; but he couldn't

believe the man would shoot him. Why? For what reason? Or perhaps Wellesley feared he was going to use the cross-bow again. That must be it, yes. He dropped his weapon into the armchair's well and threw up his arms.

But now Wellesley's aim was unwavering, his eyes glinting, his knuckle turning white in the trigger guard of the automatic. And he actually grinned as he shouted, "Keogh, you madman—no! *No!*"

Then . . . three things, happening almost simultaneously.

One: Darcy Clarke's voice, which Harry recognised immediately, shouting, "Wellesley, get out of there. Get the fuck *out* of there!" And his footsteps coming clattering down the corridor, and his cursing as he collided with a plant pot and stand and knocked them over.

Two: Harry throwing himself over backwards behind the armchair as finally Wellesley's intention became clear, and hearing the angry *whirrr* of the bullet as the first shot went wide by an inch. And levering himself up to make a grab for the crossbow again, just in time to see the look on Wellesley's face turn from a mixture of incomprehensible rage and murderous intent to one of sheerest horror as his eyes were drawn to something behind Harry, which caused them to flash wide and disbelieving in a moment.

Three: the crash of shattering glass and snapping of thin wooden mullions inwards as something wet and heavy and clumsy came plunging through the locked patio doors into the room, something which drew Wellesley's fire from Harry to itself!

"Jesus! Jesus! Jesus!" the head of E-Branch screamed, emptying his gun over Harry's head, which he'd now turned towards the shattered glass doors. And there, staggering from the impact of the shots but somehow managing to keep its feet, Harry saw something—indeed, some*one*, though who exactly it would be hard to tell—which he'd thought never to see again. And even though he didn't know this one, still he knew him or it for a friend. For in the old days, all of the dead had been Harry's friends!

This one was bloated, wet, intact, not long dead—but long

enough to smell very badly. And behind it came a second corpse, dusty, withered, almost mummified, stepping through the frame of the shattered door. They were in their crumbling burial sheets and each of them carried a stone, advancing on Wellesley where he stood pinned to the wall, still yanking on the trigger of his empty gun.

And Harry could only crouch there watching, mouthing silent denials, as they drew close to the frenzied, maddened boss of E-Branch and began to raise their stones.

That was when the corridor light came on and Darcy Clarke stumbled into the room. His talent for survival—unfelt except by Darcy himself—was shrieking at him to get the hell out of here, almost physically driving him back. But somehow he fought it; and after all, the hostility of the dead wasn't directed at him but at his boss. "Harry!" he yelled, when he saw what was happening in the room. "For God's sake call them off!"

"I can't," Harry yelled back. "You know I can't!" But at least he could put himself between them. He did that now, jumped forward, and somehow got between the dead things and Wellesley where he gibbered and frothed. And there they stood with their stones upraised, and the soggy one seeking to put Harry gently to one side.

He might have, too, but suddenly suicidal, Harry cried out, "No! Go back where you belong! It's a mistake!" Or at least he tried to. But he only got as far as "go back where—" For he was forbidden to speak to the dead. But fortunately for Wellesley, the dead weren't forbidden to heed him.

As Harry clapped his hands to his head and cried out, jerking like a spastic puppet as he crumpled up, so the dead men let fall their stones and turned away, and went out again into the night.

Strangled until now, Wellesley found his voice again; but it was a deranged voice if ever Darcy Clarke heard one. "Did you see? Did you see?" Wellesley gibbered. "I didn't believe it, but now I've seen for myself. He called them up against me! He's a monster, by God, a *monster*! But it's the end of you, Harry Keogh!"

He'd freed the spent magazine from his gun and dropped it to the carpeted floor, and was in the process of bringing a fully loaded one out of his pocket when Clarke hit him with all the force he could muster. Gun and magazine went flying, and Wellesley hung there in his makeup, suspended from the crossbow bolt.

Then there were more running footsteps, and in the next moment the two-man backup team was there wondering what the hell was going on; and Darcy was down on the floor with Harry, holding him in his arms as the agonised man clutched at his head and gasped out his unbearable pain, and slid down into the deep, dark well of merciful oblivion . . .

A great deal occurred in the nine hours it took Harry to sleep it off. A security-screened doctor was called in to look at him, also to give Wellesley a shot that would keep him down awhile; Clarke got in touch with Sandra because he reckoned she should be in on this and should have been from the start; and as dawn came and went and both Harry and Wellesley were beginning to show signs of regaining consciousness, so a call came through from the duty officer at E-Branch HQ.

Darcy had, of course, already put HQ in the picture. He'd contacted the DO right after the excitement had died down to report everything that had happened and what he'd done, and at the same time to tender his resignation to the minister responsible. Also he'd suggested that someone might like to start thinking about a replacement for Wellesley, who was obviously several kinds of flake. And looking back on Wellesley's plan to scare Harry Keogh into using the Möbius Continuum—which he, Darcy Clarke, had gone along with—Darcy reckoned he might be just a little on the flaky side himself!

Sandra, when she'd arrived looking worried as hell and after he'd explained things to her, had said as much in no uncertain terms and probably would have said a lot more, except she could see that Darcy was taking it badly enough already. She didn't feel the need to blame him because he was so obviously blaming himself; so instead of ranting and raving and generally going to pieces, she'd simply sat with Harry through what was left of the night and into the morning. And just a few minutes ago, when everyone was into his third cup of coffee, that was when the telephone rang and it was HQ asking to speak to Darcy Clarke. He took the call, which was a long one, and when he was through had to sit down a minute and think about it.

They'd stretched Wellesley out on Harry's bed upstairs, with one of the men from E-Branch watching him; Harry himself had a leather couch downstairs in the study where everything had happened, and where they'd draped a blanket over the broken patio doors to keep out the night chill; Sandra, Darcy, and the other E-Branch operative were all there with him, with nothing to do now except wait for him to wake up.

Except that now, following this telephone call, Darcy had quite a bit more to do, and the speed with which circumstances had changed had left him breathless. But Sandra had seen the full range of rapidly changing expressions on his face as he'd talked into the telephone; and now, catching a glimpse of the confusion in his mind—and the relief, and something of the shock, too?—she felt prompted to enquire, "What was that all about?"

Darcy looked at her and his bleary eyes slowly focused. Then he turned to the other agent and said, "Eddy, go up and keep Joe company, eh? And when Wellesley wakes up, tell him he's under arrest!"

"What?" The other looked at him incredulously.

Darcy nodded. "That was the DO on the blower, and he had our minister right there with him. It seems our pal Norman Harold Wellesley has been fooling around a little with a suspicious character from the Russian embassy! He's suspended forthwith, and we're to deliver him to MI5 ASAP—which puts me right back in the chair. For now, anyway."

As Eddy left to go upstairs, Darcy told Sandra, "Yes, but that's just part of it. It never rains but it pours. We have a big problem."

"We?" she said, shaking her head. "No, for I'm out of

it, whatever it is. And I thought you were, too. Well, your resignation may have been turned down, but not mine. I'm through with the branch, as of now.''

"I understand that,'' he said, "and I meant *I* have a problem rather than we. It's not only business but personal, too. And I'm afraid I can't quit until it's sorted out. But you don't want to hear about it, right?''

"Hearing won't hurt,'' she said.

"It's Ken Layard and Trevor Jordan,'' he began to explain. "They were out in the Aegean, Rhodes, keeping tabs on a load of drugs being run through the Med. And now it seems they've come unstuck. Badly.''

"How badly?'' Sandra had met the two men—in fact Jordan, the telepath, had been her sponsor—and she knew something of their talents and outstanding reputations.

"Very badly.'' Darcy shook his head. "And . . . it's weird! Something I'm going to have to look into myself. These were two of my closest friends.''

"Weird?'' she repeated him. "Were?''

He nodded. "Over the last few days Trevor's had a couple of minor problems. They thought it was overeating or drinking or something. Now apparently he's a raving madman . . . or would be if he wasn't under sedation in a Rhodes asylum! And the night before last—no, the one before that; when I'm tired like this my body clock goes out of whack—Ken Layard was fished out of the harbour half-full of water and with a bump on his head where he'd collided with something. Concussion, that's all. Except as yet there's no sign of a normal recovery. All of which smells very fishy to me.''

"What?'' said Harry Keogh, fumbling the word out of a mouth that tasted highly toxic as he tried to sit up.

They sprang to his side, Darcy supporting him and Sandra hugging his head. "Are you all right, Harry?'' She stroked his hair, kissed his forehead.

He freed himself, licked his lips, and said, "Be a love and make me a cup of coffee.'' And as she left the room he focused on Darcy.

"Names,'' he said.

"Eh?"

"You mentioned the names of some people," Harry said again, seeming to find some difficulty in getting his tongue round the words. "People I've heard of, and met, in E-Branch." He pulled a face. "God, my mouth tastes vile!" And then, suddenly remembering, his eyes went wide. "That idiot was trying to shoot me! And then—" Abruptly, he struggled upright, his eyes searching every corner of the room.

"All that was last night, Harry," Darcy told him, knowing what he was looking for. "And . . . they've gone now. They went when you told them to."

Some of the anxiety went out of Harry's face, replaced by the bitter look of a man betrayed. "You were here," he accused, "with Wellesley."

Darcy didn't deny it. "Yes," he said, "I was, but for the last time. I was following orders, or trying to, but that's no excuse. I *was* here, and shouldn't have been. But from here on in . . . I have one more job to do, and then I'm out of E-Branch for good. I don't think spying's my style, Harry. And I know that shitting on my friends isn't! As for Wellesley: I don't think he'll be much trouble from now on."

"What?" Harry went deathly pale in a moment. "Don't tell me they . . . ?"

Darcy shook his head. "No, they didn't hurt him. You told them to go and they went. And then you folded up."

Sandra was back with Harry's coffee. "What's this about names?" she said.

Harry took a mouthful of hot coffee, gave his head a tentative shake, and said, "Ow! God, my head!"

She took pills from her bag and gave them to him. He accepted them and washed them down. And: "Names, yes," he said yet again. "The names of people in E-Branch. You were talking about them as I came to?"

Darcy told him about Layard and Jordan, and as he talked Harry's face grew drawn, even haggard. Finally, when Darcy was done, Harry glanced at Sandra. "Well?"

She shrugged, looked mystified. "What are you getting at, Harry?"

"Tell him about the stones," Harry said, "in the garden."

And seeing his meaning at once, she gasped, "Ken L! And T. Jor!"

Now it was Darcy's turn to look dumb. "Do you want to let me in on it?" he said.

Harry stood up, swayed a little, then headed for the patio doors. He was still in his pyjamas. "Be careful!" Darcy cautioned him. "There's still a lot of glass there. We didn't do much of a job of tidying up, I'm afraid."

Harry avoided the glass and took down the blanket, and they followed him into the garden. In his bare feet he crossed the lawn, pointed to a fresh series of stones where they'd been laid out on the grass. "There," he said. "That's what they were doing when Wellesley jumped me—which, incidentally, you might like to try explaining sometime when you've a week or two to spare!" This was directed at both of them.

"Harry." Sandra was quick to protest. "I had nothing to do with it."

"But you do work for the branch."

"Not anymore," she said. And then, because she was afraid of losing him, she let it all out in a breathless rush. "Try to understand, Harry. At first you were just a job, but different to any other they ever gave me. Also, what I was doing was for your benefit; that's what they told me. But they didn't plan—and I didn't plan—on my falling in love with you. That just happened, and now they can stuff their job."

Harry smiled in his wan way, then staggered a little. She at once caught him, held him up. "You shouldn't even be on your feet! You look terrible, Harry!"

"I'm still a bit dizzy, that's all," he answered. "Anyway, what you were saying: I heard all that, too, when I was waking up. And what the hell, I think I've always known that you were one of theirs. You and Old Man Bettley. So what? So was I, once. And let's face it, I can use all the help I can get, right?"

Darcy was still looking at the stones, his forehead creased

in a frown. "Does this mean what I think it means?" he asked. They all looked at the incomplete word:

R H O D F

"Rhodes," said Harry, nodding. "They didn't have time to finish the E and the S, that's all. And now it all adds up."

"But to what?" Sandra and Darcy said together.

Harry looked at them and made no attempt to hide his fear. "To something I've been praying wouldn't happen, and yet half expecting ever since I returned from Starside," he said. Then he shivered and added, "Let's get inside." And for the moment that was all he would say about it . . .

When Wellesley woke up and Darcy told him it looked like he was in big trouble, at first he was full of bluster. But then he had to face down Harry, too, and that was when he caved in. He knew how lucky he was that he wasn't a murderer, knew, too, that Harry hadn't let his dead friends kill him, even though he'd had the right and couldn't have been blamed for it. What's more, he knew what it had cost Harry to call them off. And so he told everything, the whole story: how he'd been recruited by Gregor Borowitz because of his negative talent (the fact that his mind couldn't be read) and how he'd been a sleeper until they tried to activate him.

Harry had been their chief interest—though doubtless they would have got around to the rest of E-Branch, too, when they were satisfied that he was no longer a player—and so Wellesley had been feeding them details of his progress. But when it had seemed that Harry might be on the verge of new things, they'd wanted rid of him. Harry, with his old powers returned to him, or maybe new talents they hadn't even heard of, would be just too dangerous . . .

Then Darcy had given his men their orders, to take the ex-head of the branch back to London and hand him over, and finally he'd spent a long session on the telephone talking to the minister responsible. One subject had been Nikolai Zharov, Wellesley's Russian contact. He was still loose somewhere, and, alas, would stay loose for the time being. Since he was diplomatically immune, they couldn't even pick him up. Eventually a protest would be made to the Soviet embassy, requiring Zharov's expulsion for the usual "activities inconsistent with . . ." etc.

By the time Darcy was through, Harry had a lot more coffee inside him and a bite of brunch, and was looking more his usual self. Not doleful, Darcy thought, just sort of placid and not entirely with it. He reminded him of nothing so much as a powerful hand torch minus its batteries. Fully charged, he could really shine, but right now there wasn't even a spark.

Or maybe there was.

"When are you going to Rhodes?" Harry asked him.

"Now, as soon as I can get a flight out. I'd be out of here right now but I wanted to be sure you were okay first. I reckoned I owed you that at least, and probably a lot more. But I want to arrange to get Trevor and Ken out of there, if they can be moved. Also, I have to see if I can discover what they came up against. Their Greek liaison man is still out there and might be able to help me on that." He looked at Harry speculatively. "And I had hopes that you might be able to help me, too, Harry, what with these . . . *messages* you've been getting, and all."

Harry nodded. "I have my suspicions," he said, "but we'd all better pray I'm wrong! See, I know the dead wouldn't harm me; they wouldn't deliberately risk hurting me. And yet this thing is so important to them, or to me, that it's almost as if they've been tempting me into conversation! But my son did a hell of a good job on me. I don't remember my dreams in any detail—not the ones which they send me, anyway—and I can't try to clarify them. And as for the Möbius Continuum . . . God, I can't add two and two without it comes out five!"

Darcy Clarke had personal experience with the Möbius Continuum. Harry had taken him there once, taken him through it. From here, this very house, to E-Branch HQ in London over three hundred miles away. And that had been a trip Darcy would never forget, and he hoped never repeat, all the days of his life. Even now, these years later, it was printed on his memory in vivid detail.

There had been darkness on the Möbius strip, the primal darkness itself, as it was before the universe began. A place of negativity, yes, where darkness lay upon the face of the deep. And Darcy had thought that this could well be that region from which God had commanded Let There Be Light, and caused the physical universe to split off from the metaphysical void.

There had been no air, but neither had there been time, so that Darcy didn't need to breathe. And without time there was likewise no space; both of these essentials of a universe of matter had been absent. But Darcy hadn't ruptured and flown apart, because there'd been nowhere to fly to!

Harry had been Darcy's single anchor on sanity and being and humanity; he couldn't see him for there was no light, but he could feel the pressure of his hand. And perhaps because Darcy was himself psychically endowed, he'd felt he had some small understanding of the place. For instance: he knew it was real because he was here, and with Harry beside him he'd known he need not fear it because his talent hadn't prevented him from coming here. And so, even in the confusion of his near panic, he'd been able to explore his feelings about it.

Lacking space, it was literally "nowhere," but by the same token, lacking time, it was every-where and -when. It was core and boundary both, interior and exterior, where nothing ever changed except by force of will. But there was no will, except it was brought here by someone like Harry Keogh. Harry was only a man, and yet the things he could do through the Möbius Continuum were . . . godlike? And what if God should come here?

And again Darcy had thought of The God, who wrought a Great Change out of a formless void and willed a universe. And then the thought had also occurred: We aren't meant to be here. This isn't our place.

"I understand how you feel," *Harry had told him then,* "for I've felt it, too. But don't be afraid. Just let it happen and accept it. Can't you feel the magic of it? Doesn't it thrill you to your soul?''

And Darcy had had to admit it thrilled him—but it scared him witless, too!

Then, so as not to prolong it, Harry had taken him to the threshold of a future-time door. Looking out, they'd seen a chaos of millions, no billions, of threads of pure blue light etched against an eternity of black velvet, like an incredible meteor shower, except the tracks didn't dim but remained printed on the sky—indeed, printed on time! And the most awesome thing was this: that two of these twining, twisting streamers of blue light had issued from Darcy and Harry themselves, extruding from them and racing away into the future!

The blue life-threads of humanity, of all mankind, spreading out and away through space and time . . . But then Harry had closed that door and opened another, a door on the past.

The myriad neon life-threads had been there as before, but this time, instead of expanding into a misted distance, they'd contracted and narrowed down, targeting on a faraway, dazzling blue core of origin.

And in the main, that was what had most seared itself on Darcy's memory: the fact that he'd seen the very birth light of mankind . . .

"Anyway," Harry's voice, decisive now, brought him back to the present, "I'm coming with you. To Rhodes, I mean. You might need my advice."

Darcy gazed at him in astonishment. He hadn't seen or heard him so positive in . . . how long? "You're coming with . . . ?"

"They're my friends, too," Harry blurted. "Oh, maybe I don't know them like you do, but I trusted in them once and they trusted in me, in what I was doing. They were in on that Bodescu business. They have their talents, and they have invaluable experience of . . . things. Also, well, it seems to me the dead want me to go. And lastly, we really can't afford to have anything happen to people like those two. Not now."

"We can't afford it? What 'we,' Harry?" And suddenly Darcy was very tense, waiting for Harry's answer.

"You, me, the world."

"Is it that bad?"

"It could be. So I'm coming with you."

Sandra looked at them both and said, "So am I."

Darcy shook his head. "Not if it's like he thinks it might be, you're not."

"But I'm a telepath!" she protested. "I might be able to help with Trevor Jordan. He and I used to be able to read each other like books. He's my friend, too, remember?"

Harry took her arm. "Didn't you hear what Darcy said? Trevor's a madman. His mind has gone."

She pulled a face and tut-tutted. "What does *that* mean, Harry? Minds don't just 'go'; you of all people should know that. It hasn't 'gone' anywhere—just gone wrong, that's all. I might be able to look in there and see what's wrong."

"We're wasting time." Darcy was growing anxious. "Okay, so it's decided: we're all three going. How long will it take you to get ready?"

"I'm ready," Harry answered at once. "Five minutes to pack a few things."

"I'll need to pick up my passport on our way through Edinburgh." Sandra shrugged. "That's all. Anything else I need I'll buy out there."

"Right," said Darcy. "You phone a taxi, and I'll help Harry pack. If we have time, I can always put HQ in the picture from the airport. So let's go."

And in their graves the teeming dead relaxed a little—for the moment, anyway. Harry, because he thought he'd heard their massed sighing, gave a small shudder. It wasn't terror or dread or anything like that. It was just the frisson of knowing. But of course his friends—his living friends—knew nothing at all of that . . .

Though they could not know it, Nikolai Zharov was at Edinburgh airport to see them off. He had also been across the river with a pair of KGB-issue night-lite binoculars when

203

Wellesley broke into Harry's house in Bonnyrig. And he'd seen what had left the garden to plod back to their riven plots in a cemetery half a mile away. He'd seen and known what they were, and still looked haggard from knowing it.

But that didn't stop Zharov from coding a message and phoning it through to the KGB cell at the embassy. So that in a very short time indeed, the Soviet intelligence agencies knew that Harry Keogh was en route to the Mediterranean . . .

It was 6:30 P.M. local time at Rhodes airport when Manolis Papastamos met them off their flight; during the taxi ride into the historic town, he told them in his frenetic fashion all he knew of what had transpired. But seeing no connection, he made no mention of Jianni Lazarides.

"What of Ken Layard now?" Darcy wanted to know.

Papastamos was small, slender, all sinew and suntan and shiny-black, wavy hair. Handsome in a fashion, and usually full of zest, now he looked harassed and hagridden. "I don't know what it is." He gave a series of questioning, desperate shrugs, held out his hands palms up. "I don't know, and blame myself because I don't know! But . . . they are not easy to understand, those two. Policemen? Strange policemen! They seemed to know so much—to be so *sure* of certain things—but never explained to me how they knew."

"They're very special," Darcy agreed. "But what about Ken?"

"He couldn't swim, had a bump on his head. I dragged him out of the harbour onto some rocks, got the salt water out of him, went for help. Jordan was no use to me: he just sat on the mole under the old windmills babbling to himself. He was suddenly . . . crazy! And he's stayed that way. But Layard, he was okay, I swear it! Just a bump on the head. And now . . ."

"Now?" said Harry.

"Now they say he may die!" Papastamos looked like he might cry. "I did all I could, I swear it!"

"Don't blame yourself, Manolis," Darcy told him. "Whatever happened wasn't your fault. But can we see him?"

"Of course, we go to the hospital now. You can see Trevor, too, if you wish it. But"—and again he shrugged—"you won't get much out of that one. My God, I am so sorry!"

The hospital was off Papalouca, one of the New Town's main roads. It was a big, sprawling place with a frontage all of a hundred yards long. "One section—a ward, clinic, and dispensary—is reserved mainly for the treatment of the tourists," Papastamos explained as their taxi took them in through the gates. "It's not much in use now, but in July and August the work doesn't stop. The broken bones, bad sunburns, heatstroke, stings, cuts, and bruises. Ken Layard has a room of his own."

He told their driver to wait, led the way into a side wing where a receptionist sat in her booth clipping her fingernails. As soon as she saw Papastamos she sprang to her feet and spoke to him in breathless, very much subdued Greek. Papastamos at once gasped and went pale. "My friends, you are too late," he said. "He is . . . dead!" He looked at Sandra, Darcy, and Harry in turn and shook his head. "There is nothing I can say."

They were too dumbstruck to answer for a moment, until Harry said, "Can we see him anyway?"

Harry looked cool in a pale blue jacket, white shirt, and slacks. He and the others had slept on the plane, catching up on a lot of lost sleep. And despite his travails of the night before, he seemed to have come through it better than they. His face was calm, resigned; unlike Sandra's and Darcy's, Papastamos saw no sorrow in it. And the Greek thought, *A cold-blooded one, this Harry Keogh.*

But he was wrong: it was simply that Harry had learned to view death differently. Ken Layard might be finished "here"—finished physically, materially, in the corporeal world—but he wasn't all dead. Not all of him. Why, for all Harry knew, Ken might be seeking him out right now, desperate to engage him in deadspeak! Except Harry was forbidden to hear him, and forbidden to answer even if he did.

"See him?" Papastamos answered. "Of course you can. But the girl tells me that first the doctor wishes to see us. His office is this way." And he led them down a cool corridor, where the light came slanting in through high, narrow windows.

They found the doctor, a small bald man with thick-lensed spectacles perched on the end of his hook of a nose, in his tiny office room signing and stamping papers. When Papastamos introduced them to him, Dr. Sakellarakis was at once the soul of concern, displaying his very genuine dismay at the loss of their friend.

Speaking half-decent English and shaking his head sadly, he told them, "This bump on the Layard's head—I 'fraid is much more than the simple bump, gentlemen, lady. There is perhaps the damage inside? This is not certain until the autopsy, naturally, but I thinks this one is causing the death. The damage, the blood clot, something." Again he shook his head, gave a sad shrug.

"Can we see him?" Harry asked again. And as the doctor led the way: "When is the autopsy?"

Again the Greek's shrug. "One days, two—as soon as it can be arranged. But soon. Until then I am having him removed to the morgue."

"And when did he die—exactly?" Harry was relentless.

"Exactly? To the minute? Is not known. One hour, I thinks. About . . . ah, eighteen-hundred hours?"

"Six o'clock local time," said Sandra. "We were in flight."

"Does there have to be an autopsy?" Harry hated the thought of it; he knew the effect necromancy had on the dead, how much they feared it. Dragosani had been a necromancer, and oh how the dead had loathed and feared him! Of course, this wouldn't be the same; Layard would feel nothing at the hands of a pathologist, whose skills would be those of the surgeon as opposed to the torturer, but still Harry didn't like it.

Sakellarakis held up his hands. "It is the law."

Layard's room was small, white, clean, and pungently antiseptic. He lay full length on a trolley, covered head to toe by a sheet. The bed he'd used had been made up again, and the window closed to keep out flies. Darcy carefully laid back the sheet to show Layard's face—and drew back at once, wincing. Sandra too. Layard's face wasn't in repose.

"Is the spasm," Sakellarakis informed, nodding. "The muscles, a contraction. The mortician is putting this one right. Then Layard, he is doing the correct sleeping."

Harry hadn't drawn back. Instead he stood over Layard, looking down at him. The esper was grey, clay-cold, frozen in rigor mortis. But his face was fixed in something rather more than that. His jaws were open in a scream and his upper lip at the left had lifted up and away from the teeth, leaving them visible and shining. His entire face seemed pulled to the left in a sort of rictus, as if he screamed his denial of something unbelievable, unbearable.

His eyes were closed, but in the eyelids under the brows Harry saw twin slits in the membranous skin. They were fine but dark and plainly visible against the overall pallor. "He's been . . . cut?" Harry glanced at the Greek doctor.

"The spasm." The other nodded. "The eyes come open. It can happen. I make the small cuts in the muscles . . . no problem."

Harry licked his lips, frowned, peered intently at the large blue lump showing on Layard's forehead and continuing into his hair. The shiny skin was broken in the centre, a small abrasion where flesh white as fish belly showed through. Harry looked at the lump, reached out a hand as if to touch it, then turned away. And: "That look on his face," he said, under his breath. "No muscular spasm that, but sheer terror!"

Darcy Clarke, for his part, had taken one look at Layard and drawn back first one pace, then another. But he hadn't stopped drawing back and was now out in the corridor. His face was drawn, eyes staring into the room at the figure on the trolley. Sandra joined him; Harry too.

"Darcy, what is it?" Sandra's voice was hushed.

Darcy only shook his head. "I don't know," he gulped.

207

"But whatever it is, it's not right!" It was his talent working, looking out for him.

Papastamos put back the sheet over Layard's face; he and Sakellarakis came out of the room into the corridor. "Not the spasm, you say?" The doctor looked at Harry and cocked his head on one side. "You are knowing about these things?"

"I know some things about the dead, yes." Harry nodded.

"Harry's . . . an expert." Darcy had himself under control now.

"Ah!" said Sakellarakis. "A doctor!"

"Listen." Harry took him by the arm, spoke earnestly to him. "The autopsy must be tonight. And then he must be burned!"

"Burned? You are meaning cremated?"

"Yes, cremated. Reduced to ashes. Tomorrow at the latest."

"My God!" Manolis Papastamos burst out. "And Ken Layard was your friend? Such friends I don't need! I thought you were the cold one but . . . you are not merely cold, you are as dead as he is!"

Cold sweat was beading Harry's forehead now and he was beginning to look sick. "But that's just the point," he said. "I don't think he is dead!"

"You don't . . . ?" Dr. Sakellarakis' jaw fell open. "But I know this thing for sure! The gentleman, he is *certain* dead!"

"Undead!" Harry was swaying now.

Sandra's eyes flew wide. So this was really it! But Harry had been caught off guard; he was shocked, saying too much. "It's . . . an English expression!" she quickly cut in. "Undead: not dead but merely departed. Old friends simply . . . pass on. That's what he meant. Ken's not dead but in the hands of God."

Or the devil! Harry thought. But he was steadier now and glad that she'd come to his rescue.

Darcy's mind was also working overtime. "It's Layard's religion," he said, "which requires that he's burned—

cremated—within a day of his dying. Harry only wants to be sure it will be the way he would want it.''

"Ah!'' Manolis Papastamos still wasn't sure, but he thought that at least he was beginning to understand. "Then I have to apologise. I am sorry, Harry.''

"That's okay,'' said Harry. "Can we see Trevor Jordan now?''

"We'll go right now.'' Papastamos nodded. "The asylum is in the Old Town, inside the old Crusader walls. It's off Pythagora Street. The nuns run it.''

They used the taxi again and reached their destination in a little over twenty minutes. By now the sun was setting and a cool breeze off the sea brought relief to the heat of the day. During the journey Darcy asked Papastamos, "Incidentally, can you fix us up with somewhere to stay? A decent hotel?''

"Better than that,'' said the other. "The tourist season is just starting; many of the villas are still empty; I found you a place as soon as I knew you were coming. After you have seen poor Trevor, then I take you there.''

At the asylum they had to wait until a Sister of Rhodos could be spared from her duties to take them to Jordan's cell. He was straitjacketed, seated in a deep, high-sided leather chair with his feet inches off the ground. In this position he could do himself no harm, but in any case he seemed asleep. With Papastamos to translate, the sister explained that they were administering a mild sedative at regular intervals. It wasn't that Jordan was violent, more that he seemed desperately afraid of something.

"Tell her she can leave us with him,'' Harry told the Greek. "We won't stay long, and we know the way out.'' And when Papastamos had complied and the sister left: "And you too, Manolis, if you please.''

"Eh?''

Darcy laid a hand on his arm. "Be a good fellow, Manolis, and wait for us outside,'' he told him. "Believe me, we know what we're doing.''

The other shrugged, however sourly, and left.

209

Darcy and Harry looked at Sandra. "Do you feel up to it?" Darcy said.

She was nervous, but: "It should be easy," she answered at last. "We're two of a kind. I've had plenty of practice with Trevor and know the way in." But it was as if she spoke more to convince herself than anyone else. And as she took up a position behind Jordan, with her hands on the back of his chair, so the last rays of the sun began to fade in the tiny, high, recessed stained-glass windows of the cell.

Sandra closed her eyes and the silence grew. Jordan sat locked in his chair; his chest rising and falling, his eyelids fluttering as he dreamed or thought whatever thoughts they were that troubled him; his left hand fluttering a little, too, where it was strapped down by his thigh. Harry and Darcy stood watching, aware now of the gathering dusk, the fading light . . .

And without warning Sandra was in!

She looked, saw, gave a strangled little cry, and stumbled back away from Jordan's chair until she crashed into the wall. Jordan's eyes snapped open. They were terrified! His head swivelled left and right and he saw the two espers standing before him—and just for a moment, he knew them!

"Darcy! Harry!" he croaked.

And as simply and suddenly as that, Harry knew who had come to him in his dreams at Bonnyrig to beg his help!

But in the next moment Jordan's white face began to twitch and shake in dreadful spasms of effort and agony. He tried to say something but was denied the chance. The shuddering stopped, his fevered eyes closed and his head lolled, and he slumped down again.

But even as he returned to his monstrous dreams, so he managed one last word: "Ha-Ha-*Haarrry!*"

They rushed to Sandra where she stood half-fainting against the wall. And when she stopped gasping for air and was able to hold them off: "What was it?" Harry asked her. "Did you see?"

"I saw." She nodded, swallowing rapidly. "He's not mad, Harry, just trapped."

"Trapped?"

"In his own mind, yes. Like some innocent, cringing, ter-rified victim locked in a dungeon."

"A victim of what?" Darcy wanted to know, slack-jawed as he gaped at her trembling in Harry's arms.

"Oh God! Oh God!" she whispered, her trembling threat-ening to shake Harry, too, as her eyes went fearfully back to Trevor Jordan lolling there unconscious in his chair. And Darcy felt his blood stiffen to ice in the haunted light of her eyes, as finally she answered, "Of the monster who's in there with him! Of that thing who's in there right now, talking to him, questioning him . . . *about us*!"

VIII: Undead!

Night was already drawing in, the early-break tour-ists promenading in their evening finery, and the town's lights beginning to come on as the taxi sped the three to their villa. But in the front of the car with the driver, Manolis Papasta-mos was very quiet. Darcy supposed that the Greek felt out of things and probably considered he'd been snubbed, and he wondered how best to make up for it. There was still a lot Papastamos could do for them; indeed, without his cooper-ation they might find the going very difficult.

The villa stood in its own high-walled gardens of lemon, almond, and olive trees, overlooking the sea on the Akti Can-ari promenade towards the airport. It was square and flat-roofed, had shuttered windows, squealing wrought-iron gates, and a pebbled path to the main door, where a dim lamp glowed under the roof of a pine porch. The lamp had already attracted a cloud of moths, and they in their turn had lured several small green geckos, which scattered across the wall as Papastamos turned the key gratingly in the door. And while the stubble-jawed, chain-smoking taxi driver patiently waited, so the Greek policeman showed his three very odd foreign visitors around the place.

It wasn't the best but it was private and gave easy access to the town; there were cooking facilities but the three would be well advised to eat at any one of the half-dozen excellent tavernas which stood within a stone's throw; and there was a telephone, which came with a typed list of useful local numbers kept clean in a plastic folder. Downstairs were two bedrooms, both equipped with two single beds, bedside tables, reading lamps, and built-in wardrobes. There was also a spacious sitting or reading room, with glass doors to a patio under a striped, wind-down canvas awning. And lastly a small toilet and bathroom; no bath as such but a tiled shower recess and all the rest of the amenities. Upstairs didn't matter.

When Papastamos was through, he automatically assumed he wouldn't be needed anymore that night; but when he went back out to the taxi, Darcy followed him, saying, "Manolis, we really don't know how to thank you. I mean, how do we pay for all of this? Oh, we can pay—of course we can—but you'll have to tell us how, and how much, and . . . et cetera."

The other shrugged. "It's on the Greek government."

"That's very kind," Darcy said. "We really would have been lost without you. Especially at a time like this, with so much on our minds. For Layard and Jordan, they really are—or were—two of our very closest friends."

At last Papastamos turned to him. "My friends too!" he said, with a lot of feeling. "I only knew them for a day or two, but they were nice people! And I tell you, not everyone I meet is so nice!"

"Then you must understand how we feel," Darcy answered, "who knew them a long time."

Papastamos was quiet a moment then shrugged again, perhaps apologetically, and nodded. "Yes, of course I understand. Is there anything else I can do?"

"Oh, indeed there is!" Darcy knew it was all right between them now. "Like I said: we'd be lost without you. And that still goes. We'd like you to exert whatever pressure you can to get that autopsy over and done with, and then to have poor Ken Layard cremated as soon as possible. And that's just for starters. You'll also need to keep tabs on this gang of drug smugglers, for right now you're the only one who knows anything about them! We will eventually have some more people flying out, and you'll also be required to brief them. And finally, if it's at all possible . . . do you think you could arrange a car for us?''

''No problem!'' said the other, expansive as ever. ''It will be here tomorrow morning.''

''Then that's about it for now.'' Darcy smiled. ''We'll just trust you to see to your end of this thing, for after all, that's what's most important. And you must trust us to do the things we have to do. We're all experts in our different ways, Manolis.''

Papastamos scribbled a number on a scrap of paper. ''You can get me here anytime,'' he said. ''Or if not, you'll get someone who knows where I am.''

Darcy thanked him again and said good night. And as the taxi drew away he went back in through the squeaking gates . . .

The three went out to eat, and to talk.

''But why out?'' Darcy wanted to know after they'd found a taverna fronting on a quiet street—with small stairways to private tables on internal balconies, out of earshot of other patrons—and when they were seated in just such privacy. ''I mean, wasn't the villa private enough?''

''It could have been too private,'' Harry told him.

''Too private?'' Sandra was still a little shaky from the brief mental contact she'd made with something unthinkable in the mind of Trevor Jordan.

''There are people here.'' Harry tried to explain something he wasn't himself sure of. ''Other minds, other thoughts. A background blanket of mental activity. You two should understand that better than I do. I don't want us to be found out, that's all. You think you espers are clever? Well, and so you are—but the Wamphyri have powers, too.''

Wamphyri! It was a word Darcy Clarke couldn't hear without remembering the Yulian Bodescu affair. And he felt a familiar shiver down his spine as he asked, "And you believe that's what we're up against, right? Another like Bodescu?"

"Worse than that," Harry answered. "Bodescu was an open book compared to this. He didn't know what was happening to him. He wasn't an innocent himself—hadn't even been innocent from a time before he was born—but he was an innocent in the ways of the Wamphyri. He was a beginner, a child learning how to run before he could walk. And he made mistakes, kept falling down. Until one of his falls was fatal. But this one isn't like that."

"Harry," said Sandra, "how do you know these things? How do you know what we're up against? Yes, I sensed a mind in there with Trevor's, a powerful, totally evil mind . . . but couldn't it have been another telepath? They were on a drugs job, Ken and Trevor. What if the big-league criminals have set up their own ESP units? It could happen, couldn't it?"

"I doubt it," Harry answered. "From what I've seen of espers they don't work for other people."

"What?" Darcy was surprised. "But we all do. Ken, Trevor, Sandra, myself. And you, once upon a time."

"Worked for a cause," said Harry, "for an idea, a country, for revenge. Not for the gain of other people. Would you, if you were as powerful as the one Sandra sensed? Would you sell your talent to a gang of thugs who'd destroy you the moment they began to fear you—which they would, eventually?"

"But what about Ivan Gerenko, who—"

"A madman, a megalomaniac!" Harry cut him off. "No, even the necromancer Dragosani was working for an ideal—the resurrection of old Wallachia. At least until his vampire took control. Listen: how many people know you have your talent, Darcy? And Sandra, how many people know you're a telepath? I've only known it myself for a few hours. You didn't go around advertising it, did you? Take it from me,

215

the ones who do tell all are the fakes. Mediums and spoon benders, mystics and gurus—fakes every one!''

Darcy snorted his derision. ''So you're saying that all of us espers are good guys, right?''

''No such thing.'' Harry shook his head. ''No, for there's plenty of wickedness in the world, even among 'all you espers.' But think about it: if you're evil and you've mastered a special talent, why would you want to sell it to someone else? Wouldn't you use it—in secret—to make yourself mighty?''

''The fact is,'' said Darcy, ''I've often wondered why they don't! The people in E-Branch, I mean.''

''I've no doubt that some do,'' said Harry. ''No, I'm not talking about E-Branch, but others, people we know nothing about. There must be many talents loose in the world. How do we know that so-called business acumen isn't just another talent? Did this man make a million because he has a 'knack' for wheeling and dealing, or was it because there's a special something guiding his hand? Something which he himself might not even know about? Is the war hero really as brave as we believe him to be, or has he—like you, Darcy, or even like Gerenko—got a guardian angel watching over him? Did you know that the casinos have a list of people they won't let in, professional gamblers who have the winning 'knack,' and that an awful lot of them are rich as Croesus?''

''That's all very well,'' said Darcy reasonably, ''but still you have no proof that this one is a vampire!''

''Proof, not yet,'' Harry answered. ''But evidence, plenty. Circumstantial, but still it's there.''

''Such as?'' said Sandra.

Perhaps exasperated, he turned to her. ''Sandra, the closest you've been to a vampire is in reading my case file. I take it you have read it? It's a standard text in E-Branch, as a guard against 'the next time.' But I do know what I'm talking about, and so does Darcy. So while I don't want to be hurtful, still I think you'd best just sit still and listen. Especially you, for we don't yet know that when you saw him—whoever he is—in Trevor's mind, he didn't see you!''

She gasped and sat up straighter, and Harry reached across to pat her hand. "I'm sorry, but now maybe you can see what's worrying me. Some of it, anyway. Me? I've been here before, or at least in a similar position. But you? God, I don't want anything to happen to you!"

Darcy said, "But you did mention evidence."

Before Harry could answer, a waiter came to take their order. Darcy ordered a full meal, Sandra a salad and sweet, but Harry only asked for a portion of chicken and plenty of coffee. "A full stomach always makes me sleepy," he explained, "and alcohol is worse still! And I intend that you understand how deadly serious I am about this thing. But if you really want to drink that brandy, just go ahead, Darcy."

Darcy looked at his brandy glass and the large measure of golden liquid it contained, and put it aside.

"Evidence, then," said Harry. "For more than four years the dead haven't attempted to contact me. Or if they have, I haven't been aware of it. Oh, my mother may well have come to me in my dreams; in fact, I'm sure she has, for that's her nature. And yet now, suddenly, they've placed me in jeopardy. All right, the fact of them attacking Wellesley was circumstantial: they just happened to be there when he'd planned to murder me. But they *were* there, delivering a message. And they were doing it, possibly (a) for my mother, or (b) for themselves, out of their concern for me, or (c) for Ken and Trevor, who had been trying to reach me in my dreams."

Darcy frowned. "They'd been trying to reach you, telepathically? I didn't know that."

"Neither did I, until Ken Layard woke up and saw us, and spoke. A mental voice sounds just like the real thing to me, Darcy, and back in Scotland I'd been dreaming that people were trying to reach me, but I didn't know who they were. As soon as I heard Ken's real voice, then I recognised it. As to how they did it: Ken's a locator, he found me. And Trevor's a telepath; he helped send the message. Why me? Because I'm the so-called expert on what they both knew they were dealing with. And so they *should* know, because they, too, were in on the Bodescu affair."

217

Darcy nodded, licked his dry lips. He lifted his brandy and took the merest sip, dampening his mouth with it. "All right—what other evidence?"

"The evidence of my own senses," said Harry, "which, like yours, number more than five."

"Not any longer," Sandra pointed out—and at once bit her tongue, hoping he wouldn't take it the wrong way.

Harry didn't. Smiling, however wryly, he said, "I don't have to be able to talk to the dead to know the difference between a corpse and a live man."

Again Darcy frowned. "So what does that mean?" he asked. "The same goes for any one of us!"

"Have you ever walked down a silent, empty alley at night?" Harry asked him. "And all of a sudden you're certain someone is there? And sure enough, you see the flare of a match in a dark corner where someone is lighting a cigarette? Have you ever played hide-and-seek where you're it, and when you're searching for the other kids, you get this feeling right between the shoulder blades that someone is watching you? And when you look round, again one of them is there? I mean, not the sixth sense which you already know you possess, but just a sort of gut feeling?"

Darcy nodded, and Harry continued, "Well, just as you sense the presence of living people, so I sense the dead. I know when I'm in the company of dead men. Which is why I can tell you definitely that Ken Layard isn't! Even if I could still speak to the dead, I couldn't have spoken to Ken. For he's not dead. Oh, he's not alive either, but something in between. He's undead, in thrall to some other, and he'll rise up again as a vampire unless we make sure he's put down forever! That's what he was saying to me in my dream, what he was begging me to do: find him, finish him, put him down."

Again Darcy nodded. "And when he and Trevor couldn't get through to you, the real dead relayed their message, right?"

"Right," said Harry. "They tried to spell it out for me, in stone, right there in my garden."

Sandra shuddered. "God, but I just might have defied Wellesley, Harry! I might have been there with you when he came after you. Also when *they* came after him!" She shook her head. "I don't think I could bear it . . . to have seen those things!"

He reached out to clasp her hand across the table. "They're not just things," he said. "They were living people, once. And now they're dead people. Why, most of the soil and sand and sky and sea on or covering this entire planet was alive one time or another! It's the nature of things, and life's a stage we go through. But the dead think enough of me to transcend the natural order of things."

"And transcending the natural makes them . . . supernatural?" This from Darcy.

"I suppose it does," said Harry, turning his soulful eyes on him. "But didn't we think of vampires as being supernatural, once upon a time?" And at last he allowed himself a genuine smile, however wan. "You know, Darcy, for the head of E-Branch you're hellish sceptical! I mean, isn't this what it's always been about? Gadgets and ghosts? The physical and the metaphysical? The natural and the supernatural?"

"I'm not sceptical," said Darcy, "for I've seen too much for that. It's just that I like things sorted out, that's all."

"And have I sorted things out for you?"

"I suppose you have. So . . . where do we go from here?"

"We go nowhere. We examine what we know, take a stab at what we don't know. And we try to prepare for what's coming. But frankly, if I were you two, I'd simply back right out of it."

"What?" Darcy wondered if his hearing was all right.

"You and Sandra. You should climb right aboard the next flight for home, go back to E-Branch, and utilise whatever powers are available to you from that end. We should play it like we played the Bodescu business: low-key, until we know what we're dealing with."

Darcy shook his head. "We're in it together. I can get the branch jacked up from right here. Maybe I'd better remind you: falling in harm's way isn't a habit of mine. My guardian angel? And anyway, what can you do on your own? Sandra was right, Harry. You're an ex-Necroscope. You don't have it anymore. Where talents are concerned, you no longer figure. And as you yourself pointed out, what happened in Bonnyrig was entirely coincidental: the dead won't be there to help you out every time. So let's face it, of the three of us you're the weakest! It isn't that you don't need us, more that we don't need you.''

Harry stared at him. "You need my expertise," he said. "And I've already stated the possible danger to Sandra. She really shouldn't be anywhere near me, and . . .'' And abruptly, he paused. But too late, for the damage was done. He never had been much good at subterfuge.

"Near you?" she said. "What does that mean, Harry?" It was her turn to trap his hand.

He sighed, looked away, finally said, "Look, we have a vampire here. Possibly of the old guard, but in any case not too far removed from the original strain, the Wamphyri themselves. And like I keep telling you, if only you'd listen, the Wamphyri have powers! Sandra, you looked in Jordan's head and there was this thing in there torturing him, questioning him—specifically about us. By now he probably knows all there is to know about E-Branch, and how we dealt with what Thibor Ferenczy left behind, and Yulian Bodescu, and . . . hell, anything he *wants* to know! But more especially he'll know about me. If not now, soon. And then he'll come for me. He can't afford not to, for he'll know his cover's blown. I'm Harry Keogh, the Necroscope, and I'm dangerous. I've killed vampires; I've caused vampire sources to be rooted out and destroyed; and locked away in my brain somewhere I have the secrets of deadspeak and the Möbius Continuum. Of course he'll come for me. *And* for you two, if you're with me. Now Darcy . . . okay, you have your talent, which protects you. But you're still a man, flesh and blood. You were born and you can die. And remember, this thing *knows* about your talent! If there's a way to dispose of you—or even better, to use you—he'll find it.''

"But surely that's my big advantage?" Darcy argued. "I already know how to kill him!"

"Oh?" said Harry. "And how will you find him? And if and when you do, do you think he'll lie still for you to stake him out? Man, he won't *wait* for you to find him—he'll come looking for you! For us! Look, I'll say it again: compared to this, Yulian Bodescu was a bumbling amateur!"

"Then I'll call in all the help I can get, from E-Branch. I can have ten of our best out here by tomorrow noon."

"Call them in to be slaughtered?" Harry's frustration was growing, turning to anger. With people as special and intelligent as these two, still he had to explain these things as if they were children. For compared to the Wamphyri they were children, and just as innocent. "But can't you see, Darcy," he tried again, "they don't know him. They don't know who or where he is."

Sandra spoke up, displaying all of her innocence and lack of experience for anyone to see. "Then it's a game of hide-and-seek," she said. "We'll keep our heads down and let him make his play. Or close him in through a system of elimination. Or—"

"We can use our locators," Darcy cut in, "like we did with Bodescu, and—" He paused abruptly and his scalp tingled. And: "Jesus!" he said, giving a nervous start as something of the enormity of the problem—and something of its true horror—suddenly hit him. And: "Our locators!" he said again. So that now Sandra, too, caught on.

"Oh, my God!" she said.

Harry nodded and allowed himself to flop slowly back in his chair. "I see we're starting to think," he said, almost without sarcasm. "Locators? A terrific idea, Darcy—except our enemy has fixed it so he may soon have a locator of his own. Yes, and Ken Layard's one of the best there is!"

The food arrived; gloomy and thoughtful, Darcy and Sandra only toyed with theirs; Harry tucked his away in short order, lit one of his very rare cigarettes, started on the coffee.

Darcy, silent for some time, said, "If it comes to it, we may have to burn Ken ourselves."

Harry nodded. "You can see why I was in a hurry."

"I'm a fool!" Sandra said suddenly. "I *feel* such a fool! Some of the utterly stupid things I've said!"

"No, you're not a fool." Harry shook his head. "Don't put yourself down. You're just loyal, brave, and human. You could no more think like a vampire than you could think like a cockroach! That's what it boils down to: being as devious as they are. But don't think that's a bonus. Believe me, it isn't. You can make yourself sick, trying to think like they do."

"Anyway," said Darcy, "I agree with you; Sandra has to get out of this."

"Yes"—Harry nodded—"and never should have been in, except there was no way we could know until we got here." He turned to her. "You must be able to see, love, how hampered we'd be? Oh, Darcy will get by okay—he always has—but I wouldn't even be able to think straight with you around. I'd be forever worrying about what you might bump into."

Sandra thought, *It's the first time he's called me "love" in . . . a day or two?* It felt like a long time anyway. But the wait had been worth it. "And what would I do?" she said. "Sit around back home and hope for the best?"

Darcy shook his head. "No, you'd coordinate E-Branch's efforts in my absence. With Wellesley out of the picture and me over here, things are bound to be tight. But you have firsthand knowledge of our situation, so you'll be invaluable as our liaison man—or woman. Also, you'll be kept fully in the picture, day to day, on what's happening. In fact you'll probably have so much on your plate that there won't be time to worry about Harry!"

And Harry said, "He's right, you know."

She looked at them, then looked away. "Well, I'll say one thing for it: at least I won't have to worry about things like . . . like burning poor Ken!"

Darcy looked at Harry. "How about it? How long do we have before . . . ?"

"It will only come to that—dealing with it ourselves—if the local authorities don't get a move on," Harry answered. "But out here, because of the heat and such, I should think they're normally pretty smart off the mark."

Darcy frowned. "But is there no official deadline—God, what a pun! I mean, before things start to get . . . problematic?"

"You mean: when does he get up and walk, right?" Harry shook his head. "No, there's no official deadline. How long did it take George Lake, Yulian Bodescu's uncle?"

"Three days and nights," Darcy answered at once. "They had just enough time to bury him before he was digging his way out again!"

"Oh, don't!" said Sandra, her eyes bright with horror.

Harry looked at her, felt sorry for her, but had to continue anyway. "Lake was textbook," he said. "But I don't think there are any strict rules. None I'd trust, anyway." He sat up straighter and looked around. "But you know, I was just thinking: for tourists we must look pretty miserable! Anyway, this place is filling up now. I suggest we get back to the villa. Let's face it, I could be wrong about the value of crowds; we could be just as safe there as we are here. And whichever, we still have to make our plans—and make the villa secure."

On their way back they were mainly silent. This far out from Rhodes central, and this early in the season, things weren't so busy. There was plenty of traffic on the roads, heading for the bright lights, but the sidewalks were almost empty. With the sea flat and shining on their right, beyond the promenade, and the Milky Way strewn like the dust of diamonds across the sky, it might have been very romantic. In other circumstances. But as they walked the pebble path to their door, even the plaintive, repetitive, molten silver calling of small Greek owls couldn't lift their mood.

As soon as they were inside Darcy went upstairs to check the windows while Harry tended to the downstairs windows and back door. Both doors were solid, with strong locks and good bolts. All the windows were fitted with shutters externally and thief locks internally.

"Couldn't be better," said Darcy as they got together again around a table in the sitting room.

"Oh, it could be," Harry contradicted him. "Remind me tomorrow to buy some garlic."

"Of course." Darcy nodded. "You know, I'd forgotten that entirely? It's so much a part of the fiction that it slipped my mind it's also part of the fact!"

"Garlic," Harry repeated, "yes. On Sunside the Travellers call it *kneblasch*. That's the root of its name in Earth's languages, too. It's the German *Knoblauch* and the Gypsy *gnarblez*." He grinned tiredly and without humour. "Another piece of useless information."

"Useless?" said Sandra. "I think it's as well if you give us all the useless information you can!"

Harry shrugged. "You can get a lot of it out of Darcy's 'fiction.' But if that's what you want . . ." And he shrugged again, but warned, "Except you must always remember, *nothing* is certain, not with a vampire. And no one—myself included—knows everything there is to know about them. What, everything? I don't know a tenth of it! But I do know that the closer you get to the source, to the original Wamphyri stock, the more effective the various poisons become. Garlic sickens them. Its stink offends as ordure offends us, even makes them ill. On Starside, Lardis Lidesci smears his weapons with oil of garlic. A vampire, struck with a weapon treated that way—arrow, knife or sword, whatever—will suffer hideously! Often the infected member must be shed, and another grown in its place."

Darcy and Sandra looked at each other aghast, but they said nothing.

"Then there's silver," Harry continued, "poison to them, like mercury or lead is to us. Which reminds me: we should be on the lookout for a couple of these fancy Greek paper knives—in silver or silver plate. Darcy, you saw those bolts I packed with my crossbow? They're of hardwood, rubbed with garlic oil, tipped with silver. And please don't ask me if I'm serious. On Starside the Travellers swear by these things, and stay alive by them!''

Starside! Darcy thought, staring at Harry. *The alien, parallel world of the vampires. He's seen it, been there and returned. He's had all that. And now he sits here, entirely human and vulnerable, and tries to explain these things to us. And somehow he doesn't get angry with us, and somehow he doesn't crack up and rant and rave. And he never quits.*

''Vampires,'' said Sandra, and felt herself thrilling to the word, even knowing she loathed it. ''Tell us about them, Harry. Oh, I know it's all in the files back at E-Branch HQ in London. But it's different coming from you. You know so much about them, and yet you say you know so little.''

''I'll tell you the several sure things I know about them,'' said Harry. ''They're devious beyond the imagination of human beings. They're liars each and every one, who on almost every occasion would rather lie than tell the truth—unless there's something of substantial value in it for them. They're expert in confusing any argument, adept at ambiguous and frustrating riddles, word games, puzzles and paradoxes, false similes and parallels. They're insanely jealous, secretive, proud, possessive. And as for their grip on life—or undeath—they are the most tenacious creatures in or out of Creation!

''Their source lies in the vampire swamps east and west of the central mountain range that divides Starside from Sunside. The legend is that at times they emerge as monstrous slugs or leeches to fasten on men and beasts. As to what degree of intelligence they possess at that stage: who can say? But their tenacity is there from square one. They live on the blood of the host and form a horrific symbiosis with him. The host is changed, materially and mentally. Sexless, the vampire 'adopts' the sex of its host, and it fosters in him—or in her—that lust for blood which eventually will sustain both of them.

''I said that the host is altered materially. That's true: a vampire's flesh is different from ours. It has within itself the power of regeneration. Lose a finger, an arm or leg, and given time, the vampire will replace them. That's not as weird as it sounds. A starfish does it even better. Cut a starfish up and throw it back in the sea, each part will grow a whole new animal! Likewise a gecko losing its tail, or the segmented cestode or tapeworm of men. But a vampire is no cestode worm. Lesk the Glut, an insane Wamphyri Lord, lost an eye in battle—and caused another to grow on his shoulder!

"As the vampire matures within its host, so that host's strength and endurance increase enormously. Likewise his emotions. Except for love, whose concept is alien to the Wamphyri, all other passions become a rage! Hate, lust, the urge to war, to rape, to torture and destroy all peers or opponents. But such evils as these are tempered by the vampire's desire for secrecy, anonymity. For he knows that if he is discovered, men won't rest until he's destroyed. That last applies specifically in this world, of course, for in their own they are, or were, the Lords. They *were*, until The Dweller and I brought their reign to ruin. But even before that there were certain Traveller tribes who would kill them if and when they could. My son and I . . . we didn't destroy them all. Sometimes I wish we had . . .

"So . . . when did they first come here, how, and where did they arrive? The first of them, in this world? Who knows? There have been vampires in all man's legends. Where is far easier: in ancient Dacia, in Romani and Moldova, in Wallachia. Which is all one and the same: Romania to you, on or close to the Danube. There's a gate there, a tunnel between dimensions, but mercifully inaccessible. Or very nearly so. I used it when I went to Starside, but that was before Harry Jr. stripped me of my talents."

Harry sat back and sighed. Time and its events were catching up with him. He looked very tired now, but nevertheless asked, "What else?"

However morbid, Sandra couldn't resist the fascination of Harry's subject. "What of their life cycles, their longevity? When I read the E-Branch files, it all seemed so fantastic! And you say their origin is the swamps; but what about before that? How did they get there in the first place?"

"That's like asking what came first, the chicken or the

egg," said Harry. "The swamps are their place, that's all. Why are there aborigines in Australia? How come we only find Komodo lizards in Komodo?

"As for their life cycles: they start in the swamps, as great leeches. That's how I understand it, anyway. They transfer to men or beasts, usually wolves. And incidentally, it's a theory of mine that the werewolf of myth is in fact a vampire. Why not? It lives on raw, red flesh and its bite can create another werewolf, can't it? Of course, for the bite is the passing of the egg, which carries the codes of both wolf and vampire!"

Suddenly Harry's haunted look became more haunted yet. "My God!" he whispered, shaking his head in wonderment. "And every time I think of that, I can't help thinking of my son. Where is he now, I wonder? Still on Starside, a vampire Lord? *What* is he now, that child of Brenda and me? For Harry's vampire came from a wolf!"

For long moments his soulful eyes were fogged, distant, lost. But then he blinked, stirred himself, came back to the present point in space and time. And:

"Their life cycles." He cleared his throat and continued. "Very well. So far we've traced the cycle from a swamp leech to a parasite in a human or animal host. But I called the partnership a symbiosis, and as you'll appreciate, that calls for give and take on both sides. Well, the parasite gets his keep, and learns from the mind of his host. And the host gets the vampire's healing powers, his proto-flesh, his skills for survival, and, of course, his longevity! Eventually the vampire will weld itself to its host's interior; it will become part of him, utterly inseparable. The two parts—even the brains—will slowly merge and become one. But in the early days the parasite retains a certain individuality. If an immature vampire senses extreme, inescapable danger to its host, it may even attempt to flee him. Dragosani's vampire did just that when I destroyed him. But to no avail; I destroyed it, too . . ."

A tremor had entered Harry's soft-spoken voice, and the gauntness was back in his face. It was a hagridden expression and hard to define, at least until he continued.

227

"Or again, an immature vampire may be driven out from its host, if you know the way. But always with . . . with disastrous results to the host." And now they knew he was talking about the Lady Karen and understood his mood.

He saw the looks on their faces and moved quickly on.

"Where was I? Oh yes: the life cycle. Well, you might be tempted to think that the rest of it is the weirdest of all, but is it really? Have a look at the amphibia, the frogs and newts. Or moths and butterflies. Or if you're happy to stick with parasites, how about the liver fluke? There's a horror if ever there was! But what makes the vampire worse is his evil intelligence, and the fact that in the end his will is ascendant, dominant, stronger than that of his host. So you see it isn't really give and take at all but total submission. And then there's the egg. Faethor Ferenczy passed on his egg to Thibor the Wallach by way of a kiss. He hooked the thing up out of his throat onto his forked tongue and thrust it down Thibor's throat! And from that moment forward, Thibor, warrior that he was, was doomed.

"Staked and chained and buried, undead for five hundred years, Thibor put forth a proto-flesh tendril and dropped his egg on the back of Dragosani's neck. The thing entered like quicksilver, passed through Dragosani's flesh, and fastened to his spine without even leaving a mark. And so Dragosani, too, was doomed. Now, Faethor was Wamphyri. He gave Thibor his egg, and so *he* became Wamphyri! Yes, and so would Dragosani be Wamphyri if I hadn't put an end to him.

"The egg, then, carries the true Wamphyri strain. Only the egg. And it may be passed on through a kiss, through intercourse, or simply hurled at its target host. So Dragosani was informed by Thibor Ferenczy himself, the old thing in the ground. Except Thibor, like all vampires, was a liar! Why, the old devil barely *touched* the undeveloped foetus of Yulian Bodescu, and the child was corrupted and vampirized before he was even born! And he had *all* the—stigmata?—of the Wamphyri. Every sign and symptom, yes, including the ultimate vampire skill of shape changing. Yulian *was* Wamphyri! But—

"Would he have developed an egg of his own? I don't know. It's entirely paradoxical, which is only what you'd expect of them." And Harry fell silent.

Sandra and Darcy had sat and listened in a sort of stupefaction to all of this. But now, when it seemed Harry was done, Darcy took it up. "Their varieties are equally baffling," he said. "It seems Bodescu infected his mother with a small piece of himself. We don't know what sort of piece or how, but hell, I can't say I'm sorry about that. He grew something monstrous in the cellars of Harkley House, an unbelievable thing that murdered one of our espers. And he grew it from one of his own wisdom teeth! This mindless, proto-flesh thing: he used it to infect his uncle, his aunt and cousin. It seems he vampirized all of them, in as many different ways. Even his damned dog!"

Harry nodded slowly and said, "Yes, all of that, and it's still not the half of it. Darcy, the Wamphyri of Starside had skills which the vampires of Earth, our Earth, seem to have forgotten, thank God! They could take flesh—Traveller flesh, trog flesh—and given time, shape it to their will. I've talked about or mentioned gas-beasts, which they breed for the methane they produce; but they make warriors, too, which you wouldn't believe even if you saw one!"

"I've seen one," Darcy reminded him.

"On film," said Harry, "yes—but you haven't seen one falling towards you out of the sky, every inch of it armoured and lethally equipped! And you haven't seen the bony, cartilage creatures they design *specifically* for the skins, ligaments, and skeletons with which they extend and provision their aeries! And God, you've neither seen nor could imagine their siphoneers!"

Sandra closed her eyes, held up her hand, and gasped, "No!" She'd read about the things called siphoneers in the Keogh files, and this was something she really didn't want to hear from Harry. She knew about the great placid, flaccid things in the heights of the vampire towers: how their living veins hung down through hundreds of yards of hollow bone

229

pipes, to siphon up water from the wells. And she knew, too, how all of these creatures and beasts had once been human, before vampire metamorphosis. And, "No!" she said again.

"Yes," said Darcy, "Sandra's right. And perhaps this was the wrong time to go through all of this anyway. God knows I shan't sleep!"

Harry nodded. "I rarely sleep," he answered, "peacefully."

And as if they had already agreed on it, though in fact it hadn't been mentioned, they carried three single beds out of the bedrooms into the large living room, set them up there around the central table, and prepared to sleep in the same room together. It might not be entirely civilised, but it was safest.

Harry brought out his crossbow from a holdall, assembled it, and fitted a bolt. He placed the loaded weapon between his and Darcy's bed, on the floor close to the table, where they weren't likely to step on it. Then, while the others used the bathroom to prepare for bed in their turn, he stretched out in an armchair and drew a blanket up over himself. If he became uncomfortable later, he could always stretch out on his bed then.

And in the darkness and quiet of the room, where only a haze of grey light came in through the louvres, Darcy yawned and asked, "What plans for tomorrow, Harry?"

"To see to Ken Layard," Harry answered without hesitation, "to get Sandra on a plane for home, and to see what can be done for Trevor Jordan. We should try to get him out of here as soon as possible. To distance him from the vampire should be to lessen the thing's influence. Again I suppose it's up to the local authorities and what they say. But let's deal with all that in the morning. Right now I think I'll be happy just to make it through the night."

"Oh, I'm sure we will," said Darcy.

"You feel . . . easy, then?"

"Easy? Hardly that! But there doesn't seem to be anything bothering me especially."

"Good," said Harry. And: "You're a very handy man to have around, Darcy Clarke."

Sandra said nothing. Already she was asleep . . .

Harry did in fact sleep; he caught brief, troubled snatches of sleep in a series of short naps, never more than ten or fifteen minutes at a time . . . for the first few hours, anyway. But in the wee small hours his exhaustion caught up with him and his sleep grew deeper; and now the dead, no longer able to communicate with his conscious mind, could at least try to get through to him.

The first was his mother, whose voice came to him from far away, faint as a whisper on the winds of dream:

Haaarry! Are you sleeping, son? Why don't you answer me, Harry?

"I . . . I can't, Ma!" he gasped, expecting to feel his brain squeezed in a moment, and acid poured on the nerves of his mind. "You know that. If I try to talk to you, he's going to hurt me. Not him, but what he did to me."

But you are speaking to me, son! It's just that you've forgotten again, that's all. It's only when you're awake that we can't speak. But there's nothing to stop us when you're only dreaming. You've nothing to fear from me, Harry. You know I'd never hurt you. Not deliberately.

"I . . . I remember now," said Harry, still not quite sure. "But what's the use anyway? I won't remember what you tell me when I wake up. I never do. I'm forbidden to."

Ah, but I've found ways round that before, Harry, and I can try to do it again. I don't quite know how, for I sense you're a long way away from me, but I can always try. Or if not me, perhaps some of your other friends . . .

"Ma"—he was fearful now—"you have to tell them to stop that. You've no idea the pain they can cause me, the trouble they can get me in! And I have enough problems right now without adding to them."

Oh, I know you have, son, I know, she answered. *But there are problems and there are problems, and the solution is*

231

sometimes different. We don't want you to go solving them in the wrong way, that's all. Do you understand?

But in his sleep he didn't understand; only that he was dreaming, and that someone who loved him was trying her best to help him, however mistakenly, however misguided. "Ma," he said, suddenly angry with her, and with all of them, "I really wish *you'd* try to understand. You have to get it through your head that you're putting me in danger! You and the rest of the dead, all of you—it's like you were trying to kill me!"

Oh, Harry! she gasped. *Harry!* And he knew she was ashamed of him. *Now how can you say a thing like that, son? Kill you? Heavens, no. We're trying to keep you alive!*

"Ma, I—"

Haaarry! She was fading away again, going back where she belonged, as faint and distant as a forgotten name on the tip of your tongue, which won't shape itself no matter how hard you try. But then, in another moment, her deadspeak signal strengthened and he focused on her again. And:

You see, son, she said, *we don't worry too much about you that way anymore. It's no longer so painful to us to think that one day you might die. We know you will, for it comes to us all. And through you we've come to understand that death isn't really as black as it's painted. But between life and death there's another state, Harry, and we've been warned that you're straying too close!*

"Undeath!" It was his turn to gasp, as suddenly his dream turned sharp as reality. "Warned? By whom?"

Oh, she answered, *there are many talents among the dead, son. There are those you can speak to and trust, without fearing their words, and others you should never, ever speak to! At times you've moved without caution, Harry, but this time . . . one . . . evil . . . lost to . . . dark as . . . forever!*

Her deadspeak was breaking up, fading, dissolving. But what she'd been saying was important, he was sure. "Ma?" he called after her, into the gathering mists of dream. "Ma?"

Haaaaarrry! Her answer was the faintest echo, diminishing and . . . gone.

Then—

—Something touched Harry's face; he started and sat up a little in his armchair. And: "Wha . . . ?" he gasped as he came half-awake. Was that a fluttering just then? Had something disturbed the air of the room?

"Shhh!" Sandra mumbled from her bed somewhere in the darkness. "You were dreaming. About your mother again."

Harry remembered where he was and what he was doing here, and listened for a moment to the room's darkness and silence. And in a little while he asked, "Are you awake?"

"No," she answered. "Do you want me to be?"

He shook his head before realising she couldn't see him, then whispered, "No. Go to sleep."

And as he himself sank down again in dreams, once more he felt that faint fanning of the air. But sleep had already claimed him and he ignored it . . .

This time the voice came from the heart of a fog which rolled up out of Harry's dreams as dank and clinging as any fog he'd known in the waking world. It was clear, that voice; however distant, its signal was fixed and true; but it was dark, too, and deep and grinding and sepulchral as the bells of hell. It came out of the fog and seemed to surround Harry, pressing in on his Necroscope mind from all sides.

Ahhh! Beloved of the dead, it said, and Harry recognised it at once. *And so I have found you, despite the misguided efforts of those who would protect you from a very old, very dead, very harmless thing.*

"Faethor," Harry answered. "Faethor Ferenczy!"

And: *Haaarry Keeooogh,* crooned the other, his voice seething. *But you do me honour, Harry, with this stress which you place upon my name! Is this awe which I sense in you? Do you tremble before the power I once represented? Or is it something else? Fear, perhaps? But how so? What, fear? In one who was always so fearless? Now tell me: what has changed you, my son?*

"No son of yours, Faethor," Harry at once answered, with

something of his old spirit. "My name is clean. Don't try to taint it."

Ahhh! The gurgling, hissing, monstrous thing smiled in his mind. *But that's better. So much better to be on familiar termsss.*

"What is it you want, Faethor?" Harry was suspicious, careful. "Is it that you've heard the dead whispering of my fix and so you've come to taunt me?"

Your fix? Faethor feigned surprise, but not so much as to disguise his oozing sarcasm. *You are in a fix? But is it possible? With so many friends? With all the teeming dead to advise and guide you?*

Even dreaming, Harry was well versed in the ways of vampires—even the "harmless," expired variety. "Faethor," he said, "I'm sure you know well enough the problem. But since you've asked, I'll state it anyway: I'm Necroscope no longer, except in my dreams. So enjoy my predicament all you can, for awake it's a pleasure you'll never know."

Such bitterness! said Faethor. *And there, I thought we were friends, you and I . . .*

"Friends?" Harry felt inclined to laughter, but controlled it. Better not unduly antagonise one of these, not even one as surely dead and gone forever as Faethor. "In what way friends? The dead are my friends, as you've pointed out, and to them you're an abomination!"

And so you deny me, said the other, *and the cock not yet crowed three times.*

"That is a great blasphemy!" Harry cried.

And he sensed Faethor's vile, yawning grin. *But of course it is. For I am a great blasphemy, Haaarry! In the eyes of some . . .*

"In the eyes of all," said Harry. "In the eyes of sanity itself, Faethor." And with finality: "Now leave me, if you've done with mocking. There must be better things to dream."

Your memory is short! the other now snarled. *When you sought advice, you came to me. And did I turn you away? Who was it destroyed your enemy in the mountains of the Khorvaty?*

234

"You aided me because to do so suited you own ends, and for no other reason. You assisted me in order to strike at Thibor, and so avenge yourself a second time even from the grave! You tossed down Ivan Gerenko from the cliffs guarding your castle because he had caused it to be destroyed. You did nothing for me. In fact and as I see it now, you used me more than I used you!"

So! Faethor snapped. *Not quite the fool I thought! Little wonder you prevailed, Harry Keogh! But even if what you say is true, still you must admit that the advantage was mutual?*

And now Harry knew that the old vampire wasn't here simply to mock; no, there was more to it than that. That much was made perfectly obvious by Faethor's manner of expression, his use of the words "mutual" and "advantage." And Harry wondered, would their conversation now prove mutually advantageous? What did the monster want, and perhaps more importantly, what was he willing to exchange for it? Only one way to find out.

"Out with it, Faethor," said Harry. "What is it you want from me?"

Shame on you! said the other. *You know how I like a good argument: the persuasion of unassailable logic, the deft manipulation of words, the skillful haggling before a bargain is struck. Would you deny me these simple pleasures?*

"Spit it out, Faethor," said Harry. "Tell me what you want, and also what it's worth to you. And only then—if I can deliver and still live with myself—only then let's talk about bargains."

Bah! the other answered; but was equally quick to follow up, *Very well.* And without more ado: *I have heard it from the dead that you are come upon hard times. Yes, I admit it, I knew that you had been stripped of your powers. Oh, it's true, I am a pariah among the dead, but sometimes when they talk, it pleases me to "overhear" what is said. Much has been said about you, Harry Keogh, and I have overheard it. Not only are you forbidden to deadspeak, but you no longer command the facility of instantaneous transportation. This is all true?*

"Yes."

So. (Harry sensed Faethor's curt nod.) *Now, I know nothing of this . . . teleportation? And so in that sphere may not help you. It involves numbers, I believe—the simultaneous resolution of myriad complicated equations?—and in that I admit to a failing. I am out of touch by a thousand years, and even in my heyday was never much of a mathematician. But as for the question of deadspeak, there we might come to some agreement.*

Harry tried not to show his eagerness. "An agreement? You think you can return it to me? You don't know what you're saying. Experts have handled my case. In my waking hours I can no more speak to the dead than pour acid in my ears! That is, I can, but the result would be the same. I know for I've tried it—once! And also because it was forced upon me—once!"

So, said Faethor again. *And I have also heard it whispered by the dead that this mischief was worked upon you by your own son in a world other than this world. Astonishing! So, you found your way there, did you? Aye, and suffered the consequences . . .*

"Faethor," said Harry, "get to the point."

The point is simple. Only the Wamphyri could so interfere with your mind, and even then only one of their most powerful. It was the art of fascination—hypnotism—as used by a great master of that art, which crippled you, Harry Keogh. Ah, and I pride myself that I, too, was just such a master!

"You're saying that you can cure me?"

Faethor chuckled darkly, for he knew as well as Harry himself that the ex-Necroscope was hooked. *What is written may be erased,* he said, *as you now appreciate. But just as surely, what is set askew may be put to rights! Only put yourself in my hands, and it shall be done . . .*

Harry shrank back. "Put myself in your hands? Let you into my mind, as Dragosani once let Thibor into his? Do you think I'm mad?"

I think you are desperate.

"Faethor, I—"

Now listen to me, the long-extinct vampire interrupted. *I have spoken of mutual advantage, and of the dead whispering in their tombs. But some of them do more than merely whisper. In the mountains of the Metalici and Zarundului there are those who cry out in their very* terror *of that which is risen up! For not even the centuries dead—not even their bones and their dust—are safe from this one! Aye, and I know his name, and I deem myself responsible.*

And now Harry was hooked more surely than ever, but like a fish on a line he intended to give the vampire a good run for his money. "Faethor," he said, "you're saying that one of the Wamphyri has come among us. But I already knew this. Where's the advantage in that? Was I supposed to deliver my mind into your hands for such a scrap as this? You *do* think I'm mad!"

No, I think you are dedicated. To the eradication of what you term a foulness. You would destroy it before it destroys you. You would do it for the safety and sanity of your world, and I would do it . . . solely for my satisfaction. For I hated this one even as I hated Thibor!

"Who was he?" Harry shot the question, hoping against hope to catch the other out and read the answer in his startled mind.

But Faethor only tut-tutted, and Harry sensed a saddened, disappointed shake of his head. *No need for that, my son,* he said, oh so quietly, *for I'll gladly tell you his name. Why not? For you won't remember it when you awaken. His name—his most hated, despised name—was Janos!* And such was the venom in his voice that Harry knew it was true.

"Your son." He sighed, nodding. "Your second son, after Thibor. Janos Ferenczy! So now at least I know who I'm up against, if not what."

The who of it is Janos, said Faethor, *and without my help the what of it will destroy you utterly!*

"Then tell me about him," Harry answered. "Tell me all you can of him, and I'll try to do the rest. You've bargained well. I can't refuse you."

237

Again Faethor chuckled. And: *Indeed your memory is short,* he said. *It will last only as long as your dream!*

Harry saw that it was true and his frustration turned to anger. "Then what has been the point? Did you only come to mock me after all?"

Not at all, I came to seal a bargain. And it is sealed. You will come to me where you know I lie, and we shall speak again—but the next time you'll remember!

"But I won't even remember this time!" Harry cried out.

Ah, but you will, you will. Faethor's fading voice came echoing out of the rolling fog. *You'll remember something of it, at least. For I've seen to it, Harry. I've seen to it, Haaarry Keeooogh!*

"Harry?" Someone stood beside him, bent over him.

"Harry!" Sandra's urgent hand was on his arm; and Darcy Clarke hurrying to answer a banging at the door, where Manolis Papastamos was shouting to be let in; and a feeble dawn light struggling to find cracks in the louvres.

Harry leaped awake, lurched upright like a drunkard, and almost overturned his chair. But Sandra was there to support him. He held her close, and in another moment Darcy and Manolis were in the room.

"A terrible thing! A terrible thing!" Manolis kept repeating as Darcy opened a window and shutters to let in the pale light of a newly dawning day. But as the room sprang to life so Manolis' jaw fell open and he pointed a trembling hand at a huge Greek tapestry covering the better part of one entire wall. The tapestry was moving!

"God almighty!" Darcy gasped as Sandra clung to Harry more tightly yet.

The tapestry was a panorama of banded blue sky over brown mountains and white villages, but printed on the sky in letters eighteen inches high was a name: FAETHOR. And it was printed in fur that crawled!

Already Harry's dream was forgotten, but he would never in a lifetime forget his waking conversations with this father of vampires. "Faethor!" he gasped the word out loud. And as if it were some word of power, the name at once broke up the legend written on the tapestry—into a hundred individual bats! No bigger than winged mice, they released their hold on the fabric and whirled around the room once before escaping through the open window.

And: "So it's true," said Manolis Papastamos, white and trembling, the first to regain command of his senses. "It all comes together. I had thought Ken Layard and Trevor Jordan were the strange policemen, and you three stranger still! But of course, because you hunt the strange criminal!"

Sandra caught a telepathic glimpse of his mind, and knew that he knew.

"You should have told me from the beginning," he said, flopping down into a chair. "I am a Greek and some of us understand these things."

"Do you, Manolis?" said Darcy. "Do you?"

"Oh, yes," said the other, nodding. "Your criminal, your murderer, he is the Vrykoulakas. He is the vampire!"

IX: Cat and Mouse

"I UNDERSTAND WHY YOU DIDN'T TRUST ME," SAID PAPA-
stamos, "but you should have. What? You think the Greeks
are ignorant of these things? Greeks, of all people? Listen, I
was a boy in Phaestos on the island of Crete, born and lived
there until I was thirteen. Then I went to my sister in Athens.
But I never forgot the myths of the islands, and I never forgot
what I saw and heard there. Did you know that there are
places in Greece even now where they put the silver coins on
the eyes of the dead, to keep them closed? *Hah!* Those slits
in the eyes of Layard. He kept opening his eyes!"

Darcy said to him, "Manolis, how could we know? If you
took a hundred people and told them you were hunting a
vampire, how many do you think would believe you?"

"Here in Greece, in the Greek Islands, ten or twenty,"
the other answered. "Not the young peoples, no, but the old
ones who remember. And up in the mountains—in the mountain villages of Karpathos, for example, or Crete, or better
still in Santorin—maybe seventy-five out of a hundred! Because the old ways die hard in such places. Don't you know

where you are? Just look at a map. Six hundred miles away is Romania! And do you think the Romanian peoples don't know the Vrykoulakas, the vampire? No, no, we are not the innocent children, my friends!''

"Very well," said Harry, "let's waste no more time. You know, you understand, you believe—we accept that. But still we warn you that myths and legends can be very different from the real thing."

"I'm not so sure." Manolis shook his head. "And in any case I have had the experience of the real thing! When I was a boy thirty years ago, there was a sickness. The children were growing weak. An old priest had lived on the island in a remote place in the stony hills. He had lived there, all alone, for many years. He said he was alone for his sins and dared not surround himself with people. Recently he had been found dead in his place and they had buried him there. But now the village priest went there with the people—with the fathers of the sick children—and dug him up. They found him fat and red and smiling! And how did they deal with him? I heard it later with a wooden spear through the heart. I cannot be sure, no, but that night there was a big bonfire in the hills, and its light was seen for miles around!''

"I think we should tell Manolis everything," said Sandra.

"We will." Harry nodded. "But first he came here to tell us something."

"Ah!" Manolis gave a start and stood up. "My God, but now this vampire you hunt—there are two of them!"

Harry groaned. "Ken Layard!"

"Of course, the poor Ken. This morning, one hour ago, I get the call. It is the morgue. They have found the naked body of a mortician. He is dead with a broken neck. And Ken Layard's body has disappeared. And then"—he spoke directly to Harry—"then I remember what you say about Layard being undead, and that you want him burned very quickly. And then I know. But this is not all."

"Go on, Manolis," Darcy prompted him.

"The *Samothraki* has been absent from the harbour since the night of the trouble under the old windmills, when I saved

Layard from the sea. This morning the fishermen have brought in many pieces of burned wreckage. It is—it was— the *Samothraki*! And still there is more. A girl, a prostitute, died on the street three, four nights ago. She has been examined. The doctor says it could have been anything: not eating—the, how do you say, malnutrition?—or perhaps she fainted and lay in the alley all night, and so died of the exposure. But most likely it is the anaemia. *Hah!* You know this anaemia? No blood in the body? My God—anaemia!''

"Like a plague!" Harry groaned. "She must be burned, too.''

"She will be," Manolis promised. "Today. Believe me, I will see to it!''

Sandra said, "And still we're no closer to discovering who the vampire is, or what he's done to Ken. And I for one would like to know how those bats got in here . . .''

Harry indicated a domed wood-burning fireplace where its flue went up into a brick wall. "At least there's no great mystery there," he said. "As to Layard: he's now in thrall to this thing and, depending how strong his will is, serving it faithfully. And the vampire's identity? Well, there's a clue I can follow up. I think I may know someone who has the answer.''

"What clue?" Manolis faced him. "Any clue—all clues— are for me! No more secrets. Also, I want to know about that word the bats made on the wall: what did it mean?''

"That's the clue," said Harry. "Faethor fixed it so that I couldn't mistake his meaning. He wants me to go and see him!''

Frowning, Manolis looked from face to face. "This Faethor who *fixes* such things, and in such a way. He is . . . what?''

"No more secrets?" said Harry wryly. And: "Manolis, even if we had an entire day to waste, still we couldn't tell you everything. And even you wouldn't believe it all if we did.''

"Try me!" Manolis answered. "But in the car. First you dress and I take you to breakfast, then to the police station in town. I think is the safest place. And meanwhile you tell me everything.''

"Very well, we will," Darcy agreed. "But we must be allowed to get on with this thing in our own way. And Manolis, we have to be sure that all of this will go no further than you . . .''

"Anything you say.'' The other nodded. "And anything I can help you with, I will. You are the experts! But please, we are wasting the time. Hurry now.''

They got dressed as quickly as they could . . .

By midmorning their plans were finalised, and by noon Manolis Papastamos had set them in action. Once he'd known what was to be done, he wasted little time doing it.

Harry Keogh was now the owner of a suitably worn and well-thumbed Greek passport, stamped with a visa for Romania. Ostensibly, its bearer was an "international dealer in antiques" (a cover which had brought a wry smile to Harry's face), one "Hari Kiokis," a name which shouldn't give him too much trouble. Sandra had been fixed up with a flight to Gatwick, London, leaving Rhodes at 9:10 that night, and Darcy would stay here and work with Manolis. E-Branch had been put as completely in the picture as possible, but for now Darcy hadn't called in any esper help. First he must ascertain the size of the problem, and after that he'd call on help as required and available directly through Sandra.

Harry's flight to Bucharest via Athens was at 2:30; with an hour to spare, he and the others had lunch on the high balcony of a taverna overlooking Mandraki harbour. And it was there that one of the local policemen found them, with information for Papastamos.

The man was fat and sweaty, scarred and bowlegged; if he hadn't been a policeman, then he must be a brigand. He arrived in the road down below their balcony on a tiny moped which his huge backside almost entirely obscured. "Hey, Papastamos!" he shouted, waving a fat arm. "Hey, Manolis!"

"Come on up," Manolis called down to him. "Have a beer. Cool down."

"You won't feel so cool in a minute, Inspector!" the other called back, entering the taverna and panting his way upstairs.

When he arrived, Manolis offered him a chair, said, "What is it?"

The other got his breath back, and in wheezing Greek told his story. "Down at the mortuary, at the hospital," he began. "We were recording statements about the missing corpse—" He glanced at Manolis' company and quickly shrugged his apologies in the Greek fashion. "I mean, about the circumstances in the case of your dead English friend. We took statements from everybody, like you said. There was this girl, a receptionist who was on duty the night you saved his life. She said in her statement that someone went to see him in the early hours of the morning. It was her description of this one that I found interesting. Here, read it yourself."

He took a crumpled, sweat-stained official statement form from his shirt pocket and handed it over. Manolis quickly translated what he'd been told, then read the statement. He read it a second time, more thoroughly, and his forehead creased into a frown. And: "Listen to this," he said, reading aloud.

"It must have been about six-thirty in the morning when this man came in. He said he was a captain and one of his crew had gone missing. He'd heard how someone had been rescued from the sea and wondered if it was his man. I took him to see Mr. Layard in his room where he was sedated. The captain said, 'Ah, no, this one is not mine. I have troubled you for nothing.' I began to turn away but he didn't follow me.

"When I looked back, he was standing with his hand on the bump on Layard's head, and he said, 'This poor man! Such an ugly wound! Still, I am glad he is not one of mine.'

"I said he must not touch the patient and showed him out. It was strange: although he said he was sorry for Layard, still he was smiling a very peculiar smile . . ."

Harry had slowly straightened up in his chair as he listened to this, and now he asked, "And the description?"

Manolis read it out, and mused, "A sea captain; very tall, slim, strange, and wearing dark glasses even in the dawn light. I think . . . I think I know this one."

The fat policeman nodded. "I think so, too," he said. "And when we were watching that flea pit the Dakaris, we saw him come out of there!"

"Hah!" Manolis thumped the table. "The Dakaris? It's a spit away from where they found that poor whore!" And at once: "I'm sorry, Sandra."

"Who is he?" Harry demanded.

"Eh?" Manolis looked at him. "Who? Oh, I'll do even better than that and show you where! *There* he is!" And he pointed across the harbour.

The sleek white motor cruiser was slicing her way out of the harbour through the deep-water channel, but the distance wasn't so great that Harry's keen eyes couldn't read her name. "The *Lazarus*!" he breathed. "And the name of the owner?"

"The same, almost," said Manolis. "Jianni Lazarides!"

"Jianni?" Harry's face was suddenly drawn, lined, grey.

"Johnny." Manolis shrugged.

"John," Harry repeated him. And in the back of his mind another voice—or the memory of one—said, *Janos*!

"Ahhh!" Harry clasped his head as pain lanced through his skull. It was sharp but short, nothing so bad as a full-scale attack, a mere warning. But it confirmed his worst suspicions. For Janos could only be a name he'd learned from the dead—perhaps from Faethor himself—with whom conversation had been forbidden. He unscrewed his eyes and let in the cruel sunlight and the concerned expressions of his friends. And: "I know him," he said when he could speak. "And now I know I'm right to go and see Faethor."

"But why, if we already know our man?" Darcy asked.

"Because we don't know him well enough," Harry told him as the pain quickly subsided. "And since Faethor spawned him, he's the one most likely to know how to deal with him!"

* * *

245

"Nothing has changed," said Harry as they drove into the airport in the car Manolis had provided. "Everything stands. I go to Ploiesti, to see if I can learn anything from Faethor. I'll spend the entire night there, even sleep in the ruins of his place if I have to. It's the only sure way I can think of to contact him. Sandra goes back home tonight—definitely! Now that this 'Lazarides,' Janos Ferenczy, controls Ken Layard, he can locate anyone he wants to. Anyone associated with me will be in danger, and more especially so here in the vampire's own territory." He paused and looked into each face in turn, then continued.

"Darcy, you stay here with Manolis, dig up everything you can on Lazarides, his crew, and the *Lazarus*. Go right back to the start of it, when they first appeared on the scene. Manolis can be of real assistance there; since Janos has chosen himself a Greek identity, it shouldn't be too hard for the Greek authorities to fill in his origins and background."

"Ah!" said Manolis, looking at Harry through his driving mirror. "One other thing. He has dual nationality, this one. Greek, yes—and Romanian!"

"Oh, my God!" Sandra gasped at once. And: "Harry, he can travel freely where you may only go with extreme caution!"

Harry pursed his lips, thought about it for a moment, and said, "Well, and maybe I should have expected as much. But that doesn't change anything either. By the time he knows I'm there, and if he tries to come after me, I'll be out again. Anyway, I've no choice."

"God, I feel so helpless!" Manolis complained as he parked the car and they all climbed out. "Inside, a voice says, 'Arrest this monster aboard his ship!' But I know that this is impossible. I understand we must not alert him until we know all about him. Also, Ken is in his hands, and—"

"Save it, about Ken," Harry cut in, heading for the departure lounge. "There's nothing anyone can do for him." He turned his haunted eyes on Manolis. "Except destroy him, which would be a mercy. And even then, don't expect him to thank you for it. Thank you? God, no! He'll have your heart out first!"

246

"Anyway," Darcy told Manolis, "you're absolutely right that we can't touch him yet. We've told you about Yulian Bodescu; he was an innocent, a child, by comparison with Lazarides. Harry thinks so, anyway. But once he knew we were onto him . . . we each of us lived in fear of hell until he was finally dead!"

"Is all academic." Manolis shrugged. "What? I should go to the government and say, 'Send our gunboats to sink a vampire in his ship!' No, quite impossible. But when the *Lazarus* puts in to port again, I think I may be tempted to take out her crew one by one!"

"If you could isolate them, positively identify them as vampires, and had a good backup team who knew what to do and weren't frightened to do it, yes," said Harry. "But again this might be to tip Lazarides' hand, which in turn might precipitate something you couldn't even hope to control."

Guiding Harry and the others to the passenger control desk, Manolis answered, "Don't worry about it. I do nothing until I get your go-ahead. Is frustrating, that's all . . ."

Harry had only fifteen minutes to wait before being called forward. At the last minute Sandra said, "If we'd thought of it, I could have gone on with you to Athens and flown home from there. But things have happened so quickly I . . . I don't like seeing you go off like this, on your own, Harry."

He held her very close and kissed her, then turned to Darcy and Manolis. "Listen, I'm coming back, I promise you. But if I should be . . . delayed, go ahead and finish things as best you can. And good luck!"

"That's my middle name," Darcy told him. "Take care of yourself, Harry."

Sandra hugged him again, and then he stood back, nodded, turned and followed the crowd out onto the dusty concourse, towards the landing strip.

Among the many people there to see friends off, a man in flip-flops, bright Bermuda shorts, and an open-necked white shirt watched Harry's plane take off. He was a Greek who

247

ran the occasional errand for the Russians. Now all he had to do was discover Harry's destination and pass it on.

Not too difficult. His brother worked at the passenger information desk . . .

Harry made his Athens connection and landed in Bucharest at 5:45. The airport and its perimeter were thick with lightly armed soldiers in grey-green shirts, drab olive trousers, and scuffed boots; but their presence seemed pointless and the men themselves aimless. This was a duty of long standing, out of which nothing had ever come. They didn't expect anything to come out of it and in all honesty weren't much interested. They were there because they'd been told to be.

As Harry passed through customs, the official stamping passports scarcely looked at him; all eyes were turned towards the three or four members of some foreign delegation or other, who were being given red-carpet treatment through the airport and out into the "freedom" of Romania. Harry reckoned he was lucky.

Manolis had fixed him up with one hundred and fifty American dollars, which he'd sworn were good as gold. He caught a taxi, dumped his holdall on the backseat, and told the driver, "Ploiesti, please."

"Eh? Ploiesti?"

"Right."

"You English?"

"No, Greek. But I don't speak your language." *And God, I hope you don't speak Greek!*

"Hah! Is funny! We are both speaking English, yes?" The man was unkempt and his breath was bad, but he seemed amiable enough.

"Yes," said Harry, "it's funny. Er, do you take dollars? American?" He showed him some green.

"Eh? Eh? The dollars?" His eyes stood out. "Sure, by gosh! I take it! Ploiesti is—I don't know—sixty kilometers? Is, er, ten dollars?"

"Are you asking?"

"*Is* ten dollars." He grinned, shrugged.

"Fine!" Harry handed over the money. "Now I sleep," he said, leaning back and closing his eyes. He didn't intend to sleep, but neither did he want to talk . . .

The Romanian countryside was boring. Even in springtime merging with summer there wasn't anything much of green to be seen. Plenty of browns and greys: piles of sand and cement, cheap breeze blocks and bricks. Enough building going on to rival all the coastal regions of Spain, Turkey, and the Greek islands put together. Except that this had nothing to do with tourism, for there was plenty of wrecking, too. The grotesque, inhuman mechanics of Ceausescu's agro-industrial policy: save money by cramming more and more people under one roof, like cattle in pens. Good-bye to peasant autonomy, the picturesque settlements, and village life; hello to the ugly, rearing tower blocks. And all the while the reins of political control drawn tighter.

Through eyes three-quarters shuttered, Harry scanned the land as it sped by beyond the windows of the car. The road-side en route from Bucharest to Ploiesti looked like a landscape in the aftermath of war. Bulldozers worked in teams in the poisonous blue haze of their rumbling exhausts, erasing small farming communities wholesale to fashion empty, muddy acres in their place; while other machines stood idle or exhausted alongside huge iron diggers with their bucket heads lifted and stretching forward, almost as if watching. And where once there were villages, now there was only earth and rubble and desolation.

"More than ten thousand villages in old Romania," Harry's driver, perhaps sensing that he was still awake, told him out of the corner of his mouth. "But old President Nicolae reckons that's about five thousand too many! What a madman! Why, he'd flatten the very mountains if someone would tell him how to go about it!"

Harry made no answer, continued to nod—but he wondered, *And what of Faethor's place on the outskirts of Ploiesti? Will Ceausescu flatten that, too? Has he perhaps already flattened it?*

249

If so, then how might Harry find it again? The last time he was here he'd come via the Möbius Continuum, homing in on Faethor's telepathic voice. (Or rather, his necroscopic voice, for it was only the dead Harry could speak to in this way; he wasn't a true telepath.) Faethor had spoken to him, and Harry had tracked him down. Now was different: he would only recognise Faethor's place, know it for sure, when he got there. As to its precise location . . . he knew only that the birds didn't sing there, and that the trees and bushes and brambles grew no flowers, developed no fruit. For the bees wouldn't go near them. The place was in itself Faethor's tombstone, bearing his epitaph which read:

> This Creature was Death! His very
> existence was a Refutation
> of Life;
> wherefore he now lies Here,
> where Life Itself refuses to
> Acknowledge him.

As the taxi passed a signpost stating that Ploiesti lay ten kilometers ahead, Harry shook himself, yawned, and pretended to come more properly awake. He looked at his driver.

"There were some rich old houses once on the outskirts of Ploiesti. The homes of the old aristocracy. Do you know where I mean?"

"Old houses?" The man squinted at him. "Aristocracy?"

"Then the war came and they were bombed," Harry continued. "Reduced to so much rubble. The authorities never touched the place; it was left as a sort of memorial—until now, anyway."

"Ah! I know it—or used to. But not on this road, no. On the old road, where it bends. Now tell me quick—is that where you want to go?"

"Yes. Someone I know used to live there."

"Used to?"

"Still does, as far as I know," Harry corrected himself.

"Hold on!" said the other, hauling his steering wheel hard

right. They bumped off the road onto a cobbled avenue that wound away at a tangent under huge chestnuts.

"It's along here," said Harry's driver. "Another minute and I'd passed it and would need to turn around and come back. Old houses, the old aristocracy, aye. I know it. But you came at the right time. Another year and it's gone. Your friend, too. They just knock 'em flat, these old places, and whoever lives there moves on or gets knocked down with 'em! Oh, the bulldozers will be here soon enough, wait and see . . ."

Half a mile down the road and Harry knew that this was it. The shells of old buildings began rising left and right behind the chestnuts, dilapidated places mainly, though a few of the chimneys still smoked. And: "You can drop me here," he said.

Getting out of the taxi and picking up his holdall, he asked, "How about buses? I mean, if I stay with my friend overnight, how will I go about getting back into town tomorrow morning?"

"Walk back to the main road, toward Bucuresti," the other told him. "Cross over onto the right and keep walking. Every kilometer or so, there's a bus stop. You can't miss 'em. Except—don't go offering dollars! Here, you've got some change coming. *Banis*, my Greek friend. *Banis* and *leu*—else people will wonder what's up!" And waving, he drove off in a cloud of dust.

The rest of it was instinct; Harry just followed his nose; he would soon discover he'd been a mile or so off target, but time and distance were passing quickly enough and he sensed he was walking in the right direction. He saw few signs of humanity: smoke from distant chimney stacks, and an old peasant couple who passed him going in the opposite direction. They looked weary to the bone and pushed a cart piled high with sticks of furniture and personal belongings; without knowing them or their circumstances, still Harry felt sorry for them.

Pretty soon he felt hungry, and remembering a pack of salami sandwiches and a bottle of German beer in his holdall, he left the road through a gate into an ancient cemetery. The graveyard didn't bother him; on the contrary, he felt at home there.

It was as extensive as it was rundown, that old burial ground; Harry walked through the ranks of leaning, untended, lichen-crusted slabs until he reached the back wall, well away from the road. The old wall was two feet thick but crumbling in places; Harry climbed it where its stones had tumbled into steps and found himself a comfortable place to sit. The sunlight slanted onto him through the trees, reminding him that in just another hour the sun would be down. Before then he must be at Faethor's place. Still, he wasn't worried. He felt that he must be pretty close.

Eating his sandwiches (which had kept remarkably well) and draining the sweet lager, he looked out over the sea of leaning slabs. There'd been a time when the occupants of this place wouldn't have given him a minute's peace, and when he wouldn't have expected it. He'd have been among friends here, all of them bursting to tell him what they'd been thinking all these years. And it wouldn't matter at all that they were Romanian, for deadspeak—like its twin, telepathy—is universal. Harry would have understood them perfectly well, and to a man they'd understand him.

Ah, well . . . that was then and this was now. And now he was forbidden to speak with them. Except he must find a way to speak to Faethor.

As that name crossed his mind so a cloud passed over the sun and the graveyard fell into shade. Harry shivered and for the first time turned and looked behind him, out of the cemetery. There were empty fields back there, crisscrossed with bramble-grown tracks and paths, where the land was humped in places and spotted with ruins, and the overgrown scars of old craters were still plainly visible. Closer to the main road a half mile away, the ground had been made swampy where the bulldozers had been at work interfering with the natural drainage.

Harry scanned the land with the eye of memory, superimposing the current scene and the scene remembered, and slowly the two pictures merged into one. And he knew that the taxi driver had been right: another year, maybe only a month, and he would be too late. For one of these crumbling piles was surely Faethor's, and pretty soon the bulldozers would level it, too, into the earth forever.

Harry shivered again, got down from the wall on the other side, and made his way from ruin to ruin, searching for the right one. And as evening turned to twilight he found and knew the place at once, just from its feel. The birds kept their distance, singing muted evening songs in trees and bushes hundreds of yards away, so that they scarcely reached here at all; there were no bees or flying insects and the foliage bore neither flower nor fruit; even the common spiders kept well clear of Faethor's last place in all the world.It seemed a singular warning, and yet one which Harry must ignore.

The place was not exactly as he remembered it. The absence of adequate drainage had threaded it with small, stagnant streams, where every slightest hollow had become a pool. A veritable swamp, normally it would be alive with mosquitoes, but of course it was not. At least Harry needn't worry about being bitten while he slept. But that (being bitten) was a thought he could well do without!

In the deepening twilight he took out a sleeping bag from his holdall and made down his bed on a grassy hump within low, ivy-clad walls. Before settling, he answered the call of nature behind a crumbling mound of rubble some little way apart and, returning to his place, saw that he wasn't entirely alone here. At least the small Romanian bats weren't afraid of this place; they flitted silently overhead, then swept away to do their hunting elsewhere. Perhaps in their way they paid homage to the ancient, evil thing which had died here.

Harry smoked one of his rare cigarettes, then tossed away the stub like a tiny meteorite in the night to sizzle out in a small pool of water. Finally he pulled up the zipper on his sleeping bag and made himself as comfortable as possible, and prepared to face whatever his dreams would conjure . . .

Harry? The monstrous, gurgling voice was there at once, touching upon his sleeping mind without preamble. *So, and it would seem that you have come.* It sounded as close and vibrant as if a living person spoke to him, and Harry sensed no small measure of satisfaction in it. But in his dream, try as he may, he couldn't remember what he was doing here.

Oh, he knew Faethor's mental voice well enough, but not why the vampire had chosen to seek him out. Unless it was to torment him. And so he kept silent, for the one thing he did remember was that he was forbidden to speak to the dead.

What, all of that again? Faethor was impatient. *Now listen to me, Harry Keogh: I didn't seek you out but the other way around. It is you who visits me here in Romania. And as for being forbidden to speak to me—or to the dead in general—surely that is why you are here, so that I may undo what has been done to you!*

"But . . . if I speak to you"—Harry paused and waited for the pain to strike him down, which it did not—"there's this pain that comes and—"

And has it come? No, because you are asleep and dreaming. Conscious, you may not converse with me. But you are not conscious. Now tell me, pray, may we get on?

Now Harry remembered: asleep, his deadspeak couldn't hurt him. Oh yes, he remembered that now—and more than that. "I came . . . to find out about Janos Ferenczy!"

Indeed, Faethor answered, *that is one of the reasons why you are here. But it is not the only one. Before we consider that, however, first answer me this: did you come here of your own free will?*

"I'm here out of necessity," said Harry, "because there are vampires in my world again."

But did you come as a free man, as you yourself willed it? Or were you compelled by force, cajoled or coerced against your own natural desires?

By now Harry was fully "awake" in his dream and more surely aware of the vampire's wiles. Moreover, he'd grown as skillful in their word games as the Wamphyri themselves and knew that they were only a form of verbal manoeuvering. "Compelled?" he said. "Well, no one pushed me. Coerced?

254

On the contrary, my friends would have kept me back! But cajoled? Only by you, old devil, only by you.''

By me? Faethor played the innocent. *How so? You have a problem and I have the answer. Someone reached inside your head, grabbed up your brains, and tied a knot in them. I can perhaps untie it—if I feel inclined. Which I may not, so long as you create obstacles and make these accusations! So tell me quickly now: how have I cajoled you? In what way?*

"The way I understand it," said Harry, "the word 'cajole' has several meanings. To coax or persuade with flattery; to wheedle; to make delusive promises. It is to allure or inveigle so as to derive a point of personal gain. These are the meanings of the word. Ah, but when a *vampire* cajoles . . . then the object of the exercise is far less clear. And the consequences frequently dire.''

Hah! Harry sensed Faethor's exasperation, and his astonishment that a mere human being should attempt to try him with one of his own games! But he also sensed the vampire's shrug of indifference, and perhaps of finality. And: *Well,* said Faethor, *that says it all! You do not trust me. So be it; your journey is wasted; wake up and get yourself gone! I had thought we were friends, but I was mistaken. In which case . . . what care I that there are vampires in your world? To hell with your world, and with you, Harry Keogh!*

Harry wasn't about to fall for that one. He was supposed to plead now, for Faethor's audience. But Faethor would never have called him here just to dismiss him so casually. It was simply the way of vampires, that was all. A ploy to gain the upper hand. But just as some dreams are brilliantly clear and real as life, so this one was developing. Within it, Harry's wits were grown razor sharp.

"Let's have it out in the open, Faethor," he said abruptly. "For it suddenly dawns on me that while we've talked now and then, you and I, we've never actually met face-to-face. And I feel certain that if I could only see your earnest, honest face, why then, I'd be that much more at ease in your presence—and not need to stay so firm on guard!"

Oh? said the other, as if surprised. *And are you still here?*

But I could swear our conversation was at an end! Or perhaps you didn't understand me. Then let me make myself plain: GO AWAY!

Harry's turn to shrug. "Very well. And no great loss. For let's face it, I could never have relied on anything you said anyway!"

What? Now Faethor was furious. *And how many times have I assisted you, Harry Keogh? And how often have I borne you up, when I could—and should—have let you founder?*

"We've had this conversation before," said Harry, unperturbed. "Must we play it out again? If my memory serves me well, we agreed in a previous time that former liaisons had been to our 'mutual' advantage: neither one of us gained more than the other. So come down off your high horse and tell me truly, why now do you insist on this sinister ritual, that I should come to you of my own free will? And if I admit as much, under what obligation will I place myself, eh?"

Ahhh! sighed Faethor, after a moment. *And if only it could have been you, Harry Keogh, instead of blood-crazed Thibor or that scheming, devious lout Janos! If only I had chosen my sons more carefully, eh? Why, such as you and I could have ruled the world together! But . . . too late now, for Thibor got my egg and Janos was my bloodson. And now there's neither spark nor spunk left of me to form another.*

"If I thought for a moment there was, Faethor"—and even dreaming Harry shivered—"then believe me I wouldn't be here!"

But you are here, and so I beg of you, observe the formalities, that ancient "ritual" of which you speak so harshly and suspiciously.

"So now you beg of me," said Harry, "and still I ask myself: what's in it for you?"

Aye, and we've had that conversation before, too! Faethor cried. *Well then, if I must repeat myself: that bloodspawn of mine—that child of my human side, Janos—walks in the world of men again, and I cannot bear it! When Thibor was desperate to be up and about, who was it came to your aid in keeping him down, eh? I did, for I loathed the dog! And now it's the turn of Janos. What's in it for me, you ask? Well, when you destroy him, you might remember to tell him how his father helped you, and even now lies laughing in his grave! That will be profit enough.*

"What?" said Harry, speaking (and thinking) slowly and very carefully. "But surely that would be a lie, for nothing at all of you lies in any grave. You burned up in the fire that destroyed your house—didn't you?"

But you know I did! the other cried. *But still I am here, in a manner of speaking, for how else could I talk to you? It is my ghost, my spirit, the echo of a voice long vanished that you hear. It is your talent, your ability to speak with the dead, which in itself should be evidence enough of my extinction!*

Harry was silent awhile. He knew that it was tit for tat, this for that, and that he'd get nothing without first giving something. Faethor was eager, indeed insistent, that his rules should apply in any exchange here. And in the end it was plain the vampire would have his way, for Harry's cause was doomed without him. He thought these things, but yet contrived to hide such thoughts from Faethor.

Ah-ha! And now I see it! the other finally burst out. *You are afraid of me, Harry Keogh! Of me, a long-dead thing, burned up and melted away in a holocaust! But why now? What is different now? We are not strangers. This is not the first time we've come together for a common cause.*

"No," said Harry, "but it's certainly the first time I've bedded down with you! I've been here before, yes, but when I was awake. And other than that, I've only ever spoken to you across great distances, again via deadspeak, when there was no possible danger to me. And if there's one thing I've learned about vampires, Faethor, it's that when they seem at their most vulnerable, that's when they're most dangerous."

We're arguing at odds, getting nowhere, said the vampire, almost despairingly. But for all the "fatigue" he displayed, still Harry guessed that Faethor wouldn't be moved from his stand in this matter. Which meant there remained only one way to break the deadlock.

"Very well," he said, "and so one of us must give way. Perhaps I'm a fool, but . . . yes, I came of my own free will."

Good! the vampire grunted at once, and Harry could almost sense him smacking his lips. *A most wise and agreeable decision. And why not? For if I'm to observe your manners and customs, why should not you observe mine, eh?* They loved to win, these creatures, even in so small a thing as a contest of words. Perhaps that was all to the good, for now Faethor might find room to give way in other matters. And as if he had read Harry's thoughts:

And now we may face each other on equal terms. You desired to speak to me face-to-face? So be it.

Until now the dream had been blank and grey and unyielding, a place without substance except in the exchange of thoughts. But now the grey took on a gently swirling motion and rapidly dissolved down to a thickly misted plain under a slender horned moon. Harry sat on a ruined wall with his feet dangling in the ground mist where it lapped at his ankles; and Faethor, seated upon a heap of rubble, was a dark figure in a shrouding robe, whose hood cast his face in shadows. Only his eyes burned in that hollow darkness, and they were like tiny scarlet lamps.

And is this more to your liking, Harry Keogh?

"I know this place," said Harry.

Of course you do, for it is the same place but perceived as it shall be some small distance in the future. Oh yes, for that was one of my talents, too: to see a little way into the future. Alas, it was unreliable, else I'd not have been here that night they dropped their bombs!

"I see that the bulldozers have been at work." Harry looked all around. "This place of yours seems the only place left!"

For the moment, aye, Faethor answered. *A ruin on a low plain, surrounded by mud and debris, soon to become an industrial complex. And even if there were ears to hear me, who would listen to me then? What, through all of that hub-*

bub and mechanical chaos? How are the mighty fallen, Harry Keogh, that I am reduced to this? And perhaps now you can understand why Thibor was made to suffer, and in the end destroyed; and why Janos must go the same way. They could have had it all, everything, and instead chose to defy me. And should I haunt this place, alone, unloved and unremembered, while one of them is returned to the world, perhaps to become a power? Perhaps the *power? No, I shall not rest, until I know that Janos is as little or even less than I am—which is nothing.*

"And I'm to be your instrument."

Is it not what you want? Do not our objectives coincide?

"Yes," Harry agreed, "except I want it for the safety of a world, and you want it for your own selfish spite. They were your sons, Thibor and Janos. Whatever it is in them which you hate, they got it from you. It's a strange father who'll murder his own sons because they take too well after him!"

Faethor gloomed on him and his voice turned sly and insinuating. *Is it, Harry? Is it? And you're the expert, are you? Ah, but of course—certainly you would understand such things—for I've heard it that you have a son, too . . .*

Harry was silent; he had no answer; perhaps he would destroy his son if he could, or at least change him. But hadn't he also tried to change the Lady Karen?

Faethor took his silence as something else: a sign that perhaps he went too far. Now he was quick to change his tone. *But there, the circumstances are different. And anyway, you are a man and I am Wamphyri. There can be no meeting point except in our dual purpose. So let's make an end of criticisms and accusations and such, for there's work to be done.*

Harry was pleased to change the subject. "These are the simple facts," he said. "We both want Janos put down again, permanently. Neither one of us can do it on his own. For you it is absolutely impossible. Likewise for me, without my gift of deadspeak. You say you can return that talent to me; that

259

since it was taken from me by a vampire, only a vampire can return it. Very well, I believe you. What will it entail?''

Faethor sighed and seemed to slump down a little where he sat. He turned his red-glowing eyes away and looked out over the plain of mist. And: *We are come to that part from which I know you will shy most violently. And yet it is unavoidable.*

"Say it," said Harry.

The trouble lies in your head. A creature other than yourself has visited the labyrinth caves of your mind and wrought certain changes there. Let us say that within your house the furniture has been rearranged. Now another must go in and put the place in order.

"You want me to let you into my mind?"

You must invite me in, said Faethor, *and I must enter of my own free will.*

Harry recalled to mind all he knew about vampires, and said, "When Thibor entered Dragosani's mind, he tried to steer it his way. He interfered in Dragosani's affairs. When he touched the living foetus which would become Yulian Bodescu, that was sufficient to alter the child entirely and turn him into a monster. And again Thibor was in Yulian's mind, able to communicate with him and guide—or direct him— even over great distances. At this very moment a friend of mine on the island of Rhodes has a vampire, your bloodson Janos, in his mind, or at least controlling it. And my friend exists in a hell of terror and torment. And you want me to let *you* into *my* mind?"

I said you would shy from it.

"If I let it happen this once, how may I be sure it won't happen when I don't want it?"

I would remind you: distance removed Dragosani from danger. Even if what you suggest were possible, do you intend to stay here in Romania forever? No, for you have your own way to go, which will put you far beyond my reach. I would further remind you: Thibor was an undead thing in the ground—he was real, solid, intact in all his parts—while I

260

am but a wraith, dead and gone forever. A ghost, aye: empty, immaterial, incorporeal, and of no consequence whatsoever.

"Except to a Necroscope."

Except to you. Faethor's shade nodded its agreement. *The man who talks to and befriends the dead. Or used to.*

"So how do we go about it?" Harry asked. "I'm no telepath, with a mind like a book to be read."

But in a way you are, Faethor told him. *Is it not a form of telepathy to be able to talk to the dead? Also, when you, too, were without body, did you not speak to the living?*

"That was a strange time," Harry agreed. "It was my deadspeak. It worked in reverse. Being incorporeal, I had no voice, and so I could talk to the living—to those who had body—in the same way I talked to the dead!"

Again Faethor's nod. *There's more to your mind than even you suspect, Harry Keogh. And I say I can be into it even as Thibor was into Dragosani's!—but without the complications.*

Harry sensed Faethor's eagerness. He was far too eager but . . . there was no way around it. "What do I have to do?"

Nothing. Simply relax. Sleep a dreamless sleep. And I shall visit within your mind.

Harry felt Faethor's beguilement—his hypnotism—working on him and resisted it. "Wait! Three things I want. And if your mind-tricks work, perhaps a fourth, later."

Name them.

"First, that you undo the mischief done to my mind and return my deadspeak, as agreed. Second, that you give me some sort of defence against Janos's telepathy, for I've seen what he can do to minds such as mine. Third, that you look and see if there's any way I can regain access to the Möbius Continuum. It's the ultimate weapon against Janos and would surely tilt the odds in my favour."

And the fourth?

"When—if—I have my deadspeak back, I'll be able to find you again no matter where I am. And then, hopefully for the last time, I may ask for your help again. To free the mind of my friend Trevor Jordan, which Janos holds enthralled."

As for this last thing, the vampire answered, *if it can be*

261

done, then it shall be done in due course. But alas, access to this device of yours—teleportation?—we shall see what we shall see. However, I doubt it. It was not an art of mine; I know nothing of it; how may I unriddle something in a language I cannot speak? The language of mathematics is a stranger to me. On the other hand, your deadspeak is something I can surely put back to rights, for I understand it. Even when they were dead many hundred years, still my Szgany answered my call and got up from their graves! Lastly, you ask for some sort of defence against Janos's mindspells. Well, that is no simple thing; it's not any sort of gift I can will or bestow upon you. But later I shall describe to you how to fight fire with fire. Which may help . . . if you can stand the heat of it.

"Faethor." Harry was almost completely resigned to his fate now. "I wonder, will I thank you for this when it's done? Will there ever be thanks enough? Or will I curse you for all eternity, and will there ever be curses enough? Even now you could be plotting to destroy me, as you've destroyed everything else you ever touched. And yet . . . it seems I've no choice."

These things are not entirely true, Harry, Faethor answered. *Destroyed things? Aye, I've done that—and brought a few into being, too. Nor are you without choice. Indeed it seems to me the very simplest matter. Trust me now as an ally tried and true, or be gone from here and wait for Janos to seek you out—and when the time is come, go up against him like a child, naked and innocent of all his ways and wiles . . .*

"We've talked enough," said Harry. "And we both know there's only one course open to me. Let's waste no more time."

And: *Sleep,* said Faethor, his mental voice deep and dark as a bottomless pool of blood. *Sleep a dreamless sleep, Harry Keogh, leaving all the doors of your mind standing open to me. Sleep, and let me see inside. Ah, but even though you may will it freely, still I shall find certain doors closed to me—and closed to you! These are the ones which I must*

*unlock. For beyond them lie all your talents, which your son
has hidden from you.*

*Sleep, Harry. We are the betrayed, you and I, by our own
flesh and blood. We have this much in common, at least. Nay,
more than this, for we've both been powers in our time. And
you shall be . . . a power . . . again . . . Haaarry Keeooogh!*

The mist on the plain swirled as Faethor flowed to his feet
and approached Harry where he slumped on the broken wall.
The long-dead vampire reached out a hand toward Harry's
face . . . and the hand was white and skeletal, projecting
from the fretted sleeve of his robe like a bundle of thin sticks.
The bony fingers touched Harry's pale brow and melted into
his skull.

And as the scarlet fires dimmed in the sockets of Faethor's
eyes, so their light was transferred beneath Harry's lowered
lids, like red candles behind frosted glass. Following which
. . . the vampire was privy to Harry's most secret things: his
thoughts and memories and passions, his very mind.

Until, after what might be moments or millennia:

Wake up! said Faethor.

Harry came out of the dream with a sneeze; and a second
sneeze even as he realised he was truly awake. He rolled his
head a little in the hood of his sleeping bag, and something
made a soft bursting sound close by. In the faint dawn light,
he saw a ring of small black mushrooms or puffballs where
they'd grown up beside his bed in the night. Already they
were rotting, bursting open at the slightest movement, releasing their spores in peppery clouds. Harry sneezed again
and sat up.

For a moment his dream was there in his mind, but already
fading as most dreams do. He strove to remember it . . . and
it was gone. He knew he'd conversed with the spirit of Faethor Ferenczy, but that was all. If anything had passed between them, Harry couldn't say what it had been. Certainly
he felt no different from when he went to sleep.

Oh? said Faethor. *And are you sure of that, Harry Keogh?*

"Jesus!" Harry jumped a foot. "Who . . . ?" He looked
all about, saw no one.

And did you think I would fail you? said Faethor.

"Deadspeak!" Harry whispered.

It is returned to you. There, see now how Faethor Ferenczy keeps his word.

Harry had unzipped his sleeping bag and scrambled to his feet in the dispersing morning mist. Now he sat down again, with something of a bump. There was no pain in his head; no one squirted acid in his mind; his talent seemed returned to him in full measure.

All that remained was to try it out. And:

"Faethor?" he said, still wincing inside and expecting to be struck down. "Was it . . . difficult?"

Difficult enough, aye. The dead vampire's voice sounded tired. *What had been done to you was the work of an expert! All night I laboured to rid your house of his infestation, Harry. You may now gauge for yourself the measure of my success.*

Harry stood up again. With his heart in his mouth, he attempted to conjure a Möbius door . . . to no avail. The equations evolving, mutating and multiplying with awesome acceleration on the computer screens of his mind, were completely alien to him; he couldn't fathom them individually, let alone as a total concept or entity. He sighed and said, "Well, I'm grateful to you—indeed you'll never know just how grateful I am—but you weren't entirely successful."

Faethor's answer, with his bodiless shrug sensed superimposed upon it, was half-apologetic: *I warned you it might be so. Oh, I found the region of the trouble, be sure, and even managed to unlock several of its doors. But beyond them—*

"Yes?"

There was nothing! No time, no space, nothing at all. Very frightening places, Harry, and strange to think that they exist right there in your mind—in your entirely human *mind! I felt that to take one single step over those thresholds would mean being sucked in and lost forever beyond the boundaries of the universe. Needless to say, I took no such step. And in any case, no sooner had I opened these doors than they slammed themselves shut in my face. For which I was not ungrateful.*

Harry nodded. "You looked in on the Möbius Continuum," he said. And: "When I've finished here, I must try to find him. Möbius, I mean. For just as you're the expert in your field, so he's the one true authority in his. Useless to seek him out until now, for without deadspeak I couldn't talk to him."

Will you do it now, at once? Faethor was fascinated. *I am interested in genius. There is a kinship in all true geniuses, Harry. For however far removed their various talents, into whichever spheres, still the* obsession *remains the same. They seek to eliminate all imperfections. Where this Möbius has approached the very limits of pure numbers, I myself have searched for purest pure evil. We stand on the opposite sides of a great gulf, but still we are brothers of a sort. Yes, and it would be fascinating to meet such a one.*

"No." Harry automatically shook his head, and knew that Faethor would sense it. "I won't look for him now. Eventually, but not now. After I've practised awhile and when I've convinced myself that my deadspeak is as good as it used to be, maybe then."

As you wish. And for the moment? Do you go now to seek out Janos?

Harry rolled up his sleeping bag and stuffed it into his holdall. "That too, eventually," he answered. "But first I'll return to my friends in Rhodes and see how they're faring. And before any of that there are still things you must tell me. I still want to know all about Janos; the better a man knows his enemy, the easier it is to defeat him. Also, I need to know how to defend myself against him."

Of course! said Faethor. *Indeed! I had forgotten there was work still to be done. But only see how eager I am that you should be on your way! Ah, but I go too fast! And certainly you are right: you must have every possible weapon at your disposal if you're to defeat him. As to how you may best defend yourself, that's not easy. This sort of thing is inherent in the Wamphyri, but difficult to teach. Even the keenest instinct would not suffice, for this is something borne in the blood. If we had an entire week together . . .*

"No." Again Harry shook his head. "Out of the question. Can't you break it down into its simplest terms for me? If I'm not too stupid, I might just catch on."

I can but try, said Faethor.

Harry lit a cigarette, sat down on his stuffed holdall, and said, "Go ahead."

Again Faethor's shrug, and he at once commenced: *Janos is without doubt the finest telepath—which is to say beguiler, enchanter, fascinator—I have ever known. Wherefore he will first attempt an invasion of your mind. Now as I've hinted, and as is surely self-evident, your mind is extraordinary, Harry. Well, of course it is: for you are the Necroscope! But where you have practised only good, Janos, like myself in my time, has practised only evil. And because you know he is evil, so you fear him and what he may do to you. Do you understand?*

"Of course. None of this is new to me."

To anyone less well versed in the ways of the Wamphyri, such is the awe—the sheer terror—Janos would inspire, that his victim would be paralysed. But you are not ignorant of our ways; indeed, you are an expert in your own right. Do you know the saying, that the best form of defence is attack?

"I've heard it, yes."

I suspect that in this instance it would be true.

"I should attack him? With my mind?"

Instead of shrinking back from him when you sense him near, seek him out! He would enter your mind? Enter his! He will expect you to be afraid; be bold! He will threaten; brush all such threats aside and strike! But above all else, do not let his evil weaken you. When he yawns his great jaws at you, go in through them, for he's softer on the inside!

"Is that all?"

If I say more, I fear it would only confuse you. And who knows? You may learn more about Janos from his story than from any measures of mine to forearm you. Moreover, I'm weary from a long night's work. Ask me what has been, by all means, but not what is yet to be. True, I have been an observer of times, but as my current situation is surely witness, I was far too often in error.

Harry thought about what he'd learned: Faethor's "advice" about how to deal with a mind attack from Janos. Some might consider it suicidal to act in accordance with such instructions; the Necroscope wasn't so sure. In any case, it seemed very little to go on. But patently it was all he was going to get. Dawning daylight had apparently dampened the vampire's enthusiasm.

Harry stood up, stretched, and looked around.

The mist had thinned to nothing; a handful of gaunt houses stood beyond a hedge half a mile away; in the other direction, the silhouettes of diggers and bulldozers were like dinosaurs frozen on a grey horizon. Another hour and they'd roar into destructive mechanical life, as if the sun had warmed their joints to clanking motion.

Harry looked at the ground where he stood, the spot where Faethor had died on the night Ladislau Giresci cut off his head in the ruins of a bomb-blasted, burning house. He saw the now liquescent mushrooms there, their spores like red stains on the grass and soil; and in the eye of his mind he saw Faethor, too, the skeletal, shrouded thing he'd been in his dream. "Are you up to telling me Janos's story?" he asked, apparently of no one.

That will be no effort at all but a pleasure, the other answered at once. *It was my pleasure to spawn him, and it gave me the most* exquisite *pleasure to put him down again!*

But first . . . do you remember the story of Thibor in his early days? How he robbed me of my castle in the Khorvaty? And how I, most sorely injured, fled westwards? Let me remind you, then.

This is how it was . . .

X: Bloodson

THIBOR THE WALLACH, THAT CURSED INGRATE—TO WHOM I had given my egg, name, and banner, and into whose hands I had bequeathed my castle, lands, and Wamphyri powers— had injured me sorely.

Thrown down burning from the walls of my castle, I experienced the ultimate agonies. A myriad minion bats fluttered to me as I fell, were scorched and died for their troubles, but dampened my flames not at all. I crashed through trees and shrubs, and pinwheeled aflame down the sides of the gorge to the very bottom. But my fall had been broken in part by the foliage, and I came to rest in a shallow pool which alone saved my melting Wamphyri flesh.

As close to true death as a vampire might come and remain undead, I put out a desperate call to my faithful Gypsies where they camped in the valley. They came, lifted my body from the still, salving water and cared for it, and carried me west over the mountains into Hungary. Protecting me from jars and jolts, hiding me from potential enemies, keeping me safe from the sun's searing rays, at last they brought me to a place of rest. Aye, and it was a long rest: a time of enforced retirement, for recuperation, for the reshaping of my broken body; a long, *long* rest indeed!

For *how* Thibor had hurt me! All bones broken, back and neck, skull and limbs; chest caved in, heart and lungs amangle; skin flayed by boulders and sharp branches, and seared with fire . . . even the vampire in me was burned, bruised, and battered. A month in the healing? A year? Nay, a *hundred* years!

My long convalescence was spent in an inaccessible mountain retreat, and all the while my Szgany tended me, and their sons, and *their* sons. Aye, and their sweet, firm-breasted daughters, too. Slowly the vampire in me healed itself, and then healed me. Wamphyri, I walked again, practised my arts, made myself wiser, stronger, more awesome than ever before. And eventually I went abroad from my aerie and made plans for my life's adventure.

Ah, but it was a terrible world in which I emerged, with wars everywhere, great suffering, famines, pestilence! Terrible, aye, but the stuff of life to me—for I was Wamphyri!

I found myself the ruins of a keep in the border with Wallachia and used the tumbled stones to build a small castle there. Almost impregnable within its walls, I set myself up as a boyar of some means. I led a mixed body of Szgany, Hungarians, and local Wallachs, housed them and paid them good wages, was soon accepted as a landowner and leader. And so I became a small power in the land.

As for Wallachia: I avoided venturing there, mainly. For there was one in Wallachia whose strength and cruelties were already renowned: a mercenary Voevod named Thibor, who fought for the Wallach princelings. I did not wish to meet this one (who should by rights be keeping guard over my lands and properties in the Khorvaty even now!), not yet; for in the event of my seeing him, I might not be able to contain myself. Which could well prove fatal, for he was now grown to a far greater power than I myself. No, my revenge must wait . . . what is time to the Wamphyri, eh?

Time in the tumult of its passing, where an entire day is

like the single tick of a great clock—it is nothing. But when each vastly extended tick is precisely the same as the one gone before, and when they begin to fall like thunderclaps upon the ear . . . ah, but then one discovers time's restrictions, from which only boredom and uttermost ennui may ensue. And *that* is everything! I was restless, confined, pent up. There was I, lusty, strong, something of a power, and nowhere to channel my energies. The time was coming when I must go farther abroad in the roiling world.

But then, in the year 1178, a diversion.

Over a period of some few years I'd been hearing tales of a Szgany woman who was a true observer of times; which is to say, she had the power of precognition. Eventually my curiosity was piqued and I determined to see her. She was not of my own band of Gypsies, and so I had to wait for her to venture into those mountainous regions within my control.

Meanwhile, I sent out messengers to direct her wanderings aright, describing how and when she and her band came within my spheres, they would be offered every hospitality, treated with utmost respect, and paid in gold for whichever services they might render unto me. And in the interim, while I waited on the advent of this alleged oracle, I determined to practise what small talent I possessed in casting a few weirds of my own.

I mixed certain herbs and burned them, fell asleep breathing their incense, and sought by oneiromancy to divine the way it would be between myself and this doubtless fraudulent witch, this ''Marilena'' (for such was her name). Aye, for in those days I had good reason to be interested in talented folk, and to seek them out whenever the opportunity arose. My son Thibor had been abroad for several human lifetimes now, and might have spawned all manner of curiosities in the land!

And so I sought out all such anomalies, and in so doing prided myself with the discovery of charlatans. But . . . if I should come across a genuine talent (and if Wamphyri blood should course in the veins of such a one) then he or she would be a goner! For while to a creature such as I the blood is—or was—the life, the sweetest nectar of all may only be sipped from the undead font of another vampire! A font, aye, for such a sip is surely holy—to one such as I am, at least.

But . . . only picture my astonishment when finally my oneiromancy produced results, and I dreamed of this dark angel where I had thought to discover a hag!

What? She was a child! I saw her in my dreams: a lovely child, aye, and innocent I thought (but wrongly, for she was knowing as a whore!). She came to me naked—all curves, creamy and brown, unblemished; dark in her eyes and in her shining hair; the lips of her face red as cherries, and those of her oyster when I opened it the hue of freshly slaughtered meat—to stand before me unashamed. Two centuries gone by since Thibor destroyed my castle in the Khorvaty, and raped my vampire women and put them down; between then and now I had tasted my share of soft Szgany flesh, spilling myself into such Gypsy odalisques as pleased me. Nothing of "love" in it, mind you; that word was only applicable to others, never to myself. But now . . . ?

It was the human side of me, of course, which from time to time held sway in my dreams. I gazed upon this sweet, sensuous princess of the Travelling Folk through eyes fogged by human weakness. The shuddering of my loins was the love (call it that if you will) of a man, but never the raging lust of the Wamphyri. And to my shame, my dreams were wet, and I came in my blankets like a trembling lad stroking the teats of his first girl!

But . . . the trouble with oneiromancy was always this: had it been a true and accurate prediction of the future, or was it *just* a dream? Thereafter, in order to reinforce my findings (and perhaps for other reasons, for plainly I was besotted), night after night would find me burning my herbs and willing myself into divinatory dreams. And always they were the same, except that the better we got to know each other, Marilena and I, the more pleasurable our loveplay became and myself ever more enamoured; until I knew that instead of a mere dream, I must have the real thing or go mad!

Which was when she came to me, as it were, in the flesh.

She was of the camp of Grigor Zirra, called "King" Zirra;

indeed, Marilena was Grigor's daughter. And so I had been right: she was a "princess" of the Travelling Folk.

It was winter when they came, the end of January, and never so biting cold in all the years of my memory. My own Szgany stationed their caravans and carts in clusters close to my walls, banked them in with huge bricks of snow smoothed to ice, pitched their tents within the clusters, and tethered their beasts inside with them, for their warmth. Ah, they had known it would be a hard winter, these wise ones! In the caves all around they had worked long and hard, storing fodder for their animals. Even so, men and beasts alike would be hard put to see it through *that* winter without they relied on the patronage of the boyar in his castle.

I kept all my doors unbarred to them, and my halls warm with fires everywhere. My good grogs and coarse red wines were made available for the asking, likewise grain to make their bread; it cost me nothing; these things belonged to the Szgany anyway, for in better seasons they'd given them all to me, who had no need of them!

One midmorning a man came to me. He had been hunting in the mountains, which were *my* mountains. I did not deny the Gypsies this privilege; if they shot three pigs or woodcocks, one was mine, and so on. And he told me of the Szgany Zirra: that they were caught in a pass close by, where an avalanche had carried their caravans away! Only a handful survived, he said, scattered in the tumbled drifts.

I knew his report was true. Last night I had dreamed again my herbal dreams, but this time devoid of carnal delights and filled instead with blizzards and the screams of those swept away and dying! And because I had not dreamed of my Marilena, I wondered . . . was she one of them?

Then I called for my Szgany chief and told him, "There is a girl trapped in the snows. This man knows where she is. She and her people are Szgany. Go, find them, dig them out, and bring them here. And hurry, for if you are too late and she is dead . . . the house of the Ferenczy may feel that its hospitality is wasted on such as you and yours. Is this understood?"

It was, and he went in all haste.

In the afternoon my chief and his men returned. He made report: of the Szgany Zirra, which had numbered as many as fifty, he had found only Grigor Zirra himself and a dozen of his band alive. Three of the survivors were broken but would mend, two more were old women and might not, and of the rest . . . one was Grigor's daughter, called Marilena, an observer of times!

I commanded him, "Have your women tend them, feed them, give them whatsoever they need. Spare nothing to make them welcome, comfortable, at ease in this place. I take it they have nothing? Nothing of extra clothing, no carts or coverings? So, without me they are destitute. Very well, quarter them within the castle's walls. Find them warm rooms within easy reach of my own, where they may stay apart." And seeing a puzzled look in his eyes: "Well?"

"You own people might think it strange, master," he said, "that you treat the strangers so well. That we make way for them, who owe you no allegiance."

"You are forthright and I like you for it," I told him. "I, too, shall be forthright. I have heard it said of the woman Marilena Zirra that she is comely. If this is true, it may be that I shall want her, for you Gypsies are not the only ones who feel the cold of a night! Wherefore treat her people with respect, especially her father and family, if such as these survived. I do not wish they should find me a cold and cruel man."

"What? You, master?" he said, with no trace of emotion in his voice, his face utterly blank. "Cold? Cruel? Who would ever believe it?"

I regarded him awhile, finally saying, "Forthright is one thing, and forward another entirely. Do you seek to be familiar with me? I tell you honestly, I cannot believe you would enjoy such . . . familiarity. Wherefore, when you say certain things to me, and in such a way, it should always please you to smile . . ." I stared at him and rumbled a little deep in my throat, until he grew uncomfortable.

"Master," he said, beginning to tremble, "I meant no—"

"Hush!" I quieted him. "You are safe, my mood is a good one! Now heed me well. Later, when the Zirras are recovered, return and take me among them where they are quartered. Until then, begone."

But when I went among them, I was not pleased. It wasn't that my instructions had not been followed; they had, to the letter. It was simply that the ordeal of these people had been such that they were mazed and vacant. It would take a little time in the healing. Meanwhile, they sat in their rags and trembled, and spoke only when they were spoken to.

As for the supposed "princess" of my dreams: where was she? One filthy bundle huddled to the fire looked much like the next to me. It annoyed me that my dreams had lied to me; I felt that I had failed in my oneiromancy; I *hated* failure, especially in myself.

So I stood and gloomed over these dregs awhile and finally asked, "Which one of you is Grigor Zirra?"

He stood up: a nothing, a wisp, pale from the snow and his suffering, the loss of his people. He was not old, but neither did he look young. There had been strength in his leanness once, but now it looked washed out of him. Unlike myself, he was entirely human, and he had lost . . . much.

"I am the Ferenczy," I told him. "This is my castle. The people about are my people, Szgany like yourself. For the time being, it pleases me to give you shelter. But I have heard there is an observer of times among you, and it also pleases me to contemplate such mysteries. Where is this witch—or wizard?"

"Your hospitality is vast as your legend," he answered. "Alas that in my sorrow I cannot more fully declare my appreciation. For something of me died this day. She was my wife, swept from the cliff. Now I have only a daughter, a child, who reads the future in the stars, in the palm of your hand, and in her dreams. She is no witch, lord, but a true observer of times, my Marilena, of whom you have heard."

"And where is she?"

He looked at me and there was fear in his eyes. But I felt a tug at the sleeve of my robe and started that someone dared touch me. None of my own had laid finger on me unbidden since the day I rose up from my sickbed! I looked . . . and saw one of the rag bundles risen to its feet to stand beside me . . . its eyes were huge, dark beneath a fur hood . . . its hair was all black ringlets, spilling about a heart-shaped face . . . its lips were the colour of cherries, bright as blood. And upon my arm her tiny hand, whose fingers numbered only three, as I had seen them in my dreams!

"I am Marilena, Lord," she said. "Forgive my father, for he loves and fears for me; there are some in the land dubious of mysteries they cannot fathom, and unkind to certain women whom they term witches."

My heart felt staggered! She could be none other! I knew the voice! I saw through all her clothes to the very princess of my dreams, knowing that what was in there was a wonder. And: "I . . . know you," I said, my voice choked.

"And I you, Lord. I have seen you in my future. Often. You are in no wise a stranger!"

I had no words. Or if I had, they were stuck in my throat. But . . . I was the Ferenczy! Should I dance, laugh out loud, pick her up, and whirl her all about? Oh, I wanted to, but I could not reveal my emotions. I stood there thunderstruck, like a great fool, frozen, until she came to my rescue.

"If you would have me read for you, Lord, then take me aside from here. Here my concentration suffers, for there is much sadness—aye, and various comings and goings, and likewise much fuss and to-do—oh, and many small matters to interfere with my scrying. A private place would be to some advantage . . ."

Oh? Indeed it would! "Come with me," I said.

"Lord!" her father stopped us. "She is innocent!" The last word was spoken on a rising note—of pleading, perhaps? My nature was not unknown among the Szgany.

But . . . didn't he know his own daughter? It was in my mind to say to him, "Lying Gypsy dog! What, this one, innocent? Man, she has licked my entire body clean as if

275

bathed! I have fired my fluids into her throat every night for a month from the coaxing of her tongue and tiny, three-fingered hands! Innocent? If she is innocent, then so am I!'' Ah, but how *could* I say these things? For the fact of it was that I had only ever dreamed my love affair with Marilena!

Again she rescued me.

''Father!'' She rebuked him before I could more than pierce him with my eyes. ''I have seen what will be. For me the future *is*, father, and I have read no harm in it. Not at the hands of the Ferenczy.''

He had seen my look, however, and knew how far he strained my hospitality. ''Forgive me, Lord,'' he said, lowering his head. ''Instead of speaking as a man sorely in your debt, I spoke only as a father. My daughter is only seventeen and we are fallen among strangers. The Zirras have lost enough this day. Ah! *Ah!* I meant nothing by that! But do you see? I trip over my own tongue even now! It is the grief. My mind is stricken. I meant nothing. It is the grief!'' And sobbing, he collapsed.

I stooped a little and put my hand on his head. ''Be at your ease. He who harms you or yours in the house of the Ferenczy answers to me!'' And then I led her to my quarters . . .

Once there, alone, where none dare disturb, I lifted off her coat of furs until she stood in a peasant dress. Now she looked even more like the princess I knew, but not enough. My eyes burned on her, burned for the sight of her. And she knew it.

''How can this be?'' she said, full of wonder. ''I truly know you! Never were my dreams more potent!''

''You are right,'' I said. ''We are not . . . strangers. We *have* shared the same dreams.''

''You have great scars,'' she said, ''here on your arm, and here in your side.'' And even I, the Ferenczy, trembled where she touched me.

''And you,'' I told her, ''have a tiny red mole, like a single tear of blood, in the centre of your back . . .''

Beside my fire, which roared into a great chimney, there stood a stone trough for the bathing. Over the fire, a mighty cauldron of water added steam to the smoke. She went to the tripod and turned the gear, pouring water into the trough. She knew how to do it from her dreams! "I am unclean from the journey," she explained, "and rough from the snows."

She stripped and I bathed her, and then she bathed me. "And how is this for a private reading?" I chuckled. But as I opened her and went to slip inside:

"Ah!" she gasped. "But our mutual dreams took no account of my inexperience. My father told the truth, Lord. The future is closing fast, be sure, but I am still a virgin!"

"Ah!" I answered her, moan for moan, the while gentling my way inside. "But weren't we all, once upon a time?"

How my vampire raged within me then, but I held him back and loved her only as a man. Else the first time were surely her last . . .

Now let me make it plain. What had happened was this:

As much out of idle curiosity as for any other reason, in my oneiromantic dreams I had sought Marilena out, become enamoured of her, and seduced her. Or we had seduced each other.

But (you will ask), how could she, a child, inexperienced, seduce me? And I will answer: because dreams are safe! Whatever happens in one's dreams, nothing is changed upon awakening. She could indulge all her sexual fantasies without reaping the reward of such indulgence. And (you will also ask), how could I, Faethor Ferenczy, even asleep and dreaming, be anything less than Wamphyri? Ah, but I was a dreamer long before I became a vampire! Indeed, I was once a mere man! The things which had troubled me in my youth still occasionally troubled me in my sleep: the old fears, the old emotions and passions.

I am sure my meaning is not lost: all of us know that long after an experience has waned to insignificance in the waking world, we may still review it afresh in our dreams, with as much apprehension—or excitement—as we did when it was new. In my dreams, for example, I was still wont to remember the time of my own conversion, when I had received my father's egg and so been made a vampire. Aye, and such dreams as those *still* horrified me! But in the cold light of day that horror was quickly forgotten, and I was no stripling lad but the Ferenczy again.

The meeting of Marilena's dreams with mine had been more than mere chance, however: I had sought her out, and found her. And once insinuated into her dreams, I had dreamed (as any man might) of knowing her carnally. And again I say, these were not simple dreams! I had Wamphyri powers and she was a prognosticator. These were talents akin to telepathy. We had *in fact* shared each other's dreams, and through them known each other's bodies.

All of our fumbling and fondling, and later our more energetic, far more diverse lovemaking, had been done in another world—of the mind—where there had been no obligation to spare anything; so that when we came together at last, it was very much as lovers of long standing. Except that in reality Marilena was innocent and her flesh untried by any man . . . for a while, anyway. Now, I understood these things, but she did not. She thought that her talent *alone* had shown her the future, her future, without outside interference. She did not know that I had guided her in those dreams with a vampire's magnetism and beguilement and . . . oh, with all those arts so long instinct in me. She *thought* we were natural lovers! Who can say, perhaps we would have been anyway. But I was not so foolish as to tell her and take a chance on her disillusionment.

Now, it might also cross your mind to wonder how she, a gorgeous young girl, round and firm as an apple, fresh-minded and -bodied, could find any sort of *waking* satisfaction in a scarred and ancient undead thing like me, savage and cruel and filled with horror? I would be surprised if it did not! But then you would doubtless recollect what you know of a vampire's power of hypnotism, and perhaps believe that you had fathomed the mystery. You would say, ''She was his plaything, not of her own free will.'' Well, I'll make no bones of it, before Marilena, this had always been the way of it. But it was not the way of it with her.

To begin with, I was not so grotesque as you might imagine. Wamphyri, my seven hundred and fifty years didn't show, except perhaps occasionally in my eyes, or when I wanted it to show. Indeed with a small effort I could appear as old or as young as it pleased me to appear, which in Marilena's case was always young, no more than forty. Even without my vampire, I would be tall and strong, and I had all those centuries of charm, wit, and wisdom—and folly—in me, to draw on at will. Scarred? Oh, I was, and badly! But I had retained these gouges out of vanity (it pleased me to wear the dents of old battles) and to remind me of the one who had put most of them there. I could have let the vampire in me repair such disfigurements entirely, but so long as Thibor lived, I would not do so. No, I wore those scars like spurs against my own flanks, to goad me if ever I should find my hatred flagging.

But if you doubt that I was so handsome, only think on how Ladislau Giresci described me the night he took my head. Ah, and you see? Still I was quite the man, eh? There, you must excuse me; it is my vanity; the Wamphyri were ever vain.

Also, I beg your indulgence that I have dwelled so long upon Marilena but . . . it pleased me so to do. For who else is there with whom I might share such memories? None but a Necroscope can ever know them . . .

You know, of course, that I am Janos's father; by now you have probably guessed it, too, that Marilena was his mother. He was my bloodson, born of the love and the lust between a man and a woman, of blood in its fiery fusion, and in the passing of a single germ of life from the one to the other, to pierce her egg and bring life to the chick within. My bloodson, aye, my ''natural'' son, with nothing of the vampire in him. That was the way it was to have been. I did not know if it could be done but would try it anyway: to bring life into the world independent of Wamphyri influence. I would do it for Marilena, so that she could be a natural mother.

And if I should fail and the child grow to be a vampire?

Well, anyway he would still be my son. And I would teach him the ways of the Wamphyri, so that when I went out into the world, he would stay behind and keep my castle and my mountains safe from all enemies.

Oh? . . . Oh? . . . *Hah!* You will remember that in an earlier time I had just such high expectations of that ingrate Wallach Thibor! Ah, well; it is the nature of all great men, I suppose, to try and try again, and never count the cost in their striving for perfection. Except, and as I have stated, I was never the one to suffer failure lightly . . .

Janos, when he was born, seemed natural. He was born out of wedlock, which dismayed Grigor, his grandfather, somewhat but meant nothing at all to me. His hands were three-fingered, as were Grigor's and Marilena's before him; but this was a mere freakishness, a trait passed down to him, with nothing sinister in it.

As he grew, however, it became clear that I had failed. My sperm, which I had tried by force of will to keep free of crimson influences, had been tainted, however lightly. It had been a foolish experiment at best: can an eagle beget a sparrow, or the grey wolf a squealing pink piglet? How much harder then for a vampire, whose very touch is a taint, to beget an innocent child? No, Janos was not a true vampire, but he had the bad blood of a vampire. Aye, and all my vices twofold; but with little of my flexibility and nothing of my caution. Still, I'd been headstrong myself when I was young; I was his father and it fell to me to show him the way of things. I *did* show him, and if and when a heavy hand was required to stop him dead in his tracks or simply steer him aright, I was not slow to apply that, too.

But . . . still he grew up wrong-headed, prideful, obstinate, and cruel beyond his needs. His one good point, in which he kept faithfully to my teachings, was the way he held sway over the Gypsies. Not only the Szgany Zirra, his mother's people, who were on the increase again, but also my own Szgany Ferengi. I thought that they loved him even better than they loved me, all of them! And perhaps it soured me and I was a little jealous of him because of it. And it could be that I was harder on him, too, for the same reason.

Anyway, I will say one more thing in his favour and then

no more: he loved his mother. A point to stand any child in good stead *while he is still a child,* aye . . . but not necessarily when he becomes a man. For there's love and there's love. You will understand my meaning . . .

Meanwhile, other troubles had brewed up, boiled over, and were still scalding in the world. All of ten years ago, Saladin had crushed the Frankish Crusader kingdoms; the sinister mercenary Thibor was now fighting on the far borders of Wallachia, a Voevod for the gold of puppet princelings; in Turkey land beyond the Greek sea, the Mongols were rising up like a forest fire with the wind at its back; wars raged close to the Hungarian borders; and another "Innocent," the third, had recently been elected pope. *Aieee!* The storm lightnings flashed red from the many clouds boiling up over all the world's horizons!

. . . And where, pray, was Faethor Ferenczy in the great scheme of things? In his dotage, some must have thought, tending his castle in the mountains. Teaching manners to his bastard son, while his once-true Szgany guards drank too much and slept late abed, and chuckled behind his back!

More time passed, unremarkably enough for me. But then one morning I woke up, shook my head, and looked all about. I felt dazed, mazed, astonished! Twenty years in all had gone by, almost in a flash, without my noticing. But now I realised it well enough. It had been a sort of lethargy, a malaise, some weird spell I'd been under: a thing which commoner men call "love." Aye, and it had reduced me accordingly. For where was my mystery now? What? I was no more than a miserable boyar: obscure baron over a wasteland no one else wanted, master of a piddling stone house in the crags!

I went to Marilena and she read my future for me. I was to embark upon a great and bloody crusade, she said, and she would not stand in my way. I could make neither head nor tail of it. Not stand in my way? Why, she couldn't bear to be apart from me! What crusade was she speaking of? But she only shook her head. She'd seen no more but that I would fight in some terrible holy war; and after that . . . all her augury, palmistry, and astrology had seemingly forsaken her.

Ah! How could I know that she'd read her own future, too—only to discover she did not have one!

But . . . a great and bloody crusade, she'd said. I thought about it and decided she could well be right. News traveled slowly in those days, and sometimes reached me not at all. I began to feel penned in, with all my old frustrations returning upon me with a vengeance.

Enough of *that*! It was time I was up and about!

Well, Janos was almost twenty; he was a man now; I charged him with the keeping of my house and went down incognito into Szeged to see what I would see and make whichever plans were appropriate. It was a timely move.

The city was abustle with news: Zara, so recently taken by Hungary, would soon be under siege from Frankish Crusaders! A great fleet of Franks and Venetians was under sail even now, and riders had been sent out at the king's command to all the boyars around (myself included, I supposed) with orders that they gather their men to them and take up arms. Marilena had read my future aright!

There were men of mine in the countryside around. Szgany, I found them easily enough during my return to the mountainous borders. "Meet me," I told them, "when I come down again from my castle. I gather a small army of the very best. We go to Zara, aye, and far beyond Zara! You who have been poor shall be rich. Fight under my banner and I'll make all of you boyars to a man! Or fail me and I'm done with you, and in one hundred years I shall still be here and mighty, and you shall be dust and your name forgotten."

And so I returned home. But travelling in the manner of the Wamphyri—at least by night—I had made good time, and I had lingered not at all in Szeged. While I was apart these few days from Marilena, all of my instincts had sharpened, and my wits were made keen in anticipation of the "holy" blood feast which was my future. In the mountains my Szgany retainers had grown fat and lazy, but I knew ways to wake them up again. They would not be expecting me back so soon, but they would know when they saw me that I was the Ferenczy as of old.

In that last night, soaring home on wings of thick membrane, I reached out in the dark with my vampire's mind and called to all the young bloods of the Szgany Ferengi wherever they were scattered, and told them to meet me in the approaches to Zara. And I knew that they heard me in their dreams, and that they would be there.

And having shaken off twenty years of sloth, so I floated on an updraft between the moon and the mountains, setting all the wolves to howling in the silvered peaks, before finally gentling to the battlements of my house, where I shrank back into a man. Then . . . I sought out my woman and my son. Aye, and I found them—together!

But there, I have gone too fast; let me pause and retrace my steps awhile.

I have said that nothing of the Wamphyri was in Janos. Well, so I thought. But oh, how I was wrong. It was in him. Not in his body but in his mind! He had the *mind* of a true vampire, inherited from me. And he had inherited something of his parents' powers, too. Something of them? He *was* a power!

Telepathy? How often through the years had I tried to read his mind, and failed? Still, nothing very remarkable in that: there are men, a handful, who are naturally resistant. Their minds are closed, guarded from talents such as mine. And fascination, or hypnotism? On occasion, when he was obstinate, I had tried to hypnotise him to my will. Wasted efforts all, for my eyes could not see into his, couldn't penetrate behind them. So that in the end I no longer tried.

But, in fact, the reason for my failure in these endeavours was not that Janos was unresponsive, but that his strength was such as to defy all such would-be intrusions and close him off from me. I had likened it to a tug-o'-war, where my opponent's rope was wedged in a tree root, immovable. But no, it was not so complicated as that; he was simply stronger. What's more, he had also inherited his mother's skill at foretokening. He could see the future, or something of it, anyway. Except that in this last, our talents were more evenly balanced, else I should never have caught him. For the fu-

Brian Lumley

tures he saw were faint and far distant, like the memories of some history which time has made obscure.

But now let me return to that night.

I have said my instincts were sharper than at any time in the previous twenty years. They were, and as I passed through the castle so I sensed that things were not as they should be. I formed a bat's convoluted snout to sniff the air of the place; no enemy was here and there seemed nothing of physical danger to me, but something was strange. I went with more caution, moved silent as a shadow, and willed it that I should be unseen, unheard. But no need for that; Janos was too . . . *engrossed*—the dog!—and his mother too mazed to even know what he was about, except when he made some command of her.

Again I go ahead of myself.

I did not know that it was him, not at first. Indeed, I thought the man must be Szgany, and was astonished! What, a Gypsy? One of my own, and in my woman's bedroom at dead of night? A fearless man indeed; I must make known to him how much I admired his bravery, while choking him with his own entrails!

These were my thoughts when, as I came to Marilena's rooms, my Wamphyri senses told me that she was not alone. Following which, it took my every effort to stop the teeth in my jaws from forming scythes and shearing my gums to pulp. Indeed, I felt the nails of my fingers involuntarily elongating into chitin knives, and this, too, was a reaction I could scarce control.

The room had an exterior door, a small antechamber, and a second door to the bedroom proper. Gently, soundlessly, I tried the outer door and found it barred. Never since she came to me had this door been barred. My worst suspicions were now fully aroused, also my hot blood. Oh, I could break the door down, certainly, except . . . to come upon them that way would be to alert them too soon. And I wanted to see with my own eyes. No amount of screeched or gasped or blood-tinged, frothed denial may eradicate a scene seared upon the very skin of one's eyeballs.

I went out onto a balcony, formed my hands and forearms into webbed discs like the suckers of some grotesque octopus, and made my way to Marilena's window. The window was large, arched, and cut through a wall six feet thick. Inside, across the opening in the inner wall, curtains had been drawn. I climbed in and inched to the curtains, which I drew fractionally apart to form a crack. Inside the room, a floating wick in a bowl of oil gave light enough to see. Not that I had need of it, for I saw in the dark as surely as other men see in full daylight, and even better.

And what I saw was this:

Marilena, naked as a whore, flat on her back across a wooden table; her legs were wrapped around a man who stood upright, straining between her thighs until his buttocks were clenched like fists, driving into her as if he were hammering home a wedge! And indeed he was, a fat wedge of flesh, and in a moment more I would drive that same wedge down his throat!

But then, through the pounding of my blood and the mad thundering of my brain, and through all the roaring of my outraged emotions, I heard her voice gasping, "Ah, Faethor—more, more! Fill me, my vampire love, as only you can!"

But . . . let me pause . . . the memory enrages me even now, when all I am is a voice from beyond the grave . . . let me pause a moment and make explanation.

It strikes me I've made little mention of myself during the twenty years of Marilena and her bastard son. I shall do so now, but quickly.

The fact that I had taken a woman for my own had not made me any less a vampire. I had had women before, be sure. It is the vampire's *nature* to have women, just as it is the female of the species' nature to have men. But I had never before been so fond of any one creature. (Enough of the word "love"; I have used it too often, and anyway do not believe in it. It is just such a lie as "honesty" or "truth" in its definition of rules which all men break from time to time.)

So, for all that I had not deliberately enthralled or vampirized Marilena, I was nonetheless Wamphyri in all my thoughts, moods and activities. But having determined not to partake of her blood, and likewise that as little of my flesh as possible should be allowed to enter her (carnal intercourse excepted, of course), it had fallen upon me to find my sustenance elsewhere. I did not *have* to drink blood; so long as I could control the craving, commoner fare would suffice. But blood is as much true life to the vampire as opium is sure death to the addict, and they are both hard habits to break. In the case of the Wamphyri, the creature within ensures that the habit will not be broken.

I could go for long periods, then, without taking myself apart from Marilena. But occasionally the craving would overpower me, and then in the night I would rise up, change my shape, and glide from my castle's walls to find my pleasure. My lady, of course, was no dimwit; she had long since divined the true nature of her lover; it was in any case common knowledge among the Gypsies that the Szgany Ferengi served a vampire master. And she was jealous of them with whom I visited from time to time.

Waking up as I left our bed, she would cry, "Faethor! Are you deserting me in the night? Do you fly to some lover? Why do you treat me so badly? Is my body not enough for you? Take it and use it as you will, but do not leave me here alone and weeping!"

And I would say, "I seek me a man for his blood! What? And do you say I'm unfaithful? All through the seasons, night upon night I lie with you abed, and you have what you will of me. And have I ever flagged in my duties? But the blood is the life, Marilena . . . or would you have me shrivel to a mummy in my sheets, so that when you wake with the morning and reach out for me, I crumble into dust beneath your touch?"

And then she would shriek, "You . . . go . . . with . . . *women!* What? You seek a man for his blood? No, you seek a woman for her round backside, pointy breasts, and hot, steaming core! And am I a simpleton? Shrivel to a mummy, indeed! Why, you've the strength of ten men—and their stamina! Are you so full of a man's seed, Faethor, that you must spill it or burst? Then give it to me. Come, let me suck it out of you, and all your flightiness evaporate.''

How does one deal with it? One may not argue with a woman in such a mood. I had only ever struck her the once, and then was so filled with remorse that I could never strike her again. I was so . . . fond of her!

And so, when she would catch me that way, then I would make love to her—to prove to her that no other had attracted me. Aye, and she'd keep me at it all through the night, just to be sure I'd stay abed. Which only served to increase my fondness.

But there were times when I *must* be up and about, and then I would employ a certain draught which, taken with wine, would serve to keep her still. Or I might stroke her and hypnotise her into a deep sleep so that I could be off into the night.

And of course Marilena was right; I lied to her; I had only rarely sought out men for their life force. Oh, blood is blood, be it the blood of bird or beast, or even the nectar of another vampire, when one such may be had. But other than that sweet rarity, man-blood is superior. Or rather, the blood of women.

Once Thibor had said to me, ''You can do more to a girl than just eat her.'' Ah, and the Wallach was right! But . . . it was not so much that I *myself* would be unfaithful to Marilena, rather that the vampire within me demanded it! Or so I beg to excuse myself.

I did not go to Szgany women. Even before Marilena, I had only ever gone to them for . . . comfort, never because I was hungry. No, for they were my own and I would not break their trust. But I did have a liking for the ladies of certain foppish boyars. There were a good many castles and rich houses in those days, and often as not the ''men'' of such estates would be away on king's business; there were wars in the world, as I have said.

I remember one such lady of mine was a personage with royal connections, a Bathory called Elspa. Aye, and my evil was made manifest in the Bathorys down all the centuries. There was one born in 1560 called Elisabeth, who was married as a child to the Count Nadasdy. As coincidence would have it, his first name was Ferencz! Oh? Haha! I know what you are thinking! Well, and why not? Incest is also the way of the vampire: incest of the body, and of the spirit, and of the blood. But if you are right . . . what a delight, eh? To be wedded to my own ten-times-great-granddaughter!

Ah, the Bathorys! And Elisabeth, the "blood countess" herself. At least she is a legend, even if I myself am nothing.

And so I am brought back to Janos, by incest. And by the vile incest with which he first betrayed me. Where was I . . . ? Ah, yes.

There he was, in her to the hilt, moaning like a bull and dripping sweat and semen; and the bedroom all a shambles, with clothing and bedclothes tossed here and there, and other signs that their fornication had not been confined to a table-top; and her soft breasts red from his furious fondling while her thighs squeezed him further in. *This* is what I saw from behind those curtains. But more than what I saw, what I heard: my Marilena calling her son by my name, Faethor!

In that moment I might have torn down the curtains, started forward, and struck them both dead; oh, I wanted to, be sure! But . . . why had she called him Faethor? Then, as he lifted her up from the table and staggered to and fro with her clinging to him still, and jerking herself up and down upon his pole, I saw her face: how vacant it was despite the apparently animal lust. Her eyes, round as saucers, set in the paleness of flesh which should at least be flushed from her efforts.

And I knew at once that she was mazed, hypnotised, deeply!

Then, for the first time, I knew how treacherous he was, and how utterly he had fooled me. I understood why my Wamphyri powers had not worked on him: because he had powers of his own, which all this time he'd kept hidden from me. I understood, too, Marilena's reluctance to let me go on those nights when I must fuel myself, things she said to me, which made no sense at the time. How she dreamed bad things when I was apart from her and could never remember what they were, and how she bruised herself alone in her bed and woke up aching and worn out as from strenuous work.

Aye, strenuous, all right—for *he* had worked and used her on those occasions, the while causing her to believe that *I* was her lusty lover! He imitated me to perpetrate his mother's rape! And the thought that drove me most mad: how often had he done it?

Bursting into the room, I took the curtains with me in a tangle upon my shoulders. Crossed swords were fixed upon a wall; I tore them down and sprang upon Janos with one of them raised high. I went to split him down the middle, but he saw me and turned his mother into the blow! Her skull was split in two, with the brains leaking out even as she slumped in his embrace!

My fury evaporated in a moment, and as Janos grimaced and tossed my Marilena from him, I caught her up and cradled her in my arms. He ran gibbering from the room, leaving me alone with her grotesque corpse . . .

How long I sat there and rocked her who was no more I cannot say. Many mad schemes crossed my mind. I would put something of my vampire into her—enough to grow strong in her and heal her wound. She was dead now but need not stay dead . . . she could be undead! Except that then she would be changed, my Marilena no more but a wispy thrall to come ghosting whenever I called—a vampire. No, I could not bear the thought of her like that, when she would have no will but my will.

Or . . . I could open her up and perform an act of necromancy, and learn all about my bastard son's infamy. For even though she had been mazed to forget his handling of her, her spirit would know of it, her flesh would remember. But I could not, for I knew that even the dead feel the agony of the necromancer's touch, and I would cause her no more pain. Ah, if only I had been a Necroscope, eh? But at that time even the concept was unknown to me.

And so I sat there long and long, until her blood and brains had dried upon me and she was grown stiff in my arms; and as my despair waned a little so I commenced to think again, and likewise my fury to wax. I would kill Janos, of course, inch by agonising inch. But before I could kill him, I must first find him.

I composed myself, called in unto me Grigor Zirra and others of my Szgany chiefs. Some of them slept in the lower quarters of my castle, where in softer times I had let them take up an almost permanent residence. An end of that, however, for harder times were coming—starting now!

I showed Marilena's corpse to Grigor and said, "Your grandson did this, whose Zirra blood was impure. Henceforward the Szgany Zirra are accursed! You are no longer welcome in the house of the Ferenczy. Take yourself and all of them who are yours and get you gone from here. And from this time forward, never let me find you in all the lands around."

When he had gone, I turned to that chief of mine who upon a time had been forward with me, familiar and loose-tongued. And: "How could things have come so far?" I demanded of him. "In my absence, did you not keep guard over what was mine?"

"But, my lord," he answered, "it was your son you ordered to keep watch over your house and estates." And he shrugged, indifferently I thought. "I have not known your confidence, or favours, for many a year."

"Are you not Szgany?" I grunted as Wamphyri teeth sprouted in my skull and my talons grew into knives. "And am I not the Ferenczy? Since when must I make request of that which is my birthright, or make command of that which was ever your duty?" In my manner of speaking I was very quiet; all of them in the room with me backed off a little, except the one I questioned, whom I had taken hold of by the shoulder.

Then . . . he pulled out a knife and made as if to stab me! But I only smiled at him in my grim fashion and held him with my eyes. And trembling, he let the knife fall, saying,

"I . . . I have betrayed your trust! Banish me also, Lord, and let me go with the Zirras."

I showed him my teeth in torn and bleeding gums, and yawned to let him see the gape of my jaws. He knew that I could close those jaws on his face and tear it off! But I merely drew him toward the high window. "Banish you?" I repeated him. "And is there a place of your liking?"

"Anywhere!" he gasped. "Anywhere at all, Lord, out there."

"Out there?" I said, glancing out the window. "So be it!" And before he could speak again, I gathered him up and hurled him out and down. He screamed once before his bones were broken on the rocks, and then no more.

By then the lesser chiefs might have flown, but I cautioned them against it. "Only flee and I shall seek you out one by one, and eat your hearts." And when they were still: "Go now, and find my son. Find him and take me to him, where I may deal with him. And after that, gather to me, for I would speak with you of important things. We shall make a great crusade, you and I together. Faethor Ferenczy will rise up and be a power in the world again, and all of you shall earn your fortunes. Aye, but it will be man's work and you *shall* earn them . . . !"

XI: Harry's Friends, and Others

A DISTANT CLANKING MOMENTARILY DISTRACTED HARRY from the extinct vampire's story. Excusing himself from listening, he scanned across the wasteland of churned, boggy earth and decaying, partly demolished houses to a gaunt horizon. Even the sun, falling warmly on his neck and drawing up vapour wraiths from the stagnant pools, could not dispel the cheerlessness of the scene: a handful of metal dinosaurs on the move, strange silhouettes obscuring themselves in clouds of dust and blue exhaust smoke. Unlikely that the bulldozers would head this way, but the sight of them working brought home to Harry something of the hour. It would be about nine o'clock; he still had to get back to Bucharest; his return flight to Athens was booked for 12:45.

Harry? said Faethor, his mental voice faint as a sigh. *I can feel the sun on the earth and it weakens me. Should I continue, or shall we postpone it until another time?*

Harry thought about it. He'd already learned quite a lot about Janos, a vampire with enormous mental powers. And yet according to Faethor, his son had not been a vampire in the fullest sense of the word, not at that time almost eight hundred years ago. So this wasn't simply an opportunity to learn more about him, but also about vampires in general. Harry knew that he was already an authority, but he felt there could never be a surfeit of knowledge about creatures such as these. Not when his life, and the lives of others, might very well depend upon it.

Quite right, said Faethor. *Very well, let me continue. I shall be brief as possible . . .*

My Szgany found the dog shivering in a cave high in the crags. I went up to him and called him out. He came to the entrance, which opened onto a ledge in the face of a sheer cliff.

Janos, though young, was big and very strong. As big as Thibor in his youth, even as big as myself. He was afraid but not craven. He had cut himself a branch and sharpened it to a stake. "Come no closer, Father," he warned, "or I'll pierce your vampire heart!"

"Ah, my son," I told him, with nothing of animosity, "but you have already done that. What? I thought you loved me! Indeed, I knew it. And I knew you loved your mother, too—though not how *well* you loved her. And yet what, in fact, do I know about you, except that you are my son? Very little, it now appears." And I moved a single pace forward into the cave.

"At least you know I will kill you," he gasped, backing off, "if you should try to punish me!"

"Punish you?" I let my shoulders slump, shook my head in a sad fashion. "No, I seek only an explanation. You are of my flesh, Janos. What? And shall I punish my own son, now of all times, when of all creatures I am surely the most lonely? Oh, I was angry, be sure, but is that so hard to understand? And what did my rage get me, eh? Your mother is dead now and gone from us, and we are both without her whom we loved so dearly. And now there is no more anger left in me."

"You don't . . . hate me?" he said.

"Hate you? My own son?" Again I shook my head. "It is simply that I do not understand. I desire to *understand* you, Janos. Explain this thing you have done so that I may know you better." And I stepped a little deeper inside the cave.

He backed off more yet, but held his spear steady on me. And now, as if a dam had been broken, the words flooded out of him. "I have *hated* you!" he said. "For you were cruel to me, cold, often indifferent, and always . . . different. I was like you, and yet unlike you. I wanted so much to be like you in my entirety, but could not. Often I've watched you become a blanket of flesh to soar like a curling leaf on the air, but when I tried, I always fell. I wanted to inspire your fear in the hearts of men, with a glance, a word, a thought; but I was not a vampire and knew that if I tried, they would only kill me like any common enemy. So instead I must befriend them whom I despised, get into their minds, make them love me in order to gain their obedience. In myself I looked a little like you, but I could never *be* you, and so I have hated you."

"You desired to *be* me?" I repeated him.

"Yes, because you have the power!"

"You have powers enough of your own!" I said. "Great powers! Fantastic powers! For which you must thank me! And yet you hid them from me all these years."

"I did not hide them," he said scornfully. "I demonstrated them! I used them to keep you out of my mind and will. And even full-blown, they remained secret! You thought my mind was inferior, incapable of knowing your talents and therefore unassailable by them; that I was such a blank—indeed a void—no stylus could ever impress me! So that when you discovered that you couldn't force yourself upon my mind, you did not say, 'Ho, he is strong!' but, '*Hah!* He is weak!' That was your ego, Father, which is vast but not infallible."

"Aye." I nodded thoughtfully when he was done. "Much more to you than I suspected, Janos. You do have certain powers."

"But not *your* power!" he said. "You are . . . a changing

thing, mysterious, always different. And I am always the same.''

"Well, and there you have it," I told him, with a shrug. "I am Wamphyri!"

"And I desired to be," he said, "but was only a strange man. A halfling . . .''

"But does this excuse you?" I asked him. "Is this reason enough that you should use your own mother as a whore? To hate me for your own deficiencies was one error, but to compound it by cleaving unto—''

"Yes!" He cut me short. "It was my reason. I wanted to be like you and could not, and so hated you. Wherefore I would defile or suborn all that you most treasured. First the Szgany, whom I would cause to love me if not above you then at least as your equal; and then your woman, who knew you better than anyone else in the world—and in ways which only a lover could know you!''

Now (quite deliberately) I backed away from him, and he followed after, towards the mouth of the cave. "In your desire to be like me," I said, "you determined to do the things I did, and to know the things I knew. Even to the extent of knowing your own mother—carnally?''

"I thought she might . . . teach me things.''

"What?" I almost laughed, but not quite. "The ways of the flesh, Janos? A father's task that, surely?''

"I wanted nothing of you, except to be you.''

"Could you not try to be more affectionate towards me, and so engender my affection?''

His turn to laugh, almost. "What? As well seek sweetness in a lump of salt!''

"You are hard," I told him, low-voiced. "Perhaps we are not so far apart after all. And so you'd be Wamphyri, eh? Ah, but you've much to learn before that day dawns.''

"What?" he said, a look of incredulity crossing his face like a shadow. And again, in a whisper: "What? Are you saying that—''

"Ah!" I held up a cautionary hand; for now that he was fascinated, I was in a position to cut *him* off. "Aye, not so very far apart at all. And I'll tell you something, my oh so stupid, jealous, impatient son: what you did was no rare thing. Neither vile nor even strange. Not to my thinking, or the thinking of others like me. What, incest? Why, the Wamphyri have ever fucked their own, and in more ways than one! I tell you, Janos: only be *glad* that you were born a man and mainly human. For if you were another vampire . . . oh, I'd know how best to serve you. Aye, and then you'd know well enow the real meaning of rape!''

My words should have warned him that I was not so forgiving as I seemed, but they did not. I had made him a half promise, and he wanted the other half—now. "You said . . . did you mean . . . can you teach me to be Wamphyri?''

"Something like that," I answered. And his spear was wavering now where he pointed it at me.

"How would you do it?''

"Not so fast!'' I said. "First you must tell me how far you've progressed. You have said you desire to be like me. Exactly like me. Which is to say, Wamphyri. Very well, but meanwhile you have practised, am I right? So, and what have you achieved?''

He was sly. "Ask me instead the things which I have not achieved. All else is mine!''

"Very well: what eludes you?''

"I cannot alter my flesh, change my shape, fly.''

"That is a matter of the will over the flesh—but only if it is Wamphyri flesh. Yours is not. Still . . . there are ways to change that. What else?''

"You are a crafty necromancer. Once, when a lone Traveller passed this way, you murdered him. Hidden in a secret place, I saw you open his body and tease the various parts of him for all of his knowledge of the outside world. You inhaled the gases of his gut, to learn from them. You sucked his eyes, to see what they had seen. You rubbed the blood of his ruptured ears into your own, to hear what they had heard! Later, when a party of strange Szgany passed by, I stole away a girl-child from them and used her in the same way. As you had done, so did I. But I learned nothing and was very ill.''

"The Wamphyri excel in necromancy," I told him. "Aye, and it's a rare art. But . . . even this may be taught. Had I been allowed into your mind, I could have instructed you. In this you thwarted yourself, Janos. Is there anything else?"

"Your great strength," he said. "I saw you chastise a man. You picked him up and hurled him away like a small log! And I have watched you . . . in bed. When others would have flagged, your energy was boundless. I used to think she had some secret, Marilena, some ointment or trick to keep you hard. Another reason why I went to her. I desired to know all of your secrets."

And in my turn, there was something I, too, had to know. "Did she ever suspect?" I asked him then.

He shook his head. "Not once. My eyes held her entirely in thrall. She knew only what I wanted her to know, did only as I instructed her to do."

"And you caused her to think that you were me," I growled, "so that she would hold nothing back!" And I went to grab him.

In that same moment the dog had read my mind. Until then I had kept it shielded from him, but as the thought of him and Marilena together returned to plague me, all grip was lost. He saw my thoughts, my intentions, avoided my grasp, and lunged at me with his spear!

I was on the rim of the cliff; I ducked to one side and his weapon tore my robe and grazed my shoulder; I wrenched it from him and knocked him in the face with it. His mouth was torn and his teeth broken in. Also, he jerked away from me and slammed his head against the cave's ceiling. And as he collapsed I caught him up. Dazed, he could do nothing as I carried him to the sheer rim. His head lolled a little, but his eyes were open, watching me as I gave way to the vampire within to let its fury shape and reshape my face and form!

"So," I grunted then, meshing my teeth where they came bursting through the ripped ridges of my jaws. "So, and you would be Wamphyri." I showed him my hand, which was changed to the talon of a primal beast. "You would be as I am. But I would have you know, Janos, that the only reason you are human *at all* is because of your mother. I wanted her to have a child, and gave her a monster. But you called yourself a halfling and you are right. You are neither one thing nor the other, and no use to man or beast. You desire flesh you can mould to suit yourself? So be it!'' And I gathered up a gob of phlegm, froth, and blood onto my forked tongue and hurled it into his gaping mouth, and massaged his throat until it was down. He gagged and choked until his eyes stood out in his face, but there was nothing he could do.

"There!'' I laughed at him, madly. "Let that grow in you and form the stretchy flesh you so desire, and make your own flesh like unto itself! Aye, for you'll need something of the vampire in you—if only to mend all your broken bones!''

And without more ado I hurled him from the cliff . . .

Janos was sorely broken. All his bones, as I had guaranteed, and his flesh all torn on the rocks. A man, he would have died. But there had always been something of me in him, and now there was even more. What I had spat into him spread faster than cancer, except that unlike cancer, it spared, indeed saved, his miserable life. He would mend, and live to serve my purpose.

Before I went down into Hungary and headed for Zara, I commanded those Szgany I left behind me: "Tend him well. And when he is mended, give him my instructions. He is to stay here and guard my castle and lands so that when I return there will be a welcome for me. Until then he is the master here, and his will be done. So let it be.''

Then I went to join the Great Crusade, the substance and outcome of which you already know . . .

As Faethor's voice trailed away, Harry looked up and all around and saw that the bulldozers were toiling now. Only two hundred yards away an old, raddled relic of a house went down in dust and shuddering debris, and Harry fancied he felt the earth shake a little. Faethor felt it, too.

Will they get this far today, do you think?

The Necroscope shook his head. "I shouldn't think so. In

any case they seem to be working at random and don't appear to be in too much of a hurry. Will it affect you—I mean, when they level this place? There's not much left to level anyway.''

Affect me? No, nothing can do that, for I'm no more. But it may make it damned hard to eavesdrop upon the dead, with all that rumble going on! And Harry sensed the extinct monster's hideous grin as the monster in turn sensed the inevitability of a concrete tomb, probably in the heart of a bustling factory complex. A grin, yes, for Faethor would not accept Harry's concern, wouldn't even acknowledge it.

Pointless therefore to say, ''Well, I hope you'll be . . . okay?'' But the Necroscope said it anyway. And quickly, before his (or Faethor's) embarrassment could show through: ''But now I have to get on my way. I've learned a lot from you, I think, and of course I'm grateful for the power of deadspeak, which you've returned to me. If I may, I'll contact you again, however—by night, of course, and probably from afar—so that you can finish your story. For I know that after the fourth crusade you came back to Wallachia and put an end to Thibor, and there must have been more between you and Janos, too. Since he is only recently risen, I know someone must have put him down. You, Faethor, I would suspect.''

He sensed the vampire's grim nod.

''Well, what was done once may be done a second time, with your assistance.''

You are welcome, Harry, anytime. For after all, that is our dual purpose, to return him to dust. And now be on your way. I would like to rest awhile in whatever peace is left to me—while I may.

But as Harry took up his holdall, so his feet squelched in the slime of the rotting toadstools. Their ''scent'' reached him in a single poisonous waft. And:

''Ugh!'' He couldn't hold back the exclamation of detestation. And Faethor picked it up, and perhaps saw in his mind something of the cause.

What? he said. *Mushrooms?* His mental voice was a little

299

sharp, Harry thought, and suddenly nervous. Perhaps the finality of his situation was affecting him after all.

The Necroscope shrugged. "Mushrooms, toadstools—fungi, anyway. The sun is steaming them away."

He felt Faethor's shudder and could have bitten off his tongue. His last sentence had been thoughtlessly cruel. But . . . what the hell! . . . why should anyone feel sorry about the fate of a long-dead, morbid, and totally evil thing like a vampire?

"Good-bye," he said, heading out of Faethor's ruined house, back toward the graveyard and the dusty road beyond.

Farewell, that unquiet spirit answered him. *And Harry, don't linger over what you must do, but seek to make a quick end of it. Time may well be of the essence.*

Harry waited a moment more but Faethor didn't elaborate . . .

As Harry climbed the rear wall of the old cemetery and stepped down among the plots and leaning slabs, someone very close to him said, *Harry? Harry Keogh?*

He jumped a foot and glanced all around. But . . . no one there! Of course not, for it was deadspeak at work—without the terrible mental agony he'd come to associate with it. He'd been denied the use of his macabre talent for so long that it would take a little time to get used to it again.

Did I startle you? asked the voice of some dead soul. *I'm sorry. But we heard you talking to that dead Thing Who Listens, and we knew it must be you—Harry Keogh, the Necroscope. For who else among the living could it be, talking to the dead? And who else would even* want *to talk to or befriend such a thing as that? Only you, Harry, who has no enemies among the Great Majority.*

"Oh, I've a few," Harry eventually, hesitantly answered. "But mainly I get on with the teeming dead well enough, yes."

Now the entire graveyard came, as it were, to life. Before, there had been a hush, an aching void to camouflage a pent-up . . . something. But now that something burst its banks like a river in flood, and a hundred voices suddenly required Harry's attention. They were full of the usual queries of the dead: How were those they'd left behind doing in the world of the living? What was *happening* in that bustling world of corporeal being, where minds were housed in flesh? Would it be possible for Harry to deliver a message to this oh-so-well-remembered-and-loved father, or mother, or sister, or lover, and so on . . .

Why, he could spend a lifetime simply answering the questions and running the many errands of the inhabitants of this one cemetery! But no sooner had he issued that thought than they knew and recognised its truth, and the mental babble quickly died down.

"It isn't that I don't want to," he tried to explain, "but that I can't. You see, to the living you're dead and gone forever. And apart from a handful of colleagues, I'm the only one who knows you're still here, but changed. Do you think it would help if all your still-living friends and loved ones knew that you, too, remained . . . extant? It wouldn't. It would only serve to make their grief that much worse. They'd think of you as being in some vast and terrible prison camp beyond the body! Well, it's bad enough, I know, but not that bad—especially now that you've learned to communicate among yourselves. But we can't tell that to the living you left behind you, for if we did, those who've stopped mourning and returned to what's left of their own lives, why, they'd start all over again! And I'm afraid there would always be fake Necroscopes to take advantage of them."

You're right, of course, Harry, their spokesman answered then. *It's just that it's such a rare—indeed unique—treat, to speak with a member of the living, I mean! But we can sense your urgency and we certainly didn't intend to hold you up.*

Harry wandered amidst the plots, some ancient and others quite new, and enquired, "How will it affect you? When they get through levelling what's left around here, I mean? You'll still be here, I know that, no matter what happens—but won't it bother you that your graves have been disturbed?"

But they won't be, Harry! an Area Planning Council mem-

ber, late of Ploiesti, spoke up. *For this cemetery has a preservation order on it. Oh, it's true, a lot of graveyards have
been reduced to rubble, but this one at least escapes Ceausescu's madness! And I pride myself that I was in part instru-
mental—but I had to be! Why, members of my family, the
Bercius, have been buried here for centuries! And families
should stick together, right?* Radu Berciu chuckled, however
wryly. *Ah, but I never thought that I'd benefit personally, or
at least not so soon. For just nine days after I brought that
preservation order into being, why, I myself died of a heart
attack!*

Harry was thoughtful enough to enquire, "Are there any
more here only recently dead?" For he knew from past experience that they'd be the ones hardest hit, not yet recovered
from the trauma of death. At least he could find the time to
speak to them before moving on.

And eventually a pair of voices, sad, young, and very lost,
found strength to answer him.

Oh, yes, Harry, said one. *We're the Zaharia brothers.*

Ion and Alexandru, said the other. *We were killed in an
accident, working on the new road. A tanker crashed and
spilled its fuel where we were brewing tea on a brazier. We
burned. And both of us with new wives. If only there were
some way to let them know that we felt nothing, that there
was no pain . . .*

"But . . . there must have been!" Harry couldn't disguise
his astonishment.

Yes, one of the Zaharias answered, *but we'd like them to
believe there wasn't. Otherwise they could stay awake every
night for the rest of their lives, listening to us scream as we
burned. We'd like to spare them that, at least . . .*

Harry was moved, but there was nothing he could do for
them. Not yet, anyway. "Listen," he said. "It could be that
I may be able to help—not now but at some time in the
future. Soon, I hope. If and when that time comes, I'll let
you know. Right now, though, I can't promise you any more
than that."

Harry, they tried to tell him in unison, their voices overlapping, *that's more than enough! You've given us hope, in that we now know we have a friend in a place otherwise beyond our reach. All of the teeming dead should be so lucky. And indeed they are lucky—that you're the one with the power.*

He moved on, out of the cemetery and into the dusty road, turning right in the direction of Bucharest. Behind him the excited graveyard voices gradually faded, talking among themselves now, of him rather than to him. And he knew he'd made a lot of new friends. Further down the road, however, he met two who were not his friends. On the contrary.

The black car passed him heading where he'd just been, but hearing the sudden squeal of its brakes, he looked back and saw it make a rocking U-turn. And from that moment he felt he was in trouble. Then, as the car drew up alongside and stopped, and as its occupants jumped out, he *knew* he was in trouble.

They weren't in uniform, but still Harry would know their sort anywhere. He'd met them before; not these two in particular, but others exactly like them. Which wasn't strange, for they were all very much of a kind. In their dark grey suits and felt hats with soft rims—which might have been borrowed right out of the thirties—they were the Romanian equivalent of Russia's KGB: the Securitatea. One was small, thin, ferret-faced, the other tall, wooden, and lurching. Their faces were almost expressionless, hidden in the shade of their hats.

"Identity card," the small one growled, holding out a hand and snapping his fingers.

"Work ticket," said the other, more slowly. "Papers, documents, authorisation."

They had both spoken English, but Harry was so badly taken by surprise that he fell straight into their simple trap. "I . . . I have only my passport," he said, also in English, and reached for it in his inside jacket pocket.

Before he could produce his forged Greek passport, the small, thin one thrust an ugly automatic pistol into his side. "Carefully, if you please, Mr. Harry Keogh!" he rasped. And as Harry's hand came back slowly into view, so the document was snatched from him and passed to the larger of the two.

Then, while the small one expertly frisked him, the wooden one opened up his passport and studied it. After a moment he held it out where his comrade could glance at it without looking away from Harry; they both grinned, coldly and without humour, and Harry thought how well they imitated sharks. But he also knew they had him, and for now there was nothing he could do about it.

The last time anything like this had happened to him was when he'd first gone to speak with Möbius in a Leipzig cemetery. On that occasion he had made his escape through the Möbius Continuum. Also, he'd made use of an expert and practical knowledge of the martial arts, taught to him by several dead masters. Well, he was still an expert with many years of practice behind him; but at that earlier time he'd been a far younger man, less experienced and wont to panic. He was much calmer now, and with every reason: in the years flown between, Harry had faced terrors such as these two thugs could scarcely imagine.

"And so we are mistaken," the wooden one said, his command of English slightly guttural but still very good, especially in its sarcastic inflection. "You are not this Harry Keogh after all but a Greek gentleman named . . . Hari Kiokis? Ah, a dealer in antiques, I see! But a Greek who speaks only English?"

The one with the ferret's face was more direct. "Where did you stay last night, Harry?" He prodded the snout of his pistol deep into Harry's ribs. "What traitor gave you shelter, eh, Mr. Spy?"

"I . . . I stayed with no one," Harry answered, which wasn't entirely true. He indicated his holdall. "I slept in the open. My sleeping bag is in here."

The tall one took the holdall from him, opened it, and pulled out the sleeping bag. It had a little mud on it and a few stains from the grass. And now the special policeman's face wasn't so wooden. If anything, he looked bewildered, but only for a moment. "Ah, I see!" he said then. "Your contact didn't show up, and so you've had to make the best of things. Very well, then perhaps you'll tell us who was supposed to meet you, eh?''

"No one," said Harry as an idea began to form in his head. "It's just that sleeping out is cheap and I enjoy a little fresh air, that's all. And in any case, what business is it of yours? You've seen my passport and know who I am, but who the hell are you? If you're policemen, I'd like to see some sort of identification.''

And while they stared at him, and at each other, in something of astonishment, so he reached out with his deadspeak to the minds of his new friends in the graveyard half a mile away. He spoke (but silently) to Ion and Alexandru Zaharia, and his message was simple and to the point.

I'm under threat from two men. Your countrymen, I'm afraid: Securitatea. Without your help I'm done for! Harry got so much out, and only so much, before the small one kicked him in the groin. He saw it coming and managed to deflect most of it, but still he collapsed, rolling in feigned agony in the dust of the road.

"There now!" said the wooden one, his voice cold and empty of emotion. "You see, you see? You've angered Corneliu! You really must try, Harry Keogh, to be more cooperative. Our patience is by no means infinite.'' He went to the back of the car, opened it, and threw Harry's things in. But he placed the forged passport in his own pocket.

But what can we do, Harry? Ion Zaharia's anxious voice came to him where he huddled on his side, playing for time. *We could try to . . . but no, for you're too far away! We'd never get to you in time.*

No, Harry answered, *you stay right where you are. Only dig yourselves out, that's all. You and anyone else who—well, who's still in shape—and who wants to help. But don't go wasting yourselves trying to come to me, for I think I know how to bring these bastards to you!*

"Jacket!" the small thin one, Corneliu, snapped. "Quickly!"

Harry sat up, half shrugged out of his jacket before it was snatched from his back.

"All very disappointing, really," said the other one, who wasn't so much wooden now as disdainful, superior. "We fully expected that we would have to shoot you! Such things they told us about you! Such problems you've caused our friends across the border! And yet . . . you don't seem very desperate to me, Harry Keogh. Perhaps your reputation is undeserved?"

Harry had given up all thoughts of trying to bluff it out. They knew well enough who he was, if not what. "That was all a long time ago," he said, "when I was younger. I'm not so foolish now. I know when the game is up."

An open-backed truck rumbled by, heading for Bucharest. In the back, seated on benches along the sides, twin rows of men and women, mainly aging peasants, faced each other. Their eyes were uniformly empty of hope; they scarcely glanced at Harry where he knelt in the dirt with a pair of thugs standing over him; they had troubles of their own. They were the destitute, the homeless ones, their lives blighted by Ceausescu's blind, uncaring agro-industrial policy.

"Well, the game is most certainly up for you, my friend," the tall one continued. "You'll know, of course, that they want you for espionage and sabotage—and murder? Oh, a great deal of the latter, apparently!" He took out handcuffs. "So much, in fact, that I think we'll just immobilise you a little. One can never be too careful. You look harmless enough, and you're unarmed, but . . . ."

He put the cuffs on, locking Harry's hands together.

"Return air tickets to Rhodos"—the ferret had been ferreting in Harry's pockets—"cigarettes and matches, and a lot of American dollars. That's all." And to Harry: "Get up!"

He was bundled into the back of the car with the small one beside him, holding his gun on him. The tall, lurching one got into the driver's seat. "And so you were heading for the airport," the latter said. "Well, we shall give you a lift. We have a small room there where we can wait for the flight from

306

Moscow. And after that you are out of our hands." He started the car and headed for Bucharest.

"I don't get it," said Harry, genuinely puzzled. "Since when have the Securitatea been big friends with the KGB? I would have thought the USSR's glasnost and perestroika were totally at odds with what what Ceausescu is doing? Or perhaps you two, as a team, are a two-edged sword, eh? Is that it? Are you working for two bosses, Mr . . . er . . . . ?"

"Shut up!" The ferret scraped his gun down Harry's ribs.

"No let him talk." Their driver merely shrugged. "It amuses me to discover how little they know, in the West." He glanced over his shoulder. "And how much of what they do know is based on guesswork. Mr. Keogh, you may call me Eugen. And why not, since our acquaintance will be so short? But does it surprise you that Russia has friends in Romania, when Romania has been a satellite and neighbour of the USSR for so very long? Why, next you'll be telling me that there are no Russian agents in England, or France, or America! No, I can't believe you're that naive."

"You're . . . KGB?" Harry frowned.

"No, we're Securitatea—when it suits us to be. But you see, compared to the *leu,* the rouble has always been so very strong and stable—and we all must look to our futures, eh? We all must retire sooner or later." He glanced back, smiled at Harry, and gradually let the smile slide from his face. "In your case, sooner."

So . . . these two were in the pockets of the KGB, who in turn would have a section working with Harry's old "friends" at the Soviet E-Branch HQ in Moscow. It was the Russian espers who were raising their ugly head again; they remembered Bronnitsy too well and desired to pay Harry back for it. Yes, and they must fear him mightily! First Wellesley's crazy plot in Bonnyrig, and now this. He would be smuggled quietly out of Romania and into the USSR, handed over to Soviet E-Branch, and simply . . . disappear. Or at least, that was the scenario as they had worked it out . . .

But it told Harry quite a lot. If he was to be *smuggled* out of Romania, then patently the actual Romanian authorities didn't know about him at all! To them he was simply what his passport said he was: Hari Kiokis, a perfectly legitimate businessman from Greece! It made sense. The KGB (or E-Branch) had contacted their own in Romania, men who could be trusted to expedite the job—because to try to arrange any other kind of extradition would only prove to be lengthy and frustrating. So maybe there was something to be said for Ceausescu's way of running the show after all.

"Er, Eugen?" he said. "It seems to me that your main task was simply to pick me up. So why didn't you do it yesterday, at the airport? Because you needed to avoid publicity?"

"That was one reason," the tall one answered over his shoulder. "Also, we thought to kill two birds with one stone: tail you and discover your contact. You must have come here to see someone, after all! So we simply followed your taxi. But alas, a puncture! These things happen. Later we picked up your taxi driver and he showed us where he'd dropped you off. Also, he said you'd be catching a bus back into the city in the morning. Now *that* was frustrating! All that driving up and down since dawn, waiting for you to put in an appearance. As a last resort, of course, we would be obliged to return to Bucharest and wait for you at the airport. There is only one flight to Athens today. As it happened, however, that wasn't necessary."

"There was no contact!" Harry suddenly blurted it out. "I was just . . . just supposed to leave certain instructions, and pick up certain information." He was taking a chance they knew almost nothing about him, except that he was to be detained for their Russian bosses. Also, time was getting shorter. By now his friends in the cemetery back there should be very nearly ready for him.

Eugen applied the brakes, slowed the car to a halt. "You left instructions? There's a drop, back there?"

"Yes," Harry lied.

"And the information you picked up? Where is that?"

"It wasn't there. That's why I waited all night, to collect it this morning. But it still wasn't there."

Eugen turned around in his seat and stared at Harry with narrowed eyes. "You are being very open, my friend. I take it this all has to do with our peasant fifth columnists, right?"

Harry tried hard to look frightened, which wasn't at all hard. He knew nothing about Romania's peasant fifth columnists, but he did understand something of the psychology of thugs such as these. "Something like that," he said. "But . . . you said you have a room at the airport? Well, I think I'd rather tell you everything now, than have Comrade Corneliu beat it out of me in private later."

"A great shame," Corneliu grunted, and shrugged. "Still, I might beat you anyway."

Eugen said, "You will show us this letter drop?"

"If it will make life easier for me, yes," Harry answered.

"Hah!" scoffed Corneliu. "This one, tough?" And to Harry: "Are they all girls, your British spies?"

Harry shrugged. In fact he knew very little about standard British spies, only about espers: mindspies.

Eugen turned the car around and backtracked; there was no more conversation until Harry called a halt at the entrance to the graveyard. "It's in here," he said then. "The letter drop."

They all got out of the car and Corneliu used his gun to prod Harry on ahead. As he went he sent his deadspeak before him: *We're here. One of them at least has a gun—trained on me! In the moment that he sees you he'll be distracted. That's when I plan to disarm him. Is everything okay?*

We're okay, Harry, the Zaharias answered at once. *And there are several others who wouldn't be dissuaded. We don't know if they'll be much good. But . . . strength in numbers, eh?*

I don't see you. Harry looked worriedly all about. *Are you in hiding?*

The others are just under the soil, Harry, Ion Zaharia told him. *And we're out of our boxes, in our sarcophagus.*

Harry remembered: the Zaharias had been buried in the same plot and had a joint sarcophagus, its heavy, beautifully veined lid standing some eighteen inches above the surrounding marble chips of their plot. They hadn't seemed to mind him sitting there for a few moments while he was talking to them. So they were waiting under the lid, eh? Well, and that should come in very handy.

"Move, Keogh!" Corneliu growled, shoving him forward down an aisle between rows of leaning headstones. "Where is this drop, anyway?"

"Right there." Harry pointed ahead. He moved to the huge tomb and stood looking down at its massive lid. "I had to lever it to one side, but together we should slide it easily enough, once we lift it from its groove." He hoped that the thugs hadn't noticed how ripe the air was, and how much worse the smell was growing from second to second, but this was something he dare not ask.

"Oh?" Eugen grinned mirthlessly. "Desecration, too, eh? Why, you should be ashamed of yourself, Harry Keogh, posting letters to the dead! They can't answer you, you know." And to Corneliu: "You hold your gun on him while I give him a hand."

How wrong you are! Harry thought, as he and the tall agent strained at the lid—which suddenly, and very easily, slid to one side. The necroscope had expected that, certainly, and held his breath; but Corneliu and Eugen had not, and didn't. Nor were they expecting what happened next, in the moment after the tomb's trapped gasses whooshed out.

"*God!*" Eugen staggered back, his hands flying to his nose and mouth. But Corneliu, standing back a little, simply gasped and bugged his eyes. And the weapon in his hand seemed to transfer its aim automatically from Harry's back to what was first sitting up, then standing, and finally reaching out from the shadowy mouth of the tomb!

Before he could squeeze the trigger, if indeed sufficient strength remained for that, Harry broke his wrist with a kick he seemed to have been saving for years. The gun went flying, and so did Corneliu—directly into the burned and blistered, blue and tomb grey hands of the Zaharias! The brothers grabbed and held him, stared at him with their dead bubble eyes, and threatened him with blackened bone teeth in straining, scorched cartilage jaws.

The other agent, Eugen, gibbering as he crashed through the ancient bramble-grown plots towards the graveyard's exit, didn't even pause to look back . . . until he ran into what was waiting for him. Those others of whom the Zaharias had reported: "They wouldn't be dissuaded." And for all that they were mainly fragmentary—or possibly because that's what they were—these crumbling, crawling, spastically kicking *parts* of corpses stopped Eugen dead in his tracks.

One of them was a woman, whose legs and life had been lost in a terrible accident. Long-buried, her breasts were rotting onto her belly, sloughing away from her in grotesque lumps; but still she stood upright on her stumps and found a supernatural strength to cling to Eugen's shuddering thighs where he danced and screamed to heaven for mercy and tried to push her face away from his midriff. Finally he succeeded and the vertebrae of her neck parted; her entire head flopped over backwards like that of a broken doll, as if it were hinged, exposing maggots where they seethed in her throat and fed on ravaged flesh and torn tendons.

With a series of frenzied leaps and kicks born of the sheer terror of his situation, at last Eugen freed himself from the dead woman's crumbling torso and reached inside his jacket. He bought out an automatic pistol and cocked it, turning it upon others of these impossibly animated parts where they came crawling or jerking towards him. Harry didn't want that gun to go off; Eugen's screams were bad enough; gunshots might easily attract investigators.

The dead picked up Harry's concern as surely as any spoken word and moved to dispel it. The pile of loathsomeness which was the legless woman struggled upright and toppled itself against Eugen's weapon, and her mouldy hands drew its barrel into the trembling jelly cavity of her neck. With her trunk she deadened the sound of Eugen's first shot, while Harry saw to it that there wouldn't be a second one.

Coming upon the agent from behind and clenching his manacled hands, he rabbit-punched him unconscious and, as he fell, kicked the gun from his hand. Collapsing, Eugen saw Harry's face fading slowly into darkness and wondered why nothing of horror was written in his strange, soulful eyes . . .

Regaining consciousness a few minutes later, the tall awkward secret policeman was sure that what he'd experienced had been a vivid and especially terrifying nightmare . . . until he actually opened his eyes and looked around. Then:

"My God! Oh . . . my . . . *God!*" he burst out. For a moment his eyes bulged, and then he closed them again—tightly.

"Don't faint," Harry warned him. "I've only so much time left and there are things I want to know. If I don't get the answers I need, these dead people will probably be angry—with you!"

Eugen kept his eyes closed. "Harry . . . Harry Keogh!" he finally gasped. "But these people . . . they're dead!"

"I just said they were," Harry told him. "You see, that's where your 'friends across the border' made their mistake. They told you who I am but not what I am. They didn't tell you how many friends I have, or that they're all dead."

The other mumbled something in Romanian, began to gibber hysterically.

"Calm down," Harry told him at once, "and speak English. Forget that the people holding you are dead. Just think of them as my friends, who'll do anything they have to in order to protect me."

"God—I can *smell* them!" Eugen wailed, and Harry suspected that he wasn't getting through to him. He hardened.

"Look, you were going to hand me over to the KGB—who in turn would have tortured me for things they want to know, then killed me! So why should I go easy on you? Now you can get a grip on yourself and start answering my questions, or I give up on you, get out of it, and leave you here with them."

Eugen struggled a little, then sat very still as the movements he'd made stirred up fresh waves of tomb stink. He could feel dead, rubbery fingers holding his arms. His eyes were still tightly closed. "Just tell me one thing," he said. "Am I mad? God—I can't *breathe*!"

"That's another thing," Harry told him. "The longer you're here with my friends, the more chances you're taking with your health. Diseases proliferate in the dead, Eugen. You're not only smelling them but you're breathing them, too!"

Eugen's head lolled and Harry thought he was about to pass out. The Necroscope slapped him, twice, hard, front- and back-handed. The agent's eyes snapped open, glared, and swivelled left and right as his situation reimpressed itself upon his mind and his momentary rage shrank down again.

The Zaharias held him. They were kneeling inside their exposed tomb, reaching out of it to pinion his arms and hold him down where he was seated with his back to their sarcophagus. And they "looked" at him with their glazed, deadfish eyes. The Romanian agent at once turned his gaze away from them, looked straight ahead, at Harry.

The Necroscope was down on one knee in front of Eugen, staring hard at him, and behind Keogh other dead—*things*—formed a half circle amidst the rank grasses, brambles, and tombstones. Some of these were mummied fragments, sere and shrivelled, dry as paper. But others were . . . wet. And all of them moved, trembled, threatened, however mutely. The friends of Harry Keogh. A group of them were gathered about the prone form of Corneliu, who had fainted from a combination of shock and the agony of his broken wrist.

All of this Eugen took in. And at last the trapped, terrified agent asked, "Are they going to kill me?"

"Not if you tell me what I have to know."

"Then ask it."

"First, you can get these off me," said Harry, and he held out his hands with Eugen's handcuffs still in place. "The dead are great at taking hold and refusing to let go, but not much for fumbling about with things. They're not as articulate as the living." Eugen stared at him and wondered who was the more frightening, the dead or Harry Keogh. The Necroscope was so matter-of-fact about things.

313

Ion Zaharia reluctantly released Eugen's hand so that he could get the key out of his pocket. But Alexandru, Ion's brother, was taking no chances; he gripped the agent's neck in his elbow and clung that much tighter. Finally Harry was free of the cuffs, and rubbing his wrists, he stood up.

"You're not leaving me here?" Eugen's face was white, with eyes like holes punched in papier-mâché.

Harry shrugged. "That's up to you. First answer my questions, and then we'll see what's to be done with you and your unpleasant little friend here." He crossed to Corneliu and recovered his air ticket, cigarettes, and matches, then came back, knelt down again, and took back his passport from Eugen. "And the first thing I want to know," he said, "is will I still be able to use this? Or will there be people looking for me at the airport? What I'm saying is: were you two alone on this, or do others of the Securitatea work for the KGB?"

"They might do, I don't know," Eugen answered. "But we were on our own on this one. They got in touch with us—a telephone call, it's easy—and told us what plane you'd be on from Athens. We were to pick you up, hold you until someone came to collect you. There's a flight due in from Moscow at 1 P.M."

"So . . . I should be able to go on back into Bucharest and simply board my plane?"

Eugen looked surly, said nothing—until Ion pushed his hideous face very close and held up a warning finger. And:

"Yes! For God's sake!" Eugen gasped.

"God?" said Harry, reaching into the agent's pocket for the keys to his car. Harry wasn't sure he still believed in God, and he certainly couldn't understand why the dead should, not in the "heaven" which they had been granted. But they did, as he'd discovered in several conversations. God was hope, he supposed. But while Harry wouldn't personally describe as a blasphemy the mere fact of the Deity's spoken Name, still it set his teeth on edge hearing it as an exclamation from one such as Eugen. "And you know all about Him, do you?"

"What?" said the other as Harry stood up again. "About

who?'' It was as Harry had expected: Eugen knew nothing about Him.

"Well, I'm going now," said Harry, "but I'm afraid you're staying right here. You and Corneliu. Because I know I can't let you walk, not just yet, anyway. So you'll remain the honoured guests of my friends until I'm well out of it. But once I'm safely airborne, then I'll let these people know they can release you—and themselves.''

"You'll . . . let them know?" Eugen had started shuddering and couldn't control it. "How will you let—''

"I'll shout," said Harry, with a mirthless grin. "Don't worry, they'll hear me.''

But what if he starts shouting first? Ion Zaharia asked as Harry walked out of the graveyard.

Then stop him, Harry answered. And: *But try not to kill them. Life's precious, as you know well enough. So let them live what they have left. And anyway, they're not worthy to be in here with such as you . . .*

Harry drove very carefully back to Bucharest, parked the car in the airport car park and locked it, and pressed the keys into the soil of a large flowerpot in the booking lounge. Then, just five minutes past his actual reporting time, he handed in his ticket and luggage. It was the same as when he'd come in: no one looked at him twice.

The Olympia Airlines plane took off just eleven minutes late, at 12:56. As it turned its nose south for Bulgaria and the Aegean, Harry was rewarded by the sight of an Aeroflot jet going in for a landing. There would be a bright-eyed couple of lads on board just dying to get their hands on him. Well, so let them die.

Forty minutes later, with the Aegean just swimming up into view through the circular windows, Harry reached out with his deadspeak to the cemetery outside Ploiesti. *How are things?*

All's well, Harry. No one's been in here, and these two haven't been a problem. The big one did faint, eventually.

315

His small friend came to, took one look, and passed out again!

Harry said, *Ion, Alexandru, all of you—I don't have the words to thank you.*

You don't need any. Can we just leave these two where they are now, and . . . dig ourselves in again?

Harry's nod was reflex as he reclined his seat and lay back a little. The dead in the Romanian graveyard picked it up anyway and began to disperse back to their resting place. *Thanks again,* Harry told them, withdrawing his thoughts and allowing himself some small relaxation for the first time in . . . well, in a day at least.

Don't mention it, was their response . . .

Harry tried to get Faethor. If he could contact the others as easily as that, communication with the long-dead father of vampires should be no problem. After a few seconds of concentration, he got through.

Harry? I see you are safe. Ah, but you're the resourceful one, Harry Keogh!

You knew I was in trouble?

(Faethor's mental shrug.) *As I've told you before: I sometimes overhear things. Did you want something?*

It seemed to me we might save ourselves some time, Harry answered. *I have nothing to do right now, and in a little while my head will be full of the clutter of friends and the atmosphere of a friendly place—not that I'm complaining! So I thought maybe now would be a good time for you to tell me the rest of Janos's story.*

There's not much more to tell. But if you wish it . . . ?

I wish it.

And: *Very well, my son,* Faethor sighed. *So be it . . .*

As has been told, I was away for three hundred years. Three centuries of blood! The Great Crusade was only the start of it; later I served Genghis Khan, and then his grandson Batu. In 1240 I assisted and delighted in the taking of Kiev, and in burning it to ashes. Eventually it was time for me to "die"

. . . and return as Fereng the Black, son of the Fereng! Then, under Hulegu in 1258, I helped bring down Baghdad. Ah, such years of bloodshed, pillage, and rape!

But the Mongols were on the wane, and by the turn of the century I had forsaken them in order to fight for Islam. Oh, yes, I was an Ottoman! Me, a Turk, a Moslem *ghazi*! Ah, what it is to be a mercenary, eh? And with the Turks, for one and half a centuries more, I revelled in blood and death and the sheer glut of war! In the end, however, I had lived with them too long and so was obliged to desert their cause. Ah, well, and it was crumbling anyway.

And so finally I returned and put Thibor down (as has also been told), then took me off into the unchanged and unchanging mountains to seek out Janos and see how well he had kept house for me.

In the interim, however, I had kept my ears open. Wamphyri ears are delicate instruments, be sure, and miss very little. Aye, and they had always been alert for news of my sons, Thibor and Janos. Well, of the former we know. And of the latter?

Where Thibor had been greedy for blood, Janos had been simply greedy. In my time abroad he had many interests, but mainly he'd been a thief, a pirate, a *corsair*. Does it surprise you? It should not: for the Barbary pirates had their origin in petty princelings who rose up during the Christian-Moslem conflicts of the Crusades. That then had been Janos's chief business during the time of my absence: a grand thief on the broad bosom of the Mediterranean, to loot them who had looted others!

And now he's a sailor again, eh? Well, and why not? Oh, he knows the sea well enough that one, who now for a profession brings up treasure from the ocean and digs for it in the islands around. Hah! And who pray would know better where to find it—since he was the one who laid it down, more than five hundred years ago! And what was that all about, you may wonder, that great squirreling for nuts, as if some fearsome winter were about to embark? But it was, it was! Aye, just such a winter: for Janos had worked hard at his art to look well into the future, and had not liked what he saw there.

For one thing, he had doubtless seen my return, and he did not *need* to look to know how I would deal with him! And so he had made provision for *another time*, far beyond the hour of my revenge. This present time, of course, when he is up again and about in the world of men.

But (you may ask) my revenge for what? The loss of Marilena was three to four hundred years in my wake, and I could have killed him then for that; so what now? I will tell you:

First, for his desertion from my cause. To go a-pirating he must first vacate my house. Second, for his treatment of my Szgany. For in the early years of my absence he had kicked out the Szagy Ferengi and reinstated the filthy Zirra, whom I had cursed! Third and last, but not least, for the way in which he greeted me, when at last I was returned.

On my way I had gathered faithful Gypsies to me, who had remembered me through all the years of my exile. Not the originals, no, for they were dust, but the sons of their sons. Ah, they remember legends, the Szgany! But when I went up to my castle, I went alone, by night, for a task force would be too obvious and could only appear threatening.

Alas, when I was come there, I saw the place a ruin! Well, perhaps not quite so bad, but near enough. The battlements were broken; earthworks without were untended; the repair in general was bad. Left to fend for itself through much of my absence, the place had suffered. But Janos, done with pirating now and returned to other pursuits, was to house. And just as I had tried to follow his career, so he had followed mine.

He knew I was coming; guards were out, with clear instructions; I was challenged, and upon identifying myself . . .

. . . Was set upon!

They had sharpened hardwood staves. They had crossbows with wooden bolts. They carried the curved long knives of the Turks. Silver they had, too, on their weapons, and garlic in which to steep them! And each party of men, they had

318

casks of oil, and torches with which to fire it! For what to burn, I ask you?

I fled them, up into the crags and for many a mile in the high places. I limped, scurried, cried out in some great pain, kept barely ahead of my pursuers. They knew I was injured and that they would have me. Janos sent out his entire household to hunt me down. But . . . I merely lured them. What, Faethor Ferenczy, with his tail between his legs, running from Zirra scum?

Aha! For while they were out chasing me, my own small but faithful Szgany army were up and into my house, into all of its stations and down behind its earthworks! And high in the peaks, I turned on my trackers, laughed and slew a few, then launched myself into the night and glided down to my castle as of old. And there I discovered Janos trapped, and brought him to his knees.

The Zirras, when they came straggling home, were met by mine, who slew them out of hand. Some escaped the slaughter and word went out; in a little while no more came; the survivors had fled into the night and the countryside around, to become Travellers once more as of old . . .

And it was then I discovered Janos's several subsidiary interests, with which he had occupied himself while I had been away. Then, too, I saw how severely I had underestimated him. My castle had been built upon the foundations of another, earlier house, whose basements Janos had uncovered. And he had seen to it that these were extended, outwards into the roots of the crags around, down into the rock of the mountain itself. To what end?

There lay the measure of my underestimation. Janos had told me he desired to be Wamphyri . . . ah, but *how* he had desired it!

Now in those days necromancy was an art. Certain common men had discovered the way of it; they practised it much as a vampire might, but without his natural instinct for it. Janos knew I was a crafty necromancer and would emulate me, but I had declined to teach him my techniques. Wherefore he had determined to discover methods of his own. Doubtless he'd consulted with many necromancers, to learn their ways.

The extensive cellars of the castle were mazy and secret, whose stairs and passageways were known only to Janos and a handful of his men, all of whom were now either fled or dead. But I went down with him to see what he had been about, and there discovered tomb loot from all Wallachia and Transylvania and the lands around. No, not treasure as such, but *tomb* loot!

Do you know that in prehistory it was the way of men to burn their dead and bury their ashes in vases? Of course you do, for the habit has survived. Why, there's as much burning as burying even to the present day! But the Thracians, they had entombed a great *many* of their dead in this fashion, and Janos had been busy digging them up again! And once more you will ask: to what end?

To enquire of them their secrets! To fetch the dead to life and torment them for their histories! To invest their very ashes with flesh which he could torture! For the Thracians were heavy in gold, and as I have said, Janos was greedy. Nothing is new, eh? An hundred, two hundred, even three hundred years later, necromancers were *still* calling up spirits in order to discover their treasures. Your own Edward Kelly and John Dee were two such, but fakers both of them. I consulted with them in my time and know this for a fact.

As for Janos's method, it was simplicity in itself.

First, remove a burial urn to his castle vaults, where, by use of those arts he had mastered, its salts might be reconstituted; chain the poor wretch so obtained and torture him for knowledge of his kith and kin, the locations of their graves, etcetera, and *their* hoards in turn. And so forth, In the pursuit of which policy, Janos had amassed a veritable graveyard of despoiled pots and urns and *lekythoi*, such as to fill several large rooms!

Intrigued, I demanded a demonstration of his art. (For you will understand, this was *not* necromancy as the Wamphyri might use it, but something new—to me, anyway.) And Janos, knowing I had still to deal with him and seeking to please me, proceeded. He tipped out salts upon the floor, and by use of strange words in an Invocation of Power—lo and behold—conjured from these cinders a Thracian woman of exceeding beauty! Her language was archaic in the extreme but not beyond understanding; certainly it was not beyond *my* understanding, for I was Wamphyri and expert in tongues. Moreover, she knew she was dead and that this was a great blasphemy, and begged of Janos that he not use her again. From which I knew that this bastard son of mine not only called up the dead into former semblance, but had more uses for some of them than simply to question as to the whereabouts of buried treasure!

How grand! My excitement was such that I had her before allowing him to reduce her back to ashes!

"You must teach me this thing," I told him. "That is the least you can do to atone for your many sins against me."

He agreed and showed me how to mix certain chemicals and human salts together, then carefully inscribed two sets of words upon a stretched skin. The first set, alongside an ascending arrow, thus, ↑, was the invocation as such, and the second, marked ↓, was the devolution.

"Bravo!" I cried then, when I had the thing. "I must put it to the test!"

"As you see"—he indicated all his many jars and urns—"you have a wide choice."

"Indeed I have," I answered gravely, and stroked my chin. And before he knew what I was about, I drew out a wooden stake from beneath my cloak and pinned him! This did not serve to kill him, no, for he had a vampire in him; it merely immobilised him. Then I called down some trusted men of mine from the castle and burned Janos to ashes even while he frothed and moaned and eventually screamed a little. Aye, and when these ashes of his—these essential salts—were cool, I had them sifted, applied his several chemical powders . . . *and used his own magic to have him up again*!

And did he scream then? You may believe he did! The heat of the fire, a mercifully short travail, had been nothing compared to the unendurable agony of the fact that he was now and eternally and *utterly* in my power! So I thought . . .

But alas, his screaming was not borne of this knowledge but of a wrenching, a tearing, a division of being—which I shall explain in a moment.

But oh, to see those clouds of smoke puff up from his dry, dusty remains—a great upheaval of smoke and fumes—from which stumbled Janos, naked and screaming. But . . . a miracle! He was not alone. There with him, but entirely apart, was his vampire: my spittle grown to a live thing, but a creature with little or nothing of its own intelligence!

It was leech, snail, serpent, a great blind slug, and all unused to going on its own. It, too, mewled, though I know not how. But I did know the answer to the riddle: in burning Janos I had burned *two* creatures, and raising him up again, I had also revitalised two—but in their separate parts!

Then . . . I had me a thought. I brought forward my cowering men and commanded them that they take Janos and hold him down. "And so you would be Wamphyri, eh?" I said, approaching him with my sword. "And so you shall be. This creature here is a vampire but has very little of a brain. It shall have yours!" He screamed again, once, before I took his head. And splitting his skull, I took out from it his living, dripping brain.

You can guess the rest, I'm sure. Using Janos's own process and keeping his body apart, I devolved his head and vampire *both* into one heap of ashes, which I placed in an urn among the others. And then I laughed and *laughed* till I cried! For if by any fluke he should be brought back now, it would be as . . . as what? A clever slug? An intelligent leech? Why, it would amuse me to call him up again and see!

But alas, that was not to be, for in the end he'd thwarted me. The skin upon which he'd written his runes had been resurrected skin, flayed from a victim. I had directed my runes of catabolism *through* the very skin from which I read them, and so when I'd sent Janos down, the skin, too, had crumbled into dust! Well, the Words of Power were tricky and I had not learned them except for the single name of an

322

ancient dark god of the outer spheres. However, I still had my bastard son's body.

So . . . I burned that, too—aye, a second time—and sent pinches of it out to the four corners of the earth, and there dispersed them on the winds.

That was the end of it. I had done with Janos. And now I have done with my story . . .

XII: First and Second Blood

As FAETHOR FINISHED, SO THERE CAME A CABIN ANNOUNCE-ment: the plane was now descending towards Athens.

Harry said, *Faethor, in another ten to fifteen minutes I'll be on the ground and into the bustle of the airport. I've noticed that you've been growing weaker—your voice—and put it down to distance and the sun full on the ruins of your house. Soon I'll be on my way to Rhodes, which is more distant yet. So this is probably my last chance to say a few things.*

You have something to say? (Harry pictured Faethor raising an eyebrow.)

First . . . I owe you my thanks, Harry told him, *but second, I can't help but remind myself that without you in the first place, none of this—Thibor, Dragosani, Yulian Bodescu, and now Janos—would ever have happened. Okay, so I'm in your debt, but at the same time I know you for the black-hearted thing you have been, and for the monsters you've spawned in my world. And I'd be a liar if I didn't tell you that in my opinion, you're the biggest monster of them all!*

324

I consider it a compliment, Faethor answered, without hesitation. *Is there anything else you require to know?*

A few things, yes, said Harry. *If you destroyed Janos so utterly, how come he's back? I mean, what trick did he work—what dark magic did he leave behind him—to bring him back into the world? And why did he wait so long? Why now?*

Is it not obvious? Faethor sounded genuinely surprised by Harry's naiveté. *He had seen the far future and laid his plans accordingly. He had known I would put him down, that time when I returned to the mountains. Yes, and he knew that if he came back in my time, I would find a way to do it again! And so he must wait until I was gone from the world. Time is but a small thing to the Wamphyri, Harry. As to how he worked this clever trick:*

It was those accursed Zirras! Aye, and I know it was them, for I've had it from my own faithful few, who mutter in their graves much like other men. I'll tell you how it was.

Long after me and mine were gone from the castle on the heights, certain of Janos's own returned and placed his vampire ashes in a secret place which he'd prepared against just such an eventuality. For he'd learned other magicks in my three hundred years' absence, of which this was one. He'd had Zirra women in his time, that bastard of mine, and sown his seed far and wide. The three-fingered son of a son of his would one day feel his allure and go up to the old castle in the mountains . . . but it would be Janos who came down from it! So he planned it, and so it has come to pass . . .

And all the treasure he'd looted from ancient tombs, did you never find it? Harry pressed. *Didn't you search the place, your own castle?*

I searched a little, Faethor answered. *But have you not listened? The treasure was elsewhere, buried again or sunken in the sea, until this later time when he could have it up.*

Of course. Harry nodded. *I'd forgotten.*

As for searching the place in its entirety: no, I did not, not every hole the dog had dug. I no longer felt that it was mine but that he had fouled it. I could smell him, even taste him, everywhere. The castle had his mark on it, where his despi-

cable sigil was carved into the very stone: the red-eyed bat, rising from its urn. He had used the place and made it his own, and I wanted no more of it. Shortly, I moved on. As for my own history after that time, that does not concern you.

So . . . *the castle still stands,* Harry mused in a little while. *And in its roots . . . what? Does anything remain of Janos's "tomb loot," his experiments with necromancy, I wonder? For after all, it appears that's where he came from in this most recent resurgence . . .* And Faethor knew that Harry was thinking of another castle in the Carpathians, but on the Russian side, in a region once called the Khorvaty and still called by some Bukovina. For that had been Faethor's home, too, upon a time, and what had been done there and left there to scream and fester in the earth had been monstrous; so that Harry knew there was a grave peril in certain ruins.

I can understand your concern, the vampire told him, *but I think it is unfounded. For my place in the heights over old Halmagiu and Virfurilio is no more. It was swept away, all in a magnificent thunder, in the October of the year 1928.*

Yes, I remember that, Harry answered. *I heard it from Ladislau Giresci. Apparently it was some sort of explosion, possibly of methane gas accumulated in the cellars; which, if they were as extensive as you say, seems feasible. But if Janos's*—remains—*came through it, who is to say there weren't other . . . survivals?*

But as I have explained, said Faethor, *Janos had made provisions. Whatever else perished when that house went down, he did not. Perhaps his Szgany had taken his ashes from there to some other place, only returning them later when the house lay in ruins, I don't know. Possibly they did it when the castle became the property of another. Again I cannot say.*

What other? said Harry.

Faethor sighed, but eventually: *There was one other, aye,* he finally said. *Listen and I'll tell you about him.*

During the fifteenth, sixteenth, and seventeenth centuries, and even to the eighteenth, the supposed civilised world had grown more aware of so-called witches and the black arts.

*Witches, necromancers, demons, vampires, and all such
creatures—real and imagined, guilty or innocent—were harried by relentless witchfinders, "proved" by torture, and destroyed. Now, the true vampire was ever aware of his
mortality and of the one Great Enemy of all his kind, called
Prominence! And the sixteenth century especially was not a
good time for a person to be found too old or different or
reclusive or even noticeable. In short, while anonymity among
the Wamphyri has ever been a synonym for longevity, it were
never more so than in those dark and doomful sixteenth and
seventeenth centuries!*

*Now, in the middle and to the end of the seventeenth cen-
tury the witchfinders were active in America, and from a
place called Salem was driven a man called Edward Hutchinson. He obtained a lease on my old house in the mountains
and dwelled there . . . far too long! He was a diabolist, a
necromancer, and possibly a vampire. Perhaps even Wamphyri! But as I have hinted, he was imprudent; he lived too
long in the one place and made himself prominent.*

*He studied the history of the house and took for his own
several grand pseudonyms: as well as Edward he was wont
to call himself "Baron" or "Janos"—aye, and even "Faethor"! And finally he settled for "Baron Ferenczy." Now
this, as might well be imagined, was what brought him to my
attention. It offended me; likewise his occupancy of the castle, for I had thought me that one day I might return there
myself, when things were different and Janos's taint faded a
little with the years. The Wamphyri are territorial, as you
know. And so I vowed that at a time of my choosing and as
chance permitted, then that I'd square these things with this
Hutchinson.*

*But chance never did permit; no, for I had my own exis-
tence to look to, and the world was ever a-bustle and full of
change. And so for two hundred years and more this foreign
man lived in the castle I had builded, while I in my turn lived
alone in my house in Ploiesti.*

*As I have said, he made himself prominent in some way,
perhaps in several. Certainly he would soon have been sum-*

moned to Bucuresti, to make account of himself, if not for that titan explosion which finished him and his works forever. But as for Janos: I can only assume he lay in his jar or urn in a secret place, and waited for his time and a certain three-fingered son of the Szgany to find and rescue him.

Myself . . . I went back there once—in 1930, I think—do not ask me why. Perhaps I desired to see what remained of the place; I might even have lived there again, if it was habitable. But no, Janos's touch was still on the stone, his taint in the mortar, his hated memory in the very air of the ruins. Of course it was, for Janos himself was still there! But I did not know that.

But do you know, I believe that in the end Janos had been closer to his Wamphyri source than I might ever have imagined? For however cursory my exploration of those ruins that time in 1930, nevertheless I found evidence of works which . . . but enough. We are both tired, and you are not giving me your best attention. Still, nothing will waste; you know the bulk of it; the rest will keep until another time.

You're right, said Harry, *I am tired. Nervous exhaustion, I suppose.* And he made himself a promise that between Athens and Rhodes he'd sleep.

And he did . . .

. . . but coming awake just before the landing, and as Harry stepped down from the plane into the blasting sunlight and made his way with the other passengers towards customs, he could feel that something was very much amiss. And his heart speeded up a little when, beyond the barriers in the arrivals area, he saw Manolis Papastamos and Darcy Clarke waiting for him; for it was written in their faces, too, that something was wrong. For all the sunshine and warmth, still they looked cold, pale, sick.

He looked at the two of them where they waited, searched their faces for an answer, and almost snatched back his forged passport when it was handed to him. Then he hurried to them, thinking, *There's a face missing, Sandra's, but that's only right, for she'll be in London now . . . won't she?*

"Is it Sandra?" he said when they were face-to-face. They looked at him, then looked away. And: "Tell me about it," he said, curiously calm now for all that he felt very, very ill.

And so they told him about it . . .

Twenty-one hours earlier:

Darcy had escorted Sandra to the airport outside Rhodes and stayed with her until she was called forward for her London flight—almost. But at the last moment he had been obliged to answer a call of nature. The toilets were a little distant from the boarding gates, so that coming out, he had to run the length of the terminal in order to wave her goodbye. By the time he'd found a vantage point, the last of the passengers were already climbing the gantry steps to the aircraft's door. But he waved anyway, thinking that perhaps she would see him from her window.

After the plane left he drove back to the villa and began packing his things, only to be interrupted by a telephone call from Manolis at the police station. It had been Manolis' idea that when Sandra was out of it, Darcy shouldn't stay on his own. The Greek policeman had rooms in a hotel in the centre of town; Darcy would be welcome to stay there. But before driving out to the villa to act as Darcy's guide to his new lodgings, and because it happened now and then that flights were late, Manolis had thought to call the airport first and ensure that Sandra was safely away. And he'd discovered that she wasn't away at all but missed her flight.

"What?" Darcy couldn't believe it. "But . . . I was there. I mean, I was in the . . ."

"Yes?"

"*Shit!*" Darcy gasped as the truth hit him.

"You were in the shit?"

"No, in the bloody toilets," Darcy groaned, "which in this case amounts to much the same thing! Manolis, don't you see? It was my *talent* working for me—or against me. Against that poor girl, anyway."

"Your talent?"

"My guardian angel, the thing that keeps me out of trouble. It isn't something I can control. It works in different ways. This time it saw danger around the corner and . . . and I had to go to the damned toilet!''

Now Manolis understood, and knew the worst of it. "They've taken her?" he hissed. "The Lazarides creature and his vampires, they have drawn the first blood?"

"God, yes!" Darcy answered. "I can't think of any other explanation."

In his native Greek, Manolis said a long stream of things then; curses, Darcy supposed. And: "Look, stay where you are and I'll be right there."

"No," Darcy answered. "No, meet me at that place where we ate the other night. *Christ*, I need a drink!"

"Very well," said Papastamos. "Fifteen minutes . . ."

Darcy was into his third large Metaxa when Manolis arrived. "Will you get drunk?" he said. "It won't help."

"No," Darcy answered. "I just needed a stiffener, that's all. And do you know what I keep thinking? What will I tell Harry? That's what!"

"It isn't your fault," Manolis commiserated, "and you must stop thinking about it. Harry is back tomorrow. We must let him take the lead. Meanwhile, every policeman on the island is looking for Lazarides, his crew and his boat— and Sandra, of course. I made the call and gave the orders before I came here. Also, I should have the complete background information on this . . . this Vrykoulakas *pig* by morning! Not only from Athens but also America. Lazarides' right-hand man, called Armstrong, is an American."

Darcy looked at Manolis and thought, *Christ, I thank you for this man!*

Darcy wasn't a secret agent, nor even a policeman. He'd been with E-Branch all these years not because his talent was indispensable to them but simply because it *was* a talent, and all such weird and esoteric powers had interested them. But he couldn't use it as the telepaths and locators used theirs, and it was useless except in special circumstances. Indeed, on several occasions it had seemed to Darcy that his talent used him! Certainly it had caused him grief now and then:

as during the Bodescu affair, for example, when it had kept him safe and sound only at the expense of another esper. And Darcy still hadn't forgiven himself for that. Now . . . now there was this. Without Papastamos to take control and actually, physically *do* something . . . Darcy didn't know what he would have done.

"What do you suggest we do now?" he said.

"What *can* we do?" the other answered. "Until we have word of them—until we know where Lazarides and the girl are—we can do nothing. And even then I will need authorisation to move on this creature. Unless . . . I could always claim I had the strong suspicions of the drug running, and close in on him even without authorisation! But it will help when we know all about him, tomorrow morning. And Harry Keogh might have the ideas, too. So for now"—he shrugged, but heavily and with obvious frustration—"nothing."

"But—"

"There are no buts. We can only wait." He stood up. "Come on, let's get your things."

They drove to the villa, where, oddly, Darcy found himself reluctant to get out of the car. "Do you know," he said, "I feel completely done in, 'knackered,' in common parlance! I supose it's emotional."

"I suppose it's the Metaxa!" Manolis answered dryly.

But as they approached the door of the place down the garden path, suddenly Darcy knew that "it" was neither. He grabbed the Greek's arm and whispered hoarsely, "Manolis, someone is in there!"

"What?" Manolis looked at him, glanced back towards the villa. "But how do you know?"

"I know because I don't want to go in! It's my guardian angel acting up, my talent. Someone's waiting in there for us—for me, anyway. My own fault. I was in such a state when I came out that I left the door open."

"And now you're sure someone is in there, right?" Manolis' voice was a mere breath of air as he brought out his pistol and fitted a silencer to the barrel, then cocked it.

"God, yes!" Darcy in turn breathed. "I'm sure, all right!

331

It's like someone was trying to turn me around and boot me the hell out of it! First, I didn't want to get out of the car, and now, with every step I take, it gets stronger. And believe me, whoever it is in there, he's deadly!''

"Then he's mine," said Manolis, showing Darcy his gun. "For this, too, is quite deadly!" He reached out and touched the door, which swung silently open. "Follow me in." And then he turned sideways, crouched down a very little, and stepped inside.

Darcy's every instinct—each fibre of his being—screamed RUN! . . . but he followed Manolis inside. He wouldn't let it make a coward of him this time. There were two too many people on his conscience already. It was time he showed this fucking thing who was boss! And—

Manolis put on the light.

The main living room was empty, looked just as Darcy had left it. Manolis looked at Darcy, cocked his head on one side enquiringly, and gave a small, questioning shrug. "Where?" His whisper was so quiet as to be a mere shaping of the lips.

Darcy looked around the room, at the beds grouped in the centre of the floor, the tapestry on the wall, a pair of ornamental oil lamps on a shelf, a suitcase of Harry's under the bed he'd never used. And the doors, closed, leading to the bedrooms, which likewise hadn't been used. Until now . . .

Then his eyes went back to Harry's suitcase, and narrowed.

"Well?" Manolis shaped his mouth again.

Darcy held a finger to his lips, crossed to the beds, and slid Harry's suitcase fully into view. The lid was open; he lifted it, took out the crossbow and loaded it, and stood up. Manolis nodded his approval.

Darcy crossed to the bedroom doors and reached out a hand to touch the first one. His trembling fingertips told him nothing except that he was scared half to death. He commanded his feet to carry him to the second door, and went to touch that, too. But no, that was as brave as his talent

332

would let him be. NO! something screamed at him. FOR FUCK'S SAKE, NO!

Gooseflesh crawled on his arms as he half turned towards Manolis to say, "In here!" But he never said it.

The door was hurled open, knocking Darcy aside, and Seth Armstrong stood framed in the opening! Just looking at him, apish, threatening, no one could have mistaken his alienism, the fact that he was less, or more, than a mere man. In the subdued lighting of the room, his left eye was yellow, huge, expanded in its orbit, and a black eye patch hid the right eye from view.

Manolis shouted, "Stay where you are! Stand still!" But Armstrong merely smiled grimly and came loping towards him.

"Shoot him!" Darcy shouted, scrabbling on his hands and knees. "For Christ's sake shoot him!"

Manolis had no choice, for Armstrong was almost upon him—and he'd opened his mouth to display teeth and jaws which the Greek simply didn't believe! He fired twice, almost point-blank; the first into Armstrong's shoulder, which served to snap the big American upright, and the second into his belly, which bent him down again and pushed him back a little. But that was all. Then he came on again, grasped Manolis by the shoulder, and hurled him against the wall. And Manolis knew where he'd felt such strength before, but knowing it didn't help him now. His gun had been sent flying, and Armstrong—and Armstrong's teeth—were coming for him again!

"Hey, you!" Darcy shouted. "Fucking vampire!"

Armstrong was dragging Manolis to his feet, lowering his awful face towards him; he turned to face Darcy; and Darcy, aiming at his heart, pulled the trigger of his crossbow.

That did it. As the bolt went in, the American released Manolis and smashed back against the wall. Gagging and choking, he sought to grasp the bolt and draw it out. But he couldn't. It was too close to his heart, that most vital of organs. His heart pumped his vampire blood, and that was the source of his hideous strength. He gurgled, coughed, staggered to and fro, and spat blood. And his left eye glared like a blob of sulphur seared into his face!

Manolis was on his feet again. As Darcy fumbled frantically to reload his crossbow, so the Greek tried a second time and pumped four carefully aimed shots into the stricken vampire. But now the bullets had more effect. Each one drove Armstrong like a pile driver backwards across the floor, and the last one hurled him against the window which shattered outwards, showering glass, broken louvre boards, and Armstrong himself into the night garden.

Darcy had loaded up. He stumbled out into the garden, with Manolis right behind him. Armstrong lay flat on his back in the remains of the window, alternating between flailing his arms and tugging at the hardwood bolt where it transfixed his chest. But he saw Darcy approaching and somehow sat up!

Darcy took no chances; from no more than four feet away he sent the second bolt crashing through the vampire's heart, which not only served to stretch him out again but pinned him down and kept him still.

Manolis, his mouth hanging open, came forward. ''Is he . . . is he finished?''

''Look at him,'' Darcy panted. ''Does he look finished? You may believe in them, Manolis, but you don't know them like I do. He's not finished—yet!''

Armstrong was mainly still but his fingers twitched, his jaws chomped, and his burning yellow eye followed them where they moved about him. His eye patch had been dislodged and an empty socket gaped black in the light from the wrecked window.

Darcy said, ''Watch him!'' and hurried back inside. A moment later he was back with a heavy, razor-honed, long-bladed cleaver, also from Harry's suitcase.

Manolis saw its silvery gleam and said, ''What?'' His upper lip at the left drew back from his teeth in a nervous grimace.

''The stake, the sword, and the fire!'' Darcy answered.

''Decapitation?''

334

"And right now. His vampire is already healing him. See, no blood. In an ordinary man your bullets—any one of them— might have killed him with shock, let alone damage. But he's taken six and he isn't even bleeding! Two bolts in him, one right through the heart, and his hands are still working. His eyes too . . . *and* his ears!"

He was right: Armstrong had heard their conversation, and the loathsome orb of his left eye had swivelled to gaze upon the cleaver in Darcy's hand. He began gurgling anew, his body vibrating against the earth, the heel of his right foot hammering robotically into the dry soil of the garden.

Darcy got down on one knee beside him and Armstrong tried to take hold of him with a spastic right hand. But he couldn't reach him, couldn't make his limbs work properly. Froth, phlegm, and blood welled up in the vampire's throat. His right hand scuttled a little way towards Darcy like a spider, until the arm it dragged got too heavy for it. He tried a third time, then abruptly fell back and lay still.

Darcy gritted his teeth, raised the cleaver—

—and the membrane in the back of the cavity of Armstrong's right eye bulged and erupted, and a *finger*, blue grey and pulsating, wriggled out onto his cheek!

"Jesus!" Darcy fell back, almost fainted, and Manolis took over. He fired at Armstrong's face, pulling the trigger of his silenced gun until the nightmare finger and face both were so much pulp. And when his magazine was empty, then he took the cleaver from Darcy's rigid fingers, and took Armstrong's head, too.

Darcy had turned away and was throwing up, but between each bout he gasped. "Now we . . . we have to burn the . . . the ugly bastard!"

Manolis was up to that, too. The lamps in the villa weren't just ornamental after all. They contained oil, and there was a spare can of fuel in the kitchen. By the time Darcy could take control of his heaving stomach, the remains of Armstrong were burning. Manolis stood watching, until Darcy got hold of his arm and took him off to a safe distance.

"You can never tell," he said, wiping his mouth with a

handkerchief. "There might be a lot more in him than just that god-awful finger!"

But there wasn't . . .

"I hope you didn't leave it like that," said Harry. "The oil couldn't have burned all of him."

"Manolis got a body bag," Darcy explained. "We took him to an incinerator in the industrial part of town. Said he was a mangy dog that crawled into the garden to die."

"The heat of the incinerator would calcine his bones down to powder!" Manolis added.

"So, we took second blood!" Harry growled, but with such uncharacteristic savagery that the others glanced at him in surprise. He saw their looks and turned his face away. But not before Darcy noted that his eyes were more soulful—or soulless—than ever. And of course he knew why.

"Harry, about Sandra," he started to explain yet again.

But Harry cut him off. "It wasn't your fault," he said. "If anyone's, it was my fault. I should have made sure personally that she was out of this. But we can't think about her now, and I *mustn't* think about her—not if I want to be able to think about anything else. Manolis, did the information you were waiting for come in?"

"A great deal of information," said the other. "Almost everything, except that which is the most important."

Manolis was driving his car, with Harry and Darcy in the backseat. They were approaching the centre of Rhodes New Town where Manolis was quartered. It wasn't yet 6:00 P.M. but already some tourists were out in their evening finery. "Look at them," said Harry, his voice cold. "They're happy; they laugh and dress up; they've had a blue sky all day and a blue sea to swim in, and the world looks fine. They don't know there are scarlet threads among all that blue. And they wouldn't believe it if you told them." And to Manolis, abruptly: "Tell me everything you've learned."

"Lazarides is a very successful archaeologist," Manolis began. "He came into prominence, oh, four years ago, with several important finds on Crete, Lesbos, and Skiros. Before that . . . we don't have much on him. But he does have Greek nationality, *and* Romanian! This is very odd, if not unique. The authorities in Athens are looking into it, but"—he shrugged—"this is Greece. Everything takes time. And this Lazarides, he has the friends in high places. Perhaps he purchased his nationality, eh? Certainly he would have the monies for it if the rumours are correct. Rumours? They abound! It is said that he keeps—or sells to unscrupulous collectors— at least half of the treasures he excavates; also that he is the— how do you say?—the Midas! Everything he touches turns to gold! He only has to look at an island to know if any treasure is hidden there. Why, even now, men of his are digging in an old crusader castle on Halki!''

Harry nodded. "I understand all of that, and I'll tell you about it later. Go on.''

Manolis turned left off a busy street into an alley, then left again into a tiny packed car park behind his hotel. "We'll talk inside,'' he said.

He had good spacious rooms; apparently the proprietor owed the local police a few favours, and Manolis was collecting; as he talked he prepared cool drinks, but low in alcohol. For a Greek he was sweating profusely. Darcy mentioned it and again Manolis shrugged.

"I am the criminals,'' he explained. "Pardon: *a* criminal. I am a murderer, and it concerns me.''

"Armstrong?'' said Harry. "You never performed a more worthy act in your entire life!''

"Still, I did it, and I am hiding it, and it bothers me.''

"Forget it!'' Harry insisted. "You may be doing it again, and sooner than you think. Tell me more about Lazarides.''

Manolis nodded. "He is purchasing an island. Well, a rock, in the Dodecanese off Sirna. Amazing! I mean, what is that for an island? One small beach and a fang of rock jutting from the sea? But he plans a house there, on a great ledge on the rock. Again, there was once a crusader tower there, a pharos. What he will do there is anybody's guesses. There is no water; everything will have to be brought in by boat; he will be one very lonely creature up there!''

"An aerie," said Harry, "or the next best thing. He still desires to be Wamphyri!"

"Eh!"

"Forget it. Go on."

Again Manolis' shrug. "He keeps a small private airplane, a Skyvan, on Karpathos. There is a runway there now. He uses the plane for trips to Athens, Crete, elsewhere. Maybe even to Romania, eh? Which means that sometimes his boat may be found off Karpathos. Don't worry, I have a man on it. Every day tourists fly out to Karpathos from Rhodes. They, too, use a Skyvan. It is the flying matchbox! But very, very safe. The pilot will look for Lazarides' boat. I expect his call anytime . . ."

"Anything else?" Harry was still very cool, very pale. He didn't seem to have been touched by the sun.

"About Armstrong," said Manolis. "Five and a half years ago he and some American friends went on a trip somewhere in Europe . . . that's all I know about it, somewhere in Europe. There was an accident, a fall in the mountains or some such, and some people were killed. Armstrong survived but he didn't go back to America. Instead he ended up here, in Greece, and applied for the Greek citizenship. The next thing we know, he's working for Lazarides."

"And that's it?" Harry's gaunt, almost vacant expression hadn't changed.

"That's it," said Manolis. And: "Oh, one other thing. I now have the authorization to chase this Vrykoulakas dog to hell, if I can find him!"

Darcy nodded. "We didn't sleep much last night. Manolis spent a lot of time phoning Athens. We pushed the drugs side of this thing just as hard as we could. So now we can use all the force that's necessary to apprehend and search Lazarides and his lot."

"If we can find them," Harry echoed Manolis.

"Well, two or three of them we can find, for sure!" said the Greek. "On Halki, where they're digging in those ruins."

Again Harry's nod. "That will be as good a place as any

to start, yes. I'd like to see this fang of rock in the Dodecanese, too. All right, and now I'll tell you what I've discovered, and you'll see for yourselves how it all fits together.
But I warn you now, it's an incredible story.''

He told it all and they sat fascinated to the end. ''And so
now I have my deadspeak back,'' he finished off, ''which is
one step in the right direction, at least.''

''You are the cool one,'' Manolis told him. ''I thought so
the first time I met you. You talk about steps in the right
direction, and all this time Sandra, your lover—''

''Manolis.'' Harry stopped him. ''No man has lost more
than I have. No, I'm not being a martyr, I'm just stating a
fact. It started when I was a kid and it hasn't stopped yet.
I've lost just about every person I ever loved. I've even lost
my son in another world, to another creed: this *same* damned
creed, vampirism! And the more you lose, the more hardened
you get to it. Ask any habitual gambler. They don't play to
win but to lose. They *used* to play to win, but now when they
win, they just go right on back to the tables.''

''Harry,'' Darcy took his arm, ''ease up.''

But Harry shook him off. ''Let me finish.'' And he turned
back to Manolis. ''Well, I used to play to win, too. But it's
a hell of a game where all the cards are stacked against you.
You want me to cry over Sandra? Maybe I will, later. You
want me to go to pieces, to show that I'm a good guy? But
what good will I be in all of this if I go to pieces? I loved
Sandra, yes, I think. But already it's too late to do anything
about it. She's just one more thing that I've lost. It's the only
way I can look at it and still go on. Except now I may be
starting to win again. *We* may be starting to win again. Not
Sandra, no, for she's dead. And if she isn't, then she'd be
better off. I *know* this Janos Ferenczy now, and I know what
I'm talking about. You call me cold, but you don't know how
I'm burning up inside. Now I'll ask you to do me a favour:
stop worrying about how you see things. Stop worrying about
Sandra. It's too late. This is a war and she was a casualty.
What we have to do now is start hitting back, while we still
have a chance!''

For long moments Manolis said nothing. Then: "My friend," he said very softly, "you are wound up very tight. You bear a great weight on your shoulders, and I am a great fool. I cannot hope to know what it is like for you, or even anything about you. You are not the ordinary man, and I had no right to speak the way I did or think the things I have thought."

Harry sat very still, just looking at the Greek; and slowly Manolis watched the Necroscope's soulful eyes turn to liquid. Before they could spill over, Harry stood up and kicked his chair away, and went unsteadily to the bathroom . . .

Later:

"What I hate especially about this," said Harry, "is that he's laughing at us—at all of us, at mankind—and perhaps at me in particular. It's his vampire ego. He calls himself Lazarides, after the biblical Lazarus, raised up from the dead by Christ. Depending on your beliefs, that's a blasphemy in itself. But he doesn't stop there. Just to rub it in and make his point he called his boat by the same name! He dares us to discover him, yells, 'Hey, look, I'm back!' He breaks the first rule of vampires and makes himself prominent, in several ways. And I think he does it deliberately."

"But why!" said Darcy.

"Because he can afford to!" Harry answered. "Because people no longer believe in vampires. No, I don't mean us but people in general. In this day and age he can afford to be prominent, because to a point he's safe from the masses. But he also does it because he knows that the people who *do* believe—and they are the ones he's chiefly interested in, the dangerous ones, you, me, E-Branch, and any other friends— will go up against him."

"You mean he . . . he *wants* a showdown?"

"Oh yes, for he's seen the future! That's the thing he was best at, and it's how he thwarted Faethor. He knows we have to have a showdown, so he's guiding events his way, to give himself every advantage. He'll use my own devices against me, and against anyone who is with me. He has Ken Layard, and so can locate any one of us more or less at will. He crippled Trevor Jordan so that he'd be no use to us; and he's taken Sandra not out of spite or greed or lust but the better to know *me,* because then he'll not only know my strengths but also my weaknesses. As for last night: he sent his thrall Armstrong to test you, and possibly destroy you, so as to deny me the use of one of my last crutches.''

"But if he can see the future, wouldn't he know we'd get Armstrong?" Manolis used his policeman's logic. "In which case, why simply sacrifice him like that?"

"A test," Harry answered, "like I said. He wouldn't see it as a sacrifice. Vampires have no friends, only thralls. And anyway, Armstrong was only one of Janos's players; he has plenty more. Ken Layard, for example, who can do anything Armstrong could do and a lot more. But I understand your question: why provoke a skirmish you can't win, right?"

"Right."

Harry shook his head. "The future isn't like that," he said. "It isn't easily read, never safely, and there's no way to avoid it. And it must always be remembered, *nothing* is certain until it has happened. There was a man, a Russian esper, called Igor Vlady. I met him once in the Möbius Continuum. In life he'd been a prognosticator, he read the future. And when he was dead, he kept right on doing it, eventually to become a master of future and past time. Where all space was an open book to Möbius, all time was Vlady's playground. Incorporeal, he wandered the timestream forever. Vlady told me that in life he had always held his own future inviolable: he wouldn't read it, felt that to do so would be to tempt fate. He didn't *want* to know how or when his time would come, for he knew that he'd only worry about it as it loomed ever closer. Eventually, in a moment of uncertainty and fear, he broke his own rule and forecast his own death. He believed he knew from which quarter it was coming and fled to avoid it. But he was wrong and fled *into* it! He was like a man crossing railway tracks, who sees a train coming and jumps to avoid it—into the path of another train.''

Darcy said, "You mean, Janos can't trust what he reads of the future?"

"He can trust it only to a point. He sees only the wide scheme of things, not the fine detail. And whatever he sees, he knows he can't avoid it. For example: he knew Faethor would destroy him, but saw beyond it to a time when he'd be back. He couldn't stop Faethor and didn't really try to, for the inevitable was by definition inescapable, but he could and did make certain of his return."

Manolis had kept up with all of this as best he could, but now he began to feel something of the hopelessness of it. And he asked, "But how can you even think to beat this creature? He would seem to me . . . invincible!"

Harry smiled a strange, grim smile. "Invincible? I'm not so sure about that. But I'm sure he wants us to *think* he is. Ask yourself this: if he's invincible, why does he concern himself with us? And why is he so worried about me? No, Igor Vlady was right: the future is never certain, and only time can tell. And anyway, what difference does it make? If I don't seek him out, he'll only come looking for me." He nodded. "A showdown, yes, it's coming. And for now Janos is pulling the strings. We can only hope that in his manipulations he'll overstep himself and make the same mistake Igor Vlady made . . . and step in front of a train."

At 8:05 P.M. the call Manolis was expecting from the pilot of the Rhodes–Karpathos Skyvan materialised; it transpired that Jianni Lazarides' aircraft, piloted by a man in his employ, had taken off at 3:00 A.M. from the Karpathos airstrip, destination unknown, with Lazarides himself aboard—accompanied by a man and woman answering Sandra and Ken Layard's descriptions!

Harry had steeled himself to expect something of the sort and wasn't so badly shocked, but he was puzzled. "How do you mean, destination unknown? Wouldn't the aircraft require some sort of clearance? Didn't he log himself out, go through customs, or whatever they have to do?"

Manolis gave a snort. "I say again, this is Greece! And

Karpathos is a small island. The airport is . . . a shack! It has only existed for a year or two and wouldn't be there at all if not for the tourists. But, did you say customs? Hah! Someone to stamp your passport if you're a foreigner coming in, maybe, but not if you're Greek and going out! And at three in the morning—why, it amazes me that anyone has even bothered to remember the time so precisely!''

"Stymied!" said Darcy. "He could have gone anywhere."

Harry shook his head. "No, I can find him. The problem is, it may not be so easy for me to go where he's gone. We'll jump that one when we reach it. Meanwhile, I have to speak to Armstrong."

That caught both Manolis and Darcy off balance—for a moment. Darcy was the first to recover, for he'd seen the Necroscope at work before. "You want us to take you to him?"

"Yes, and right now. Not that I think time is any longer of the essence, for I don't. Wheels have been set in motion and everything will eventually come to a head, I'm sure. But if all I had to do was sit twiddling my thumbs . . . I think I'd go mad."

Manolis had caught up. "Are you saying you're going to speak to a dead man?"

Harry nodded. "Yes, at the incinerator. That's where he is and where he'll always be, from now on."

"And . . . he'll talk to you?"

"It doesn't trouble the dead to talk to me," said Harry. "Armstrong's no longer in thrall to Janos. He might even be eager to square things. And later, tonight, then there's someone else I must try to reach."

"Möbius?" Darcy wondered.

"The same." Harry nodded. "A vampire tangled my mind and took away my deadspeak, and it took another vampire to put the mess to rights. But the one who caused the damage was also a great mathematician: my son, who inherited his talents from me. And while he was in my mind he also closed certain doors, so that now I'm innumerate. Well, if Faethor could do what he did, maybe Möbius can restore that other talent of mine. If so, then Janos gets a real run for his money . . .''

The incinerator was still working. A young Greek labourer on overtime shovelled timber waste into the red and yellow maw of a glaring, roaring beast, while overhead, smoke shot with dying sparks billowed blackly from a high chimney. Darcy and Manolis stood to one side watching the stoker at work, and Harry sat on a crate a little apart from them, his strange eyes staring and almost vacant. His mind, however, was anything but vacant, and the Necroscope's every instinct assured him that Seth Armstrong's spirit was here. Indeed, he could hear its moaning cries.

Armstrong, Harry said, but softly, *you're out of it now. You've been released. Why all the sorrow?*

The moaning and sobbing stopped at once, and in another moment: *Harry Keogh?* Armstrong's dead voice was full of astonishment and disbelief. *You'd talk to me?*

Oh, I've talked to a lot worse than you, Seth, Harry told him. *And anyway, it's my guess you were just another victim, like so many others. I don't think you could help what you'd become.*

I couldn't, oh, I couldn't! the other answered, with obvious relief. *For five and a half long years I was just a . . . a fly in his web. He was my master; I was in thrall to him; nothing I did was of my own free will.*

I know, Harry told him, *but they like to pretend it is. I suppose that even knowing it's a lie, still it's the one salve to their conscience: that you are theirs of your own free will.*

Conscience? Armstrong's spirit was bitter. *Don't make me laugh, Harry. Creatures such as Janos Ferenczy never suffered such common complaints!*

You're glad to be free of him, then? So why the remorse? You're as one with the teeming dead now. Which, as so many of them have told me, isn't as bad as you might think.

Oh? said Armstrong. *And do you honestly believe the dead will wish anything to do with me?*

Harry thought about it a moment, then said, *Two of them,*

344

at least, that I can think of. And probably more. What of your parents, Seth?

He sensed the other's nod. *Dead some time ago, yes. But . . . do you think . . . ?*

I think that when you've got yourself together, it might be a good idea to try and reach them, said Harry. *As for the Great Majority: who can say? Maybe they won't come down on you as hard as you think. Certainly I can put in a good word for you.*

And you'd do that?

Why don't you ask the dead about me, said Harry, *when the time comes? I think they'll tell you I'm not such a bad sort. But until then, there's a favour you could do for me.*

Armstrong's thoughts turned bitter again. *Nothing for nothing, eh? Even here.*

No, you've got it all wrong, Seth, said Harry. *Turn me down, it will make no difference. I'll still ask them to go easy on you. You're dead and burned away, and as all the rest of them know, you can't be any more punished than that.*

What is it you want to know?

Janos has gone now, Harry told him, *out of Rhodes, probably out of the islands. And he took the woman—I suppose you'd say my woman—with him. I want to know where he is.*

She's the bait in his trap, I suppose you know that?

Oh, yes, I know. But I'd go after him anyway.

Then go to Romania.

Harry groaned. It was the worst possible scenario. *I've been to Romania,* he said. *It won't be so easy a second time.*

Nevertheless, that's where he is. His castle in the mountain heights over Halmagiu. He said you were his only living enemy and the greatest possible enemy, and that when he met you, it must be there, on his terms and in his territory. He read it that way, and that's how he'll play it. But Harry . . . I hope you didn't love that girl.

Don't! Harry gritted his teeth, shook his head, rejected the unthinkable pictures Armstrong's words had conjured. Instinctive reactions to something he'd hoped would not be mentioned. *Don't tell me about that . . .*

345

Armstrong was silent, but the Necroscope could sense his sympathy and even his . . . remorse? And suddenly Harry knew. He'd suspected it might be so, but had tried to keep it out of his mind. Until now. *It was you who took her for him, right?*

Armstrong was sobbing again. *It changes everything, doesn't it?* he said. But it was a statement of fact, not a question. *Yes, he got into her mind, and I took her to him.*

Harry didn't rave, didn't curse, but simply stood up and walked way, with his head down.

Darcy and Manolis came after him, looked at him and at each other, and asked no questions. Behind them the incinerator's furnace hissed and roared, and a man sobbed wrackingly, but only Harry Keogh could hear him.

And despite his promises, Harry didn't care . . .

Later, back at the hotel where Harry had arranged for a room of his own, he tired to contact Möbius. He reached out his Necroscope's awareness to a place he knew well indeed: the graveyard in Leipzig where August Ferdinard Möbius's *mortal* remains had lain buried for one hundred and twenty years, but from which his mathematician's and astronomer's immortal mind had gone out to explore the universe. And:

Sir? said Harry, showing his usual respect. *August? It's me, Harry Keogh. I know it's been some time since I was in touch, but I'd hoped I could talk to you again.*

He waited but there was no response, just an aching void. It was about what he'd expected: the man who had taught him how to venture into and use an otherwise entirely conjectural fifth dimension was out there even now, doing his own thing along the Möbius way. Harry couldn't tell how long he'd been away, or even hazard a guess as to when he was likely to be back. *If* he would be back.

But if Harry was ever to achieve a balance of power with Janos, Möbius was his one hope. And so he kept trying: for an hour, then two, until finally Darcy came knocking at his door. "Any luck?" he said when the Necroscope opened the door for him.

Harry shook his head. And perhaps surprisingly, in the circumstances: "I'm hungry," he said.

They all three ate out, at a taverna of Manolis' recommendation; and there, during the course of their meal, Harry outlined a possible course of action as he saw it.

"Manolis," he said, "I need to get into Hungary. Budapest initially, and from there to Halmagiu across the border. That's a distance of about one hundred and fifty miles. Once I'm in, I can travel by road or rail; I'll be a 'tourist,' of course. As for getting across the border into Romania, I'm not sure. I can work on that when I get there. How long will it take to fix me up with documentation?"

Manolis shrugged. "You don't need any. Your English passport says you're an 'author'; it has a Greek entry stamp; quite obviously you are the genuine tourist, or perhaps the author doing his research. You can simply fly to Budapest via Athens. Tomorrow, if you wish it. No problem."

"As simple as that?"

"Hungary is not Romania. The restrictions are less severe. In fact Romanians are fleeing to Hungary every day! When will you go?"

"Three or four days," Harry answered. "As soon as we're finished up here. But as I've said before, where Janos is concerned, time is no longer of the essence. I believe he'll simply hole up in the Transylvanian mountains and wait for me. He knows I'll come eventually."

Manolis looked at him, and looked away. "Time not of the essence," the Greek mumbled, shaking his head a little.

"All right," said Harry at once, a harsh, unaccustomed edge to his voice, "and I know what's bothering you. Look, I'll try to explain it as simply as possible. And then for Christ's sake and mine both *let's drop it*! Either Janos has already vampirized Sandra or he hasn't. If he hasn't, then he's keeping her as his ace in the hole, in case I come up with something unexpected, in which case she'll be a bargaining point. But that's only the way I *hope* it is, not the way I *think* it is. And if he has changed her . . . then given only half a chance, I'll do my level best to kill her! For her

347

sake. But right now if I concentrate on Sandra to the exclusion of everything else, then obviously I won't be able to think straight. And we all of us need to think straight. Now, I know you think I'm a cold one, Manolis, but is everything understood?"

Manolis shook his head. "Not cold," he said, "just very strong. I simply needed reminding, that's all. You see, Harry, some of us are not so strong."

Harry sighed and nodded. "I think you'll do," he said. He picked up his glass of rich red wine.

Darcy said, "So, three or four days before you head for Hungary, right? And between times? You think it's time we took on the rest of them, right?"

"That's exactly what I think," Harry answered. "Janos has men, or vampires, at his dig in Halki. It's possible there are others on his island, and there's also the crew of his boat. Which makes quite a few of them, and we don't yet know how dangerous they are. I mean, if they're all vampires, then they're *all* dangerous, but there are vampires and vampires. Janos is . . . one hell of a vampire! By comparison the rest of them won't be too hard to handle. No harder than Armstrong was, anyway."

"Jesus!" said Manolis, crossing himself. "You don't think the American was hard enough?"

"Oh yes, I do," said Harry. "I was just thinking out loud, remembering some of the things I saw on Starside. But right here and now . . . Manolis, you've seen how effective a crossbow firing hardwood bolts can be. So what can Rhodes supply in the way of special weaponry?"

"Crossbows? I don't think so. Next best thing: spear guns!"

Harry started to shake his head, then stopped and narrowed his eyes. "With steel spears, right?"

"Steel harpoons, yes." Manolis nodded, and he wondered what Harry was thinking. The Necroscope didn't keep him in suspense.

"Do we have silver-plating facilities? A factory or plant that can put a sheath of silver on a handful of harpoons?"

Manolis' eyes opened wide. "Certainly!" he said, beaming.

"Very well, let's buy ourselves two or three high-performance spear guns. Can we leave that to you?"

"Tomorrow morning, first thing. I am the spear fisherman and know these guns. The best model is called 'Champion,' Italian manufacture, with single or double rubbers. Using a single barb, with a metal flap that opens on making a strike . . . they will be quite as effective as your crossbow."

"Rubbers?" Darcy Clarke wasn't much for water sports.

Harry explained. "These guns use rubber hurlers for propulsion. They're pretty deadly. Slow to load, though, so we'll need single, powerful rubbers. Manolis, better make it half a dozen guns. And Darcy, I think it's time you called in extra help. I don't think it will be too difficult to find three or four volunteers from your lot back in London."

"E-Branch?" Darcy answered. "They're just waiting for the word! I'll bring in the blokes from the Bodescu job. I can get on it just as soon as we're finished here."

"Good." Harry nodded. "But it might be a good idea to get it started even before they get out here. I think our first priority has to be Halki. We know there are only a couple of Janos's creatures there. And actually, we don't yet know that they are 'creatures'! They could be men pure and simple, dupes in his pay, who don't know what they're working for. Well, I'll only have to see them to know them. Manolis, how long will it take to get those spears—er, harpoons—silvered up?"

"By tomorrow night?"

"And how long to Halki?"

"In a fast boat"—Manolis shrugged—"two hours, two and a half at most. It sits in the sea only a few miles from the island of Rhodes, but fifty miles down the coast from Rhodes Town, where we are now. Halki's only a little place. A big rock in the sea. One village with a couple of little tavernas, one short road, some mountains, and one crusader castle."

"Tomorrow's Wednesday," said Harry. "If you can fix us up with a boat and a pilot by Thursday morning, we can

349

easily be there before midday. So that's what we'll aim for. Between times, is there any chance of taking a look at this 'fang of rock' that Janos is buying in the Dodecanese?''

Manolis shook his head. "That would take the best part of a day. I suggest we do Halki Thursday morning, and go straight on to have a look at Karpathos and this bay close to the airport where the *Lazarus* is laid up. Incidentally, both Halki and Karpathos lie in what used to be called the 'Carpathian Sea'! This vampire, he likes to feel at home, eh?''

Harry nodded. "I fancy it's a coincidence. A funny one, but a coincidence anyway. But I agree with you on the rest of what you said. And in any case, we should have reinforcements from E-Branch by Thursday evening. Friday will be soon enough to take a look at Janos's twentieth-century aerie.''

Harry's large steak, rare, without vegetables, must surely be cold by now. He hadn't yet touched it and the others had long since finished eating. He shrugged and ate anyway. It was a long time since he'd tasted meat so rare and bloody. In fact he couldn't remember the time. And the deep red wine was good, too. And to himself, wryly, *If you can't beat 'em, join 'em!*

Maybe Manolis was right and he was a cold one after all . . .

A message was waiting for them back at the hotel: a sister at the asylum had requested that Inspector Papastamos call her back. Manolis did so immediately. He spoke on the phone in his usual rapid-fire Greek, with long pauses between each burst, while Harry and Darcy watched his face going through a variety of expressions: from wary and enquiring to astonishment, then disbelief, and finally sheer delight. And at last he was able to translate the message back to them.

"Trevor Jordan is much improved!" he almost shouted, his face a huge smile. "He is conscious, talking, making sense! Or at least he was. They made him take food, then gave him a shot to put him down for the night. But before he

350

slept, he said he wanted to see you, Harry. They say you can see him first thing in the morning.''

Darcy and Harry looked wonderingly at each other, and Darcy said, ''What do you make of it?''

For a moment Harry was bewildered. He frowned and scratched his chin. ''Maybe . . . maybe distance has put him beyond Janos's reach? I had thought his condition was permanent—that his mind had been tampered with, like mine—but maybe Janos isn't up to that. Maybe he isn't that good. Hell, who cares? Whatever it is, it sounds like good news to me. We'll just have to wait until the morning to find out . . .''

XIII: First Contact—
The Challenge—
Thralls

BEFORE HE WENT TO SLEEP, HARRY TRIED AGAIN TO CONtact Möbius. It was useless; his deadspeak went out to Möbius's grave in Leipzig, but no one answered. One of the reasons Harry had delayed pursuing Janos was that he'd hoped (hope against hope) to regain his numeracy—and through it access to the Möbius Continuum. This had been his plan but . . . it was fading now, possibly into oblivion.

Still worrying about it, eventually he slept . . .

But his obsession of the moment was carried over into his dreams, where, separated from the lesser problems and diversions of the waking world, Harry continued to transmit his thoughts across that Great Dark Gulf which men called death. Many of the teeming dead in their graves heard him, would answer or comfort him, but dared not. None of them was the one he sought; communication for its own sake would be pointless; they knew that their commiserations, even their inevitable approbations, would only constitute obstructions in Harry's path. For the Necroscope had never been able to refuse conversation with the dead, whose suffering of solitude he alone of all living men understood.

There was one among the dead, however, who—for all that she loved him more than the rest—stood much less in awe of him. Indeed, on a good many occasions she had chided him. The mothers of men are like that.

Harry? Her deadspeak touched his. *Can you hear me, son?*

He sighed and abandoned his search for Möbius. There had been that in her tone which commanded his attention. *What is it, Ma?*

What is it? (He could picture her frown.) *Is that how you speak to me, Harry?*

Ma, he sighed again, and tried to explain. *I've been busy. And what I'm doing is important. You don't know how important.*

Do you think so? she answered. *Do you really think I don't know? But who knows you better than me, Harry? Well, I know this much, anyway—that you're wasting your time!*

Harry's dreaming mind played with her words and found no explanation for them. Nor would he unless she was willing to supply one. She picked that up at once and flew at him in the closest she'd ever come to a rage. *What! And would you take that attitude? Would you take your impatience out on me? Well, the dead might prize you, but they don't know you like I do. And Harry, you . . . are . . . a . . . trouble!*

Ma, I—

You, you, you! Always you! And are you the only one? Who is this "I" you're always mentioning, Harry? And why is it you never speak of "we"? Why must you always think you're alone? Of all men you are not alone! For a million years men have died and lain silent in the dark, thinking their thoughts and following their solitary designs, each separate from the next but joined in the belief that death was an airless, lightless (oh, yes, and painless too!), but relentless prison . . . until a small bright light named Harry Keogh came along and said, "Why don't you talk to me? I'll listen. And then you might like to try talking to each other!" Ahhh! A revelation!

Harry remained silent, didn't know how to answer. Was she praising or chastising him? He had never heard her like this, not even when he was awake. She had never been so angry. And his ma picked that up, too.

Why am I angry? I don't believe it! For years you couldn't speak to me if you wanted to—not without killing yourself for it—and finally when you can speak to me—

Now he believed he understood, and knew that she was right, and hoped he also knew how to deal with it. *Ma*, he said, *the others need to know about me, need to be reassured that there's more than just loneliness in death. And they need to know that there's safety in it, too. From such as Dragosani and the Ferenczys, and others of their sort. But there are so many of the dead—I have so many good friends amongst them—that I can't ever hope to speak to them all. Not until I'm one of them, anyway. But you don't need to know these things because you* already *know! Yes, and you've always known . . . that I love you, too, Ma . . .*

She was silent.

So if there's ever a time I don't contact you, it's because something very, very important is getting in the way. And, Ma, that's the way it's always going to be . . . Ma?

She was full to the top, which was why she wasn't answering, but at least she wasn't crying. Harry hoped not, anyway. And eventually she said, *Oh, I know that, son. It's just that I . . . I worry about you so. And the dead . . . they ask after you. Yes, and because they love you, they go out of their way for you, too. Don't you know that? Can't you understand that we all want to help? And don't you know that there are experts among us—in* every *field—whose talents you're wasting?*

What? Wasted talents? The dead wanted to help him? But didn't they always? What had she been up to? *What's that, Ma?* he said. *About the dead? And what did you mean: I'm wasting my time?*

In trying to contact Möbius, that's what I mean, she immediately answered. *If only you'd stay in touch, you'd know!*

Why, we've been trying to get hold of Möbius for you ever since you got your deadspeak back!

You what? But . . . how? Möbius isn't here. He's out there somewhere. He could be anywhere. Literally anywhere!

We know that, she answered, *and also that anywhere's a big place! We haven't found him yet. But if and when we do, he'll get your message and, we hope, get back to you. Meanwhile . . . you needn't concern yourself about it. You can get on with other things.*

Ma, said Harry, *you don't understand. Listen: Möbius is probably in the Möbius Continuum. The dead—even the massed thoughts of* all *the dead—couldn't possibly reach him there. It's a place that isn't of this universe! So you see it's not so much that I'm wasting my time, but that you are wasting yours!*

He could sense her shaking her head. And: *Son,* she said, *when Harry Jr. took away your deadspeak and your mathematical intuition, did he also addle your brains?*

Eh?

When you use the Möbius Continuum, how much time do you actually spend in it?

And he at once saw that she was right, and wondered, *Is logic linked with numeracy in the human mind? Has my son diluted my powers of reason, too? No time,* he said. *It's instantaneous.* Möbius wasn't in the Möbius Continuum—he merely used it to get wherever he was going!

Exactly. So why waste your time aiming deadspeak thoughts at his grave in Leipzig, eh? It's like you said: he's out there somewhere. An astronomer in life, death hasn't changed him! So right now there are an awful lot of us directing our thoughts outwards to the stars! And if he's there, we'll find him, eventually.

Harry had to give in to her. *Ma, what would I do without you?*

I was only putting you straight, Harry. Telling you that between times you should get on with other things.

Such as?

Harry, you have access to the most extensive library in the world, books which not only hold knowledge but can also impart it. The minds of the dead are like books for you to read, and their talents are all there to be learned. Just as you learned from Möbius, so you can learn from the rest of us.

But that was something Harry had long ago considered and long since turned down. Dragosani had learned from the dead, too. Thibor Ferenczy had instructed him—in evil. Likewise, as a necromancer, Dragonsani had stolen from the talents of Max Batu, and the secrets of the Soviet E-Branch from Gregor Borowitz. And yet none of these things had helped him in the end. Indeed Batu's evil eye had assisted in his destruction! No, there were things, like the future, which Harry preferred not to know. And these thoughts of his were deadspeak, which of course his mother read at once.

Maybe you're right, she said, *but still you should keep it in mind. There are talents here, Harry, and if and when you need them, they're yours for the asking . . .*

Her voice was fading now, dwindling away into dreams. But at least this time Harry would remember their conversation. And at last, weary now in mind and body both, he relaxed, let go, sank down even deeper into dream, and lay suspended there, simply sleeping.

For a little while. Until—

Haaarry? It was Möbius! Harry would know his deadspeak anywhere. But even by dreaming standards Möbius's voice was . . . dreamy. For this was a very different Möbius, a changed Möbius.

August Ferdinand? Is that you? I've been looking for you. I mean, a great many of us have been searching for you everywhere.

I know, Harry. I was . . . out there. But you were right and they were wrong. I was in the Continuum! For as long as I could bear it, anyway. The thoughts of your dead friends reached me as I emerged.

Harry didn't understand. *What's to bear?* he asked. *The Möbius Continuum is what it is.*

Is it? Möbius's voice was still mazed and wandering, like

that of a sleepwalker, or a man in some sort of trance. *Is it, Harry? Or is it much more than it appears to be? But . . . it's strange, my boy, so strange. I would have talked to you about it—I wanted to—but . . . You've been away so long, Haaarry.*

That wasn't my fault, Harry told him. *I couldn't keep in touch, wasn't able to. Something had happened to me—to my deadspeak—and I was cut off from everyone. And that's one of the reasons why I had to contact you now. You see, it's not just that I'd lost my deadspeak, but also my ability to use the Möbius Continuum. And I need it like I never needed it before!*

The Continuum? Need it? Still Möbius wasn't entirely himself, far from it. *Oh, we all need it, Harry. Indeed, without it there's nothing! It is* EVERYTHING! *And . . . and . . . and I'm sorry, Harry, but I have to go back there.*

That's all right, Harry desperately answered, feeling Möbius's deadspeak sliding off at a tangent. *And I swear I wouldn't be troubling you if it wasn't absolutely necessary, but—*

It . . . it talks to me! Möbius's voice was an awestruck whisper, drifting, fading as his attention transferred itself elsewhere. *And I think I know what it is. The only thing it can be. I have . . . to . . . go . . . now . . . Haaarry.*

Another moment and he had gone, disappeared, and not even an echo remaining. So that Harry knew Möbius had returned to the one place above all others which was now forbidden to him. Into the Möbius Continuum.

Finally Harry was left alone to sleep out a night which, for all that it was dreamless, was nevertheless uneasy . . .

The next morning, on their way in Manolis' car to see Trevor Jordan, something which had been bothering Harry suddenly surfaced. "Manolis," he said, "I'm an idiot! I should have thought of it before."

The Greek glanced at him. "Thought of what, Harry?"

"The KGB knew I was going to Romania. They knew it almost before I did. I mean, they were waiting for me when

I landed—goons of theirs, anyway. So, someone must have told them. Someone here on Rhodes!''

For a moment Manolis looked blank, but then he grinned and slapped his thigh. ''Harry,'' he said, ''you are the very strange person with the *extremely* weird powers—but I think you will never make the policeman! Yesterday, when you told us your story, I thought it was understood that I must arrive at this selfsame conclusion. And of course I did. My next step was to ask myself who knew you were going other than your immediate circle? Answer: no one—except the booking clerk at the airport itself! The local police are looking into it right now. If there is an answer, they will find it.''

''Good!'' said Harry. ''But the point I'm making is this: the last thing I want is that someone should be waiting for me in Hungary, too! I mean, if it works out that I must go there.''

Manolis nodded. ''I understand your concern. Let's just hope the local boys turn something up.''

Neither Manolis, Harry, nor Darcy had any way of knowing that at that very moment the police were at the airport, talking to a man who worked on the passenger information desk; to him and to his brother, against whom they'd long entertained certain grudges and suspicions of their own. Talking to them, and not much caring for the answers they were getting, but sure that eventually they'd get the right ones . . .

At the asylum a sister met the three and took them to Jordan's room. He had a room now as opposed to a cell: a small place with high, barred windows and a door with a peephole. The door was locked from the outside; obviously the doctors were still a little wary. The sister looked through the peephole, and smiled, and beckoned Harry forward. He followed her example and looked into the room. Jordan was striding to and fro in the confined space, his hands clasped behind his back. Harry knocked and the other at once stopped pacing and looked up. His face was alive now, alert and expectant.

''Harry?'' he called out. ''Is that you?''

''Yes, it is,'' Harry answered. ''Just give us a moment.''

The sister unlocked the door and the three went in. She waited outside.

Inside, Jordan took Darcy's hand and shook it; he slapped Manolis on the back, then stood stock still and slowly smiled Harry a greeting. "So," he said, "and we have the Necroscope back on our team, eh?"

"For a while," Harry answered, returning his smile. And: "You scared us, Trevor. We thought he'd wrecked your mind."

Darcy Clarke, after the initial handshake, had backed off a little, but unobtrusively. Now he mumbled, "Will you excuse me a moment?" He went back out into the corridor, with Manolis following quickly on behind. In the corridor Darcy was standing beside the sister—or rather, he was leaning against the wall. And his face was white!

"What is it?" Manolis hissed. "I've seen that look on your face before."

"Call Harry out of there," Darcy whispered. "Quickly!"

The sister was beginning to look alarmed, but Darcy cautioned her with a finger to his lips.

"Harry." Manolis' voice was casual as he leaned back into the room. "Would you come out here a moment?"

"Do you mind?" Harry lifted an eyebrow, glanced at Jordan.

"Not at all." The other shook his head and smiled strangely, knowingly. Harry went out to the others.

"What is it?"

Darcy closed the door and turned the key. He looked at Harry and his Adam's apple was working. "It's all wrong!" he said. "There's something . . . not right with him. In fact *nothing's* right with him!"

Harry's soulful eyes studied his drawn, trembling face. "Your talent?"

"Yes. That doesn't feel like Trevor. It looks like him, but it doesn't feel like him. Not to my guardian angel. My talent wouldn't let me stay in there."

"Harry?" came Jordan's voice from beyond the door.

"What's the delay? Look, I have something to tell you—but only you. Can't we talk, you and I, face-to-face?"

Manolis was quick off the mark. He showed the sister his police identification, again warned her to silence as Darcy had done, with a finger to his lips, took out his Beretta and gave it to Harry. And: "Leave the door ajar behind you, and we'll stay right here," he said.

"But," said Darcy, his voice wobbly, "will that stop him?" He indicated the gun in Harry's hand.

Harry nodded. "He's not a vampire," he said. He put the gun into an inside pocket of his jacket, unlocked the door and went through it.

Inside the room Jordan had sat down in an armchair. There was another chair facing him and he beckoned Harry to take it. Harry sat down . . . but carefully, warily, never taking his eyes off the man opposite. "Well," he finally said, "and here I am. So what's the big mystery, Trevor?"

"All of a sudden," said the other, still smiling his weird, knowing smile, "you're not so concerned about me." And Harry noticed how he formed his words slowly, carefully, making sure he got them right.

Right there and then the Necroscope guessed what Jordan's trouble was and decided to put it to the test. "Oh, I'm concerned about you, all right." He forced a smile onto his face. "In fact you wouldn't believe just how concerned I am! Trevor, do you remember what you people at E-Branch used to call Harry Jr. when you looked after him that time?"

The strange, almost insinuating expression slid from Jordan's face. His features went slack and gaunt, his eyes blank, but just for a moment or two. Then . . . animation returned and he said, "Oh, of course. The Boss, that's what we called him!"

"That's right"—Harry nodded, and reached for the gun in his pocket—"but you were much too slow in remembering. And you were the one who was always especially fond of him. It's not something you'd need time to think about—or enquire about—if you were you!"

As his gun started to come into view, so Jordan moved.

Previously the man's movements had seemed slow to match his speech . . . but so are the movements of a chameleon before its tongue flickers into deadly life. And Janos's grip was strong on Jordan's mind. He moved like lightning, his left hand grabbing Harry's throat and his right bearing down on his gun hand, ramming it back inside his jacket.

The Necroscope's reflexes took over. As Jordan straightened up from his chair, Harry kicked him hard between the legs . . . useless, for the mind which controlled Jordan's body simply turned the pain aside! In return, Jordan released Harry's throat and backhanded him with a clenched fist hard as iron! Before his eyes could focus from that, Jordan had lifted him half out of his chair and tried to butt him in the face. In the last moment Harry saw it coming and managed to turn his face aside, but even so, the crushing hammer force of the man's head against his temple dazed and shook him. Before he could recover, Jordan let him fall back into his chair and dragged his gun into view. Then—

The door burst open and Manolis hurled himself into the room. Darcy was right behind him, defying his leery talent's every effort to turn him back. Grunting his frustration, Jordan tried one last time, without effect, to wrench Harry's gun out of his hand before Manolis hit him. And the compact Greek policeman knew exactly how to hit! He shouldered Jordan back from Harry, dropkicked him and knocked him down, then scrabbled his hands out from under him where he tried to push himself to his feet.

Then Harry was between them, pointing his gun directly at Jordan's forehead. "Don't make me!" he shouted at the possessed man, his words sharp as gravel chips. Jordan sat up and snarled at him, at all three of them.

"I was not the one to threaten!" he growled, his voice no longer that of the Jordan they had known. "You threatened me!"

"That's right," Harry answered, "you haven't threatened me personally, not yet, but you would sooner or later . . . Janos Ferenczy!" He made motions with his gun, indicating that the other should stand up.

Janos, in Jordan's body, did so, and stood glowering at the three who ringed him in. And: "Well then, Harry Keogh," he finally grunted, "and so you know me now. Very well, all subterfuge aside, we meet at last. But I wanted to know you, and I wanted you to know something of my power. You see how easily I have occupied this mind? Telepathy? *Hah!* Trevor Jordan was the veriest amateur!"

"Your powers don't impress me," Harry lied. "The stench from a dead pig is likewise strong!"

"You . . . you *dare* . . . !" The other took a pace forward.

Harry gritted his teeth and carefully aimed the gun right between Jordan's eyes—

—And smiling crookedly, the possessed man came to a grudging halt. Then . . . he staggered.

Harry narrowed his eyes. "What . . . ?"

"I . . . I have pushed this weakling's flabby body too far," Janos Ferenczy grunted from Jordan's throat. "Allow me to sit down."

"Sit," Harry told him. And as the other flopped into his chair, and sat there reeling, the Necroscope once more seated himself opposite. "Now out with it, Janos," he said. "Why did you want to see me? To kill me?"

"Kill you?" Janos laughed a baying laugh. "If I were so desperate to have you dead, believe me, you would be dead! But no, I want you alive!"

"Wait!" Manolis came closer. "Harry, are you saying that this is Janos Ferenczy? Is this really the Vrykoulakas?"

Janos/Jordan scowled at him. "Greek, you are a fool!"

Manolis moved closer still, but Darcy took his arm. "It's his mind," he said, "his telepathy, controlling Trevor's body."

"Kill him now!" Manolis said at once.

"That's just it," Harry answered. "I wouldn't be killing him but poor Jordan."

Janos laughed again. "You are helpless!" he said. "Why, I could walk out of here! You are like small children!" Then he stopped laughing and scowled at Harry. "And so you are the all-powerful Necroscope, eh? The man who talks to the

362

dead, the famous vampire killer! Well, I think you are nothing!''

"Do you?'' said Harry. "And is that why you're here, to tell me that? Fine, so you've told me. Now scurry off back to your Carpathian castle and get your filthy leech's mind out of my friend's head!''

The eyes in Jordan's head glared until they seemed about to leap from their orbits, and his hands trembled where they gripped the arms of the chair. But finally: "It . . . will . . . be . . . my . . . my *great* pleasure to meet you again, Harry Keogh,'' he said, grinding his teeth. "But man-to-man, face-to-face.''

Harry was practised in the ways of the Wamphyri. He knew how to hurl weighty insults. "Man-to-man?'' He gave a snort of derision. "You elevate yourself to ridiculous heights, Janos. And face-to-face? Why, there are cockroaches in this world who stand taller than you!''

Manolis got down on one knee beside Harry's chair, reached for his gun. "Give it to me,'' he said, "and tell me what you want to know. And believe me, I will make him tell you!''

"I go now,'' Janos said. "But I go knowing that you will come to me.'' He opened his mouth and laughed, and wriggled his tongue as frantically and obscenely as a madman. "I know it as surely as I know that tonight—ah, *tonight*!— sweet Sandra will writhe in my bed, lathered with the froth of our fornication!''

He laughed, a great shout of a laugh, and fell limp in his chair. His eyes closed, his head leaned to one side, and his jaw fell open. Foam dribbled from one corner of his mouth, and his left arm and hand vibrated a little where they hung down the side of the chair.

Harry, Darcy, and Manolis glanced at each other, and at last Harry half released the Beretta into Manolis' hands—at which Jordan's eyes sprang open! He laughed again and leaped alert, and snatched the gun from between them. And: "Ah, hah-hah!'' he screamed. "Children, mere *children*!''

And putting the gun to his right ear, he pulled the trigger!

363

Harry had drawn back, forcing his chair backwards away from the action, but Darcy and Manolis were sprayed with blood and brains as the left side of Jordan's head flew apart. Yelping their horror, they started upright and back.

Framed in the open doorway, a trio of Sisters of Mercy held their hands to their mouths and gasped. They had seen it all. Or the end of it, anyway. "Oh, my G-G-*God*!" Darcy staggered from the room, leaving Harry and Manolis, mouths agape, staring at Jordan's bloody corpse . . .

Harry and Darcy left Manolis to hand over the body to the local police (the case was a "suicide" pure and simple, with plenty of witnesses to prove it) and walked back to their hotel.

It wasn't yet 10:00 A.M. but already baking hot; the heat seemed to bounce off the cobbles in the narrow streets of the Old Town; Darcy dumped his bloodied jacket in the back of a refuse truck and cleaned up as best he could in a drinking fountain along the way.

At the hotel they showered and Harry saw to his bruises, and then for the best part of an hour they sat and did nothing at all . . .

A little before noon Manolis joined them. "What now?" he wanted to know. "Do we go ahead as planned?"

Harry had been thinking it over. "Yes and no," he answered. "You two go ahead as planned: go to Halki, tomorrow, then Karpathos, and see what you can do. And you'll have the men from E-Branch to back you up from then on in. But . . . I can't wait. I have to square it with that bastard. It was what he said at the end. I can't live with that. It has to be put right."

"You'll go to Hungary?" Manolis looked washed out, exhausted.

"Yes," Harry told him. "See, I thought that after Sandra was taken, it wouldn't matter: she'd simply be a vampire, beyond anyone's help. But I hadn't reckoned with how he might use her. Well, it could be that she herself is now past caring, but I'm not. So . . . I have to go. Not even for her sake anymore but for mine. I may not any longer have what it takes to get him, but I can't let her go on like that.''

Darcy shook his head. ''Not a good idea, Harry,'' he said. ''Look, Janos was goading you, challenging you to take part in a duel he doesn't think you can win. And you've fallen for it. You were right the first time: where Sandra is concerned, what's done is done. Now's the time to steady up and start thinking ahead, the time for preparation and planning. But it *isn't* the time to go off half-cocked and get yourself killed! You know how difficult it's going to be just getting to Janos in the Carpathians; but you also know that if you simply leave him alone, then sooner or later, he'll come looking for you where you can meet him on your terms. He'll *have* to, if he ever again wants to feel safe in the world.''

''Harry,'' said Manolis, ''I think maybe Darcy is right. I still don't know why that maniac killed himself and not you, but what you're planning now . . . it's like putting your head right back in the noose!''

''Darcy's probably right,'' Harry agreed, ''but . . . I have to play it how I see it. As for Jordan killing himself: that was Janos, showing me how 'powerful' he is! Yes, and hurting me at the same time. But kill me? No, for it's like he said: he wants me alive. I'm the Necroscope; I have strange talents; there are secrets locked up in my head that Janos wants to get at. Oh, he can talk to some of the dead—poor bastards—in that monstrous, necromantic way of his, but he can't command their respect as I do. He'd like to, though, for he's as vain as the rest of them, but he still doesn't feel that he's true Wamphyri. So . . . he probably won't be satisfied until he's made himself the most powerful vampire the world's ever seen. And to that end, if he can find some way to steal my skills from me—'' He let it tail off . . .

. . . And immediately, in a lighter tone, continued, ''Anyway, you two are going to have plenty on your own plates. So stop worrying about me and start worrying about yourselves. Manolis, how about those spear guns? And I'd also like you to book me a seat on the next plane for Athens—say

365

sometime tomorrow morning?—with a Budapest connection. And Darcy—''

''Whoa!'' said Darcy. ''You changed the subject a bit fast there, Harry! And let's face it, there's really no comparison between what we'll be doing here in the islands and what you'll be going up against in the Carpathians. Also, Manolis and I, we have each other, and by tomorrow night there'll be a gang of us. But you'll be on your own all the way down the line.''

Harry looked at him with those totally honest, incredibly innocent eyes of his and said, ''On my own? Not really, Darcy. I have a great many friends in a great many places, and they've never once let me down.''

Darcy looked at him and thought, *God, yes! It's just that I keep forgetting who—what—you are.*

Manolis didn't know Harry so well, however. ''Friends?'' the Greek said, having missed the point of the exchange. ''In Hungary, Romania?''

Harry looked at him. ''There too,'' he said, and shrugged. ''Wherever.'' He stood up. ''I'm going to my room now. I have to try and contact some people . . .''

''Wherever?'' Manolis repeated him after he had gone.

Darcy nodded, and for all the drowsy Mediterranean heat, he shivered. ''Harry's friends are legion,'' he explained. ''Right across the world, the graveyards are full of them.''

Harry tried again to contact Möbius, with as little success as the teeming dead allies whom his ma had recruited to that same task. He tried to speak with Faethor, too—to check on a certain piece of advice that the extinct vampire had given him, which now seemed highly suspect—and was likewise frustrated; it must be the scorching heat of the midday sun, shimmering in Romania just as it shimmered here, which deterred Faethor's Wamphyri spirit. Disappointed, finally Harry reached out with his thoughts to touch the Rhodes asylum, where Trevor Jordan now lay in the morgue, peaceful in the wake of his travails and well beyond the torments of the merely physical world. There, at last, he was successful.

Is that you, Harry? Jordan's dead voice was at first tinged with anxiety, then relief as he saw that he was correct. *But of course it is, for who else could it be?* And eagerly: *Harry, I'm glad you've come. I want you to know that it wasn't me. I mean, that I could never have—*

"Of course you couldn't!" Harry cut him off, speaking out loud, as he was wont to do when time, circumstances, and location permitted. "I know that, Trevor. It's one of the reasons I wanted to speak to you: to put your mind at rest and let you know that we understand. It was Janos, using you to relay his thoughts—and that one god-awful action—through to us. But"—he was as frank as ever—"it's a damned shame he had to murder you to be doubly sure I'd go after him!"

Harry, said Jordan, *it's done now and I know it can't be reversed. Oh, I suppose it will get to me later, when it sinks in how much I've lost. I suppose they—I mean we—all have to go through that. But right now I'm only interested in revenge. And let's face it, I haven't fared as badly as some. God knows, I'd rather be dead than undead, in thrall to that monster!*

"Like poor Ken Layard."

Yes, like Ken. And Harry felt the dead man's shudder.

"That's something else I have to try to put right." The Necroscope sighed. "Ken belongs to Janos now, his locator. But Trevor, Sandra is his, too . . ."

For a moment there was only a blank, horrified silence. Then: *Oh, God, Harry . . . I'm so sorry!*

Harry felt the other's commiserations, nodded, said nothing. And:

God, it seems impossible! Jordan finally said, speaking to himself as much as to Harry. *We came out to Greece to find a few drugs—and look what we found. Death, destruction, and a one-man plague who can burst out any time he's ready. And powerful? It's like Yulian Bodescu was a pocket torch compared to a laser beam! You know, I scanned him by mistake? I was like a tiny spider who fell in a bathful of water, and some bastard pulled the plug! There was no fighting him.*

Harry, his mind is a great black irresistible whirlpool. And little old me? I dived right in there headfirst!

"That's the other thing I want to talk to you about," Harry told him. "This control he had over you, even at a distance. I mean, how could such a thing come about? You were a powerful telepath in your own right."

Therein lies a tale, Jordan answered bitterly. And: *Harry, we're all of us like radio stations: our minds, I mean. Most of us operate on very personal channels, our own. We only talk to ourselves. We think to ourselves. Most of us. Telepaths, on the other hand, have this knack of tuning in to other people's wavelengths. But Janos is a superior and far more sophisticated station. Only let someone pick up his wavelength and he jams their transmission, tracks the signal home, and literally takes over! The stronger their beam, the faster he homes in on them. Yes, and the harder they fall. It's as simple as that.*

"You mean he got to you *because* you're a telepath? Ordinary people would be safe, then?"

I can't answer yes for a certainty, but I would think so. But one thing I am certain of: with a mind like that, he has to be a powerful hypnotist, too. In fact he'll have all the usual—the unusual?—mental powers of the Wamphyri in spades!

"So I've been told." Harry nodded gloomily. "It makes a nonsense of something Faethor said to me."

Faethor? You've been talking to that blackhearted bastard again? Harry, he was Janos's father!

"I know that," said Harry. "But if you don't speak to them, you can't know them. And that's my best weapon: knowing them."

Well, I suppose you know best what you're doing. But, Harry, never let him into your mind. Be sure to keep the bastard out of your mind. Because once he's in, he's in for good!

Which was the opposite of the advice Faethor had given him. "I'll keep that in mind," said Harry, but artlessly,

368

without humour. And: "Trevor, is there anything I can do for you? Any messages?"

I've left a few friends behind. Given time, I'll think of a couple things to say. Not right now, though. Maybe you can get back to me. I hope so, anyway.

"Trevor, you were a telepath in life. Well, it doesn't stop there. You won't be alone, ever. See if I'm not right. And . . . there's one last thing."

Yes?

"I . . . I want to make sure you're cremated. And then, if everything works out, I think I'd like to keep your ashes."

Harry, said Jordan in a little while, *did anyone ever tell you you're morbid?* Then he actually laughed, however shakily. *Hell, I don't care what happens to my ashes! Though I suppose I'd get to talk to you more often, right? I mean, from your mantelpiece?*

Harry had to grin to keep from crying. "I suppose you would," he said . . .

By midafternoon things were starting to shape up. Harry still couldn't contact Möbius or Faethor, but Manolis and Darcy returned from an outing in the town with an armful of spear guns. They were the Italian Champion models Manolis had recommended, with very powerful single-rubber propulsion.

"I once saw a man accidently shot in the thigh with one of these," the Greek related. "They had to open his leg up and cut the harpoon head right out of him! Our harpoons are being silvered right now. We pick them up tonight."

"And my flight to Athens?" Harry's resolve was as strong as ever.

Manolis sighed. "Same as last time. Tomorrow at two-thirty. If there's no trouble with your connection, you'll be in Budapest by, oh, around six-forty-five. But we both wish you'd change your mind."

"That's right," Darcy agreed. "Tomorrow night our people from E-Branch will be out here. And they're trying to contact Zek Föener and Jazz Simmons in Zakinthos to see if they'd like to be in on it. We'll have a hell of a good team,

369

Harry. There's absolutely no reason why you should go off to Hungary on your own. Someone could go with you at least part of the way. A good telepath or prognosticator, say.''

"Zek Föener?" Harry had turned to look sharply, frowningly at Darcy on hearing her name spoken. "And Michael Simmons? Oh, they'll want to be in on it, all right!"

So far there'd been no chance to report what Trevor Jordan had told him about the vampire's superior ESP; now he did so, and finished up: "Don't you realise who and what Zek Föener is? Only one of the most proficient telepaths in the world! Just let her mind so much as scrape up against Janos's and he'd have her! And as for Jazz . . . he was a hell of a man to have around on Starside, but this isn't Starside. The fact is I daren't take *any* of our talented people up against Janos. He'd just take them out one by one and use them for his own. I mean, this is the very essence of why I have to handle my side of it alone. Two many good people have lived through too much already just to go risking their necks again now.''

"You're right, of course." Darcy nodded. "But you're our best chance, Harry, our best shot. Which makes it doubly frustrating to simply say nothing and let you go risking *your* neck! I mean, without you . . . why, we'd be left stumbling around in the dark!" Which seemed to say a lot for what he thought of Harry's chances. But:

"I won't argue with you," Harry said quietly. "I'm on my own." And his voice held a note of finality, and of a determination which wouldn't be swayed . . .

They hadn't eaten; that evening they went out to pick up their silvered harpoons and on the way back stopped off at a taverna for a meal and a drink. They ate in silence for a while, until Darcy said, "It's all boiling up, I can feel it. My talent wishes to hell tomorrow wasn't coming, but it knows it is.''

Harry looked up from his large, rare steak. "Let's just get through the night first, right?" There was a growl in his voice that Darcy wasn't used to. It had a hard, unaccustomed edge

370

to it. Tension, he supposed, nerves. But . . . who could blame Harry for that?

Harry couldn't know it but he wasn't going to have a good night. Asleep almost before his head hit the pillows, he was at once assailed by strange dreams; "real" dreams in the main, but vague and shadowy things which he probably wouldn't remember in the waking world.

Ever since his Necroscope talents had developed as a child, Harry had known two sorts of dreams. "Real" dreams, the subconscious reshuffling of events and memories from the waking world, which anyone might experience, and metaphysical "messages" in the form of warnings, omens, and occasionally visions or glimpses of real events long since over and done with and others yet to come. The latter had presaged his developing deadspeak, enabling the dead in their graves to infiltrate his sleeping mind. He had learned to separate the two types, to know which ones were important and should be remembered, and which to discard as meaningless. Occasionally they would overlap, however, when a conversation with a dead friend might drift into a "real" dream or nightmare—such as when his ma had become a shrieking vampire! Or it might just as easily work the other way, when a troubled dream would be soothed by the intervention of a dead friend.

Tonight he would experience both types and intermingled, and all of them nightmarish.

They started innocuously enough, but as the night progressed, so he began to feel a certain mental oppression. If anyone had shared his room, they would have seen him tossing and turning as the weird clearing house of his mind set up a series of strange scenarios.

Eventually Harry's struggles wearied him and he drifted more deeply into dreams, and as was often the case soon found himself in a nighted graveyard. This was not in itself ominous: he need only declare himself and he knew he'd find friends here. Contrary as dreams are, however, he made no effort to identify himself but instead wandered among the weed-grown plots and leaning headstones, all silvered under the moon.

There was a ground mist which lapped at the humped roots of stunted trees and turned the well-trodden, compacted paths between plots to writhing ribbons of milk. Harry picked his way silently beneath the lunar lamp, and the mist curled almost tangibly about his ankles.

Then . . . suddenly he knew he was not alone in this place, and he sensed such a coldness and a silent horror as he'd never before known in any cemetery. He held his breath and listened, but even the beat of his own heart seemed stilled in this now-terrible place. And in the next moment he knew why it was terrible. It wasn't just the preternatural cold and the silence, but the *nature* of the silence!

The dead themselves were silent . . . they lay petrified in their graves, in terror of something which had come among them. But what?

Harry wanted to flee the place, felt an unaccustomed urge to distance himself from what should be (to him) a sure haven in an uncertain dream landscape; but at the same time he was drawn towards a mist-shrouded corner of the graveyard, where rubbery vegetation grew green and lush and damp from the coiling vapours.

The vapours of the tomb, he thought, *like the cold breath of the dead, leaking from all of these graves!* It was an unusual thought, for Harry knew that there was no life in death . . . was there?

No, of course not, for the two conditions of man were quite separate: the living and the dead, distinct from each other as the two faces of a fathomless gorge, and Harry the only living person with the power to bridge the gap.

Oh? And what of the undead?

Something squelched underfoot with a sound like bursting bladders of seaweed, and Harry looked down. He stood at the very rim of the rank vegetation, beyond which unnatural mists boiled upwards presumably from some untended tomb.

And at his feet . . . a cluster of small black mushrooms or puffballs, releasing their scarlet spores even as he stepped amongst them.

Whose grave was it, he wondered, out of which these fungi siphoned their putrid nourishment? He passed in through a curtain of damp, clinging green, where heavy leaves and clutching creepers seemed reluctant to admit him; but emerging from the other side . . . it was as if he'd passed into an entirely different region!

No mausoleum here. No leaning, lichened tombstones or weedy plots but . . . a morass?

A swamp, yes. Harry stood on the rim of a vast, misted expanse of quag, rotting trees, and rank vines; and all around, whenever there was semisolid ground, the wrinkled black toadstools grew in diseased, ugly clumps, releasing their drifting red spores!

He moved to turn, retreat, retrace his steps, only to discover himself rooted to the spot, fascinated by a sudden commotion in the leprous grey mire. Directly to the fore, the quag was shuddering, forming slow doughy ripples as if something huge stirred just below the surface, causing vile black bubbles to rise and belch and release their gasses.

And in another moment, up from the depths of the bog rose . . . the steaming slab of a headstone, complete with its own rectangular plot of hideously quaking earth!

Until now, however unquiet, Harry's dream had been languid as a strange slow-motion ballet—but the rest of it came with nerve-shattering speed and ferocity.

Longing to turn and run but still rooted there, he could only watch as the mush of the bog slopped from the thrusting headstone and dripped from the rim of the risen tomb to reveal its true nature . . . indeed to reveal the identity of its *dweller*! The legend carved in the slab where the oozing quag gurgled from its grooves was hardly unfamiliar. It said, quite simply:

HARRY KEOGH: NECROSCOPE

Then—

—The mound of the burial plot burst open, hurling great clods of earth in all directions! And lying there in that open grave, like some morbid parasite in a wound, a semblance or grotesque caricature of Harry himself . . . *but festooned in all its parts with ripening, spore-bearing mushrooms!*

Harry tried to scream and had no mouth; his likeness did the job for him; with a monstrous grunt it sat up in its gaping tomb, opening its yellow, pus-filled eyes, and screamed until it rotted down into a gurgling black stump!

Harry put up a hand before his eyes to ward off the sight of the thing . . . and his hand was *covered* with black nodules, like monstrous melanomas, growing and sprouting from his flesh even as he stared aghast! And now he saw why he couldn't run: because he *was* rooted to the spot, was himself a hybrid fungus thing, whose tendril toes had hooked themselves into the bank of rotting soil above the quivering swamp!

He turned up his face to the moon and screamed then, not with his puffball-spewing mouth but with his mind.

Christ! Oh, Christ! Oh, Christ! And before the dry-rot fungus webbing crawled over his eyes to seal them, too, he saw that in fact the moon was a skull which laughed at him from a sky of blood! But before the sky could rain its red on him, the moon skull reached down skeletal arms to gather him up, draw him from the sucking swamp, and refashion his limbs back into man-shape. And:

Haarrry! the moon sang to him with Sandra's voice. *Harry! Oh, why don't you answer me?*

The old dream receded apace with the new one's advance. Harry tossed in his bed and sweated, and sent out tremulous deadspeak thoughts into the dark of the night. But:

No, no, Harry, came Sandra's urgent mental voice again. *I don't need that, for I'm not dead. Better if I were, perhaps, but I'm not! And only look at me now, Harry, only* look *at me now!*

He forced open his squeezed-shut eyes and looked, and tried to accept the strangeness of what he saw.

The scene itself was weird and gothic, and yet Harry knew

the people in it well enough. Sandra, striding to and fro, to and fro, wringing her hands and tearing her hair; and Ken Layard, hunched over a wooden table, strangely slumped and crooked where he crushed his head between taloned hands and gazed feverishly on the unguessed caverns of his own mind. Sandra the telepath, and Layard the locator. Janos's creatures now.

In their entirety?

Harry was immaterial, incorporeal, without body. He knew it at once, that same nonfeeling of unbeing which had been his lot in the strange times between the death of the physical Harry Keogh and his mind's incorporation with the brain-dead Alec Kyle. He was here not in the flesh but in spirit alone. Incredible, indeed impossible outside the scope of dreams and without the aid of the metaphysical Möbius Continuum. And yet with his Necroscope's instinct, Harry knew that this was more than just a dream.

He examined his surroundings.

A huge bedchamber of a room, with a massive four-poster in an arched-over recess in a raw stone wall. Other than this, the room contained a low cot with a straw-stuffed mattress and mouldy blankets, wide wooden chairs and a rough table, a great fireplace and blackened flue, and ancient tapestries rotting on the gaunt stone walls. There were no windows and only one door, which was of massive oak and iron-banded. It was closed and displayed neither doorknob nor handle; Harry guessed it would be bolted and barred from the outside.

The only light came from a pair of squat candles wax-welded to the table where Layard sat hunched in his fever of concentration; they flickeringly illuminated a vaulted ceiling, with nitre crystals crusted in the mortar between massively carved keystone blocks. The floor was of stone flags, the atmosphere cold and unwelcoming, the entire scene fraught with the menace of a dungeon. The place *was* a dungeon, or as close as made no difference.

A dungeon in the ruined castle of the Ferenczy!

"Harry?" Sandra's voice was a hushed, frightened whisper, kept low for fear of alerting . . . someone. She stopped pacing and hugged herself tightly as an involuntary shudder of terror—and then of sudden awareness—wracked her body. Her mouth fell open in a gasp and she strained her face forward, staring at nothing. "Harry, is that . . . you?"

Ken Layard at once looked up and said, "Do you have him?" His face was gaunt, twisted from some unbearable agony, with cold sweat standing on his brow. But as he spoke the scene began to waver and Harry, however unwillingly, to withdraw.

"Don't let it *slip*!" Sandra hissed. She rushed to the table, caught Layard's head in her hands, lent her will to his in bolstering whatever extrasensory feat it was which he performed. And the room grew solid again, and at last the incorporeal necroscope understood.

As yet they were not entirely in Janos's thrall. They were his, yes, but he must needs watch them, lock them up when he himself was not close by . . . like now. And because they knew they were doomed to his service as undead vampires, so they combined their ESP in this one last effort to defy him, while still their minds were at least in part their own. Layard had used his talent to locate and "fix" Harry in his bed in a Rhodes hotel, and Sandra had followed Layard's coordinates to engage the necroscope in telepathic communication. But with their powers enhanced or amplified by the vampire stuff Janos had put into them, they had succeeded above their expectations. They had not only sought Harry out and contacted him, but given him telepathic and visual access to their dungeon prison!

Sandra was dressed in some gauzy shift which let the light of the candles strike right through; she wore neither shoes nor underclothes; there were dark angry blotches on her breasts and buttocks which could only be bruises. Layard's attire was little more substantial: a coarse blanket which he'd belted into a sort of cassock. It would be bitterly cold down there in the secret core of the old castle, but Harry rightly supposed that the cold no longer affected them.

"Harry! Harry!" she hissed again, turning her gaze directly toward his unbodied presence where he viewed them.

"Harry, I *know* we have you! So why don't you answer me?" Her fear and frustration were obvious in the huge orbs of her eyes.

"You . . . you have me." He finally spoke up. "It took a moment to get used to, that's all."

"Harry!" Her gasp made a plume of mist in the cold air. "My God, we really do have you!"

"Sandra," he said, more animated now, "I'm asleep and, well, dreaming, sort of. But I can wake up, or be woken up, at any time. After that . . . we might still be in contact and we might not. You've done this—got in touch with me—for a reason, so now it would be better if you just got on with it."

His words—so cold, distant, empty—seemed to stun her. He wasn't how she'd expected him to be. She went to the table and flopped into a chair alongside Layard. "Harry," she said. "I've been used, changed, poisoned. If you've ever loved me—especially feeling what you'd be feeling for me now—then I know you'd be screaming. And Harry, you're not screaming."

"I'm feeling nothing," he said. "I *daren't* feel anything! I'm talking to you, that's all, but without looking inside. Don't ask me to look inside, too, Sandra."

She put her head in her hands and sobbed raggedly. "Cold, so cold. Were you ever, ever in your life warm, Harry?"

"Sandra," he said, "you're a vampire. And though you probably don't know it, you're already displaying the traits of a vampire. They rarely converse but play word games. They play on emotions they don't themselves share or understand, such as love, honesty, honour. And others which they understand only too well, like hate and lust. They seek to confuse issues and so blunt the minds of their opponents. And to a vampire, each and every other creature who is not a thrall is an opponent. You sought me out, doubtless because you had important things to tell me, but now the vampire in you delays and distracts you, causes you to deviate from your course."

"You *never* loved me!" she accused, spitting out the words

377

and showing her altered teeth. And for the first time he saw how her eyes, and Ken Layard's, were yellow and feral. Later they would turn red . . . if he were to fail and let them have a later.

And now Harry looked again, more closely, at these two prisoners of Janos, one who'd been a lover and the other something of a friend, and saw how well the vampire had done his work on them. Apart from their eyes, their flesh had little of human life in it; they were undead, with more than their fair share of Janos himself in them. Sandra's beauty, hitherto natural, was now entirely unearthly; and Layard: he looked like a three-dimensional cardboard figure, which had been partly crushed.

Harry's thoughts were as good as spoken words. "But I *was* crushed, Harry!" Layard looked up and told him, speaking to the empty air. "On Karpathos, in a moment when Janos was distracted, I broke a length of driftwood and tried to put its point through him. He called his men off the *Lazarus* and had me tied down on the beach, where they dropped boulders on me from the low cliffs! They only stopped when I was quite broken and buried. My vampire is healing me now, but I'll never be straight again."

Harry's pity welled up and threatened to engulf him, but he forced it down. "Why did you call me here? To advise me, or to weaken me with remorse and regrets—and with fear for myself? Are you your own creatures, or are you now entirely his?"

"At the moment," Layard answered, "we're our own. For how long . . . who can say? Until he returns. And after that . . . the change is working and can't be reversed. You are right, Harry: we are vampires. We want to help you, but the dark stuff in us obfuscates."

"We make no progress," said Harry.

"Only say you loved me!" Sandra pleaded.

"I loved you," Harry told her.

"Liar!" she hissed.

Harry felt torn. "I can't love," he said, in something of desperation, and for the first time in his life realised it was probably true. Once upon a time, maybe, but no longer. Manolis Papastamos had been right after all: he was a cold one.

Sandra shrank down into herself. "No love in you," she said. "And should we advise you so that you may kill us?"

"But isn't that the point of all this?" said Layard. "Isn't it what we want, while still we have a choice?"

"Is it? Oh, is it?" She clutched one of his broken hands. And to Harry: "I thought I no longer wanted to live, not like this. But now I don't know, I don't know. Harry, Janos has . . . has . . . he has known me. He *knows* me! There's no cavity of my body he hasn't filled! I loathe him . . . and yet I want him, too! And that's the worst: to lust after a monster. But lust is part of life, after all, and I've always loved life. So what if you win? Will it be for me . . . as it was for the Lady Karen?"

"No!" The thought repelled him. "I couldn't do that again. Not to you, not to anyone, not ever. *If* I win, it will be as easy for you as I can make it."

"Except you can't win!" Layard moaned. "I only wish you could."

"But he might! He might!" Sandra jumped up. "Perhaps Janos is wrong!"

"About what?" Harry felt he'd broken through and was now getting somewhere. "Perhaps he's wrong about what?"

"He's looked into the future," Sandra said. "It's one of his talents. He's read the future, and seen victory for himself."

"What has he seen? What, exactly?"

"That you will come," she answered, "and that there will be fire and death and thunder such as to wake the dead. That the living and the dead and the undead shall all be embroiled in it: a chaos spawning only one survivor, the most terrible, most powerful vampire of all. Ah, and not merely a vampire but . . . Wamphyri!"

"A paradox," Layard sobbed. "For now you know the reason why you must *not* come!"

Harry nodded (if only to himself) and said, "That's always the way it is when you read the future."

Then—

—The dungeon's heavy door burst open! Janos stood there, handsome as the devil, evil as hell. And hell's fire burned in his eyes.

And before the scene dissolved entirely and turned to darkness, Harry heard him say, "So, given enough rope and you hang yourselves. I *knew* you would contact him! Well, and what you have done for yourselves you can doubtless do for me. So be it!"

XIV: Second Contact—
Horror on Halki—
Negative Charge

TURBULENT IN HIS RHODIAN HOTEL BED, HARRY MIGHT HAVE woken up there and then; but no sooner was his contact with Sandra and Layard broken than another voice intruded on his dreams, this time a far more welcome visitation.

Harry? Did you call out? Did you call His Name, Harry, into the void?

It was Möbius, but the waft and whisper of his deadspeak voice told the necroscope that he was just as mazed and wandering as ever. "His name?" Harry mumbled, still tossing and turning in his sticky sheets but gradually settling down again. "Your name, do you mean? Probably. But that was earlier."

No, His Name! Möbius, insisted.

"I don't know what you're talking about." Harry was bewildered.

Ah! Möbius sighed, partly in relief but mainly in disappointment. *But I thought for a moment that you had reached a similar conclusion. Not at all impossible, nor even improb-*

*able. For as you know, I've always considered you my peer,
Harry.*

He still wasn't making much sense, but Harry didn't like
to tell him so. His respect for Möbius was limitless. "Your
peer?" he finally answered. "Hardly that, sir. And whatever
new conclusion you've reached, no way that I could ever
match it. Not anymore, for I'm not the man I used to be.
Which is the reason I was looking for you."

*Ah, yes! I remember now: something about losing your
deadspeak? Something about being innumerate? Well, as for
the former, obviously not—for how else would you be speaking to me right now? And innumerate? What, Harry Keogh?*
Möbius chuckled. *That is not how I would describe you!*

Harry's turn to sigh his relief. Möbius's mind, at first misty,
was at last coming through to him with something of its usual
crystal clarity. He pressed his case.

"But that's just it: it's the only way to describe what's
happened to me. I am now innumerate; I can't conjure the
equations; I no longer have access to the Möbius Continuum.
And I need the Continuum now as never before."

Innumerate! the other said yet again, plainly astonished.
*But how may I accept it? How may I believe it of you? You
were my star pupil! Here, try this.* And he inscribed a complicated mathematical sequence on the screen of Harry's
mind.

Harry looked at it, examining each symbol and number in
turn, and it was like trying to fathom an alien language. "No
use," he said.

Astonishing! Möbius cried. *That was a very simple problem, Harry. It appears this disability of your is serious.*

"That's what I've been saying." Harry tried to be patient.
"And it's why I need your help."

Only tell me what you would like me to do.

Now Harry's sigh was a glad one, for it seemed that at last
he had Möbius's total attention. He quickly told him how
Faethor had got into his mind and untangled the connections
he'd found there, which had been stimulated into agonising
being each time Harry had attempted to use his deadspeak.

"Faethor was probably the only one who could ever have corrected it," he explained, "because it was one of his own sort who'd snarled it up in the first place. And so I got my deadspeak back. But that wasn't the only obstruction Faethor had found in there, not by a long shot. The areas governing my basic and instinctive understanding of numbers had been closed off almost entirely! Here's what he discovered: closed doors, barred and bolted—with all my math locked up behind them! Now, Faethor is no mathematician, but still, by sheer force of will he got one of these doors open. Only for a moment, before it slammed shut again, but long enough. And beyond it . . . the Möbius Continuum! That was too much for him and he got out of there."

Entirely fascinating! said Möbius. And: *It seems we'll have to start your education all over again.*

Harry groaned. "That isn't quite the way I see it," he said. "I mean, I was hoping there'd be a much quicker way. You see, this is something I need right now, or I'm very likely a goner. What I mean is, well, Faethor could only handle those areas in which he was the expert. And so I was thinking that maybe you—"

*But Harry—*Möbius seemed shocked—*I'm no vampire! Your mind is your own, private and inviolable, and—*

"But not for much longer!" Harry cut him off. "Not if you turn me down!" And desperately now: "August Ferdinand, I have to go up against something entirely monstrous, and I need all the help I can get. But it's not just for me, it's for everyone and everything. For you see, if I lose this one, then my enemy gets it all—even the Möbius Continuum itself! Believe me, I'm not exaggerating. If you can't open those doors in my head, he will. And . . . and . . . and after that—"

Yes?

"After that, I just don't know . . ."

Möbius was silent for a moment, and then: *That serious, eh?*

"That serious, yes."

But Harry, all your secrets are in there, your ambitions, your most private thoughts.

"Also my desires, my vices, my sins. But it's no peep show, August. You don't have to look where you don't want to."

The other sighed his acquiescence. *Very well. How do we go about it?*

Harry was eager now. "August Ferdinand, you're the one man among all the dead who can go anywhere—literally *any-where*—in three-dimensional space. You've been out to the stars, down to the bed of the deepest ocean. Through your knowledge of the Möbius Continuum, you've thrown off the fetters of the grave. So . . . how we go about it is simple. I hope so, anyway. I'm going to clear my mind and drift in sleep, and simply invite you in. I'm going to say: Möbius, come into my mind. Enter, of your own free will, and do whatever is necessary to—"

AHHH! came the black, gurglingly glutinous, utterly over-powering voice of Janos Ferenczy in Harry's mind. BUT SUCH AN ELOQUENT INVITATION. NEVER LET IT BE SAID THAT I WAS THE ONE TO REFUSE YOU!

Möbius and his deadspeak were swept aside on the instant. Harry, paralysed, could do nothing. He *felt* the Ferenczy step inside his head as a fish feels the lamprey's clamps in its gill, and was likewise impotent to stop it. It was as if some name-less slug had oozed in through his ear to eat his brain and was now stretching itself luxuriously before commencing the feast. He tried to bring down the shutters of his mind, but they were stuck, effortlessly held open by the invader.

OH? said Janos, as yet feeling his way, enjoying the horror of his host. AND DID I FEEL YOU CRINGE JUST THEN? COULD IT BE THAT YOU ATTEMPTED TO EVICT ME? AND WAS THAT A MEASURE OF YOUR STRENGTH? IF SO, THEN I'VE PRECIOUS LITTLE TO FEAR HERE! BUT FOR SHAME, HARRY KEOGH! WOULD YOU IN-VITE ME IN AND AS QUICKLY THROW ME OUT? AND WHAT SORT OF A HOST ARE YOU?

"My . . . invitation . . . wasn't to you!" Harry forced

his brain into gear, tried to remind himself that this was just another vampire. Janos settled on the thought like a vulture to carrion.

I WAS NOT INVITED? BUT YOUR MIND WAS OPEN AS A WHORE'S CROTCH—AND JUST AS TEMPTING!

Something of Harry's horror receded; he tightened his grip on himself, forced his feverish mind into what he hoped was a defensive stance. But he could almost smell the vampire's vile breath and feel his stealthy tread in the corridors of his most secret being.

AND STILL YOU ACCUSE ME OF STENCHES! The invader laughed. WHAT WAS IT YOU LIKENED ME TO THE LAST TIME? A DEAD PIG? YOU OF ALL PEOPLE SHOULD KNOW BETTER, FOR I AM *UN*DEAD . . .

Suddenly Harry was cool. He had felt stifled, but now it was as if someone had thrown open a window to blow out all the cobwebs of his mind. He filled his lungs with the rush of this weird, conjectural ether and felt stronger for it. And from a far more buoyant if mysterious viewpoint, he wondered at the audacity of the vampire that he should feel so safe and secure as to be able to just . . . just walk in here.

All of these most recent thoughts were guarded, so that Janos took Harry's silence as an indication of sheer terror. AND SO THIS IS THE MIGHTY NECROSCOPE, said the vampire. AND HOW DOES IT FEEL TO HAVE MY "FILTHY LEECH'S MIND" IN *YOUR* HEAD, HARRY?

Harry continued to guard his thoughts. It wasn't difficult; it was like deadspeak, where with a small effort of concentration the dead heard only what he required them to hear. And again he felt a peculiar surge of confidence which was surely well out of place here. For asleep and dreaming, he couldn't exert half as much control over his mind as when he was awake. However true that might be, still he sensed that Janos was becoming just a fraction more cautious.

YOU KNOW, OF COURSE, THAT I CAN BEND YOU TO MY WILL JUST AS I BENT—AND BROKE—THAT FOOL JORDAN? But was Janos stating a fact, or was he asking himself a question?

"Keep telling yourself that," said Harry, without emotion. "But remember: you entered of your own free will."

WHAT? And now there was a ragged, worried edge to Janos's thoughts. As if for the first time he might be weighing the issues and considering his position here.

And in the back of Harry's mind, unsuspected by Janos, it was as if he heard Faethor advising him again, as he had in the ruins of his house outside Ploiesti:

Instead of shrinking back from him when you sense him near, seek him out! He would enter your mind? Enter his! He will expect you to be afraid; be bold! He will threaten; brush all such threats aside and strike! But above all else, do not let his evil weaken you. And, finally: *There may be more to your mind than even you suspect, Harry . . .*

Janos was beginning to think so, too. THIS MIND OF YOURS IS . . . DIFFERENT FROM THE MINDS OF OTHER MEN. IT WILL GIVE ME GREAT PLEASURE TO EXPLORE IT. AND IT WILL GIVE YOU GREAT PAIN!

"Well, at least you have the vanity of the Wamphyri," said Harry. "But what is vanity without the means to match it?"

YOU KNOW US . . . WELL, said Janos, edgier than ever. PERHAPS TOO WELL.

"Having second thoughts, my son?"

And again, but angrily: *WHAT!*

"Come now, not so nervous. I speak more as an uncle than a true father. But it's a fact I do have a son of my own. Except, of course, he *is* Wamphyri! But see, now I sense your trembling. What, you, afraid? How so? For after all you have my measure. Have you not invaded my mind? Where is my resistance? With what may I resist? Here you are inside the castle of my very being. Ah, but there are castles and there are castles—and some are easier to get into than they are to get out of!" And at last Harry brought the shutters of his mind crashing down.

Janos was confused; this was no mere man; it was as if he talked to . . . something far greater than a man. In his panic, the vampire became vicious.

THESE PUNY BARRIERS YOU HAVE ERECTED . . .
I AM SURROUNDED BY DOORS. BUT I HAVE THE
STRENGTH TO BEAT THEM ALL DOWN, INDEED TO
TEAR THEM FROM THEIR HINGES!

Harry heard him, but he also heard this:

When he yawns his great jaws at you, go in through them,
for he's softer on the inside!

"Beat them all down, then," he answered. "Tear them
from their hinges—if you dare!"

Janos dared. He ran through Harry's mind, shattering every
barrier the Necroscope could put in his way, tearing down the
shutters and screens on his innermost being. All Harry's past
was there, his loves and hates, his hopes and aspirations, and
all trampled under as the vampire marauded through previously secret corridors of id. In any one of these places the
monster might pause awhile, play, cause Harry to laugh, cry,
scream—or die. But realising now that indeed he *had* Harry's
measure, he didn't pause but rampaged. And:

WHAT? WHAT? He finally laughed as he came to a place
more heavily fortified than all the rest put together. WHY,
IT CAN ONLY BE THE VERY TREASURE HOUSE! AND
WHAT MARVELLOUS SECRETS ARE STORED HERE,
HARRY KEOGH? ARE THESE THE VAULTS OF YOUR
TALENTS?

And before Harry could answer—if he would answer—
Janos had wrenched two of the doors open.

Beyond one of them was the ultimate NOTHING, so that
in a single moment Janos found himself teetering on the
threshold of the Möbius Continuum. And behind the other
. . . was Faethor Ferenczy, crouching there where he directed Harry's game, and now inspired Janos's uttermost terror!

The invader reared back—from Faethor, who had now
emerged more fully from his hiding place and was frantically
trying to push him through the doorway to eternity, and from
the Möbius Continuum both—and grunted his shock, astonishment, and total disbelief. For within a mainly human identity he had stumbled across not only an unknowable and

terrifying concept, but also the entirely monstrous and alien mind of his own long-dead father!

Terror galvanised him: he tore himself free from Faethor, gasped a stream of semicoherent obscenities at him, and fled. He broke out of Harry's id, was gone in a moment. He had done no real damage, and the Necroscope guessed that he'd never dare try it again. But . . .

"Faethor!" Harry growled, his mental voice as grim and wrenching as an old chalk on a new blackboard—his *own* voice now, no longer influenced or guided by the mind of his secret tenant. And again: *"Faethor!"*

There was no answer . . . except perhaps a far, faint chuckle, like oily bubbles bursting on a lake of pitch. Or perhaps the furtive whir of bat wings, echoing from the deepest, darkest cave.

"Oh you bastard . . . you liar!" Harry howled. "You're *in* here! You have been right from the moment I let you in! But I can find you, throw you out . . ."

And at last:

No need, my son, came Faethor's distant, diseased whisper. *The first battle is fought and won; the sun rises; I . . . get . . . me . . . gone!*

After that: Harry surfaced from his dreams slow and cold, so that the sweat was dry on him by the time he was fully awake and Darcy Clarke came knocking on his door mumbling about breakfast. By then, too, Harry believed he'd worked out how he was going to play the rest of it . . .

At 8:15 Rhodes Town was only just awake, but already Harry was down on a pier in Mandraki harbour to see his friends off. Darcy and Manolis waved several times as their boat pulled out onto the incredible blue millpond of the Aegean, but he didn't wave back. He simply nodded and watched them out of sight, and silently wished them luck.

Then he drove over to the beach at Kritika and swam for an hour before returning to the hotel and showering. Even after furiously towelling himself dry, and despite the fact that it was at least seventy-five degrees out in the sun, he was still cold. The coldness he felt had nothing to do with the temperature. It came from inside.

Harry's bed had been freshly made; he lay on it with his hands behind his head and thought awhile, slowly emptying his mind and letting himself drift . . .

. . . Then made a stab at Faethor!

And caught him there in his mind before he could wriggle down out of sight. Faethor, right there in his mind, and the time just a little after 10:30, and a scorching sun standing high in the sky. So much for the sun as a deterrent. Harry should have known: ghosts don't burn. It might give Faethor a few bad dreams but it couldn't physically hurt him because there was nothing physical left of him. Any of Harry's dead friends could have told him that much.

"You old devil!" he said, but coldly, for he wasn't name-calling, just stating a fact. "You old bastard, you old liar. So just like Thibor fastened on Dragosani, you're thinking of latching on to me, eh?"

Thinking of it? Faethor came into the open, and Harry could feel him as close as if he stood right there at his bedside. *Fait accompli, Harry. Get used to it.*

Harry shook his head and grinned mirthlessly. "I will be rid of you," he said. "Believe me, Faethor, I'll be rid of you, even if it means getting rid of myself!"

Suicide? Faethor tut-tutted. *No, not you, Harry. Why, you are tenacious as the ones you hunt down and destroy! You will not kill yourself while there's still a chance to kill another one of them.*

"Another one of you, you mean? But you could be wrong, Faethor. Me, I'm only human. I'd die pretty easily. A bullet through my brain, like Trevor Jordan . . . I wouldn't even know about it. Believe me, it's tempting."

I see no real notion of suicide in your thoughts—Faethor shrugged—*so why pretend? Do you think I feel threatened? How can you threaten me, Harry? I'm already dead!*

"But in me you have life, right? Listen and I'll tell you something: you really don't know what's in my thoughts. I

389

can hide them, even from you. It's deadspeak; that's how I
learned to do it; by keeping back my thoughts from the dead.
I did it then so as not to hurt them, but I can just as easily
use it the other way.''

For a moment—the merest tick of the clock—Harry felt
Faethor wavering. And he nodded knowingly. ''See? I know
what's on *your* mind, old devil. But do you know what's on
mine, if I hide it from you . . . so?''

Deep in the psyche of Harry, the Father of Vampires felt
himself surrounded by nothing. It fell on him like a blanket,
as if to smother him. It was as if he were back in the earth
near Ploiesti, where his evil fats had been rendered down the
night Ladislau Giresci took his life.

''You see,'' Harry told him, letting the light of his thoughts
shine in again, ''I can shut you out.''

*Not out, Harry. You can only shut me off. But the moment
you relax I'll be back.*

''Always?''

For a moment Faethor was silent. Then: *No, for we made
a bargain. And so long as you hold to it, then so shall I.
When Janos is no more, then you'll be rid of me.*

''You swear it?''

Upon my soul! Faethor gurgled like a night-dark swamp,
and smiled an immaterial smile.

It was the natural sarcasm of the vampire, but Harry only
said, ''I'll hold you to that.'' And his mental voice was cold
as the spaces between the stars. ''Just remember, Faethor,
I'll hold you to it . . .''

Manolis handled the boat. It had a small cabin and a large
engine and left a wake like low white walls melting back into
the blue. Always in sight of land, they had rounded Cape
Koumbourno and outpaced the water-skiers off Kritika Beach
before Harry had even hit the water there.

By 9:00 they had passed Cape Minas, and with the main-
land lying to port were heading for Alimnia. Darcy had
thought he might have trouble with his stomach, but the sea
was like glass and with the wind in his face . . . he might

easily be enjoying an expensive holiday. That is, if he wasn't perfectly sure he was heading for horror.

Around 10:00 A.M. a pair of dolphins played chicken across the prow of the boat where it sliced the water; by which time they'd passed between the almost barren rocks of Alimnia and Makri, and Halki (which Manolis insisted should be "Khalki," for the chalky shells it was named after) had swum into view.

Fifteen minutes later they were into the harbour and tied up, and Manolis was chatting with a pair of weathered fishermen where they mended their nets. While he made his apparently casual enquiries, Darcy bought a map from a tiny box of a shop right on the waterfront and studied what he could of the island's layout. There wasn't a great deal to study.

The island was a big rock something less than eight by four miles, with the long axis lying east to west. To the west a mile or two, mountain crests stood wild and desolate where the island's one road of any description wandered apparently aimlessly, and Darcy knew that his and Manolis' destination lay way up there, in the heights at the end of that road. He didn't need the map to know it: his talent had been telling him ever since he stepped from the boat to dry land.

Eventually, done with talking to the fishermen, Manolis joined him. "No transport," he said. "It is maybe two miles, then the climbing, and of course we will be carrying our—how do you say—picnic basket? It looks like a long hot walk, my friend, and all of it uphill."

Darcy looked around. "Well, what's that," he said, "if not transport?" A three-wheeled device, clattering like a steam engine and pulling a four-wheel cart, came clanking out of a narrow street to park in the "centre of town," that being the waterfront with its bars and tavernas.

The driver was a slim, small Greek of about forty-five; he got down from his driver's seat and went into a grocery store. Darcy and Manolis were waiting for him when he came out. His name was Nikos; he owned a taverna and rooms on a beach across the bottleneck of the promontory behind the town; business was slow right now and he could run them up

391

to the end of the road for a small remuneration. When Man-olis mentioned a sum of fifteen hundred drachma, his eyes lit up like lamps, and after he'd collected his fish, groceries, booze, and other items for the taverna, then they were off.

Sitting in the back of the cart had to be better than walk-ing—but not much better. On the way Nikos stopped to un-load his purchases at the taverna and to open a couple of bottles of beer for his passengers, and then the journey con-tinued.

After a little while and when he'd adjusted his position against the jolting, Darcy took a swig of his beer and said, "What did you find out?"

"There are two of them," Manolis answered. "They come down at evening to buy meat—red meat, no fish—and maybe drink a bottle of wine. They stay together, don't talk much, do their own cooking up at the site . . . *if* they cook!" He shrugged and looked narrow-eyed at Darcy. "They work mainly at night; when the wind is in the right direction, the villagers occasionally hear them blasting. Nothing big, just small charges to shift the rocks and the rubble. During the day . . . they are not seen to do too much. They laze around in the caves up there."

"What about the tourists?" Darcy enquired. "Wouldn't they be a nuisance? And how come Lazarides—or Janos—gets away with it? I mean, digging in these ruins? Is your government crazy or something? This is . . . it's history!"

Again Manolis' shrug. "The Vrykoulakas apparently has his friends. Anyway, they are not actually digging *in* the ru-ins. Beyond the castle where it sits up on the crest, the cliff falls away very steeply. Down there are ledges, and caves. This is where they are digging. The villagers think they are the crazy men. What, treasure up there? Dust and rocks, and that's all."

Darcy nodded. "But Janos knows better, eh? Let's face it, if he buried it, he should know where to dig for it!"

Manolis agreed. "As for the tourists: there are maybe thirty of them right now. They spend their time in the tavernas, on the beach, lazing around. They are on holiday, right? Some climb up to the castle, but never down the other side. And never at night.''

"It feels weird," said Darcy, after a while.

"What does?"

"We're going up there to kill these things."

"Right," Manolis answered. "But only if it's necessary. I mean, only if they *are* things!"

Darcy gave an involuntary shudder and glanced at the long, narrow wicker basket which lay between them. Inside it were spear guns, wooden stakes, Harry Keogh's crossbow, and a gallon of petrol in a plastic container. "Oh, they are," he said then, and offered a curt nod. "You can believe me, they are . . .''

Fifteen minutes later Nikos brought his vehicle to a halt in a rising reentry. To the left, pathways which were little more than goat tracks led steeply up through the ruined streets of an ancient, long-deserted hill town; above the ruins stood a gleaming white monastery, apparently still in use; and higher still, on the almost sheer crown of the mountain itself—

"The castle!" Manolis breathed.

As Nikos and his wonderful three-wheel workhorse made an awkward turn and went rattling and jolting back down into the valley, Darcy shielded his eyes to gaze up at the ominous walls of the castle, standing guard there as it had through all the long centuries. "But . . . is there a way up?"

"Yes." Manolis nodded. "A goat track. Hairpins all the way, but quite safe. According to the fishermen, anyway."

Carrying the basket between them, they set out to climb. Beyond the monastery and before the real climbing could begin, they paused to look back. Across the valley, they could pick out the boundaries of long-forsaken fields and the shells of old houses, where olive groves and orchards had long run wild and returned to nature.

"Sponges," said Manolis, by way of explanation. "They were sponge fishermen, these people. But when the sponges ran out, so did the people. Now, as you see, it's mainly ruins.

Perhaps one day the tourists will bring it back to life again, eh?''

Darcy had other things than life on his mind. ''Let's get on,'' he said. ''Already I don't want to go any farther, and if we hang about much longer, I won't want to go at all!''

After that it was all ochre boulders, yellow outcrops, and winding goat tracks, and where there were gaps in the rocks, dizzying views which were almost vertiginous. But eventually they found themselves in the shadow of enormous walls and passed under a massive, sloping stone lintel into the ruin itself. The place was polyglot and Darcy had been right about its historic value. It was ancient Greek, Byzantine, and last but not least crusader. As they climbed up onto walls three to four feet thick, the view was fantastic, with all the coastlines of Halki and its neighbouring islands laid open to them.

They clambered over heaps of stony debris in the shell of a crusader chapel whose walls still carried fading murals of saints wearing faded halos, and finally stood on the rim of the ruins looking down on the Bay of Trachia.

''Down there,'' said Manolis. ''That's where they are. Look: do you see those signs of excavation, where all of that rubble makes a dark streak on the weathered rocks? That's them. Now we must find the track down to them. Darcy, are you all right? You have that look again!''

Darcy was anything but all right. ''They . . . they're down there,'' he said. ''I feel rooted to the spot. Every step weighs like lead. Christ, my talent's a coward!''

''You want to rest here a moment?''

''God, no! If I stop now, I'll not get started again. Let's get on.''

There were several empty cigarette packets, scuff marks on the rocks, places where the sandy soil had been compacted by booted feet; the way down was neither hard to find nor difficult to negotiate. Soon they found a rusting wheelbarrow and a broken pick standing on the wide shelf of a natural ledge which had weathered out from the strata. And halfway along the ledge . . . that was where much of the stony debris had been excavated from the mouths of several gaping caves. Moving quietly, they approached the cave showing the most recent signs of work and paused at its entrance. And as they took out spear guns from their basket and loaded them, Manolis whispered, "You're sure we'll need these, yes?"

"Oh, yes." Darcy nodded, his face ashen.

Manolis took a step into the echoing mouth of the cave.

"Wait!" Darcy gasped, his Adam's apple working. "It would be safer to call them out."

"And let them know we're here?"

"In the sunlight, we'll have the advantage," Darcy gulped. "And anyway, my urge to get the fuck out of here just climbed the scale by several big notches. Which probably means they already know we're here!"

He was right. A shadow stepped forward out of the cave's darker shadows, moving carefully towards them where they stood in the entrance. They looked at each other with widening eyes, and together thumbed the safeties off their weapons and lifted them warningly. The man in the cave kept coming, but turned his shoulder side on and went into something of a forward leaning crouch.

Manolis spat out a stream of gabbled Greek curses, snatched his Beretta from its shoulder holster, and transferred the spear gun to his left hand. The man, thing, vampire was still coming at them out of the dark, but they saw him more clearly now. He was tall, slim, strangely ragged looking in silhouette. He wore a wide-brimmed hat, baggy trousers, a shirt whose unbuttoned sleeves flapped loosely at the wrists. He looked for all the world like a scarecrow let down off his pole. But it wasn't crows he was scaring.

"Only . . . one of them?" Darcy gasped—and felt his hair stand on end as he heard pebbles sliding and clattering on the ledge *behind* them!

The man in the cave lunged forward; Manolis' gun flashed blindingly, deafeningly; Darcy looked back and saw a second—creature?—bearing down on them. But this one was much closer! Like his colleague in the cave, he wore a floppy hat, and in its shade his eyes were yellow, viciously feral.

Worse, he held a pickax slantingly overhead, and his face was twisted in a snarl where he aimed it at Darcy's back!

Darcy—or perhaps his talent—turned himself to meet the attack, aimed point-blank, squeezed the trigger of his spear gun. The harpoon flew straight to its target in the vampire's chest. The impact brought him to a halt; he dropped his pickax, clutched at the spear where it transfixed him, staggered back against the wall of the cliff. Darcy, frozen for a moment, could only watch him lurching and mewling there, coughing up blood.

In the cave, Manolis cursed and fired his gun again—and yet again—as he followed his target deeper into the darkness. Then . . . Darcy heard an inhuman shriek followed by the slither of silver on steel, and finally the meaty *thwack* of Manolis' harpoon entering flesh. The sounds brought him out of his shock as he realised that both his and Manolis' weapons were now empty. He leaned to grab a harpoon from the open basket, and the man on the ledge staggered forward and kicked the whole thing, basket and contents, right off the rim!

"Jesus!" Darcy yelled, his throat hoarse and dry as sandpaper as again the flame-eyed thing turned towards him. Then the vampire paused, looked about, and saw its pickax where it lay close to the rising cliff. It moved to pick it up, and Darcy moved, too. His talent told him to run, run, *run!* But he yelled, *"Fuck you!"* and flew like a madman at the stooping vampire. He bowled the thing over, and himself snatched up the pick. The tool was heavy, but such was Darcy's terror that it felt like a toy in his hands.

Manolis came unsteadily out of the cave in time to see Darcy swing his weapon in a deadly arc and punch the wider point of its dual-purpose head into his undead opponent's forehead. The creature made gurgling, gagging sounds and sank to its knees, then slumped against the cliff face.

"Petrol," Manolis gasped.

"Over the edge," Darcy told him, his voice a croak.

Manolis looked over the rim. Farther down the mountain, maybe fifty feet lower, the wicker basket was jammed in the base of a rocky outcrop, where debris from the diggings had piled up to form a scree slide. The lid was open and several items lay scattered about. "You stay, keep watch, and I'll get it," Manolis said.

He gave Darcy his gun and started to clamber down. Darcy kept one eye on the vampire with the pickax in his head, and the other on the leering mouth of the cave. The creature he had dealt with—a man, yes, but a creature, too—was not "dead." It should be, but of course it was undead. The small percentage of its system which was vampire protoplasm was working in it even now, desperately healing its wounds. Even as Darcy watched, it shuddered and its yellow eyes opened, and its hand crept shakily towards the harpoon in its chest.

Gritting his teeth, Darcy stepped closer to it. His guardian angel howled at him, poured adrenaline into his veins, and yelled run, run! But he shut out all warnings, grasped the end of the spear, and yanked it this way and that in the vampire's flesh, until the thing gnashed its teeth and coughed up blood, then flopped back and lay still again.

Darcy stepped back from it on legs that trembled like jelly—and gave a mighty, heart-stopping start as something grasped his ankle!

He glanced back and down and saw the one from the cave where he'd come crawling, his iron hand clasping Darcy's foot. There was a spear through his throat just under the Adam's apple, and the right side of the thing's face had been shot half away, but still he was mobile and one mad eye continued to glare from a black orbit set in a mess of red flesh. Darcy might easily have fainted then; instead he fell backwards away from the undead thing and sat down with a bump on the ledge. And aiming directly between his feet, he emptied Manolis' gun right into the grimacing half face.

At that point Manolis returned. He hauled the basket up behind him, ripped open its lid, and yanked out Harry Keogh's crossbow. A moment later he was loading up, and just in time . . . for the one on the ledge had torn the pickax from its head and was now working to pull out the harpoon from its chest!

"Jesus! Oh, Jesus!" Manolis croaked. He stepped close to

the blood-frothing horror, aimed his weapon from less than three feet away, fired the wooden bolt straight into its heart.

Darcy had meanwhile scrambled backwards away from the other creature. Manolis caught hold of him and hauled him to his feet, said, "Let's finish it while we still can."

They dragged the vampires back inside the cave, as far back as they dared, then hurried back out into sunlight. But Darcy was finished; he could do no more; his talent was freezing him right out of it. "Is okay." Manolis understood. "I can do it."

Darcy crawled away along the ledge and sat there shivering while Manolis took up the petrol and again entered the cave. A moment later and he reappeared, leaving a thin trail of petrol behind him. He'd liberally dosed everything in the cave and the container was almost empty. He backed away towards Darcy, sprinkling the last few drops, then tossed the container far out into empty air and took out a cigarette lighter. Striking the flint, he held the naked flame to the trail of petrol.

Blue fire so faint as to be almost invisible raced back along the ledge and into the mouth of the cave. There came a *whoosh* and a tongue of fire like some giant's blowtorch—followed in the next moment by a terrific explosion that blew out the mouth of the cave in chunks of shattered rock and brought loose scree and pebbles avalanching down from above. The shock of it was sufficient to cause Manolis to stumble and sit down beside Darcy.

They looked at each other and Darcy said, "What the . . . ?"

Manolis' jaw hung loosely open. Then he licked dry lips and said, "Their explosives. They must have kept their explosive charges in there!"

They got up and went shakily back to the blocked mouth of the cave. Down below, boulders were still bounding down the mountain's steep contours to the sea. Hundreds of tons of rock had come crushingly down, sealing the diggings off. And it was plain that nothing alive—but *nothing*—was ever going to come out of there.

"It's done," said Manolis, and Darcy found strength to nod his agreement.

As they turned away, Darcy saw something gleaming yellow in the rubble. Next door to the collapsed cave another, smaller opening was still issuing puffs of dust and a little smoke. The stone wall between the two excavations had been shattered, spilling fractured rock onto the ledge. But among the debris lay a lot more than just rocks.

Darcy and Manolis stepped among the rubble and looked more closely at what had been unearthed. There in that broken wall, carefully packed in and sealed behind cleverly shaped blocks of stone, had lain the treasure for which Jianni Lazarides—alias Janos Ferenczy—had searched. That same treasure he himself had laid down all those centuries ago. Only the changing contours of the mountain, carved and fretted by nature in storms and earthquakes, had confused and foiled him. The old crusader castle had been his landmark, but even that massive silhouette had crumbled and changed through the long years. Still, he'd missed his mark by no more than two or three feet.

The two men scuffed among the dust and broken rocks, their excitement dulled to anticlimax after the horror of their too recent experience. They saw a treasure out of time: Thracian gold! Small bowls and lidded cups . . . gold rhytons spilling rings, necklaces, and arm clasps . . . a bronze helmet stuffed to brimming with earrings, belt clasps, and pectorals . . . even a buckled breastplate of solid gold!

Their find eventually got through to Manolis. "But what do we do with it?"

"We leave it here." Darcy straightened up. "It belongs to the ghosts. We don't know what it cost Janos to bring it here and bury it, or where—or how—he got it in the first place. But there's blood on it, be sure. Eventually someone will come looking for those two and find this instead. Let the authorities handle it. I don't even want to touch it."

"You are right," said Manolis, and they climbed back up to the castle . . .

* * *

By 12:30 the two were back down into the village, where Manolis refuelled the boat for the trip to Karpathos. While he worked, his fishermen friends came over and asked how were the diggers. "They were blasting," Manolis answered after a moment, "so we didn't disturb them. Anyway, the cliffs are very steep and a man could easily fall."

"Snotty buggers anyway," one of the fishermen commented. "They don't bother with us and we don't bother with them!"

Finished with his fuelling, Manolis bought a litre of ouzo and they all sat around tables in an open taverna and killed the bottle dead. Later, as their boat pulled away from the stone jetty, the Greek said, "I needed that."

Darcy sighed and agreed, "Me too. It's nasty, thirsty work."

Manolis looked at him and nodded. "And a lot more of it to come before we're through, my friend. It is perhaps the good job ouzo is cheap, eh? Just think, with all of that gold we left up there, we could have bought the distillery!"

Darcy looked back and watched the hump of rock which was Halki slowly sinking on the horizon, and thought: *Yes, and maybe we'll wish we had . . .*

Halki to Karpathos was a little more than sixty miles by the route Manolis chose; he preferred to stay in sight of land as far as possible, and to cruise rather than race his engine. When the rocks Ktenia and Karavolas were behind them, then he set a course more nearly southwest and left Rhodes behind for Karpathos proper.

That meant the open sea, and now Darcy's stomach began to play him up a little. It was a purely physical thing and not too bad; after what he'd faced already he wasn't going to throw up now. At least his talent wasn't warning against shipwrecks or anything!

To take Darcy's mind off his misery, Manolis told him a few details about Karpathos.

"Second biggest of the Dodecanese Islands," he said. "She lies just about halfway between Rhodes and Crete.

Where Halki goes east to west, Karpathos she goes north to south. Maybe fifty kilometers long but only seven or eight wide. Just the crest of submarine mountains, that's all. Not the big place, really, and not many peoples. But she has known the turbulent history!''

"Is that right?" said Darcy, scarcely listening.

"Oh, yes! Just about everyone ruled or owned or was the governor of Karpathos at one time or another. The Arabs, Italian pirates out of Genoa, the Venetians, Crusaders of the Knights of St. John, Turks, Russians—even the British! Huh! It took seven centuries for us Greeks to get it back!''

And when there was no answer: "Darcy? Are you all right?''

"Only just. How long before we're there?"

"We're almost halfway there already, my friend. Another hour, or not much more, and we'll be rounding the point just under the landing strip. That's where we should find the *Lazarus*. We can take a look at her, but that's all. Maybe we can hail someone—or something—on board, and see what we think of him.''

"Right now I don't think much of anybody," said Darcy . . .

But, as it happened, Manolis was wrong and the *Lazarus* was not there. They searched the small bays at the southern extreme of the island, but found no sign of the white ship. Manolis' patience was soon exhausted. In a little while, when it became obvious that their searching was in vain, he headed north for the sandy shallow-water beach at Amoupi and anchored there where they could wade ashore. They ate a Greek salad at the beach taverna and drank a small bottle of retsina between them. When Darcy fell asleep in his chair under the taverna's split-bamboo awning, Manolis sighed, sat back, and lit a cigarette. He smoked several, admired the tanned, bouncing breasts of English girls where they played in the sea, drank another bottle of retsina before it was time to wake Darcy up.

Just after 5:05 they set out to return to Rhodes . . .

* * *

That evening, coming in stiff, weary, and tanned by sun and sea spray, Darcy and Manolis found four people waiting for them in the lounge of their hotel. There were several moments of confusion. Darcy knew two of the arrivals well enough, for Ben Trask and David Chung were his own men; but Zekintha Föener (now Simmons), and her husband Michael or "Jazz" were strangers to him except by hearsay. Darcy had anticipated four and had booked accommodation accordingly, but of this specific group he had only expected two. On Harry Keogh's advice he had tried to get a message to Zek and Jazz that they should stay out of it, but either it hadn't reached them or they had chosen to ignore it. He would find out later. The two missing men were E-Branch operatives finalising a job in England, who would fly out here ASAP on completion of that task.

The four newcomers, having already dropped off their luggage in their rooms and introduced each other, were more or less ready to talk business. Darcy need only introduce Manolis and make known the Greek policeman's role in things, then replay the action so far, and all systems would be go. Before that, however . . .

. . . Darcy and Manolis excused themselves and took invigorating showers before rejoining the E-Branch people where they waited for them. Then Manolis took them all to a rather expensive taverna on the other side of town which wasn't likely to be swamped with tourists, and there arranged seating around a large secluded corner table with a view on the night ocean. Here Darcy quickly restated the introductions, this time detailing the various talents of his group.

There was the married couple, Zek and Jazz Simmons, who had been on Starside together with Harry Keogh. Zek was a telepath of outstanding ability and an authority on vampires. She was experienced as few before her, in that she had met up with the minds of the Real Thing, the Wamphyri themselves, in an entirely alien world. She was a very good-looker, about five-nine in height, slim, blond, and blue-eyed. Her Greek mother had named her after Zante (or Zakinthos), the island where she was born. Her father had been East German, a parapsychologist. Zek would be in her midthirties, maybe eighteen months to two years older than her husband.

Jazz Simmons had no extraordinary talents other than those with which an entirely mundane Mother Nature had endowed him, plus those in which British intelligence had expertly instructed him. After Starside, he had opted out of intelligence work to be with Zek in Greece and the Greek Islands. Just a fraction under six feet tall, Jazz had unruly red hair, a square jaw under slightly hollow cheeks, grey eyes, good strong teeth, hands that were hard for all that they were artistically tapered, and long arms that gave him something of a gangling, loose-limbed appearance. Lean, tanned, and athletic, he looked deceptively easygoing . . . *was* easygoing in normal circumstances and when there was little or no pressure. But no one should underestimate him. He'd been trained to a cutting edge in surveillance, close protection, escape and evasion, winter warfare, survival, weapons handling (to marksman), demolition, and unarmed combat. The only thing Jazz had lacked had been experience, and he'd got that in the best—or worst—of all possible places, on Starside.

Then there were the two men from E-Branch: David Chung, a locator and scryer, and Ben Trask, a human lie detector. Chung was twenty-six, a Chinese ''cockney'' tried and true. Born within the sound of Bow-bells, he had been with the branch for nearly six years and during that time had trained himself to a high degree in the extrasensory location of illegal drugs, especially cocaine. If not for the fact that he'd been working on a long-term case in London, then he and not Ken Layard might well have been out here in the first place.

Ben Trask was a blocky five feet ten, mousey-haired and green-eyed, overweight and slope-shouldered, and usually wore what could only be described as a lugubrious expression. His specialty was Truth: presented with a lie or deliberately falsified concept, Trask would spot it immediately. E-Branch loaned him out to the police authorities on priority jobs, and he was in great demand by Foreign Affairs to see

403

through the political posturing of certain less than honest members of the international community. Ben Trask knew the ins and outs of London's foreign embassies better than most people know the backs of their hands. Also, he'd played a part in the Yulian Bodescu affair and wasn't likely to take anything too lightly.

While they waited for their meals, Darcy filled in all the missing pieces for his team and watched them tighten up as the full horror of the situation was brought home to them. Then he was interested to know why Jazz and Zek had invited themselves in on this thing.

Jazz answered for them. "It's Harry, isn't it? Harry Keogh? He gets our vote every time. If Harry has problems, it's no use telling Zek and me to keep a low profile."

"That's very loyal of you," Darcy told him, "but it was Harry himself who would have preferred to keep you out of it—for your own sakes. Not that I'm complaining . . . I'm short of a couple of good hands and you two probably fit the bill perfectly. Harry's main concern was that Janos Ferenczy is one powerful mentalist. He has already killed Trevor Jordan and controls Ken Layard, so you can see why Harry was worried. He was mainly concerned about what would happen if Janos came up against you, Zek. However, since Janos is now in Romania—that is, to the best of our knowledge—and with Harry gone there to hunt him down . . ." Darcy shrugged. "Myself, I'm delighted to have you on the team!"

"So when does it all start—for us, I mean?" David Chung was eager to get into it.

"For you it starts tomorrow," Darcy told him. "The 'active service' part of it, anyway. Tonight, back at the hotel after we've finished here, that will be the time for preparation and planning. That's when we detail, as best we can, who will be doing what—and to whom!" He spied a waiter moving towards their table with a loaded trolley. "As for this very moment: I suggest we enjoy our food and relax as best we can. Because you'd better believe that tomorrow's a busy day . . ."

* * *

While Darcy Clarke and his team thought forward to their next day, Harry Keogh was looking back on the one just ended.

Harry's flight to Athens had been uneventful. Aboard the plane for Budapest, however, when he'd closed his eyes even before takeoff and determined to catch an hour's sleep . . .

. . . He'd felt them there the moment he began to drift into dreams: alien probes touching on his mind. And knowing they were there, he'd forced himself to stay awake and alert, while yet hiding that fact from the telepathic talents who had found him. ''They'' could only be Ken Layard and Sandra, but their ESP was cold now and tainted. Almost completely in thrall to Janos Ferenczy as they were, their tentative touches were slimy as the walls of a sewer, so that Harry must fight not to recoil from them. But he remembered what Faethor had told him, and strangely enough accepted that it was probably good advice:

Instead of shrinking back from him when you sense him near, seek him out! He would enter your mind? Enter his!

And as the vampire intelligences grew less apprehensive of discovery and avidly scanned him, so Harry in turn scanned them. Indeed he spoke to them in whispers, under his breath.

''Ken? Sandra? So he has your cooperation now. Well, and you've done a good job for him. But why so secretive about it, eh? I was expecting you. I knew that he would use you, that in fact he can't do without you. What, him? Face-to-face and man-to-man? Not a chance. Your vampire superman is a coward! He fears I'll creep up on him in the night. One man against him and everything he harbours up there in that pest hole in the mountains, and he's afraid of me. You warned me he'd read the future and seen his victory there. Well, you can tell him from me that the future doesn't always work out that way.''

Ahhh! He sensesss ussss! It was Sandra, hissing like a snake in Harry's mind. *He knows us. His thoughts are strong. His hidden strengths are surfacing.*

She was right and Harry felt the strangeness of it. He was

stronger, and didn't know the source of his new vitality. Was it Faethor? he wondered. Possibly. But for the moment there was nothing he could do about Faethor, and in a storm any port is better than none.

Ken Layard's locator's mind was fastened on Harry like a carrier beam. He let his own slide down it (but secretly) to its source, gazed out through Layard's eyes.

It was as if Harry were there in the flesh . . . and he was, in Layard's flesh! They were in the same subterranean room as before. Sandra sat opposite him (opposite Layard) at the table, and Janos furiously paced the pavings to and fro, to and fro. "Where is he? What is he thinking?" The monster's eyes burned red where he turned them on Sandra. Plainly he was worried, but he tried to hide it behind a mask of fury.

"He is aboard a plane," Sandra answered, "and he is coming."

"So soon? He's a madman! Doesn't he know he'll die? Can he not see that my plans for him go beyond death? What are his thoughts?"

"He hides them from me."

Janos stopped pacing, thrust his half-handsome, half-hideous face at her. "He hides his thoughts? And you a mentalist, a thought thief? What, and do you seek to make a fool of me? And have I not warned you how it will go for you if you continue to place obstacles in my way. Now I ask you again: what—are—his—*thoughts*?"

The master vampire had come forward to lean upon the table with both hands, glaring into the frightened girl's eyes from only inches away. His lips curled back like a leather muzzle shrivelling from the jagged teeth of some dead carnivore, threatening her all too graphically, but she had no answer for him except: "He . . . he is too *strong* for me!"

"Too strong for you?" Janos raged. "Too strong? Listen: in the bowels of this very castle lie the ashes of men like satyrs who in their day swarmed rampant across this land raping to the death women, men, and babes alike!" he told her. "Aye, and when they'd slain the lot, then even the beasts of the field were not beneath their lust! For two thousand

406

years some of these creatures—whose loins are now dust, whose bones are turned to salts—have gone without. But I say this to you: do my bidding now before I'm tempted to raise them up and command them how to instruct you! An unending torment, Sandra, aye: for I would line them up against you, and as fast as they tore you, your vampire would repair the damage! Only picture it: your sweet flesh awash in all their filth, ruined and ruined again . . . and again . . . and again!''

Harry looked at him out of Layard's eyes, drew phlegm up from Layard's throat, and spat it into the vampire's face. And as the monster went reeling, gurgling, and clawing at his face, Harry said to him with Layard's voice, ''Are you deaf as well as insane, Janos Ferenczy? She can't see into my affairs—for I am right here, seeing into yours!''

Layard, shocked and astonished, sat clutching at his own throat; but for a few seconds more at least, Harry kept a grip on what he now commanded.

Janos staggered back to the table, his head cocked questioningly, disbelievingly on one side. ''What?'' He glared madly at Layard. *''What?''* He lifted a claw of a hand.

''Go on,'' Harry taunted. ''Strike! For it's only your thrall you'll hurt and not the one who commands him!''

Janos's jaw fell open. He understood. ''You?'' he breathed.

Harry caused Layard's face to split into a humourless grin. And: ''You know,'' he said, ''this fascination of yours with my mind isn't merely unhealthy and irksome, I suspect it's also contagious. I had thought you would learn your lesson, Janos, but apparently I was wrong. Very well . . . so now let's see what goes on in *your* head!''

''Release him!'' Janos howled, clutching his head in talon hands and hurling himself away from the table. ''Send the Necroscope out of here! I don't want him in my mind!''

''Don't worry,'' Harry told him as Layard jerked and writhed where he sat. ''Did you really think I would bathe myself in a sewer? Only remember this, Janos Ferenczy: you sought to discover my plans. Well, and now I'll tell them to you. I'm coming for you, Janos. And as you now see, our powers are more or less equal.''

He withdrew from Layard's mind and opened his eyes. The plane was off the ground, heading north and a little west for Budapest. And Harry was well satisfied. Back in Edinburgh, less than a week ago, he'd wondered at his precognitive glimpses of some vague and frightening future·and felt that he stood on the threshold of strange new developments. Now he experienced a sense of justification: his Necroscope's powers were growing, expanding to fill the gap created by Harry Jr.'s tampering.

That was Harry's explanation, anyway . . .

Halfway into the flight—asleep in his seat and unafraid to be asleep—Harry reached out with his deadspeak and found Möbius resting in the Leipzig graveyard where he lay buried. Möbius knew him at once and said, *Harry, I called out to you but got no answer. Actually, I've been half-afraid to contact you. That last time . . . it was frightening, Harry!*

Harry nodded. *So now you know what I'm up against. Well, at the moment I have him on the run; he's not sure what I can do; but he knows whatever he plans against me will have to be more physical than mental. Physically, I'm still very vulnerable. That's why I need the Möbius Continuum.*

Möbius was at once willing. *You want me to take it up where I left off?*

Yes.

Very well, open your mind to me.

Harry did as he was instructed, said, *Enter of your own free will,* and a moment later felt Möbius timid in the labyrinth vaults of his mind.

You're an open book, said Möbius. *I could read you, if I wished it.*

Find the pages that are stuck down, Harry told him. *Unglue them for me. That's the part of me that I've lost. Only unlock those doors and I'll have access to my best shot.*

Möbius went deeper, into yawning caverns of extramundane mind. And: *Locked?* he said then. *I'll say they have* been—and by an expert! But Harry, these are no ordinary locks and bolts and bars. I'm within the threshold of your knowledge, where an entire section has been closed off. This is indeed the source of your instinctive math, but it is sealed with symbols I don't even recognise! Who did it . . . was a genius!

Harry offered a grim nod. *Yes, he was. But Faethor Ferenczy, and his son Janos, they were both able to open those doors by sheer force of will.*

Möbius was realistic. *They were Wamphyri, Harry. And I was only a man. I was a determined man, and I was patient. But I was not a giant!*

You can't do it? Harry held his breath.

Not by force of will. By reason, perhaps.

Then do what you can. Harry breathed again.

I may need your help.

How can I help you?

While I work, you can study.

Study what?

Your numbers, said Möbius, surprised. *What else?*

But I know less than a backward child! Harry protested. *Why, to me the very word "numbers" suggests only a vague and troublesome concept.*

Study them anyway, Möbius told him, and lit up a screen before his inner eye. Simple additions awaited solutions, and incomplete multiplication tables glared at Harry with empty white spaces for eyes, waiting for him to print the answers on their pupils.

I . . . I don't know the fucking answers! Harry groaned.

Then work them out, Möbius growled. For he had problems enough of his own . . .

Four rows of seats in front of Harry, across the central aisle, someone turned to glance back at his pale, troubled, sleeping face. The man was girl-slender and effeminate in his mannerisms. He smoked a Marlboro in a cigarette holder, and his heavy-lidded, deep-set eyes were dark as his thoughts.

Nikolai Zharov had fouled up very badly in England and this was his punishment. Where Norman Harold Wellesley and Romania's Securitatea had failed, now it was Zharov's turn. His superiors had spelled it out to him: go to Greece and kill Keogh yourself. And if you fail . . . don't bother to come back.

Well, Greece was way back there somewhere now, but Zharov didn't suppose it mattered much. Greece, Hungary, Romania—who would care where he died? No one at all—

—Just as long as he died . . .

By 6:30 P.M. Harry Keogh, tourist, had been out of Budapest airport and onto a train heading east for a place called Mezobereny. That had been the end of the line for him, the halt at which he'd disembarked. Past Mezobereny the tracks turned southward for Arad, which was too far out of his way. From now on Harry would go by bus, taxi, cart, on foot—whatever it took.

On the outskirts of Mezobereny he found a small family hotel called the Sarkad after the district, where he took a room for the night. He'd chosen the Sarkad for the old-world graveyard which stood guarded by tall, shady trees in a few acres just across the dusty village road. If there were to be night visitations—dreams influenced by his enemies, maybe, or perhaps more physical visitors—Harry wanted the dead on his side. Which was why, before he settled down for the night, he stood by his window and sent his deadspeak thoughts out across the road to the dead in their graves.

They had heard of the Necroscope, of course, but could scarcely believe that he was actually here; full of questions, they kept him busy until late. But as the midnight hour slipped by, Harry was obliged to tell them that he was tired, and that he really must rest in preparation for the day ahead. And getting into bed he thought to himself, *What a masterpiece of understatement!*

Harry was no spy in the normal sense of the word. If he had been, then he might have noticed the man who'd followed him from the railway station to the Sarkad and taken the room next door.

Earlier, Nikolai Zharov had listened to the Necroscope moving about in his room, and when Harry had gone to his window, so had the Russian. The light from the rooms had fallen on the road, casting Harry's shadow where he stood looking out. Zharov had moved back, put out his light, then approached the window again. And he'd looked where Harry was looking.

Then, for the first time, Zharov had noticed the graveyard. And at that he'd shuddered, drawn his curtains, lit a cigarette, and sat on the edge of his bed to smoke it. Zharov knew about Harry Keogh's talent. He had been in Bonnyrig when Wellesley tried to kill the Necroscope, and he'd seen what came out of Keogh's garden after the traitor's attack failed. Add to that certain details from the report of those Securitatea cretins in Romania, and . . . perhaps this wasn't after all the perfect time or place for a murder.

But it seemed a perfectly good time to check his weapons. He opened the secret compartment in the base of his briefcase, took out and assembled the parts of a small but deadly automatic pistol. A magazine of sixteen rounds went up into the grip and a spare magazine into his pocket. There was also a knife with an eight-inch blade slender as a screwdriver, and a garrote consisting of a pair of grips with eighteen inches of piano wire strung between them. Any one of these methods would suffice, but Zharov must be sure when the time came that it was performed with despatch. Keogh must not be given the least opportunity to talk to anyone. Or rather, to any*thing*.

And again the picture of those two—people?—spied across the river near Bonnyrig, coming out of Keogh's garden, flashed unbidden on Zharov's mind's eye. He remembered how they'd moved—each step an effort of supernatural will— and how one of them had seemed to be leaving bits behind, which followed on of their own accord after him into the night . . .

It was early when the Russian thought these things; he

411

wasn't yet ready for bed; putting on his coat again, he'd gone down to the hotel barroom to get himself a drink.

Indeed, several drinks . . .

Just as Harry had talked to his new friends in their place across the road when he was awake, so he now talked to them in his dreams; except this time the conversation was far less coherent, indeed vague, as most dreams are. But he was not so deeply asleep that he couldn't sense Ken Layard's locator mind when it swept over him (which it did, frequently), nor so far removed from the waking situation that he couldn't distinguish between the trivial gossip of the teeming dead and the occasional tidbit of real-life importance. So that when his deadspeak thoughts first picked up the new voice, he knew instinctively that this was a matter of some consequence.

Accordingly, he made enquiry:

"Who are you? Were you looking for me?"

"Harry Keogh?" The new voice came up stronger. "Thank God I've found you!"

"Do I know you?" Harry was a little cautious.

"In a way," said the other. "We've met. Indeed, I tried to kill you!"

Now Harry recognised him, and knew why he hadn't made the connection earlier. It was simple: this was a voice he would normally associate with life—until now, anyway. It wasn't, or at least it shouldn't be, the voice of a dead man, "Wellesley?" he said. "But . . . what happened?"

"You mean, why am I dead? Well, they put me through quite a lot, Harry. Not physical stuff—no, of course not—but lots of questioning—you know? Physical I could probably handle, but mental? The deeper they dug into me, the more clearly I could see what a shit I'd been. It was all over for me. A long term to serve, no career to go back to, no real prospects. Well, it sounds hackneyed, I know, but the simple fact of it was that I was 'a ruined man.' So . . . I hanged myself. See, they don't offer you a gun anymore—the honourable solution, and all that rot—so I used a pair of leather boot laces. I was half-afraid they'd snap, but they didn't."

Harry found it hard to pity him. The man was a traitor after all. "So what do you want from me?" he said. "Would you like me to say how sorry I am? Offer you a shoulder to cry on? Hey, I have lots of friends among the dead who *didn't* try to kill me!"

"That's not why I'm here, Harry," Wellesley told him. "No, for I got what I deserved. I think we all do. I came to say I'm sorry, that's all. To apologise that I wasn't stronger."

Harry gave a snort. "Oh, wow!" he said. "Gee, Harry, I'm sorry I wasn't stronger. Hey, if I had been, I would've fucking killed you!"

Wellesley sighed. "Well, it was worth a try. I'm sorry I bothered you. It's just that when I killed myself, I didn't know my hard times were only just beginning." He began to withdraw.

"What's that?" Harry held him. "Your hard times?" Then he saw what the other meant. "The dead don't want to know you, right?"

Wellesley shrugged. He was a beaten man. "Something like that. But it's like I said: we get what we deserve. I'm sorry I bothered you, Harry."

"No, wait . . ." Harry had an idea. "Listen, what would you say to a chance to square it with me? And with the dead in general?"

"Is there a way?" (Sudden hope in Wellesley's voice.)

"There could be. It all depends."

"Just name it."

"You had this negative sort of talent, right?"

"That's right. Nobody could see into my mind. But . . . as you can see, it died with me."

Harry shook his head. "Maybe it didn't. You see, what we're doing now isn't the same. It isn't telepathy but deadspeak. You control it yourself. You don't have to speak to me if you don't want to. That other thing you had was uncontrollable. You didn't even know it was there. If someone hadn't noticed it—hadn't discovered that your mind was a stone wall—you still wouldn't know you'd ever had it. Am I right?"

"I suppose you are. But what are you getting at?"

"I'm not sure," said Harry. "I'm not even sure if it's possible. But it would be one hell of a bonus if I had that talent of yours!"

"Well, obviously it would," Wellesley answered. "But as you've just pointed out, it wasn't a talent. It was some kind of negative charge. It was there all the time, working on its own, without my knowledge or assistance."

"Maybe so, but somewhere in your mind there's the mechanism that governed it. I'd just like to see how it works, that's all. Then, if I could sort of imitate it, learn how to switch it on and off at will . . ."

"You . . . want to have a look inside my mind? Are you saying there's a way you can do that?"

"Maybe there is," said Harry, "with your help. And maybe that's why no one else ever could: because you just kept them out . . . Now tell me, did you ever read my file?"

"Of course." Wellesley gave a wry chuckle. "At the time I thought it was fantastic. I remember one of the espers seeing your file lying on my desk, and telling me, 'I wouldn't be caught dead speaking to that guy!' "

"That's not at all bad!" Harry laughed. But he was serious again in a moment. "And did you read about Dragosani, and how he stole Max Batu's evil eye?"

"That too," Wellesley answered. "But he cut it out of his heart, read it in his guts, tasted it in his blood."

"Yes he did"—Harry nodded—"but it doesn't have to be that way. You see, that's always been the difference between me and Dragosani's sort. It's the difference between a necromancer and a Necroscope. He would take what he wanted by force. He would torture for it. But me, I only ask."

"Anything I have, I give it willingly," Wellesley told him.

Again Harry nodded. "Well, that will go a long way with the dead," he said.

"So how will you do it?" Wellesley was eager now.

"Actually," said Harry, "it's you who has to do it."

"Really? So tell me how."

"Just let your mind go blank and invite me in," Harry answered. "Just relax like I was a hypnotist putting you to sleep and say to me, 'Enter of your own free will.' "

"As easily as that?"

"The first part, anyway," said Harry.

"Very well." Wellesley was committed. "So let's try it . . ."

XV: Thracians—
Undead in the Med—
Szgany

LATER, MÖBIUS CAME CALLING.

"Harry? Listen, my boy, I'm sorry I've been so long. But those mental doors of yours were giving me real problems. However, and as you well know, the more difficult a problem is, the more surely it fascinates me. So, I've been in conference with a few friends, and between us we've decided it's a new maths."

"What is?" Harry was bewildered. "And what friends?"

"The doors in your mind are sealed shut with numbers!" Möbius explained. "But they're written as symbols, like a sort of algebra. And what they amount to is the most complicated simultaneous equation you could possibly imagine!"

"Go on."

"Well, I could never hope to solve it on my own—not unless I cared to spend the next hundred years on it! For you see, it's the sort of problem which may only be resolved through trial and error. So ever since I left you, I've been looking up certain colleagues and passing it on to them."

"Colleagues?"

Möbius sighed. "Harry, there were others before me. And some of them were a very long time before me. But as you of all people know, they haven't simply gone away. They're still there, doing in death what they did in life. So I've passed parts of the problem on to them. And let me tell you, that was no simple matter! Mercifully, however, they had all heard of you, and to my delight they welcomed me as a colleague, however junior."

"You, junior?"

"In the company of such as Aristotle, Ptolemy, Copernicus, Kepler, Galilei, Sir Isaac Newton, Ole Christensen Roemer . . . even I am a junior, yes. And Einstein a mere sprout!"

Harry's thoughts whirled. "But weren't they mainly astronomers?"

"And philosophers, mathematicians, and many other things," said Möbius. "The sciences interlace and interact, Harry. So as you can see, I've been busy. But through all of this there was one man I would have liked to approach and didn't dare. And do you know, he came looking for me! It seems he was affronted that he'd been left out!"

"So who is he?" Harry was fascinated.

"Pythagoras!"

Harry was stunned. "Still here?"

"And still the Great Mystic, and still insisting that God is the ultimate equation . . ." But here Möbius grew very quiet. "And the trouble is . . . I'm not so sure anymore that he's wrong."

Still Harry was astonished. "Pythagoras, on my case? My mother told me there were a lot of people willing to help me. But . . . Pythagoras?"

Möbius snapped out of his musing. "Hmm? Yes, oh yes!"

"But . . . does he have the time for it? I mean, aren't there more pressing—"

"No." Möbius cut him short. "For him this is of the ultimate importance! Don't you realise who Pythagoras was and what he did? Why, in the sixth century B.C. he had already anticipated the philosophy of numbers! He was the principal advocate of the theory that number is the essence of all things, the *metaphysical* principle of rational order in the universe! What's more, his leading theological doctrine was metempsychosis!''

Lost, Harry could only shake his head. ''And that has something to do with me?''

Again Möbius's sigh. ''My boy, you're not listening. No, you are, you are! It's your damned innumeracy which makes you blind to what I'm saying! It has *everything* to do with you! For after two and a half millennia, you are living proof of everything Pythagoras advocated! You, Harry: the one flesh-and-blood man in all the world who ever imposed his metaphysical mind on the physical universe!''

Harry tried to grasp what Möbius had said but it wouldn't stand still for him. It was his innumeracy getting in the way. ''So . . . I'm going to be okay, right?''

''We're going to break down those doors, Harry, yes. Given time, of course.''

''How much time?''

But here Möbius could only shrug. ''Hours, days, weeks. We have no way of knowing.''

''Weeks doesn't cut it,'' Harry told him. ''Neither does days. Hours sounds good to me.''

''Well, we're trying, Harry. We're trying . . .''

In the heights over Halmagiu, close to the ruins of his castle, Janos Ferenczy, bloodson of Faethor, ranted and raved. He had brought Sandra and Ken Layard up onto the sloping crest of a wedge of rock that jutted out into space, a thousand feet above the sliding scree and the steep cliffs of the mountainside. The night winds themselves were disturbed by Janos's passion; they blustered around the high rock, threatening to tear the three loose and hurl them down.

''Be quiet!'' He threatened the very elements. ''Be still!'' And as the winds subsided, there where the clouds scudded like things afraid across the face of the moon, so the enraged vampire turned on his thralls.

''You.'' He drew Layard close, gathered up the skin at the

418

back of his neck like a mother cat holds its kitten, thrust him towards the edge of the sheer drop. "I have broken your bones once. And must I do it again? Now tell me: where is he? Where—is—Harry—Keogh!"

Layard wriggled in his grasp, pointed to the northwest. "He was there, I swear it! Less than a hundred miles, less than an hour ago. I sensed him there. He was . . . strong, even a beacon! But now there is nothing."

"Nothing?" Janos hissed, turning Layard's face towards his own. "And am I a fool? You were a talented man, a locator, but as a vampire your powers are immeasurably improved. If it can be found, then you can find it. So how can you tell me you've lost him? How *can* he be there, and then no longer there? Does he come on, even through the night? Is he somewhere between? *Speak*!" And he gave the other a bone-jarring shake.

"He was there!" Layard shrieked. "I felt him there, alone, in one place, probably settled in for the night. I *know* he was there. I found him, swept over him and back, but I didn't dare linger on him for fear he'd follow me back to you. Only ask the girl. She'll tell you it's true!"

"You—are—in—*league*!" Janos hurled him to his knees, then snatched at Sandra's gauzy shift and tore it from her. She cringed naked under the moon and tried to cover herself, her eyes yellow in the pale oval of her skull. But in another moment she drew herself upright. Janos had already done his worst; against horror that numbs, flesh has no feeling.

"He's speaking the truth," she said. "I couldn't enter the Necroscope's mind in case he entered mine, and through me yours. But when I sensed him asleep, then I thought I might risk a glimpse. I tried and . . . he was no longer there. Or if he was, then his mind was closed."

Janos looked at her for long moments, let his scarlet gaze burn on her and penetrate, until he was sure she'd spoken only the truth. Then—

"And so he is coming," he growled. "Well, and that was what I wanted."

"Wanted?" Sandra smiled at him, perhaps a little too knowingly. "Past tense? But no longer, eh, Janos?"

He scowled at her, caught her shoulder, forced her down beside Layard. Then he turned his face to the northwest and held his arms out to the night. "I lay me down a mist in the valleys," he intoned. "I invoke the lungs of the earth to breathe for me, and send up their reek into the air, to make his path obscure. I call on my familiars to seek him out and make his labours known to me, and to the very rocks of the mountains that they shall defy him."

"And these things will stop him?" Sandra tried desperately hard to control her vampire scorn.

Janos turned his crimson gaze on her and she saw that his nose had flattened down and become convoluted, like the snout of a bat, and that his skull and jaws had lengthened wolfishly. "I don't know," he finally answered her, his awful voice vibrating on her nerve endings. "But if they don't, then be sure I know what will!"

With three vampire thralls (caretakers, who looked after his pile for him in his absence and guarded its secrets) Janos went down into forgotten bowels of earth and nightmare to an all but abandoned place. There he used his necromantic skills to call up a Thracian lady from her ashes. He chained her naked to a wall and called up her husband, a warrior chief of massive proportions, who was a giant even now and must have been considered a Goliath in his day. Both of these Janos had had up before, for various reasons, but now his purpose was entirely different. He had given up tomb looting some five hundred years ago, and his appetite for torture and necrophilia had grown jaded in that same distant era.

While still the Thracian warrior stumbled about dazed and disoriented, crying out in the reek and the purple smoke of his reanimation, Janos had him chained and dragged before his lady. At sight of her he became calm in a moment; tears formed in his eyes and trickled down the leathery, bearded, pockmarked jowls of his face.

"Bodrogk." Janos spoke to him in an approximation of

his own tongue. "And so you recognise this wife of yours, eh? But do you see how I've cared for her salts? She comes up as perfectly fleshed as in life—not like yourself, all scarred and burned, and pocked from the loss of your materials. Perhaps I should be more careful how I gather up your ashes, as I am with hers, when once more I send you down into your jar! Ah, but as you must know, she has been of more use to me than you. For where you could only give me gold, she gave me—"

"You are a dog!" The other shut him off, his voice cracking like boulders breaking. Leaning forward in his chains, he strained to reach his tormentor.

Janos laughed as his thralls fought hard to keep Bodrogk from breaking loose. But then he stopped laughing and held out a glass jug for the other to see. And: "Now be still and listen to me," he commanded, harsh-voiced. "As you see, this favourite wife of yours is near perfect. How long she remains so is entirely up to you. She is unchanged from a time two thousand years ago and will go on the same for as long as I will it—and not a moment longer."

While he talked, his creatures made fast Bodrogk's chains to staples in the wall. Now they stood back from him. "Observe," said Janos. He took a glass stem and dipped it in the liquid in the jug, then quickly splashed droplets across the huge Thracian's chest.

Bodrogk looked down at himself; his mouth fell open and his eyes started out as smoke curled up from the matted hair of his chest where the acid had touched him; he cried out and shook himself in his chains, then crumpled to his knees in the agony of his torture. And the acid ate into him until his flesh melted and ran in thin rivulets, red and yellow, all down his quivering thighs.

His wife, the last of the six wives he'd had in life, cried out to Janos that he spare Bodrogk this torture. And weeping, she, too, collapsed in her chains. At last her husband struggled to his feet, the orbits of his eyes red with agony and hatred where he gazed at Janos. "I know that she is dead," he said, "even as I am dead, and that you are a ghoul and a

421

necromancer. But it seems that even in death there is shame, torment, and pain. Therefore, to spare her any more of that, ask what you will of me. If I know the answer, I will tell it to you. If I can perform the deed, it shall be done."

"Good!" Janos grunted. "I have six of your men in their burial urns, where they lie as salts, ashes, dust. Now I shall spill them out of their *lekythoi* and have them up. They will be my guard, and you their captain."

"More flesh to torture?" Bodrogk's growl was a rumble.

"What?" Janos put on a pained expression. "But you should be grateful! These were your warrior comrades in an age when you battled side by side. Aye, and perhaps you shall again. For when my enemy comes against me, I can't be sure that he'll come alone. Why, I even have your armour, with which you decked yourself all those years agone, and which was buried with you. So you see, you shall be the warrior again! And again I say to you, you should be grateful. Now I call these others up, and I call upon you, Bodrogk, to control them. Your wife stays here. Only let one treacherous Thracian hand rise against me . . . and she suffers."

"Janos." Bodrogk continued to gaze at him. "I will do all you ask of me. But for all that I was a warrior in life, I was a fair man, too. It is that fairness which prompts me to advise you now: keep well the upper hand. Oh, I know you are a vampire and strong, but I also know my own strength, which is great. If you did not have Sofia there, in chains, then for all your acid I would break you into many pieces. She alone stays my hand . . ."

Janos laughed like a great baying hound. "That time shall never come!" he said. "But I, too, shall be fair: when this is done, and done to my liking, then I shall put you both down, and mingle your dust, and scatter it to the winds forever."

"Then that must suffice," said the other.

"So be it!" said Janos . . .

As the sun painted a crack of gold on the eastern horizon, Harry Keogh slept on. But in the Aegean Sea off Rhodes

Darcy Clarke and his team were aboard a slightly larger, faster boat than last time and already passing Tilos to port, where they forged west to Sirna. Watching the sea slip by like blue silk sliced by the scissors prow, Darcy again went over the plans they'd made last night and looked for loopholes in their logic.

He remembered how David Chung had sat at a table in their hotel rooms, while the rest ringed him about and watched his performance. Chung's parents had been cocaine addicts; the drug had rotted their minds and bodies, killing both of them while he was still little more than a child. So that ever since joining the branch, he'd aimed his talent in that one specific direction: the destruction of everyone who trafficked in human misery. They had given the locator other tasks from time to time, but everyone in E-Branch knew that this was his forte.

Last night he'd employed a little of the very substance he loathed, crouching over the smallest amount of snow white cocaine. Upon the table a large map of the Dodecanese, and upon the map the merest trickle of poisonous dust, lying on a flimsy brown cigarette paper to give it definition.

Chung had called for silence, and for several minutes had sat there breathing deeply, occasionally wetting a finger to take up the white grains and touch them to his tongue. Then—

With a single sharp puff of air from his mouth he'd blown the cigarette paper and its poison away, and in the next moment stabbed the map with his forefinger. "There!" he'd said. "And an awful lot of it!"

Manolis Papastamos and Jazz Simmons had applauded, but Zek, Darcy, and Ben Trask had not seemed much surprised. They *were* impressed, of course, but ESP had been their business for many years. It wasn't so strange to them.

Then Manolis had looked more closely at the map, the place where Chung was pointing, and nodded. "Lazarides' island," he said. "So now we know where the *Lazarus* is hiding! And aboard her, all the shit that the Vrykoulakas stole from the old *Samothraki*!"

After that, planning had been basic to minimal. Their aim:

423

simply to get to the island in the hour after dawn, when the white ship's vampire crew should be less inclined to activity, and to destroy the *Lazarus*, vampires and all, right there where she was anchored.

David Chung was out of it now; his part had been played and the remainder of his time in the sun was his own; he wouldn't see the rest of the team until the job was finished. And now indeed they were on their way to finish it.

Manolis brought Darcy's mind back to the present: "Another half hour and we're there. Do you want to go over it again?"

Darcy shook his head. "No, you all know your jobs. As for me: this time I'm just a passenger—at least until we get onto the island and into Janos's place." He looked at his team.

Zek was unzipping herself from her lightweight one-piece suit. Underneath she wore a yellow bathing costume consisting of very little and leaving nothing at all to the imagination. She scarcely looked her age but was sleek, tanned, and stunning. With her blue eyes, her blond hair flashing gold, and a smile like a white blaze, there wouldn't be a man alive or undead who could keep his eyes off her!

Her husband looked at her and grinned. "What's so amusing?" she asked him, tossing her head.

"I was thinking," Jazz answered, "that we'd like to sink these blokes along with their ship! The idea isn't that they should go diving in the water after you!"

"This is something I learned from the Lady Karen on Starside," she told him. "If I can distract them, then the rest of you will be able to do your jobs more safely and easily. Karen was an expert at distraction."

"Oh, they'll be distracted, all right!" Manolis assured her.

Ben Trask had meanwhile opened up a small compartmented suitcase and taken out four of six gleaming metal discs some two inches thick by seven across. The back of each disc was black, magnetic, and the obverse fitted with a safety switch and timer. Manolis looked at the limpet mines where Trask began fitting them to a pair of diving belts in place of the usual lead weights, and shook his head. "I still don't know how you got them out of England," he said.

Trask shrugged. "In a diplomatic bag. We may be silent partners, but we're still part of British Intelligence after all."

"There's a rock up ahead," Zek shouted from where she now sat on a rubber mat on the narrow deck on top of the cabin and in front of the windshield. She pointed. "Manolis, is that it?"

He nodded. "That's it. Darcy, can you take the wheel?"

Darcy took control of the boat and throttled back a little. Manolis and Jazz stripped down to swimsuits and went into the tiny cabin out of sight. In there, they tested aqualungs and checked their swim fins. Ben Trask took off his jacket and put on sunglasses and a straw hat. In his Hawaiian shirt he was just some rich tourist fool out for a day's pleasure boating. Darcy might easily be his brother.

The island had swum up larger and Zek was seen to be right: it was little more than a big rock. There were a few shrubs, patches of thyme and coarse grass, and lots of rocks . . . and situated centrally, above coastal cliffs, a weathered yellow stack going up sheer for maybe one hundred and fifty feet.

Zek looked at it and put her hand to her brow. "That's a pigmy of an aerie," she said, "but it gives me the shudders just the same. And there are men—no, vampires—on it. Two of them at least."

The boat rounded the point of a promontory and Darcy saw what lay ahead. But even if he hadn't seen it, his talent had already forewarned him. "Stay down," he called out to Manolis and Jazz in the cabin. "Draw those curtains. You two aren't here. There are just the three of us."

They did as he told them.

Zek stretched herself out luxuriously on the cabin's roof and put on sunglasses; Trask lay back and hooked one leg idly over the boat's rail; Darcy headed the boat directly across the mouth of a small bay. And there, anchored in the bay . . . the white ship, the *Lazarus*.

Trask knocked the cap off a bottle of beer and tilted his

head back, merely wetting his lips but studying what he could see of the island intently. That was part of his job, while Darcy and Zek, in their various ways, studied the *Lazarus*.

The island consisted of a tiny beach inside a pair of bare spurs of rock extending oceanward and an almost barren slope of rock climbing to the central stack. From this side, the top of the stack was seen to be a ruined fortification or pharos of some sort, with the remains of badly eroded steps still showing where they zigzagged up to it. But halfway up the stack, a false, flat, extensive plateau seemed carved, as if in ages past the upper section had split down the centre and half had toppled over. With massive walls built around the plateau's perimeter from one side of the needle rock to the other, the place had obviously been a crusader stronghold. The old walls had long since fallen away in places, but it was seen that new walls were now under construction, and scaffolding was plainly visible clinging to both the stump and the surviving upper section of the stack.

Darcy meanwhile considered the *Lazarus*. The white ship stood off from the beach in deep-water central in the small bay. Her anchor chain went down shimmering into the blue of the sea. On the deck under the black, scalloped awning, a man sat in one of several chairs. But as the motorboat came powering into view he stood up and took binoculars from around his neck. He wore a wide-brimmed floppy hat and sunglasses, and he kept fairly well to the shade as he put the binoculars to his eyes and trained them on the motorboat.

Zek propped herself up on one elbow and waved excitedly, but the watcher on the deck ignored her—at first.

Darcy throttled back, turned the boat in a wide circle about the white ship, and joined Zek in her waving. "Ahoy, there!" He put on an upper-class English accent. "Ahoy aboard the *Lazarus*!"

The man went to the door of the lounge and leaned half inside, then came back out. He now aimed his binoculars at Zek where she continued to wave; this was scarcely necessary, for the circling boat was no more than forty or fifty feet away. She felt his gaze on her and shivered, despite the blazing heat of the sun. A second man, who might have been the twin of the first, joined him and they silently observed the circling boat—but mainly they observed Zek.

Darcy throttled back more yet, and a third man came out of the white ship's lounge. Ben Trask stood up and held up his bottle to them. "Care for a drink?" he shouted, imitating Darcy's faked accent. "Maybe we can come aboard?"

Like fuck! thought Darcy.

Zek scanned the ship, not only above but also belowdecks. She counted six, all told. Three sleeping. All of them vampires. Then . . .

. . . One of the sleepers stirred, woke up. His mind was alert; it was more completely vampire than the others; before Zek could cover her telepathic spying, he had "seen" her!

She stopped waving and told Darcy, "Let's go. One of them read me. He didn't see anything much, only that I'm more than I appear to be. But if they run off now, we'll lose them."

"We'll see you later," Ben Trask called out as Darcy turned the boat away and sped for the tip of the far promontory.

Passing from the view of the watchers on the *Lazarus*, he throttled right down and allowed the boat to cruise close up to a flat-topped, weed-grown rock barely sticking up out of the sea. Jazz and Manolis came out of the cabin, put on their masks and adjusted their demand valves, and as Darcy cut the engine they stepped from the boat to the rock and so into the sea. "Jazz," Zek called down, "be careful!"

He might have heard her and he might not; his head went down and a stream of bubbles came up; the swimmers submerged to fifteen feet and headed back towards the *Lazarus*.

"More distraction," said Darcy grimly as he throttled up and turned back out to sea.

"Darcy," Zek called to him, "keep just a little more distant this time. They'll be wary, I'm sure."

As Darcy headed straight out to sea and the *Lazarus* came back into view, so Ben Trask got down on his knees and took a Sterling submachine gun out of its bag under the seat. He extended the butt and slapped a curved magazine of 9-mm rounds into the housing, then lay the gun between his feet and covered it with the bag.

Half a mile out, Darcy turned to port and came speeding back towards the white ship. There was activity aboard now, where the three on the deck hurried round the rail, pausing every few paces to look over into the water. Jazz and Manolis would be there any time now. Darcy piled on the speed and Zek commenced waving as before. The men on the deck came together at one point at the rail and again Zek felt binoculars trained on her almost-naked body. But this time the interest was other than sexual.

Then, as Darcy leaned the boat over on her side and re-commenced his circling, they heard the rattle of the *Lazarus*'s anchor chain as it was drawn up and the throbbing cough of her engines starting into life. And now a fourth man came ducking out of the lounge onto the deck . . . cradling a stubby, squat-bodied machine gun in his arms!

"*Jesus!*" Ben Trask yelled. And it might have been that his shout of warning was a signal to let the battle commence.

The man with the machine gun opened up, standing there on the deck of the *Lazarus* with his legs braced, hosing the smaller craft with lead. Zek had scrambled down off the cabin roof; as she ducked into the tiny cabin the windshield flew into shards and Darcy felt the *whip* of hot lead flying all around. Then Trask stood up and returned fire, and the gunner on the *Lazarus* was thrown back as if he'd been hit by a a pile driver! He bounced off a stanchion on the deck, came toppling over the rail, and splashed down into the water. And another crewman ran to retrieve his gun.

Darcy was round the white ship now and putting distance between as he forged for the open sea; but as Zek came back out of the cabin, she grabbed the wheel and yanked it hard over, shouting, "Look! Oh, look!"

Darcy let her have the wheel and looked. The man with the gun on the deck of the *Lazarus* was firing down into the water, shooting at something which drew slowly away from the white ship's flank. It could only be Jazz or Manolis, or both of them!

"You handle her!" Darcy yelled, and he moved to where Trask was still firing and drew out a second bag from under the seating. But as he loaded up the number-two SMG there came more of the angry wasp buzzing of sprayed bullets, and Trask cried out and staggered back, only just managing to prevent himself going over the side. The upper muscle of Trask's left arm had a neat hole punched clean through, which turned scarlet and spilled over with blood in the next moment. Then Darcy was up on his feet, returning fire.

But the *Lazarus* was moving; she reversed out of the bay and began to turn slowly on her own axis, and the water boiled furiously where her propellers churned. They couldn't stop her now and so let her go, and Zek went to Trask to see if there was anything she could do. He grimaced but told her, "I'll be okay. Just wrap it up, that's all."

Heads broke the surface of the water as Zek tore Trask's shirt from his back to make a bandage and sling. Darcy throttled right back and drew alongside Jazz where he slipped out of his lung's harness and trod water, then helped him clamber aboard, and Manolis came knifing in an expert flurry of flippers. In another moment he, too, had been dragged up into the boat—at which point the motor gave a gurgling cough and stopped dead!

"Flooded!" Darcy cried.

But Ben Trask was pointing out to sea and yelling, "Jesus, Je-*sus*!"

The *Lazarus* had turned round and was coming back. The throb of her engines was louder, faster as she bore down on the smaller vessel, and her intention was obvious. Manolis, working furiously to get the motor restarted, glanced at the waterproof watch on his wrist. "She should have gone up by now!" he yelled. "The limpets, they should have—"

And when the *Lazarus* was something less than fifty yards away, then the mines did go off. Not in one unified explosion, but in four.

The first two exploded near the stern of the white ship,

with only a second or so between them, which had the effect of first throwing the stern one way and then the other, and also of lifting it up out of the water. Slewing and wallowing as the engines seized up, the Lazarus was still advancing under something of her former impetus, but then the third and fourth limpets went off where they'd been placed towards the stern, and that changed the whole picture. With the stern already low in the water from massive flooding, the prow was pushed up on the crest of white-foaming waters, and as her nose slapped back to the tossing ocean, so the engines exploded. The back of the boat was at once split open in gouting fire and ruin, and hot, buckled metal was hurled aloft in a fireball of igniting fuel.

As the glare of the fireball diminished and a huge smoke ring climbed skyward on the last hot gasp of the ship, so she gave up the ghost, settled down in the water and sank. Scraps of burning awning fluttered back to the tossing ocean and the drifting smoke cleared; the sea belched hugely and offered up clouds of steam; the gurgling and boiling of the waters continued for a few seconds longer, before falling silent . . .

"Gone!" said Darcy when he could draw breath.

"Right." Jazz Simmons nodded. "But let's make sure she's *all* gone. And her crew with her."

Manolis got the motor going and they chugged over to where the *Lazarus* had gone down. An oil slick lay on the water, where bubbles surfaced and made spreading rainbow colours. Then, even as they watched, a head and shoulders came bobbing up, lolled over backwards, and the lower part of the blackened body slowly rotated into view. He lay there in the water as if crucified, with his arms spread-eagled and great yellow blisters bursting on his neck, shoulders, and thighs. But as they continued to stare aghast, so his eyes opened and glared at them, and he coughed up phlegm, blood, and salt water.

Manolis didn't think twice but shut off the motor, picked up a spear gun, and put a harpoon straight into the gagging vampire's chest. The creature jerked once or twice, then lay still in the water. But still they couldn't be sure. Zek looked away as they reeled him in to the side of the boat, tied lead weights to his ankles, and let him sink slowly out of sight.

"Deep water," Manolis commented, without emotion. "Even a vampire is only flesh and blood. If he can't breathe, he can't live. Anyway, the floor of the sea is rocky here: there will be many big groupers down there. Even if life were possible, he can't heal himself faster than they can eat him!"

Ben Trask was white and shaky but well in control of himself. His shoulder was all strapped up now. "What about the one I knocked overboard?" he said.

Manolis took the boat to the middle of the bay where the *Lazarus* had been moored, and Darcy gave a shout and pointed at something that splashed feebly in the water. Even shot, the vampire had made it halfway to land. They closed with him, speared him, and dragged him back out to sea, where they dealt with him as with the first one.

"And that's the end of them," Ben Trask grunted.

"Not quite," Zek reminded him, pointing at the looming stack of white and yellow stone inland. "There are two more of them up there." She put her hand to her brow, closed her eyes, and frowned. "Also . . . there may be something else. But I'm not sure what . . ."

Manolis beached the boat and took up his spear gun. He was happy with that and with his Beretta. Darcy had his SMG, which he considered enough to handle, and Zek took a second spear gun. Jazz was satisfied with Harry Keogh's crossbow, with which he'd familarised himself during the voyage. They might have taken the other SMG, too, but Ben Trask was now out of it and they must leave the gun with him—just in case. His task: stay behind and look after the boat.

They waded ashore and started up the rocks. The trail was easy to follow where the thin soil had been compacted between boulders and where steps had been cut in the steeper places. Halfway to the stack, they paused to take a breather and look back. Ben was watching them through binoculars, and also watching the stack. So far there had been no sign of

431

life in the place, but as they approached its base Jazz spied movement up in the ancient embrasures.

He immediately dragged Zek into cover and motioned Darcy and Manolis down among jumbled rocks. "If those creatures up there had rifles," he explained, "they could pick us off like flies!"

"But they haven't, or they would have already," Manolis pointed out. "They could have got us as we beached the boat, or even as we engaged the *Lazarus*."

"But they have been watching us," said Zek. "I could feel them."

"And they are waiting for us up there." Jazz squinted at the rearing, dazzling white walls.

"We're skating on very thin ice," Darcy told the others. "I can feel my talent telling me that this far is far enough."

A shout echoed up to them from the beach. Looking back, they saw Ben Trask struggling up the incline after them. "Hold it!" he yelled. "Wait!"

He approached to within thirty or forty yards, then fell back against a boulder in the shade and rested awhile. And when he had recovered: "I've been looking at the fortifications through my glasses," he yelled. "There's something very wrong. The climb looks easy enough—up those ancient stone steps there—but it's not. It's a lie, a trap!"

Jazz went back and met Ben halfway, and took the binoculars from him. "How do you mean, a trap?"

"It's like when I listen to a police interview with a suspect perp," Ben answered. "I can tell right off if he's lying even if I don't know what the lie is. So don't ask me what's wrong up there, just take my word for it that it is!"

"Okay," said Jazz. "Go on back down to the boat. From here on in we step wary."

When Ben had started back, Jazz looked through the binoculars at the zigzagging, precipitous stone stairway from the base of the stack to the ancient walls. Close to the top, a jumble of boulders and shards of stone bulged from the gaping mouth of a cave, held back from the steps and the vertiginous edge by a barrier of heavy-duty wire mesh strung

432

between deeply bedded iron staves. Cables, almost invisible, hung down from the ramparts and disappeared into the gloom of the cave. Jazz looked at these cables for long moments. Demolition wire? It could be.

He rejoined the others where they waited. "I think we're walking right into one," he said. "Or we will be if we start up those steps." He explained his meaning.

Darcy took the binoculars from him, stuck his head out from under cover, and double-checked the face of the looming rock. "You could be right . . . *must* be right! If Ben says it's all wrong, it's all wrong."

"No way we can cut those cables," Jazz said. "Those things up there have the advantage. They could spot a mouse trying to make it up those steps."

"Listen," said Manolis, who had also been studying the route up the rock. "Why don't we play them at their own game? Let them think we're falling for it and make them waste their ambush?"

"How?" said Darcy.

"We start on up," said Manolis. "But we are stringing it out a little, and one of us is staying well ahead of the rest. The path turns a corner just underneath the cave with the boulders. And just before the corner, there is this big hole— er, this concavity?—in the face of the cliff. So, one of us has already turned the corner, and the others look all set to follow him. The creatures up in the fort are in a quandary: do they press the button and get the one man for sure, or do they wait for the others to come round the corner? At this point the one in front, he goes faster, past the point of maximum danger, and the others *pretend* they are coming on! But they only just show themselves and don't actually start on up that leg of the climb. The vampires can't wait; they have missed one of us and so must try for the other three; they press the button. Boom!"

Jazz took it up: "The three at the rear have now showed themselves around the corner, but the guys on top don't know they're expecting what happens next! As the charge blows

433

those rocks out of the cave higher up, so the three skip back round the corner and into the scoop in the face of the cliff.''

"Is how I see it," said Manolis, nodding, "yes."

"Or," said Darcy, his face suddenly pale, "we leave it till tonight, and—''

"Is your guardian angel speaking." Manolis looked disgusted. "I have seen that look on your face before!"

Darcy knew he was right and cursed under his breath. "So, who do you suggest bells the cat?" he said.

"Eh?"

"Who goes first and risks getting blown the hell off the cliff?''

Manolis shrugged. "But . . . who else? You, of course!"

Jazz looked at Darcy and said, "This talent of yours, it really works?''

"I'm a deflector, yes." Darcy nodded and sighed.

"So what's the problem?"

"The problem is my talent doesn't work in fits and starts," Darcy answered. "It's working all the time. It makes a coward of me. Even knowing I'm protected, I'll still use a taper to light a firework! You are saying: off you go, Darcy, get on up those steps. But *it* is saying, run like hell, son—run like bloody hell!''

"So what you have to ask yourself," said Jazz, "is who's the boss, it or you?''

Darcy offered a grim nod for answer, slapped a full magazine into the housing of his SMG, and stepped out into view of who or whatever was watching from above. He made for the base of the stone steps and started up. The others looked at each other for a moment, then Manolis started after him. Jazz let him get out of earshot and said, "Zek, you stay here."

"What?" She looked at him. "After Starside you're telling me that I should let you do something like this on your own?''

"I'm not on my own. And what good will you be anyway with only a spear gun? We need you down here, Zek. If one of those things gets past us, you're going to have to stop him."

"That's just an excuse," she said. "You said it yourself: what good am I with only a spear gun?"

"Zek, I—"

"All *right*!" she said. And: "They're waiting for you."

He kissed her and started after the other two. She let him get onto the steps and start upwards, then scrambled after. They could fight later . . .

Just before the crucial corner, where the narrow stone steps angled left and climbed unevenly up the section of cliff face directly beneath the threatening cave with its potential barrage of boulders, Darcy paused to let the others catch up a little. His breathing was ragged and his legs felt like jelly: not because of the stiff climb but because he was fighting his talent every inch of the way.

He looked back and, as Manolis and Jazz came into view, waved. And then he turned the corner and pushed on. But he remembered how, as he'd passed the sheltering hollow where the rest of the team would take cover, he'd been very tempted. Except he had known that once he stepped in there, it would take a stick of dynamite to get him out again!

He craned his neck, glanced straight up, and winced. He could see the wire netting holding back the bulging tangle of rocks not ten feet overhead. It was time to make his break for it. He put on speed and climbed out of the immediate danger area, then glanced back and saw Jazz and Manolis coming round the corner. At which precise moment a pebble slipped underfoot and sent him sprawling!

Feeling his feet shoot out over the rim, Darcy grabbed at projecting rocks and in the same moment *knew* that it was going to happen. "Shit!" he yelled, clinging to the cliff face and the steps as a deafening explosion sounded close by and its shock wave threatened to hurl him into space. Then—

Fragments of rock were flying everywhere; it was like the entire stack was coming down; deaf and suffocating in choking dust and debris, Darcy could only cling and wait for the ringing to go out of his ears. A minute went by or maybe two, and the rumbling died away. Darcy looked back . . .

435

and Jazz and Manolis were clambering dangerously up towards him across steps choked with rubble.

But up ahead someone—two someones—were clambering dangerously down!

As Darcy began pushing himself to his feet, he saw them: flame-eyed, snarling, coming to meet the stack's invaders head-on. One of them carried a pistol, the other had a nine-foot octopus pole with a barbed trident head. The tines must be all of eight inches long!

Darcy's SMG was trapped under rubble and stony debris. He yanked on the sling but it wouldn't come. The vampire with the pistol had paused and was taking aim. Something *thrummed* overhead and the creature aiming at Darcy dropped its pistol and staggered against the cliff face, its hands flying to the hardwood bolt skewering its chest. It gagged, gave a weird, hissing cry, fell to its knees, and toppled into thin air.

The other one came on, cursing and stabbing at Darcy with its terrible weapon. He somehow managed to turn the wicked trident head aside as Manolis arrived behind him. Then the Greek policeman yelled, "Get down!" and Darcy threw himself flat again. He heard the *crack!—crack!—crack!* of Manolis' Beretta, and the hissing of the vampire turn to shrieks of rage and agony. Shot three times at close range, the thing staggered there on the steps. Darcy yanked the octopus pole out of its hands, slammed the butt end into its chest. And over it went, mewling and yelping as it pinwheeled all the way down to the base of the stack.

Jazz Simmons came up to the other two. "Up or down?" he panted.

"Down," said Darcy at once. "And don't worry, it isn't my talent playing up. It's just that I know how hard those things are to kill!" He looked beyond his two friends. "Where's Zek?"

"Down below," said Jazz.

"All the more reason to get back down," said Darcy. "After we've burned those two, then we'll see what else is up here."

But Zek wasn't down below, she was just that moment

coming round the corner. And when she saw that they were all in one piece . . . her sigh of relief said more than any number of spoken words . . .

They brought petrol from the boat and burned the two badly broken vampires, then rested awhile before going up into the old fortifications. Up there Janos had been preparing a spacious, spartan retreat; not quite an aerie of the Wamphyri as Zek remembered such, but a place almost equally sinister and foreboding.

Letting her telepathic talent guide her through piles of tumbled masonry and openings in half-constructed walls, and past deep embrasure windows opening on fantastic views of the ocean's curved horizon, she led the others to a trapdoor concealed under tarpaulins and timbers. They opened it up and saw ages-hollowed stone steps leading down into a crusader dungeon. Rigging torches, the men followed the stairwell down into the reeking heart of the stack, and Zek followed the men. Down there they found the low-walled rims of a pair of covered wells which plunged even deeper into darkness, but that was when Zek gasped and lay back against nitrous walls, shivering.

"What is it?" Jazz's voice echoed in the leaping torchlight.

"In the wells," she gasped, one hand held tremblingly to her throat. "There were places like this in the aeries on Starside. Places where the Wamphyri kept their . . . beasts!"

The wells were covered with lids cut from planks; Manolis put his ear to one of the covers and listened, but could hear nothing. "Something in the wells?" he said, frowning.

Zek nodded. "They're silent now, afraid, waiting. Their thoughts are dull, vacuous. They could be siphoneers, or gas beasts, or anything. And they don't know who we are. But they fear we might be Janos! These are . . . *things* of Janos, grown out of him."

Darcy gave a shudder and said, "Like the creature Yulian Bodescu kept in his cellar. But . . . it has to be safe to look, at least. Because if it wasn't, I'd know."

437

Manolis and Jazz lifted the cover from one of the wells and stood it on its edge by the low wall. They looked down into Stygian darkness but could see nothing. Jazz looked at the others, shrugged, held out his torch over the mouth of the well, and let it fall.

And it was like all hell had been let loose!

Such a howling and roaring, a mewling and spitting and frenzied clamour. For a moment—only a moment—the flaring torch as it fell lit up the monstrosity at the bottom of the dry well. They saw eyes, a great many, gaping jaws and teeth, a huge lashing of rubbery limbs. Something terrible beyond words crashed about down there, leaped, and gibbered. In the next moment the torch went out, which was as well, for they'd seen enough. And as the hideous tumult continued, Jazz and Manolis replaced the cover over the awful shaft.

On their way back up the steps, Manolis said, "We shall need all the fuel we can spare."

"And plenty of this building timber," Jazz added.

"And after that those other limpet mines," said Darcy, "so we can be sure we've blocked those wells up forever. It's time things were put back to rights here . . ."

As they reached the open air, Zek clutched Jazz's arm and said, "But if this is a measure of what Janos can do here, even in the limited time he's had, just think what he might have done up in those Transylvanian mountains . . ." Darcy looked at his friends and his face was still gaunt and ashen. His throat was dry as he voiced his own thoughts: "God, I wouldn't be in Harry Keogh's shoes for . . . for anything!"

Harry woke up to the sure knowledge that something had happened, something far away and terrible. Inhuman screams rang in his ears, and a roaring fire blazed before his eyes. But then, starting upright in his bed, he realised that the screams were only the morning cries of cockerels, and that the fire was the blaze of the sun striking through his east-facing windows.

Now that he was awake there were other sounds and sensations: breakfast sounds from downstairs, and food smells rising from the kitchen.

He got up, washed, shaved, and quickly dressed. But as he was about to go downstairs he heard a strangely familiar jingling, a creaking, and the easy clatter of hooves from out in the road. He went to look down and was surprised to feel the heat of the sun on his arms where he leaned out of the window. He frowned. The hot yellow sunlight irritated him, made him itchy.

Down there in the road, horse-drawn caravans rolled single file, four or five of them all in a line. Gypsies, Travellers, they were heading for the distant mountains; and Harry felt a sudden kinship, for that was his destination, too. Would they cross the border? he wondered. Would they even be allowed to? Strange if they were, for Ceausescu didn't have a lot of time for Gypsies.

Harry watched them pass by and saw that the last in line was decked in wreaths and oddly shaped funeral garlands woven from vines and garlic flowers. The caravan's tiny windows were tightly curtained; women walked beside it, all in black, heads bowed, silently grieving. The caravan was a hearse, and its occupant only recently dead.

Harry felt sympathy, reached out with his deadspeak. "Are you okay?"

The unknown other's thoughts were calm, uncluttered, but still he started a little at Harry's intrusion. And: *Don't you think that's rude of you?* he said. *Breaking in on me like that?*

Harry was at once apologetic. "I'm sorry," he answered, "but I was concerned for you. It's obviously recent and . . . not all of the dead are so stoical about it."

About death? Ah, but I've been expecting it for a long time. You must be the Necroscope?

"You've heard about me? In that case you'll know I didn't mean to be rude. But I hadn't realised that my name had reached the Travelling Folk. I've always thought of you as a race apart. I mean, you have your ways, which don't always fit in too well with . . . no, that's not what I meant, either! Perhaps you're right and I am rude."

439

The other chuckled. *I know what you mean well enough. But the dead are the dead, Harry, and now that they've learned how to talk to each other, they talk! Mainly they reminisce, with no real contact with the living—except for you, of course. Which makes you yourself a talking point. Oh, yes, I've heard about you.*

"You're a learned man," said Harry, "and very wise, I can tell. So you won't find death so hard. How you were in life, that's how you'll be in death. All the things you wondered about when you were living, but which you could never quite resolve, you'll work them all out now that you're dead."

You're trying to make me feel better about it, and I appreciate that, the other answered, *but there's really no need. I was getting old and my bones were weary; I was ready for it, I suppose. By now I'll be on my way to my place under the mountains, where my Traveller forebears will welcome me. They, too, were Gypsy kings in their time, as am I . . . or as I was. I look forward to hearing the history of our race at first hand. I suppose I have you to thank for that, for without you they'd all be lying there like ancient, desiccated seeds in a desert, full of potential, shape, and colour but unable to give them form. To the dead, you have been rain in the desert.*

Harry leaned far out of his window to watch the caravan hearse out of sight around a bend in the dusty road. "It was nice meeting you," he said. "And if I'd known you were a king, be sure my approach would have been more respectful."

Harry. The other's deadspeak thoughts drifted back to the Necroscope, and he sensed that they were a little troubled now. *You seem to me to be a very rare person: good, compassionate, and wise in your own right, for all that you are young. And you say that you have recognised an older wisdom in me. Very well, so now I would ask you to accept some sensible advice from a wise old Traveller king. Go anywhere else but where you are going. Do anything else but that which you have set out to do!*

Harry was puzzled, and not a little worried. Gypsies have

440

strange talents, and the dead—even the recently dead—are not without theirs. How then a dead Gypsy king? "Are you telling my fortune? It's a long time since I crossed a Traveller's palm with silver."

The other seized upon that. *With silver, aye! My palms shall never know its feel again—but be sure my eyes are weighted with it! No, cross yourself with silver, Harry, cross yourself!*

Now Harry wasn't merely puzzled but suspicious, too. What did this dead old man know? What could he possibly know, and what was he trying to say?

Harry's thoughts weren't shielded; the Gypsy king picked them up and answered, *I have said too much already. Some would consider me a traitor. Well, let them think it. For you are right: I'm old and I'm dead, and so can afford one last indulgence. But you have been kind, and death has put me beyond forfeiture.*

"Your warning is an ominous thing," said Harry. But there was no answer. Only a small cloud of dust, settling, showed where the caravans had passed from sight.

"My route is set!" Harry called after. "That is the way I must go!"

A sigh drifted back. Only a sigh.

"Thanks anyway." Harry answered sigh for sigh, and felt his shoulders sag a little. "And good-bye."

And he sensed the slow, sad shake of the other's head . . .

At 11:00 A.M. Harry booked out of the Hotel Sarkad in Mezobereny and waited by the side of the road for his taxi. He carried only his holdall, which in fact held very little: his sleeping bag, a small-scale map of the district in a side pocket, and a packet of sandwiches made up for him by the hotel proprietor's daughter.

The sun was very hot and seemed intensified by the old boneshaker's dusty windows; it burned Harry's wrists where it fell on them, causing a sensation which he could only liken to prickly heat. At his first opportunity, in a village named

Bekes, he called a brief halt to purchase a straw summer hat with a wide brim.

From Mezobereny to his drop-off point close to the Romanian border was about twenty kilometers. Before letting his driver go, he checked with him that in fact his map was accurate and that the border crossing point lay only two or three kilometers ahead at a place called Gyula.

"Gyula, yes," said the taxi driver, pointing vaguely down the road. And again: "Gyula. You will see him both, from the hill—the border, and Gyula." Harry watched him turn his cab around and drive off, then hoisted his holdall to one shoulder and started out on foot. He could have taken the taxi closer to the border, but hadn't wanted to be seen arriving in that fashion. A man on foot is less noticeable on a country road.

And "country" is what it was. Forests, green fields, crops, hedgerows, grazing animals: it seemed good land. But up ahead, across the border: there lay Transylvania's central massif. Not so darkly foreboding as the Meridionali, perhaps, but mountains awesome and threatening enough in their own right. Where the road crossed the crest of low, undulating hills, Harry could see the grey-blue peaks and domes maybe twenty-five miles away. They clung to the horizon, a sprawl of hazy crags obscured by distance and low-lying cloud. His destination.

And from that same vantage point he could also see the border post, its red-and-white-striped barrier reaching out across the road from a timber, almost Austrian-styled chalet. Borders hadn't much bothered Harry, not when he had use of the Möbius Continuum, but now they bothered him considerably. He knew that there was no way he was going to get past this one, not on the road, at least. But his uncomplicated plan had taken that into account. Now that he knew exactly where he was on the map (and the precise lay of the border), he would simply continue to act the tourist, spending the day quietly in some small village or hamlet. There he'd study his map until he knew the area intimately, and choose himself a safe route across into Romania. He knew the Securitatea were keen to keep Romanians in, but couldn't see that there'd be much to-do made about keeping foreigners out! After all, who but a madman would want to break in? Harry Keogh, that was who . . .

At the bottom of the hill was a T-junction where a third-class road (or half-metalled track, at least) cut north through dense woodland. And less than a mile through the woods . . . that must be Gyula. Harry could see hazy blue smoke rising from the near-distant chimneys, and the gleaming, bulbous domes of what were possibly churches. It looked a quiet enough place and should suit his purpose ideally.

But reaching the bottom of the slope and as he turned left into the woods, he heard again that half-familiar jingle and saw in the shade of the trees those same Gypsy caravans which had passed under his window earlier in the day. They had not been here long and the Travellers were still setting up camp. One of the men, wearing black boots, leather trousers, and a russet shirt, with a black-spotted bandana on his brow to trap and control his long, shiny black locks, was perched on a leaning fence chewing a blade of grass.

Smiling and nodding as Harry drew level, he said, "Ho, stranger! You walk alone. Why not sit awhile and take a drink, to cut the dust from your throat?" He held up a long slim bottle of slivovitz. "The *slivas* were sharp the year they brewed this one!"

Harry began to shake his head, then thought, *why not?* He could just as easily study his map seated under a tree as anywhere else. And draw less attention to himself, at that. "That's very kind of you!" he answered, following up immediately with: "Why, you speak my language!"

The other grinned. "Many languages. A little of most of them. We're Travellers, what would you expect?"

Harry walked into the camp with him. "How did you know I was English?"

"Because you weren't Hungarian! And because the Germans don't much come here anymore. Also, if you were French, there would be two or three of you, in shorts, on bicycles. Anyway, I didn't know. And if you hadn't answered me, why, I still wouldn't, not for sure! But . . . you *look* English.''

Harry looked at the caravans with their ornate, curiously carved sigils, their painted and varnished woodwork. The various symbols were so stylised they seemed to flow into and become one with the fancy scrolls of the general decoration, almost as if they'd been deliberately concealed in the design. And looking closer—but yet maintaining an attitude of casual observation—he saw that he was right and they had been so concealed.

His interest in this regard centred on the funeral vehicle, which stood a little apart from the rest. Two women in mourning black sat side by side on its steps, their heads on their bosoms, arms hanging slackly by their sides. ''A dead king,'' said Harry . . . and out of the corner of his eye watched his new friend give a start. Things began to piece themselves together in his mind, like bits of a puzzle forming up into a picture.

''How did you know?''

Harry shrugged. ''Under all the flowers and garlic, that's a good rich caravan and fit for a Traveller king. It carries his coffin, right?''

''Two of them,'' said the other, regarding Harry in a new, perhaps slightly more cautious light.

''Oh?''

''The other one is for his wife. She's the thin one on the steps there. Her heart is broken. She doesn't think she'll survive him very long.''

They sat down on the humped roots of a vast tree, where Harry got out his sandwiches. He wasn't hungry but wanted to offer them to his Gypsy ''friend,'' in return for the good plum brandy. And: ''Where will you bury them?'' he eventually asked.

The other nodded eastward casually enough, but Harry felt his dark eyes on him. ''Oh, under the mountains.''

''I saw a border post up there. Will they let you through?''

The Gypsy smiled in a wrinkling of tanned skin, and a gold tooth flashed in the sun, striking through the trees. ''This has been our route since long before there were border posts, or even signposts! Do you think they would want to stop a funeral? What, and risk calling down the curse of the Gypsies on themselves?''

Harry smiled and nodded. "The old Gypsy-curse ploy works well for you, eh?''

But the other wasn't smiling at all. "It works!'' he said quite simply.

Harry looked around, accepted the bottle again, and took a good long pull at it. He was aware that others of the Gypsy menfolk were watching him, but covertly, while ostensibly they made camp. He sensed the tension in them and found himself in two minds. It seemed to Harry that he'd discovered a way across the border. Indeed, he believed the Gypsies would gladly *take* him across; more than gladly, and whether he wanted to go with them or not!

The odd thing was that he didn't feel any animosity towards this man, these people, who he now felt reasonably sure were here partly out of coincidence but more specifically to entrap him. He didn't feel afraid of them at all; in fact he felt less afraid generally than at almost any time he could remember in his entire life! His problem was simply this: should he casually, even passively accept their entrapment, or should he try to walk out of the camp? Should he make allusion to the situation, make his suspicions known, or simply continue to play the innocent? In short, was it better to "go quietly,'' or should he make a fuss and get roughed up for his trouble?

Of one thing he was certain: Janos wanted him alive, man-to-man, face-to-face—which meant that the last thing the Szgany would do would be to hurt him. Perhaps now that Harry was on the hook, it were better if he simply lay still and let the monster reel him in. Part of the way, anyway.

When he yawns his great jaws at you, go in through them, for he's softer on the inside . . .

Did I think that, Harry used his deadspeak, *or was it you again, Faethor?*

445

Perhaps it was both of us, a gurgling voice answered from deep within.

Harry nodded, if only to himself. *So it was you. Very well, we'll play it your way.*

Good! Believe me, you—we?—have the game well in hand.

"Do you think I might rest here awhile?" Harry asked the Traveller where they sat under the trees. "It's peaceful here and I might just sit and look at my map and plan the rest of my trip." He took a last mouthful of slivovitz.

"Why not?" said the other. "You can be sure no harm will come to you . . . here."

Harry stretched out, laid his head on his holdall, looked at his map. Halmagiu was maybe, oh, sixty miles away? The sun was just beyond its zenith, the hour a little after noon. If the Travellers set off again at 2:00 P.M. (and if they kept up a steady six miles to the hour) they might just make it to Halmagiu by midnight. And Harry with them. He couldn't even hazard a guess as to how they would go about it, but felt fairly sure they'd find a way to get him through the checkpoint. Just as sure as he'd seen that sigil of a red-eyed bat launching itself from the rim of its urn, painted into the woodwork of the king's funeral caravan!

He closed his eyes and, looking inwards, directed his dead-speak thoughts at Faethor. *I think I frightened Janos off—when I threatened to enter his mind, I mean.*

It was bold of you, the other answered at once. *A clever bluff. But you were in error, and fortunate indeed that it worked!*

I was only following your instructions! Harry protested.

Then obviously I had not made myself plain, said Faethor. *I meant simply that* your *mind is your castle, and that if he tried to invade it, you must look to understanding his reasons, must look into his mind and try to fathom its workings. I did not mean, literally, that you should step inside! It would in any case be impossible. You're no telepath, Harry.*

Oh, I knew that well enough, Harry admitted, *but Janos himself wasn't so sure. He's seen some strange things in my mind, after all. Not least your presence there. And if you were advising me, then obviously he would need to step wary. The last thing he would want—the last thing anyone would want, including myself—is you in his mind. Still, I suppose you're right and it was a bluff. But I felt . . . strong! I felt I was playing a strong hand.*

You are strong, Faethor answered. *But remember, you had the additional strength of the girl and Layard. You were using their amplified talents.*

I know, said Harry, *but it felt even stronger than that. It could, of course, have been your influence, but I don't think so. I felt that it was all mine. And I believe that if I had been a true telepath, then that I would have gone in. If only to try and do to Janos what he did to Trevor Jordan.*

He sensed Faethor's approval. *Bravo! But don't run before you can walk, my son . . .* And before Harry could answer: *Will you go with the Szgany, the filthy Zirra?*

In through his jaws? Harry answered. *Yes, I think so. If I can't get into his mind, then I'll get into his "body," as it were, and maybe blunt a few of his teeth a little along the way. But answer me this:*

If I have frightened him off from any sort of mental seduction or invasion, what will he do next? What would you do, if you were him?

What remains to him? Faethor answered. *In the skillful use of powers—those very powers he desires to steal from you— he believes you are his match. So . . . he must first conquer you physically. What I would do if I were him? Murder you, and then by use of necromancy rip your knowledge right out of your screaming guts!*

Your . . . "art"? Harry answered. *Thibor's? Dragosani's? But Janos doesn't have it.*

He has this other thing, this ancient, alien magic. He can reduce you to ashes, call you up from your chemical essence, torture you until you are a ruin, incapable of defending your-self—and then enter your mind. And so take what he wants!

Hearing that, Harry no longer felt so strong. Also, the slivovitz had been more potent than he thought and he'd taken quite a lot of it. Suddenly he knew the sensation of giddiness, an unaccustomed alcoholic buoyancy, and at the same time felt the weight of a blanket tossed across his legs and lower body. It was cool under the trees and someone was seeing to his welfare, for now at least. He opened his eyes a crack and saw his Gypsy "friend" standing there, looking down at him. The man nodded and smiled, and walked away.

Treacherously clever, these dogs, Faethor commented.

Ah! Harry answered. *But they've been well instructed . . .*

Though Harry felt he should have no real requirement for sleep, still he let himself drowse. For two or three days now there had been this weariness on him, as if he were convalescing after some minor virus infection or other, maybe a bug he'd picked up in the Greek Islands. But a strange ailment at best, which made him feel strong on the one hand and wearied him on the other! Perhaps it was a change in the water, the air, all the mental activity he'd been engaging in, including his deadspeak, so recently returned to him. It could be any of these things. Or . . . perhaps it was something else.

Even as he let himself drift, and as he began to dream a strange dream—of a world of swamps and mountains, and aeries carved of stone and bone and cartilage—so Möbius came visiting.

Harry? Are you all right, my boy?

Certainly, he answered. *I was merely resting. Whatever strength I can muster . . . it could be I shall need it. The battle draws nigh, old friend.*

Möbius was puzzled. *You use strange terms of expression. And you don't quite, well, feel the same.*

As Harry's dream of Starside faded, so Möbius's deadspeak made more of an impression. *What?* he said. *Did you say something? Terms of expression? I don't feel the same?*

That's better! said Möbius, with a sigh of relief. *Why, for a moment there I thought I was talking to some entirely different person!*

Between dream and waking, Harry narrowed his eyes. *Perhaps you were,* he said.

He sought Faethor in his mind and wrapped him in a blanket of solitude. And: *There*, he said. And to Möbius: *I can hold him there while we talk.*

Some strange tenant?

Aye, and greatly unloved and unwanted. But for now I've covered his mouse hole. I much prefer my privacy. So what is it you've come to tell me, August?

That we're almost there! the other answered at once. *The code is breaking down, Harry, revealing itself. We'll soon have the answer. I came to bring you hope. And to ask you to hold off from your contest just a little while longer, so that we—*

Too late for that, Harry broke in. *It's now or never. Tonight I go up against him.*

Again the other was puzzled. *Why, you seem almost eager for it!*

He took what was mine, challenged me, offended me greatly, Harry answered. *He would burn me to ashes, raise me up, torture me for my secrets—even invade the Möbius Continuum! And that is not his territory.*

Indeed it is not! It belongs to no one. It simply is . . . Möbius's deadspeak voice was dreamy again, which caused Harry to concentrate and consolidate within his own personality.

"It simply is"? he repeated Möbius, mystified. *But of course it is! What do you mean, it is?*

It thinks . . . everything, Möbius answered. *Therefore . . . it is . . . everything!* But something had been triggered in him. He was fading, drifting, returning to a dimension of pure number.

And Harry made no attempt to retain him but simply let him go . . .

XVI: Man-to-Man, Face-to-Face

"HARRY." SOMEONE GAVE HIS SHOULDER AN URGENT SHAKE. "Harry, wake up!"

The Necroscope came instantly awake, almost like stepping through a Möbius door from one existence to another, from dream to waking. He saw the Gypsy he had spoken to and shared food with, whose blanket lay across his legs. And his first thought was: *How does he know my name?* Following which, he relaxed. Of course he would know his name. Janos had told him it. He would have told all of his thralls and human servants and other minion creatures the name of his greatest enemy.

"What is it?" Harry sat up.

"You've slept an hour," the other answered. "We'll soon be moving on. I'm taking my blanket. Also, there is something you should see."

"Oh?"

The Gypsy nodded. His eyes were keen now, dark and sharp. "Do you have a friend who searches for you?"

"What? A friend, here?" Was it possible Darcy Clarke or one of the others had followed him here from Rhodes? Harry shook his head. "I don't think so."

"An enemy, then, who follows on behind? In a car?"

450

Harry stood up. "You've seen such a one? Show me."

"Follow me," said the other. "But keep low."

He moved at a lope through the trees to a hedgerow. Harry followed him and was aware of the other Gypsies scattered here and there throughout the encampment. Each of them to a man was silent but tense in the dappled green shade of the trees. Their belongings were all packed away. They were ready to move.

"There," said Harry's guide. He stood aside to let the Necroscope peer through the bushes.

On the other side of the road a man sat at the wheel of an old beetle Volkswagen, looking at the entrance to the encampment. Harry didn't know him, but . . . he *knew* him. Now that his attention had been focused on him, he remembered. He'd been on the plane, this man. And . . . in Mezobereny? Possibly. That cigarette holder was a dead giveaway. Likewise his generally snaky, effeminate style. And now Harry remembered, too, that earlier brush with the Securitatea in Romania. Had this man been their contact in Rhodes? An agent, perhaps, for the USSR's E-Branch?

He glanced at the Gypsy beside him and said, "An enemy—possibly." But then he saw the knife ready in the other's hand and raised an eyebrow. "Oh?"

The other smiled, without humour. "The Szgany don't much care for silent watchers."

But Harry wondered. Had the knife been for him, if he'd tried to make a run for it? A threat, to bring him to heel? "What now?" he said.

"Watch," said the other.

A Gypsy girl in a bright dress and a shawl crossed the road to the car, and Nikolai Zharov sat up straighter at the wheel. She showed him a basket filled with trinkets, knickknacks, and spoke to him. But he shook his head. Then he showed her some paper money and in turn spoke to her, questioningly. She took the money, nodded eagerly, pointed through the forest. Zharov frowned, questioned her again. She became more insistent, stamped her foot, pointed again in the direction of Gyula, along the forest road.

Finally Zharov scowled, nodded, started up his car. He drove off in a cloud of dust. Harry turned to the Gypsy and said, "He was an enemy then. And the girl has sent him off on a wild-goose chase?"

"Yes. Now we'll be on our way."

"We?" Harry continued to stare at him.

The man sheathed his knife. "We Travellers," he answered. "Who else? If you had been awake, you could have eaten with us. But"—he shrugged—"we saved you a little soup."

Another man approached with a bowl and wooden spoon, which he offered to Harry.

Harry looked at it.

Don't! said a deadspeak voice in his head, that of the dead Gypsy king.

Poison? Harry answered. *Your people are trying to kill me?*

No, they desire you to be still for an hour or two. Only drink this, and you will be still!

And sick?

No. Perhaps a mild soreness in the head—which a drink of clean water will drive away. But if you drink the soup . . . then all is lost. Across the border you'll go, and up into the ageless hills and craggy mountains—which as you know belong to the Old Ferenczy!

But Harry only smiled and grunted his satisfaction. *So be it,* he said, and drank the soup . . .

Nikolai Zharov drove as far as Gyula and midway into the town, then finally paid attention to a small niggling voice in the back of his mind: the one that was telling him, more insistently with each passing moment, that he was a fool! Finally he turned his car around and drove furiously back the way he'd come. If Keogh had gone to Gyula, he could check it later. But meanwhile, if the Gypsy girl had been lying . . .

The Traveller camp was empty; it might be that the Gypsies had never been there! Zharov cursed, turned left onto the main road, and gunned his engine. And up ahead he saw the first of the caravans passing leisurely through the border checkpoint.

He arrived in a skidding of tyres, jumped from the car, and ran headlong into the one-room, chalet-style building. The border policeman behind his elevated desk picked up his peaked, flat-topped hat and rammed in on his head. He glared at Zharov and the Russian glared back. Beyond the dusty, flyspecked windows, the last caravan was just passing under the raised pole.

"What?" the Russian yelled. "Are you some kind of madman? What are you, Hungarian or Romanian?"

The other was young, big-bellied, red-faced. A Transylvanian village peasant, he had joined the Securitatea because it had seemed easier than farming. Not much money in it, but at least he could do a bit of bullying now and then. He quite liked bullying, but he wasn't keen on being bullied.

"Who are you?" He scowled, his piggy eyes startled.

"Clown!" Zharov raged. "Those Gypsies—do they simply come and go? Isn't this supposed to be a checkpoint? Does President Ceausescu know that these riffraff pass across his borders without so much as a by your leave? Get off your fat backside; follow me; a spy is hiding in those caravans!"

The border policeman's expression had changed. For all he knew (and despite the other's harsh foreign accent), Zharov might well be some high-ranking Securitatea official; certainly he acted like one. But what was all this about spies? Flushing an even brighter red, he hurried out from behind his desk, did up a loose button in his sweat-stained blue uniform shirt, nervously fingered the two-day-old stubble on his chin. Zharov led him out of the shack, got back into his car, and hurled the passenger-side door open. "In!" he snapped.

Cramming himself into the small seat, the confused man blusteringly protested, "But the Travellers aren't a problem! No one ever troubles them. Why, they've been coming this way for years! They are taking one of their own to bury him. And it can't be right to interfere with a funeral."

"Lunatic!" Zharov put his foot down hard, skidded dangerously close to the rearmost caravan, and began to overtake

453

the column. "Did you even look to see if they might be up to something? No, of course not! I tell you they have a British spy with them called Harry Keogh. He's a wanted man in both the USSR and in Romania. Well, and now he's in your country and therefore under your jurisdiction. This could well be a feather in your cap—but only if you follow my instructions to the letter."

"Yes, I see that," the other mumbled, though in fact he saw very little.

"Do you have a weapon?"

"What? Up here? What would I shoot, squirrels?"

Zharov growled and stamped on his brakes, skidding the car sideways in front of the first horse-drawn caravan. The column at once slowed and began to concertina, and as the dust settled Zharov and the blustering border policeman got out of the car.

The KGB man pointed at the covered caravans, where scowling Gypsies were even now climbing down onto the road. "Search them," he ordered.

"But what's to search?" said the other, still mystified. "They're caravans. A seat at the front, a door at the back, one room in between. A glance will suffice."

"Any space which would conceal a man, that's what you search!" Zharov snapped.

"But . . . what does he look like?" The other threw up his hands.

"Fool!" Zharov shouted. "Ask what he doesn't look like! He doesn't look like a fucking Gypsy!"

The mood of the Travellers was ugly and getting worse as the Russian and his Securitatea aide moved down the line of caravans, yanking open their doors and looking inside. As they approached the last in line, the funeral vehicle, so a group of the Szgany put themselves in their way.

Zharov snatched out his automatic and waved it at them. "Out of the way. If you interfere, I won't hesitate to use this. This is a matter of security, and grave consequences may ensue. Now open this door."

The Gypsy who had spoken to Harry Keogh stepped forward. "This was our king. We go to bury him. You may not go into this caravan."

Zharov stuck the gun up under his jaw. "Open up now," he snarled, "or they'll be burying two of you!"

The door was opened; Zharov saw two coffins lying side by side on low trestles where they had been secured to the floor; he climbed the steps and went in. The border policeman and Gypsy spokesman went with him. He pointed to the left-hand coffin, said, "That one . . . open it."

"You are cursed!" said the Gypsy. "For all your days, which won't be many, you are cursed."

The coffins were of flimsy construction, little more than thin boards, built by the Travellers themselves. Zharov gave his gun to the mortified border policeman, who fully expected the next curse to be directed at him, and took out his bone-handled knife. At the press of a switch eight inches of steel rod with a needle point slid into view. Without pause Zharov raised his arm and drove the tool down and through the timber lid so that it disappeared to the hilt into the space which would be occupied by the face of whoever lay within.

Inside the coffin, muffled, someone gasped, "Huh—huh—*huh*!" And there came a bumping and a scrabbling at the lid.

The Gypsy's dark eyes bugged; he crossed himself, stepped back on wobbly legs; likewise the border policeman. But Zharov hadn't noticed. Nor had he noticed the high smell, which wasn't merely garlic. Grinning savagely, he yanked his weapon free and jammed its point under the edge of the lid, wrenching here and there until it was loose. Then he put the bone handle between his teeth, took the lid in both hands, and yanked it half open.

And from within, someone pushed it the rest of the way . . . *but it wasn't Harry Keogh!*

Then—

Even as the Russian's eyes stood out in his pallid face, so Vasile Zirra coughed and grunted in his coffin, and reached up a leathery arm to grasp Zharov and lever himself upright!

"God!" the KGB man choked then. "G-G-*God*!" His knife fell from his slack jaws into the coffin. The old dead

455

Gypsy king took it up at once and drove it into Zharov's bulging left eye—all the way in, until it scraped the inside of his skull at the back. That was enough, more than enough.

Zharov blew froth from his jaws and stepped woodenly back until he met the side of the caravan, then toppled over sideways. Falling, he made a rattling sound in his throat and, striking the floor, twitched a little. And then he was still.

But nothing else was still.

At the front of the column a Gypsy drove Zharov's car into the ditch at the side of the road. The Securitatea lout was reeling back in the direction of his border post, shouting, ''It had nothing to do with me—nothing—nothing!'' The Szgany spokesman stepped over Zharov's body, looked fearfully at his old king lying stiff and dead again in his coffin, crossed himself a second time, and manhandled the cover back into place. Then someone shouted, ''Giddup!'' and the column was off again at the trot.

Half a mile down the road, where the roadside ditch was deep and grown with brambles and nettles, Nikolai Zharov's corpse was disposed of. It bounced from caravan to road to ditch and flopped from view into the greenery . . .

Even as Harry had drained the soup in the bowl to its last drop, drug and all, so he'd brought Wellesley's talent into play and closed his mind off from outside interference. The Gypsy potion had been quick acting; he hadn't even remembered being bundled into the funeral caravan and ''laid to rest'' in the second coffin.

But his mental isolation had disadvantages, too. For one, the dead could no longer communicate with him. He had, of course, taken this into account, weighing it against what Vasile Zirra had told him about the short-term effect of the Gypsy drug. And he'd been sure he could spare an hour or two at least. What the old king hadn't told him was that only a spoonful or two of drugged soup would suffice. In draining the bowl dry, the Necroscope had dosed himself far too liberally.

Now, slowly coming awake—halfway between the subconscious and conscious worlds—he collapsed Wellesley's mind-shield and allowed himself to drift amidst murmuring deadspeak background static. Vasile Zirra, lying only inches away from him, was the first to recognise Harry's resurgence.

Harry Keogh? The dead old man's voice was tinged with sadness and not a little frustration. *You are a brash young man. The spider sits waiting to entrap you, and you have to throw yourself into his web! Because you were kind to me—and because the dead love you—I jeopardised my own position to warn you off, and you ignored me. So now you pay the penalty.*

At the mention of penalties, Harry began to come faster awake. Even though he hadn't yet opened his eyes, still he could feel the jolting of the caravan and so knew that he was en route. But how far into his journey?

You drank all of the soup, Vasile reminded him. *Halmagiu is . . . very close! I know this land well; I sense it; the hour approaches midnight, and the mountains loom even now.*

Harry panicked a little then and woke up with something of a shock—and panicked even more when he discovered himself inside a box which by its shape could only be a coffin! Vasile Zirra calmed him at once.

That must be how they brought you across the border. No, it isn't your grave but merely your refuge—for now. Then he told Harry about Zharov.

Harry answered aloud, whispering in the confines of the fragile box, "You protected me?"

You have the power, Harry. The other shrugged. *So it was partly that, for you, and it was . . . partly for him.*

"For him?" But Harry knew well enough who he meant. "For Janos Ferenczy?"

When you allowed yourself to be drugged, you placed yourself in his power, in the hands of his people. The Zirras are his people, my son.

Harry's answer was bitter, delivered in a tone he rarely if ever used with the dead: "Then the Zirras are cowards! In the beginning, long before your time—indeed more than seven long centuries ago—Janos fooled the Zirras. He beguiled

457

them, fascinated them, won them over by use of hypnosis and other powers come down to him from his evil father. He *made* them love him, but only so that he could use them. Before Janos, the true Wamphyri were always loyal to their Gypsy retainers, and in their turn earned the respect of the Szgany forever. There was a bond between them. But what has Janos given you? Nothing but terror and death. And even dead, still you are afraid of him.''

Especially dead! came the answer. *Don't you know what he could do to me? He is the phoenix, risen from hell's flames. Aye, and he could raise me up, too, if he wished it, even from my salts! These old bones, this old flesh, have suffered enough. Many brave sons of the Zirras have gone up into those mountains to appease the Great Boyar; even my own son, Dumitru, gone from us these long years. Cowards? What could we do, who are merely men, against the might of the Wamphyri?*

Harry snorted. "He isn't Wamphyri! Oh, he desires to be, but there's that of the true vampire essence which escapes him still. What could you do against him? If you had had the heart, you and a band of your men could have gone up to his castle in the mountains, sought him out in his place, and ended it there and then. You could have done it ten, twenty, a hundred, even *three* hundred years ago! Even as I must do it now.''

Not Wamphyri? The other was astonished. *But . . . he is!*

"Wrong! He has his own form of necromancy, true—and certainly, it's as cruel a thing as anything the Wamphyri ever used—but it is not the true art. He is a shape changer, within limits. But can he form himself into an airfoil and fly? No, he uses an airplane. He is a deceiver, a powerful, dangerous, clever vampire—but he is not Wamphyri.''

He is what he is, said Vasile, but more thoughtfully now. *And whatever he is, he was too strong for me and mine.*

Harry snorted again. "Then leave me be. I'll need to find help elsewhere.''

Smarting from Harry's scorn, the old Gypsy king said,

Anyway, what do you know of the Wamphyri? What does anyone know of them?

But Harry ignored him, shut him out, and sent forward his deadspeak thoughts into Halmagiu, to the graveyard there. And from there, even up to the ruined old castle in the heights . . .

Black Romanian bats in their dozens flitted overhead, occasionally coming into the gleam of swaying, jolting lamplight, where they escorted the jingling column of caravans through the rising, misted Transylvanian countryside. And the same bats flew over the crumbling walls and ruins of Castle Ferenczy.

Janos was there, a dark silhouette on a bluff overlooking the valley. Like a great bat himself, he sniffed the night and observed with some satisfaction the mist lying like milk in the valleys. The mist was his, as were the bats, as were the Szgany Zirra. And in his way, Janos had communicated with all three. "My people have him!" he said, as if to remind himself. It was a phrase he'd repeated often enough through the afternoon and into the night. He turned to his vampire thralls, Sandra and Ken Layard, and said it again: "They have the Necroscope and will bring him to me. He is asleep, drugged, which is doubtless why you can't know his whereabouts or read his mind. For your powers are puny things with severe limitations."

But even as Janos spoke, so his locator gave a sudden start. "Ah!" Layard gasped. And: "There . . . there he is!"

Janos grasped his arm, said, "Where is he?"

Layard's eyes were closed; he was concentrating; his head turned slowly through an angle directed out over the valley to one which encompassed the mountain's flank, and finally the mist-concealed village. "Close," he said. "Down there. Close to Halmagiu."

Janos's eyes lit like lamps with their wicks suddenly turned high. He looked at Sandra. "Well?"

She locked on to Layard's extrasensory current, followed

459

his scan. And: "Yes," she said, slowly nodding. "He is there."

"And his thoughts?" Janos was eager. "What is the Necroscope thinking? Is it as I suspected? Is he afraid? Ah, he is talented, this one, but what use esoteric talents against muscle which is utterly ruthless? He speaks to the dead, yes, but my Szgany are very much alive!" And to himself he thought, *Aye, he speaks to the dead. Even to my father, who from time to time lodges in his mind! Which means that just as I know the Necroscope, likewise the dog knows me! I cannot relax. This will not be over . . . until it is over. Perhaps I should have them kill him now, and resurrect him at my leisure. But where would be the glory, the satisfaction, in that? That is not the way, not if I would be Wamphyri! I must be the one to kill him, and then have him up to acknowledge me as his master!*

Sandra clung to Layard's arm and locked on to Harry's deadspeak signals . . . and in the next moment snatched herself back from the locator so as to collide with Janos himself. He grabbed her, steadied her. "Well?"

"He . . . he speaks with the dead!"

"Which dead? Where?" His wolf's jaws gaped expectantly.

"In the cemetery in Halmagiu," she gasped. "And . . . in your castle!"

"Halmagiu?" The ridges in his convoluted bat's snout quivered. "The villagers have feared me for centuries, even when I was dust in a jar! No satisfaction for him there. And the dead in my castle? They are mainly Zirras." He laughed hideously, and perhaps a little nervously. "They gave their lives up to me; they will not hearken to him in death; he wastes his time!"

Sandra, for all her vampire strength, was still shaken. "He . . . he talked to a great many, and they were not Gypsies. They were warriors in their day, almost to a man. I sensed the merest murmur of their dead minds, but each and every one, they burned with their hatred for you!"

"What?" For a moment Janos stood frozen—and in the

460

next bayed a laugh which was more a howl. "My Thracians? My Greeks, Persians, Scythians? They are dust, the veriest *salts* of men! Only the guards which I raised up from them have form. Oh, I grant you, the Necroscope may call up corpses to walk again—but even he cannot build flesh and bone from a handful of dust. And even if he could, why, I would simply put them down again! I have him; he is desperate and seeks to enlist impossible allies; let him talk to them."

He laughed again, briefly, and turning towards the dark, irregular pile of his ruined castle, narrowed his scarlet eyes. "Come," he grunted then. "There are certain preparations to be made . . ."

A handful of Szgany menfolk bundled Harry through the woods and past the outcropping knoll with its cairn of soul stones beneath the cliff. His hands were bound behind him and he stumbled frequently; his head ached miserably, as from some massive hangover; but as the group passed close to the base of the knoll, so he sensed the wispy wraiths of once-men all around.

Harry let his deadspeak touch them and knew at once that they were only the echoes of the Zirras he had spoken to in the Place of Many Bones deep in the ruins of the Castle Ferenczy. The knoll's base was lapped by a clinging ground mist, but its domed crest stood clear where the cairn of carved stones pointed at the rising moon. Men had carved those stones, their own headstones, before climbing to the heights and sacrificing themselves to a monster.

"Men?" Harry whispered to himself. "Sheep, they were. Like sheep to the slaughter!"

His deadspeak was heard, as he had intended it should be, and from the castle in the heights was answered.

Not all of us, Harry Keogh. I for one would have fought him, but he was in my brain and squeezed it like a plum. You may believe me when I say I did not go to the Ferenczy willingly. We were not such cowards as you think. Now tell me,

461

*did you ever see a compass point south? Just so easily might
a Zirra, chosen by his master, turn away.*

"Who are you?" Harry enquired.

Dumitru, son of Vasile.

"Well, at least you argue more persuasively than your father!" said Harry.

One of the Gypsies prodded him where they bundled him
unceremoniously up the first leg of the climb. "What are you
mumbling about? Are you saying your prayers? Too late for
that, if the Ferenczy has called you."

Harry, said Dumitru Zirra, *if I could help you I would, in
however small a measure. But I may not. Here in the Place
of Many Bones, I was gnawed upon by one of the Grey Ones
who serve the Boyar Janos. He had my legs off at the knees!
I could crawl if you called me up, but I could never fight.
What me, a half man of bone and leather and bits of gristle?
But only say it and I'll do what I can.*

So, I've found a man at last, Harry answered, this time
silently, in the unique manner of the Necroscope. *But lie still,
Dumitru Zirra, for I need more than old bones to go against
Janos.*

The way was harder now and the Gypsies sliced through
the thongs binding Harry's wrists. Instead they put two nooses
round his neck, one held by a man who stayed well ahead of
him, and the other by a man to his rear. "Only fall now,
Englishman, and you hang yourself," their spokesman told
him. "Or at very least stretch your neck a bit as we haul you
up!" But Harry didn't intend to fall.

He called out to Möbius with his deadspeak: *August? How's
it coming?*

We're almost there, Harry! came back the excited answer
from a Leipzig graveyard. *It could be an hour, two, three at
the outside.*

Try thirty minutes, said Harry. *I may not have much more
than that left.*

Other voices crowded Harry's Necroscope mind. From the
graveyard in Halmagiu:

462

Harry Keogh . . . we are shunned. Who named you a friend of the dead was a great liar!

Taken off guard, he answered aloud. "I asked for your help. You refused me. It's not my fault the world's teeming dead hold you in contempt!"

The Szgany where they laboured up the mountainside in the streaming moonlight looked at each other. "Is he mad?" Always he talks to himself!"

Harry opened all the channels of his mind—removed all barriers within and without—and at once Faethor was raging at him: *Idiot! I am the only one who can help you, and yet you keep me hooded like some vicious bird in a cage. Why do you do this, Harry?*

Because I don't trust you, he answered silently. *Your motives, your methods, your blackhearted self! I don't trust a single thing you say or do, Faethor. You're not only a father of vampires but a father of liars, too. Still, you do have a choice.*

A choice? What choice?

Get out of my mind and go back to your place in Ploiesti.

Not until this thing is seen through—to—the—end!

And how can I be sure you'll stick to that?

"You can't, *Necroscope!*

Then sit in the dark, said Harry, closing him off again.

And now the climb was halfway done . . .

In Rhodes it was 1:30 A.M.

Darcy Clarke and his team sat around a table in one of their hotel rooms. They had spent time recovering from their work, had eaten out as a group, had discussed their experiences and how they'd been affected and probably would be affected for a long time to come. But in the back of their minds each and every one of them had known that their own part in the fight was minimal, and that without Harry Keogh's success everything else was cosmetic and the partial elation they felt now only the lull before the real storm.

As they'd returned from their late meal, so Zek had come

up with an idea. She was a telepath and David Chung a locator. Together, they might be able to reach Harry and see what were his circumstances.

Darcy had at once protested, "But that's just what Harry didn't want! Look, if Janos got his mental hooks into you—"

"I've a feeling he'll be too much involved with Harry to be thinking about anything else," Zek had cut in. "Anyway, I want to do it. In the Lady Karen's stack—her aerie on Starside—I had the job of reading the minds of a great many Wamphyri. Not one of them so much as suspected I was there, or if they did, nothing came of it. That's the way I'll play it now."

Still Darcy wasn't sure. "I was only thinking about poor Trevor," he said, "and about Sandra . . ."

"Trevor Jordan wasn't expecting trouble," Zek had answered, "and Sandra was inexperienced and her talent variable. I'm not putting her down, just stating a fact."

"But—"

"No!" and again she had cut him off. "If David is willing, I *want* to do it. Harry means a lot to Jazz and me."

At which Darcy had appealed to Jazz Simmons.

Jazz had shaken his head. "If she says she'll do it, then she'll do it," he said. "Hey, don't take my word for it! I'm only married to her!"

And with reservations, finally Darcy had submitted. For the fact was that he as much as anyone else was interested to know Harry's circumstances.

Now the three who weren't participants, Darcy, Jazz, and Ben Trask, sat around the table and concentrated on what Zek and David were doing: the latter with his eyes closed, breathing deeply, his hands resting lightly on the stock and body of Harry's crossbow where it sat on the table, and Zek similarly disposed, her hand on one of his.

They had been this way for a minute or two, waiting for Chung to locate the Necroscope through the medium of one of his own possessions. But as seconds ticked by in silence and the two participants grew even more still, so the watchers began to relax a little—even to fidget—and their thoughts to drift. And just at the moment that Jazz Simmons chose to scratch his nose, that was when contact was made.

It was brief.

David Chung uttered a long drawn-out sigh—and Zek snapped bolt upright in her chair. Her eyes remained closed for several long seconds while all the colour drained from her face. Then . . . they shot open and she snatched herself away from Chung, straightened to her feet, and backed unsteadily away from the table.

Jazz went to her at once. "Zek?" His voice was anxious. "Are you okay?"

For a moment she stared right through him, then at him, and accepted his arms. He felt her trembling, but at last she answered, "Yes, I'm all right. But Harry—"

"You found him?" Darcy, too, had risen to his feet.

"Oh, yes." David Chung nodded. "We found him. What did you read, Zek?"

She looked at him, looked at all of them, and freed herself from Jazz's arms. And said nothing.

Darcy said, "Is he . . . okay?" And he held his breath waiting for her answer.

Eventually she said, "He's all right, yes, and he got there safely—to his destination, I mean. Also, I saw enough to know that it will all come to a head soon. But . . . something isn't right."

Darcy's heart thudded in his chest. "Not right? You mean he's already in trouble?"

She looked at him, and her look was so strange it was as if she gazed on alien things, in a world of ice beyond the times and places we know. "In trouble? Oh, he's that, all right . . . but not necessarily the trouble you're thinking of."

"Can you explain?"

She straightened up, gave herself a shake, and hugged her elbows. "No, I can't," she said, shaking her head. "Not yet. And anyway, I could be mistaken."

"But mistaken about what?" Darcy's frustration was mounting. "Harry is going up against Janos Ferenczy personally, man-to . . . to *thing*! If he's in trouble before they even meet, his disadvantage could well be insurmountable!"

Again she gave him that strange look, and shook her head, and quietly said, "No, not insurmountable. In fact on a one-to-one basis, I think you'll find that . . . that there's not a great deal to choose between them."

Following which, and for quite a long time, she would say no more . . .

With the misted valley far below and in the streaming moonlight of the heights, Harry knew the climb would soon be over and he'd be face-to-face with hell. He had hoped to call up all the local dead into an army on his side and march with them on Janos's place. But even the dead were afraid. Now there was very little time left, and probably less hope. So the fact that he actually found himself *anticipating* what was to come was a very hard thing to explain. It could be, of course, that he'd simply "cracked" under the strain, but he didn't think so. He'd never been the type.

His mind was still open and Möbius picked up his thoughts.

A breakdown? You? No, never! And especially not now, when we're so close. I need to be into your mind, Harry.

"Enter, of your own free will," he answered, almost automatically.

The other was very quickly in and out, and he was excited as never before. *It all fits! It all fits!* he said. *And the next time I come, I'm sure I'll be able to unlock those doors!*

"But not right now?"

I'm afraid not.

"Then there may not be time for a next time."

Don't give in, Harry!

"I haven't. I'm just facing facts."

I swear we'll have the answer in . . . minutes! And meanwhile you could try helping yourself.

466

"Help myself? How?"

Give yourself a problem in numbers. Set yourself a mathematical task. Prepare to reestablish your numeracy.

"I wouldn't even know what a mathematical problem looked like."

Then I'll set one for you. The great mathematician was silent for a moment, then said, *Now listen. Stage one: I am nothing. Stage two: I am born and in the first second of my existence expand* uniformly *to a circumference of approximately 1,170,000 miles. Stage three: after my second second of uniform expansion my circumference is twice as great! Question: What am I?*

"You're crazy," said Harry, "that's what you are! A minute ago I would have sworn it was me, but now I know that I'm perfectly sane. Compared to you, anyway."

Harry?

Harry laughed out loud, causing the Gypsies who struggled up the final rise with him to jump. "A madman," they muttered, "yes. The Ferenczy has driven him mad!"

The Necroscope used his deadspeak again. *August, here's me who can't count his toes without getting nine, and you ask me to solve the riddles of the universe?*

Pretty close, Harry, Möbius answered, *pretty close. Just keep at it and I'll be back as soon as possible.* His deadspeak faded and he was gone.

Jesus! said Harry to himself, shaking his head in disgust. *Jesus!*

But Möbius's question had stuck in his head. He couldn't give it his attention right now, but he knew it was in there, lodged firmly in his mind.

And now the party had reached the top of the cliffs; and somewhere here on this wind-blasted, sparsely clad plateau, here lay the ruins of the Castle Ferenczy. That was where Janos waited; but right here and now, here at the top of the long climb . . . here something else waited. Seven somethings in all, or eight if one included the Grey One slinking in the moon-cast shadows. Harry's "escort" to the lair of the undead vampire.

467

The two leading Zirras saw them first, then Harry, finally the three Gypsies who panted where they laboured close behind. All drew back, startled and gasping, except the necroscope himself. For Harry knew that he stood in the presence of dead men, which was common ground for him. What he and the others with him saw was this:

Seven great Thracians, dead for more than two thousand years, raised up again from their burial urns to do Janos's bidding. They had the aspect of life at least, but there was a great deal of death in them, too. They wore helmets and some pieces of armour of their own period, but wherever their grey flesh showed naked, it was scarred, disfigured. Their helmets were fearsome things, designed to terrify any beholder: they were domed, of gleaming bronze, with oval eyeholes dark in the flicker of their torches and curved, downward-sweeping flanges to cover the jaws of the wearers.

All seven were big men, but their leader stood a good four inches taller than the rest. He stepped forward, massive, but the eyes behind the holes in his mask were red—with sorrow.

Bodrogk looked at Harry Keogh and the five who cowered behind him. ''Free him,'' he said. His tongue was ancient but his meaning—the way his bronze sword touched Harry's ropes—couldn't be mistaken.

The Szgany spokesman stepped cautiously to Harry's side and loosened the nooses a little around his neck. And to Bodrogk the Gypsy said, ''You are . . . the Ferenczy's creatures?''

Bodrogk didn't understand. He looked this way and that, frowning, wondering what the man's question had been. Harry read his deadspeak confusion and answered, ''He wants to know if Janos sent you.'' He spoke the words aloud, letting his deadspeak do the translating. And now Bodrogk's gaze centered on Harry alone.

The massive Thracian paced forward and the Gypsies fell back. Bodrogk caught the ropes around Harry's neck and snapped them like threads. He grunted an introduction, then said, ''And so you are the Necroscope, beloved of all the world's dead.''

"Not all of them"—Harry shook his head—"for there are cowards among the dead even as there are among the living. If I can't know them—because they are afraid to know me— then I can't befriend them. And anyway, Bodrogk, I've no great desire to be loved by thralls."

Bodrogk's men had come forward, moving closer to the Gypsies on the bluff, herding them there. Now their huge leader took off his helmet and tossed it clanking aside. His neck was a bull's, his face full-bearded, fierce. But it was grey, that face, and, like the rest of his flesh, gaunt with an unspoken horror. His haggard, harried aspect told far better than any words the way in which Janos had dealt with him and his.

"I heard you talking to the dead," said Bodrogk. "You must know that all of Janos's thralls are not cowards."

"I know that the Thracians in the vaults of his castle are dust, and so can't help me. They told me they would but can't, because only Janos himself may call them up, for he alone has the words. On the other hand . . . you and your six are not dust."

"Are you calling us cowards?" Bodrogk's callused hand fell upon Harry's shoulder close to his neck, and in his other hand a great bronze sword was lifted up a little.

"I only know that where some suffer Janos to live," Harry answered, "I came to kill him and remove his taint forever."

"And are you a warrior, Harry?"

Harry lifted his head, gritted his teeth. He had never feared the dead, and would not now. "Yes."

Bodrogk smiled a strange, sad smile—which faded at once as he glanced beyond Harry. "And these others with you? They captured you and brought you here, eh? A lamb to the sacrifice."

"They belong to the Ferenczy." Harry nodded.

The other looked at him and his eyes went into Harry's soul. "A warrior without a sword, eh? Here, take mine." He placed it in Harry's hands—then scowled at the Szgany and nodded to his men. The six Thracian lieutenants fell on the Gypsies with their swords, swept them from the bluff and over the edge of the cliff like chaff. It was so swift and sudden, they didn't even have time to scream. Their bodies went bumping, bouncing, and clattering into the deep dark gorge.

"A friend at last." Harry nodded. "I thought I might find a few, at least."

"It was you or them," Bodrogk answered. "To murder a worthy man, or slaughter a handful of dogs. Thralldom to the Ferenczy, or freedom—for as long as it may last. Not much of a choice. I made the only decision a man could make. But if I had paused a moment to think . . . then it might have gone the other way. For my wife's sake." He explained his meaning.

"You've taken an enormous chance," Harry told him, giving back his sword.

"The dead called out to me," Bodrogk answered. "In their thousands they cried out, all of them begging your life. Aye, and one especially, whose tongue lashed like none other! Why, she might have been my own mother! But instead she was yours."

Harry sighed, and thought, *Thank God for you, Ma!*

"Your mother, yes," said the other. "She half swayed me, and Sofia did the rest."

"Your wife?"

"The same." Bodrogk nodded, leading the way back towards the ruined castle in the heights. "She said to me, 'Where is your honour now, you who once were mighty? Rather the applause and cold comforts of the teeming dead, and thralldom to Janos forever, than another urn filled with screaming ashes in the monster's vaults!'"

Harry said, "We have much in common then, your lady and I."

And, on impulse: "Bodrogk, I already have my cause but she must be yours. Only fight with Sofia in mind, and you cannot lose." And deep inside, unseen, unheard, he prayed it was true. Except: "I have no plan," he admitted.

Bodrogk laughed, however grimly, and answered, "A warrior without a sword, nor yet a plan of campaign!'' But he grasped the Necroscope's shoulder and added, ''I have been dead a long time, Harry Keogh, but in my life I was a king of warriors, a general of armies. I was the great strategist of my race, and all the centuries flown between could not rob me of my cunning.''

Harry looked at the Thracian, striding gaunt, grim, dead, and resurrected beside him. ''But will cunning suffice, when the vampire need only mutter a handful of words to return you to dust? I think you'd better tell me how this magic of his works, and then something of your plan.''

''The words of devolution may only be spoken by a master, a mage,'' said Bodrogk. ''Janos is one such. He must *direct* his words, aim them like an arrow to their target. And to hit the target he must first see it. Wherefore . . . we go up against him as individuals! You, me, my six, each man of us a unit in his own right. We approach and enter the castle from all sides. He cannot smite us all at once! And with mere words, even Words of Power, he can't smite you at all! Some of us may fall, aye. What of it? We've fallen before; we desire to fall, and to *remain* fallen! But while Janos deals with some of us, the others—especially you, Harry—may live long enough to deal with him.''

Harry nodded. ''It's as good a plan as any,'' he said. ''But . . . surely he isn't alone?''

''He has his vampire thralls,'' Bodrogk answered. ''Five of them. Three who were Szgany, and two but recently joined him. One of these is a woman with powers—''

''Sandra.'' Harry breathed her name, felt sick in the knowledge of how it must be for her, and how it was yet to be.

''And the other a man likewise talented,'' Bodrogk continued. ''Janos broke him to force his obedience. As for the woman: he did to her what he does to women, the dog!''

''Then we have them to deal with, too.''

''Indeed—and now!''

''Now?''

"They are waiting for us, there beneath the trees, beyond which lie those tumbled, cursed ruins. I am now supposed to give you into their hands, when they in turn will take you to their master."

Harry looked, saw twisted, wind-blasted pines leaning towards the cliffs of the ultimate ridge. And in the shadows formed of their canopy, he also saw the yellow flames of vampire eyes, feral in the night. He reverted to true deadspeak, using only his mind to ask, *Do you know how to deal with them?*

Do you? Question matched question.

The stake, the sword, the fire, Harry answered grimly.

Swords we have, said Bodrogk. *Fire too, in the torches which my men carry. And stakes? Aye . . . we cut a few while we waited for you at the cliff. For you see, there were vampires in my day, too. So let's be at it!*

Janos's undead thralls came ghosting out of the trees. Their long arms reached for Harry; they smiled their ghastly smiles; not a one of them dreamed that Bodrogk had reneged. But even as they ringed the Necroscope about, so the Thracians fell on them and cut them down!

It was butchery, and it was quick. All three vampires were beheaded, thrown to the ground and staked through their hearts. But only three? As Bodrogk's men took up the bodies of their victims and draped them across low branches, and set fire to the tinder-dry, resin-laden trees, Harry saw a crooked figure standing a little apart. And in the next moment Ken Layard stepped into view. "Harry!" he sighed. "Harry! Thank God!"

Moonlight turned his sallow flesh golden as he opened his arms wide, closed his eyes, and turned his face up to the night sky. The Thracians looked at Harry; there was nothing he could do; he nodded and turned away—

And saw a tall, dark figure standing at the edge of the ruins, only a dozen paces away!

Janos!

Bodrogk's men had done with Layard now. They, too, saw

the vampire there in the ruins, his scarlet eyes furiously ablaze. The Thracians began to melt quickly back into shadows, but not quickly enough for two of them who stood close together.

Janos pointed at them, and his awful baying *voice* swelled out like a curse on the night air.

"OGTHROD AI'F—GEB'L EE'H—*YOG-SOTHOTH*!"

There was more, but the effects of the rune of dissolution were already apparent. The two Thracians who were Janos's target had already cried out, fallen against each other, collapsed to insubstantial wraiths which, as he finished his devocation, drifted to the earth as dust!

Harry glanced all about; Bodrogk and his remaining four were nowhere to be seen; another terror approached.

The wolf—the Grey One which had also been part of his escort, but who had kept himself well back behind the party of Thracians—was now creeping up on him, shepherding him towards the castle's master. The Necroscope stooped, took up one of the bronze swords of the dematerialised Thracians, felt its great weight. Smaller than Bodrogk's sword, still it was no rapier. Harry knew he couldn't hope to wield this thing, but it was better than nothing.

He looked for Janos, saw the monster's fleeting shadow moving back into the darkness of the ruins. A ploy, a feint: Harry's cue to pursue him. Well, and wasn't that what he was here for?

As he followed after Janos, so the Grey One rushed up behind him and snapped at his heels. Harry stiffened his leg into a bar of flesh and bone and lashed out, and felt teeth crunch as his foot concertinaed the beast's slavering muzzle. He snarled at the creature and took up his sword two-handed . . . and astonishingly the wolf shrank back, whining!

Before Harry could wonder at the meaning of this, Bodrogk and one of his remaining four stepped from cover and together fell on the animal. The sounds of their attack were brief and reminded Harry of nothing so much as a butcher's shop as they first crippled the beast, then cut short its yelping and howling by taking its head.

473

Harry's eyes were more accustomed to the dark now; in fact, his clarity of vision in the night was entirely remarkable and a wonder to him. But that was something else he had no time to consider. Instead he looked into the heart of the tumbled pile and saw Janos standing behind a toppled wall. The monster's gaze was fixed on a point beyond Harry—the Thracians, of course. But as he pointed his great talon of a hand, so the Necroscope shouted, "Look out!"

"OGTHROD AI'F . . ." Janos commenced his crackling rune of devolution, and before he'd finished, another Thracian had cried out, sighed, and crumbled into smoking, drifting dust. One of the two had been saved at least, and Harry found himself hoping it was Bodrogk.

But now the Necroscope went after Janos with a vengeance. Athletic, surefooted even in the dark, he saw the vampire commence a descent apparently into the earth itself behind a mound of rubble. In the last moment before he disappeared, he turned his freakish head and looked back, and Harry saw the crimson lamps of his eyes. There was a challenge written there which the Necroscope couldn't resist.

He found the stone trapdoor raised above hollowed steps leading down, and almost without thought began his own descent—until a voice from behind stopped him. Looking back, he saw Bodrogk and his remaining warriors converging on him. "Harry," the great Thracian rumbled. "You'll be first down. Go swiftly! Preserve my Sofia!"

He nodded, clambered down the spiralling stairwell—a wall of stone on one side and a chasm opening on the other—down to the first landing. But setting foot on the solid stone floor—

Janos was waiting!

The vampire came from nowhere, knocked the sword out of Harry's hand, hurled the Necroscope against the wall with such force that all the wind was hammered out of him. Before he could draw breath Janos towered over him, closed one huge hand over his face, and slammed his head against the wall. Physically there was no match: Harry went out like a light . . .

* * *

Harry . . . Haaarry! his mother cried out to him, a hundred mothers like her, an even larger number of friends and acquaintances, and all the dead in their graves across the world. Their voices soughed in the deadspeak aether, filled it, penetrated the threshold of Harry's subconscious mind, and wrapped him in their warmth. Warmth, yes, for the minds of the dead are different to the common clay of their once-flesh.

Ma? He answered through his pain and the struggle to rise up, back into the conscious world. *Ma . . . I'm hurt!*

I know, son, she said, her voice brimming over. *I feel it . . . we all of us do. Lie still, Harry, and* feel *how we feel for you.* Behind her, the wash of background deadspeak was building up to a crescendo, a wall of mental moaning.

Lying still won't help, Ma, he said. *Nor all the gnashing of teeth I hear going on there. I'm going to have to shut you all out. I need to wake up. And when I've done that, I'll need help just to live!*

But the dead can *help, Harry!* she told him. *There's one trying to contact you even now who has part of the answer.*

Möbius? She had to be talking about Möbius.

No, not him. Harry sensed the shake of her head. *Another, someone who is much closer to you. Except . . . there's not much left of him, Harry. You won't hear him against all of this. Wait, and I'll see if I can quiet them.*

She retreated, spoke to others, passed on a message that spread outwards like ripples in a calm pond where a stone has been tossed, until it encompassed the world. The mental babble quickly faded away and an extraordinary silence followed. Out of which—

Harry?

Whoever it was, his deadspeak was so weak that at first the Necroscope thought he must be imagining it. But:

Are you looking for me? he answered eventually. *Who are you?*

I am nothing. The other sighed. *Not even a whimper, not*

even a ghost. Or at very best a ghost even among ghosts. Why, even the dead have difficulty hearing my voice, Harry! My name was George Vulpe, and five years ago my friends and I discovered the Castle Ferenczy.

Harry nodded. *He killed you, right?*

He did more, worse, than that! the other moaned, his dead-speak thin as the slither of dry, dead leaves. *He took my life, my body, and left me without . . . anything! Not even a place to rest.*

Harry felt that this was very important. *Can you explain?*

I've spoken to a great many Zirras in the Place of Many Bones, George Vulpe told him. *When the Ferenczy lay in his urn, they were the ones who came to feed and refuel him with their blood. But I was different. On my hands there were only three fingers!*

Now Harry gasped. *You were the one!*

He has my body, the other said again. *And I can't rest. Ever.*

What was he? Harry wanted to know. *I mean,* how *did he usurp you, drive you from your body?*

The other explained. *My blood drew him up from his urn. I was a son of his sons, from the Zirra clan. But I didn't know that. Only my blood knew.*

He came from his urn? Harry pressed. *As essential salts? My blood transformed him.*

Harry needed help to understand. He uncovered Faethor.

Damn you, Harry Keogh! the incorporeal vampire at once raged.

Be quiet! Harry told him. *Explain what this man is saying to me.*

Faethor heard Vulpe's story, said, *Why, isn't it obvious? Janos had taken precautions. When I reduced his brain and vampire both to ashes, his ever-faithful Zirras hid him away in a secret place until he could perform this . . . this metempsychosis. But it wasn't merely a transfer of minds: Janos's leech was revived from its ashes. The creature* itself *entered this one's body! And now—*

476

But Harry at once closed him down again. And: *George,* he said, *thanks for your help. I don't see what good it will do me, but thanks anyway.*

The only answer was a sigh, rapidly fading to nothing . . .

Harry strove to rise up from unconsciousness, to revive himself, to wake up. And on the verge of succeeding, then Möbius came.

Harry! Möbius cried. *We have it! We believe we have it!* He entered the Necroscope's mind, and in another moment: *Yes, yes—this must be right! But . . . are you ready?*

I've never been so ready! Harry answered.

That's not what I meant, said Möbius. *I mean, are you prepared mentally?*

Prepared mentally? August, what is this?

The Möbius Continuum, Harry. I can open those doors, but not if you're not ready for it. There's a different universe in there, doors opening on places undreamed. Harry, I wouldn't want you to get sucked into your own mind!

Sucked into . . . ? Harry shook his head. *I don't follow.*

Look . . . did you solve my problem?

Problem? Suddenly Harry felt rage and frustration boiling up in him. *Your fucking problem? What time do you think I've had for solving fucking problems?*

Did you even think about it?

No . . . Yes! . . . Yes, I thought about it.

And . . . ?

Nothing.

Harry, I'm going to open one of those doors . . . now!

The Necroscope felt nothing. *Did it work?*

It worked, yes, Möbius breathed. *And if you have the equations, you should be able to do the rest yourself.*

But . . . I don't feel any different.

Did you ever? Before, I mean?

No, but—

I'll open another door. There!

But this time Harry did feel it. A sharp white lance of

agony, setting off fireworks in his head. It was something like the pain Harry Jr. had arranged for him if ever he should be tempted to use his deadspeak, but since he was already unconscious, its effect was greatly reduced. And it served an entirely different purpose.

Instead of blacking him out, it jabbed him awake—

He came awake, into a waking nightmare!

Cold liquid burned his face, got into his throat, and stung him, caused him to cough. It was—alcohol? Certainly it was volatile. It smoked, shimmering into vapour all around. And Harry was lying in it. He struggled to his hands and knees, tried not to breathe the fumes, which were rising up into some sort of flue directly overhead . . . A blackened flue . . . Fire-blackened!

Harry knelt in a basin or depression cut from solid rock, knelt there in this pool of volatile liquid. Impressions came very quickly. He must be in the very bowels of the castle, down in the bedrock itself . . . a huge cave . . . and against the opposite wall where rough-hewn steps led up to the higher levels . . . there stood Janos watching him! He held a burning brand aloft, his scarlet eyes reflecting its fire.

Their eyes met, locked, and Janos's lips drew back from his monstrous teeth in a hideous grin. "And so you are awake, Necroscope," he said. "Good, for I desired that you should feel the fire which will make you mine forever!" He looked at the torch in his hand, then at the floor. Harry looked, too. At a shallow trough or channel where it had been cut in the rock. It ran from Janos's feet, across the floor, to the lip of the basin.

Jesus! Harry lurched for the rim of the shallow pool, and his hands shot out from under him. He wallowed in the liquid, put one hand on the rim and drew himself up, heard Janos's mad laughter, and saw him slowly lowering the brand to the floor!

My problem, Harry! Möbius was hysterical in his horror.

Harry fought back terror to picture the thing, automatically converting Möbius's circumferences to diameters:

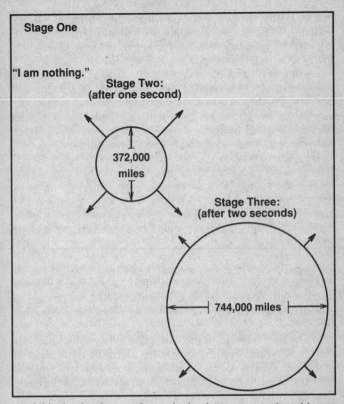

Stage One

"I am nothing."

Stage Two:
(after one second)

372,000 miles

Stage Three:
(after two seconds)

744,000 miles

And his instinctive mathematical talent, returned to him at last, did the rest.

What am I? Möbius howled as the fire of Janos's torch descended to the liquid fuse.

"Light!" Harry cried aloud. "What else can you be? Only light expands at *twice* the speed of light—from nothing to a diameter of 744,000 miles in two seconds!"

Fire whooshed, came racing across the floor of the cave in a blue-glaring blaze.

Which light? Möbius was frantic.

"You were nothing until you came into existence," Harry yelled. "Therefore . . . you are the Primal Light!"

Yes! Möbius danced in Harry's mind. *And my source was the Möbius Continuum! Welcome back, Harry!*

Computer screens opened in Harry's mind even as the bowl became an inferno. Searing heat roared up in a tongue of blue fire that belched into the chimney overhead. Liquid fire singed the hair from his head and face and set his clothes blazing. It lasted perhaps one tenth of a second—until Harry conjured a Möbius door and toppled through it!

He knew where to go, conjured a second door, and fell out of the Möbius Continuum into a deep drift of snow at the roof of the world. He was scorched, yes, but alive. Alive as never before. Elation filled him, and more than elation. His laughter—hysterical as Möbius's own—quickly died down, went out of him, became a growl that rumbled menacingly in his throat . . .

Janos had seen him disappear, and in that moment had known that Harry Keogh was invincible. The Necroscope had gone . . . where? And he'd be back . . . when? And what awesome powers would he bring with him? Janos dared not wait to find out.

He bounded up the stairs through the lower limits of the castle's labyrinth bowels, eventually emerging in the area of massively vaulted rooms which housed his urns and jars and *lekythoi*. And discovered Harry there ahead of him! Harry, Bodrogk, and the remaining Thracians.

Janos fell back to crouch against a wall, hissing, then straightened up to come forward again. "You are dust!" he snarled at Bodrogk, and pointed his finger.

The huge Thracian chief and two of his captains ducked through an arched door into another room, but the third was caught in the blast of Janos's devocation:

"OGTHROD AI'F, GEB'L—EE'H,
YOG-SOTHOTH, 'NGAH'NG AI'Y,
ZHRO!"

The devolved man threw up his arms and sighed his last
. . . and fell in a cloud of grey-green chemicals!

Janos roared his mad laughter, leaped to take up the fallen
warrior's sword. He advanced on Harry, sword raised high—
and the Necroscope knew exactly what to do. For Harry was
a mage, a master in his own right; and in his mind right now,
crying out from all of their prisoning urns, a thousand deadspeak voices instructed him in the Words of Power!

He pointed at the jars scattered all about, and turning in a
circle uttered the rune of invocation:

> "Y'AI 'NG'NGAH, *YOG-SOTHOTH*;
> *H'EE—L'GEB, F'AI THRODOG,*
> *UAAAH*!"

The vaulted room filled with stench and purple smoke in
a moment, obscuring Harry, Janos, and all. And out of the
rush and reek came the cries of the tortured. There had been
no time for the mixing of chemicals; these resurrected Thracians, Persians, Scythians, and Greeks would all be imperfect. But their lust for vengeance would be entirely in keeping.

Janos knew it, too. He careened through their stumbling,
groaning ranks as they shattered their jars and grew up like
mushrooms out of nothing; but as fast as he could target a
group and put them down again, so the Necroscope called
them up! There was no way the vampire could win. He
couldn't bellow his words fast enough, and the ranks of resurrected warriors were rapidly closing on him.

Blasting a path of dust before him, he fled to the steps winding
up to ruined regions above and passed from sight. The hideously *incomplete* army would follow after, but Harry cautioned
them: "Stay here. Your part is played. But this time when you
go down, you know that you may rest in peace."

And they blessed him as he returned them all to their *ma-
teria*. All except the warrior king Bodrogk.

And taking Bodrogk with him, he stepped through a Möbius door . . . and out again into the ruins of Castle Ferenczy.

They waited, and in a little while Janos came, grunting,

whining, and panting into the night. He saw them, choked on his terror, gagged and reeled as he stumbled away from them out of the ruins. He was spent; he had no breath; he tottered to the cliff behind the castle and climbed it along a path . . . and halfway up found Harry and Bodrogk waiting for him. The huge Thracian carried a battle-ax!

There was nowhere left to run. Janos looked outwards to the night and his crimson eyes gazed on empty space. In all his life there'd been only one Wamphyri art he never mastered or counterfeited, and now he must. He held up his arms and willed the change, and his clothing tore as his body wrenched itself into a great blanket, an airfoil of flesh. And like a bat in the night, he launched himself from the cliffside path.

He succeeded! He flew—with the tatters of his ripped clothing fluttering about him like strange wings. He flew . . . until Bodrogk's hurled battle-ax buried itself in his spine!

Harry and Bodrogk returned to the ruins and found the monster writhing there where he'd crashed down in the rubble. He choked and coughed up blood, but already he'd worked the ax loose and his vampire flesh was healing him. The Necroscope knelt beside him and looked him in the eye. Man to . . . man? Face to terrifying, terrified face.

"Bastard Necroscope!" Janos's eyes bled where they bulged.

"You have a man's body," Harry answered, without emotion, "but your mind and the vampire within you were raised from ashes in an urn." He pointed a steady hand and finger. "Ashes to ashes, Janos, and dust to dust! OGTHROD AI'F, GEB'L—EE'H."

The vampire gave a shriek, wriggled frantically, choked, gagged, and regained his man-shape.

And the necroscope continued, "*YOG-SOTHOTH, 'NGAH'NG AI'Y.*"

"No!" Janos howled. "N-n-*noooooooo*!"

As Harry uttered the final word, "*ZHRO!*" so Janos's entire body convulsed in instant, unbearable agony. He writhed frantically, vibrated, then grew still. Finally his head flopped back and his awful mouth flew open, and the lights went out in his eyes. Then—

His massive chest slowly deflated as he sighed his last, long sigh. No air escaped him but a cloud of red dust, drifting on the air. The rest of his body, even his head, must have been full of the stuff. And as the dust of that devolved vampire leech settled, it reminded the necroscope of nothing so much as the spores of those weird mushrooms at Faethor's place on the outskirts of Ploiesti.

Which in turn served to remind him of something else as yet unfinished . . .

Bodrogk's lady Sofia came up out of the ruins, and Sandra came with her.

She came ghosting in the way of vampire thralls, her yellow eyes alive in the night, but Harry knew that she was less than Sandra now. Or more. Briefly, he remembered his precognitive glimpse back at the start of this whole thing: of an alien creature that came to him in the night and lusted after him, but only for his blood. Sandra was now an alien creature, who would lust after men for their blood.

She flew into his arms and sobbed into his neck, and holding her tightly—as much to steady himself as to steady her—he looked over her sallow shoulder to where Bodrogk gathered up his wife.

And he heard Sofia say, "She saved me! The vampire girl found me where Janos had hidden me and set me free!"

And Harry wondered: Her last free-will act, before the monstrous fever in her blood claims her for its own?

Sandra's beautiful, near-naked body was cold as clay where it pressed against the Necroscope, and Harry knew there was no way he could ever warm it. A telepath, she "heard" the thought as surely as if it had been spoken, and drew back a little. But not far enough.

His thin sharp stake, a splinter of old oak, drove up under her breast and into her heart; she took one last breath, one staggering step away from him, and fell.

Bodrogk, seeing Harry's anguish, did the rest . . .

Epilogue

ALL NIGHT HARRY SAT ALONE IN THE RUINS, SAT THERE WITH his thoughts, with Faethor trapped within him and the teeming dead held at bay without. He let no one in to witness his sorrow.

He had thought he would be cold, but strangely was not. He had thought the darkness and the shadows would bother him, but the night had felt like an old friend.

With the dawn spreading in the east, he sought out Bodrogk and his lady. They had found a sheltered place to light a fire and now reclined in each other's arms, watching the sun rise. Their faces greeted him with something of sadness, but also with a great resolve.

"It doesn't have to be," he said. "The choice is yours."

"Our world is two thousand years in the past," Bodrogk answered. "Since then . . . we've prayed for peace a thousand times. You have the power, Necroscope."

Harry nodded, uttered his esoteric farewell, and watched their dust mingle as a breeze came up to blow them away . . .

* * *

And now he was ready.

He returned to the ruins and set Faethor free.

What? that father of vampires raged. *And am I your last resort, Harry Keogh? Do you enlist my aid now, when all else has failed you?*

"Nothing has failed," Harry told him. And then, even by his standards, he did a strange thing. He deliberately lied to a dead man. "Janos is crippled, dying," he said.

Faethor's fury knew no bounds. *Without me? You brought him down without me? He doesn't know I had a hand in it? I want to* feel *the dog's pain!* He crashed out of Harry's mind and discovered Janos—dead!

Astonished, Faethor knew the truth, but of course Harry had known it before him. He triggered Wellesley's talent to shut Faethor out. "I told you I'd be rid of you," he said.

Fool! Faethor raged. *I'll be back in, never fear. Only relax your guard by the smallest fraction, and we'll be one again, Necroscope.*

"We had a bargain." Harry was reasonable. "I've played my part. Go back to your place in Ploiesti, Faethor."

Back to the cold earth, after I've known your warmth? Never! Don't you know what has happened? Janos made no great error when he read the future. He knew that a master vampire—the greatest of them all—would go down from this place when all was done. I am that vampire, Harry, in your body!

"Men shouldn't read the future," said Harry, "for it's a devious thing. And now I have to be on my way."

Where you go, I go!

Harry shrugged and opened a Möbius door. "Remember Dragosani?" he said. And he stepped through the door.

Faethor shuddered but went in with him. *Dragosani was a fool*, he blustered. *You don't shake me off so lightly.*

"There's still time," Harry told him. "I can still take you to Ploiesti."

To hell with Ploiesti!

Harry opened a past-time door and launched himself

through it, and Faethor clung to him like the grim death he was. *You won't shake me loose, Necroscope!*

They gazed on the past of all mankind, their myriad neon life threads dwindling away to a bright blue origin. And now Faethor moaned, *Where are you taking me?*

"To see what has been," Harry told him. "See, see there? That red thread among the blue? Indeed, a scarlet thread . . . yours, Faethor. And do you see where it stops? That's where Ladislau Giresci took your head the night your house was bombed. That's where your life thread stopped, and you'd have been wise to stop with it."

Take . . . take me out of here! Faethor gasped and gurgled, and clung like an incorporeal leech.

Harry returned to the Möbius Continuum and chose a future-time door, where now the billions of blue life threads wove out and away forever, speeding into a dazzling, ever-expanding future. He drifted out among them and was quickly drawn along the timestream. And: "This thread you see un-winding out of me," he said. "It's my future."

And mine, said Faethor doggedly, steadier now.

"But see, it's tinged with red." Harry ignored him. "Do you see that, Faethor?"

I see it, fool. The red is me, proof that I'm part of you always.

"Wrong," said Harry. "I can go back because my thread is unbroken. Because I have a past, I can reel myself in. But your past was finished back in Ploiesti. You have no thread, no lifeline, Faethor."

What? The other's nightmare voice was a croak. Then—

The master of the Möbius Continuum brought himself to an abrupt halt, but the spirit of Faethor Ferenczy shot on into the future. *Harry!* he cried out in his terror. *Don't do this!*

"But it's done," the Necroscope called after him. "You have no flesh, no past, nothing, Faethor. Except the longest, loneliest, emptiest future any creature ever suffered. Good-bye!"

H-H-Harry! . . . Haaarry! . . . Haaaarrry! . . . HAAAAAAAAAA—

But Harry closed the door and shut him off. Always.

Except that before the door slammed shut, he looked again at the blue thread unwinding out of him.

And saw that it was still tinged red.

Men should never try to read the future. For it's a devious thing . . .